What readers are saying about
The Breakable Vow

"Finally, practical advice for teenagers about dating violence in the form of a novel! *The Breakable Vow* is a long overdue page turner. There isn't a woman alive who won't relate to Annie McGowan's plight. Clarke's heroine may very well do more to prevent domestic violence than all of our efforts in the last twenty years."

The Honorable Colleen McSweeny Moore
Circuit Court Judge
Cook County, Illinois

"I couldn't put it down. So real I had shivers up my spine. A book every young woman should read. *The Breakable Vow* is the greatest awareness tool I've seen in the battered woman's movement."

Karla Fiaoni
Project Director
Domestic Violence Unit
Chicago Heights Police Department

"I was surprised and delighted to see the involvement and enthusiasm of a multi-cultural population of young women who could relate to this heroine. Obviously, dating violence is a phenomenon that crosses religious, racial, and socioeconomic lines."

Susan M. Sanders PhD
Associate Professor
Public Services Graduate Program
DePaul University
Chicago, Illinois

"This book provides the reader with the shocking reality of dating abuse. It allows the reader to enter the world and, at the same time, evaluate their own."

Sr. Mary Therese
Mt. Assisi Academy
Lemont, Illinois

"Because I've never experienced this type of violence firsthand, the novel and program helped me gain insight into dating violence." *Michelle Golich*

"*The Breakable Vow* is funny, insightful, emotional, and helpful. It's full of valuable information that every young woman must know!" *Gretchen Madsen*

"Before this program, dating violence was just a term. Now I have gained a clear realization of the different stages and, more importantly, the warning signs." *Nora McCarthy*

"I feel privileged to have read this book. People who read it will be able to spot the signs of abuse, and I hope they will spread the word!" *Bridget Duggan*

"*The Breakable Vow* is very helpful for people in a violent relationship. The characters are realistic and show what really happens." *Lisa Brown*

"Nobody knows where it all starts, but we are where it can end." *Kathy Johnson*

"I couldn't put the book down! It transformed a one dimensional scenario of dating violence into a riveting and real-life experience." *Daina Ringul*

"Excellent. Two thumbs up!" *Chrissy Fidacz*

"This novel and program, if offered to other young women, will save many lives. It was a great experience!" *Nicole Kaiser*

"From now on, I will always be careful about my relationships." *Mara Stankicwicz*

"This dating violence program made me very aware. The novel was an excellent source." *Jen Faron*

"I cried through the whole thing. Annie McGowan could have been me. I knew something was wrong, even when I married him. I just didn't know what it was. If I'd read this story at 16, I might have spared myself and my children 20 years of abuse and torture. It's too late for us, but *The Breakable Vow* will spare others. I'm certain of it." *Anonymous battered woman*

"I saw myself throughout the book. First it made me angry. Then it made me scared. I broke up with my boyfriend. He was Kevin, and I would have been Annie if I'd stayed." *Anonymous woman*

The Breakable Vow

by
Kathryn Clarke

www.thebreakablevow.com

ADAMS PRESS CHICAGO

Adams Press
#236
6167 North Broadway
Chicago, Illinois 60660
info@adamspress.com

This book is humbly dedicated
to the united hearts of
our Savior, Jesus Christ,
and His Blessed Mother Mary.

Acknowledgments

I would like to acknowledge the following persons:

My father, Richard Jennings, who told me not only that I could write this book but that I should. He is a knowledgeable writer, an able mentor, a source of constant encouragement, and my dearest friend.

My husband, Jimmy, the ultimate team player, who makes me laugh and smile every day. He gave me the time and the courage.

My brothers and sisters, Bobby, Richy, Mary, Therese, Veronica, Nancy, and Julie, who make my whole life, even the rough times, so manageable. I truly cannot imagine a world without their laughter and wisdom.

My mother, Mary, R.I.P, who was generous enough to give me such a large and humorous family.

My children, Maggie, Annie, Bob, Mary Kathryn, Frank, and little Veronica.

Colleen, my friend, who suffered through the chapter reads, the rewrites, the typing, and everything else in my life.

Celeste, my friend, who helped me subdue the personality disorder lurking in my computer.

Sister Margaret Johnson, RSM, who liked me when nobody else did.

Father Bill Quinn, for his tremendous kindness and support.

To all of the unsung heros who work tirelessly in the cause of domestic violence. May God strengthen, bless, and reward you.

To each and every battered woman and man. May you find the courage and strength to bring peace back to your life.

Contents

Chapter One

In the early seventies, Chicago neighborhoods were strong, with clear boundaries. The tumultuous events occurring in the world were, for the most part, ignored. Hushed adult conversations were dull and usually not worth listening to. The McGowan children, from the city's South side, concerned themselves with school, sports, and staying out of trouble.

The fourth of five children, Annie McGowan was known as precocious. On a bad day, she was classified a little less kindly and sensed her father's frustration. Snapping green eyes reflected her impatience with the generally slow pace of life. Dark-haired Annie knew at a young age that she belonged to an elite group who were Irish and American, in that order.

At age thirteen, Annie McGowan entered eighth grade. Life was a whirl of sporting events including volleyball. cheerleading, and boy chasing. She ran in a pack with ten other girls from St. Malachy's Catholic School. The children spent most of their free time roaming the local park in search of each other. On Halloween this ritual was observed but with a twist. Eggs, shaving cream, and toilet paper were stockpiled. Fully armed, marauding revelers wandered through the dark assaulting whatever struck their fancy. Trees, houses, cars, and buses were obvious targets. The war waged with the boys, however, was easily the highlight of the evening. A modernized ritual was practiced in which a boy would particularly target the girl for whom he had special feelings. On this night, even a shy boy could send a subtle message with a can of shaving cream.

That year, Annie was dressed and ready. Perched on the front porch, she nestled a bowl of candy in her lap and distributed treats to the relentless stream of trick-or-treaters. Inside was a blitz of slamming doors and yelling voices as four motherless McGowan children prepared for the evening's activities. Their father, a widower, supervised the pandemonium.

As usual, the weather was hostile. A light but determined drizzle conspired with a brisk breeze to sabotage the evening for the ballerinas and princesses. Forced to don outer wear, they wore deflated looks and marched from house to house with glazed eyes. Streetlights did little to illuminate the evening. Except for a small glow at the top of each pole, the darkness remained intact. Annie glanced at the sky. A light mist was acceptable. Downpours could spoil the night.

After an eternity, Marla and Rene, her closest friends, arrived. The girls melted into the river of children heading toward the park. Their extended group of friends, boys and girls, fought a valiant war that evening. A new boy in particular interested Annie. Kevin Griffin. With dark curly hair and soft brown eyes, he had been blessed in appearance. Dark olive skin belied his Irish name. Approaching six feet, his frame was evenly distributed, and he moved smoothly. Observing him, Annie noticed he was watching her.

After exchanging a smile, she approached him.

"You're pretty small," he observed with a grin.

At just over five feet, Annie was indeed on the short side. It was not until this split second in time, however, that she noticed her size.

"Compared to some." This she delivered with a sweet and genuine smile. The message was received, and he smiled again. Both were stumbling through this banal conversation until their initial awkwardness could be bridged. The evening wore on, and she glanced at him whenever she could. On several occasions their eyes met, assuring Annie of his reciprocal interest.

Annie was rummaging through her pillowcase for her last can of shaving cream when Rene approached. Damp hair straggled around Rene's tense features, and Annie laughed out loud at the sight of her best friend. The girls conferred in whispers until a shout forced them to look up. One of the girls was holding her backside. Hastening to her side, they asked in alarm, "What happened?"

"That obnoxious bastard kicked me," said their schoolmate through sobs.

"What obnoxious bastard?" Annie asked.

Indicating Kevin, their friend continued to cry while Annie took control. "Stop crying. Don't give him the satisfaction. We'll get Julie to walk you home."

In minutes the injured reveler was dispatched. Annie looked at Rene grimly, and Rene nodded. It was time to go home.

The girls began their trek across the park. Riddled with sodden toilet paper, the dreary landscape matched their mood. Halfway home, they heard their names called and turned to see Marla approaching with their friend Terry. Kevin Griffin ambled slowly behind them.

"Thanks for leaving without me," Marla greeted. "Did you hear what Sue did to Kevin?"

Annie and Rene exchanged a glance. "No," Annie replied. "But we heard a nasty story about what Kevin did to Sue."

"Well, you heard it wrong," Terry Joyce said with feeling. A core member of the St. Malachy's group of eighth grade boys, his opinion carried weight. "She came up behind him and smashed an egg right into the back of his head."

Kevin kept his head down.

"You didn't have to kick her," Annie said to Kevin.

Kevin appealed to Rene. "You saw what she was doing to me. I asked her to leave me alone about a hundred times."

"That's true, Annie," Rene swayed. "She was driving him nuts."

The group merged and walked companionably home, discussing the event. By the end of the journey, Annie was persuaded that Kevin had been sorely victimized. When they arrived at Annie's home, the others casually withdrew, leaving Kevin with Annie.

"I'm glad I met you, Annie," Kevin offered shyly.

"I'm glad I met you," she returned playfully. "I'm sorry Sue was such a nightmare."

Kevin held up his hand. "It was my fault. I should have left. I feel terrible about the whole thing."

"Don't be ridiculous," said Annie. "She's lucky you didn't punch her. It was not your fault, Kevin." She looked up into his dark eyes.

Smiling down at her, Kevin spoke gently, "I think you are the nicest girl I've ever met, Annie."

Something tightened in Annie's throat. Since the death of her mother, she carried a dull, but constant ache of loneliness. It shifted just the slightest bit. As Kevin bent down to kiss her gently on the forehead, it shifted again. She gazed up at him and fell hopelessly in love.

Annie McGowan had no idea she would spend the next eight years making excuses for Kevin Griffin.

Chapter Two

Eighth grade flew by. Kevin's leisure time was minimal and left the couple short of time together. Kevin was an athlete. His interest in sports was fueled by the enthusiasm of his various coaches. He was currently playing football, baseball, and basketball, in addition to hockey. Sometime that winter, Kevin stopped enjoying sports. It became too serious. Coaches routinely called his parents with offers of special lessons and sports camps. Bewildered, Kevin soon felt that being an athlete was now a job. Expectations were high. His father closely monitored his free time. When Kevin was not attending a structured practice, he was expected to be conditioning. Hours of running, drilling, and power eating left him exhausted. Quite naturally, Kevin resented the regimented lifestyle. But two unpleasant confrontations with his father persuaded him that he was without options. If he wanted to get a high school scholarship, he would need to stay focused; "the party" was over.

"What party is he talking about?" Kevin complained to Annie.

The two ambled slowly through the park on a wet March night. Their friends, fifty feet ahead, had long since grown accustomed to the couple's need for privacy. The group wore jeans and winter coats with hats. All except Kevin. Attired in sweats and a warm-up jacket, he was supposed to be doing sprints at the park.

"Can your father really think you're going to sprint through the park in the rain on Saturday night?" Annie asked incredulously.

"If he thought I wasn't, Annie, he would drive up here and take me home. Then I'd have to lift weights in the basement. He's obsessed with me. What kills me is that he never cared before."

"I'm sure he did, Kevin." Annie appreciated Kevin's confidences but sometimes felt on shaky ground. It was no secret that Kevin was unhappy at home. Indeed, they spent a great deal of time discussing his parents. Annie understood his resentment. What was more difficult to grasp was his docile acceptance of the situation.

"You must talk to your mother, Kevin," she said grimly. "Tell her this is outrageous and you're not going to do it any more."

"I keep telling you, Annie. She won't say anything to him. It's like she's afraid of him." Kevin paused. "She's great, though."

Annie was unconvinced. "If she's so great, why does she let him torture you like this?"

Kevin stopped. "Don't ever say that again. You don't know anything about her. How dare you blame her? I'm sorry I tell you anything. You don't even try to understand."

Shocked and devastated, Annie stared.

"You think you are so perfect," Kevin continued, his face contorted in rage. "Your father didn't even notice you pierced your ears for six months. At least my father cares about me."

Jolted from her silence, Annie retorted, "My father not only cares about me, he cares about every one of his five kids. Your father didn't know your name until your coach called and told him you could catch a football."

"Go to hell, Annie McGowan." Kevin turned and walked away.

Open-mouthed, Annie began to cry. She walked quickly for fear someone would see her. Arriving home, she looked through the living room window of her house. The clock gave her another hour. Annie dried her eyes and took stock. If she went in now, her father would question her. Too fragile for conversation, she turned back to meet her friends. Kevin had obviously gone home. Annie was getting used to being on her own. Kevin was rarely allowed out, and it made him uncomfortable if Annie went out without him.

Too bad, Annie thought to herself. He had no right to say that about my poor father. He can damn well apologize.

She turned resolutely and walked back to the park. Feeling self-righteous, she decided to tell no one of the fight. She could not share Kevin's problems without being disloyal. Anyway, she was above that. He would appreciate her discretion later, after he apologized and they made up. Parents were hell sometimes, she mused. But what did he mean about his mother being afraid to tell his father anything? Annie had little recollection of her parent's relationship. One thing she knew. Her mother had not been afraid to tell Mr. McGowan anything. Quite loudly if necessary. Her father said you needed a bit of fight in you, and Annie heartily agreed. That's what Kevin needs, she thought. Gumption.

Spying her friends across the park, Annie took several gulps of cold air and put her hood up. "Hello everyone," she greeted them.

"What are you doing here?" asked Rene.

"Do I need an invitation?" Annie quipped. "Kevin went home, and I came to see what you were doing."

"What are you talking about?" Rene asked. "Kevin said you were rude to him, and you had gone home. He's gone to change, but he's coming back. He said you were in a bad mood. He also said you didn't want to stand around with a bunch of boring people." Rene looked miffed. "I had no idea we weren't exciting enough for you."

Looking around, Annie realized no one else had greeted her. "Rene, what are you talking about? Kevin and I had a fight, and he stormed off. I assumed he went home."

"I'm telling you he came over here and said you were in a bad mood and went home," Rene repeated.

"Well, I was in a fine mood until he began to insult my father. What's with this boring stuff?"

"That's what he said. He said you thought we were all boring."

"Rene, you are my best friend. I would hardly be friends with you if I thought you were boring. Kevin was just mad."

"Well, you better tell those guys that," Rene indicated the rest of the group with a wave. "They get the feeling you think you're too good for us."

"Are you serious?"

"They're not mad exactly, just a little insulted." Rene spoke gently now. "Go over and talk to them. I'll tell them you didn't say that."

"Give me a break, Rene. I'll tell them myself." Annie strode over to her friends. "Hi, everyone. Apparently Kevin is confused. I never said you were boring," Annie said lightly. "I could hardly say you were boring without calling myself boring. You're my friends, right?"

Terry Joyce spoke for the group. "Are you saying Kevin lied, Annie?"

"Of course not," Annie replied patiently. "I'm saying Kevin misunderstood."

Terry turned his back on Annie. "Here he comes now. Ask him yourself what he said."

Annie turned. Sure enough, Kevin was striding toward them in jeans and an overcoat.

"Don't you look casual," Annie greeted him. "How did you get out?"

Kevin eyed her coldly and addressed the boys. "Does anyone want to go and get a can of pop?"

"Sure," Terry replied. Turning to the others, he said, "C'mon."

The group left. Annie and Rene stood alone.

"Screw them!" Annie cried in disbelief

"That must have been some fight, Annie," Rene said sympathetically. "Let's go and try to talk to them."

"No way," Annie exclaimed, her pride wounded. "I'm going home."

"I'll walk you," Rene offered, loyal to the end.

The girls began their homeward journey.

"Are you sure you never said anything like that?"

Annie was frowning. "Remember last week when everyone was going skating?" Rene nodded. "Well, Kevin felt bad because he couldn't go. Naturally, I told him I wouldn't go either. We agreed to meet up here for an hour while he was sprinting. He said he felt terrible that he was ruining my fun. I told him I didn't mind because it would be boring anyway. I was trying to make him feel better."

Rene nodded. "I see what you mean. Annie, you really should have gone anyway." Rene spoke as though she had held her peace long enough. "You can't stop your life because Kevin has a lunatic for a father. You should do things without him."

"How can you say that, Rene?" Annie searched for an explanation. "It's like I'm his best friend. If I go without him, he'll feel even worse. He feels bad enough already."

"Well!" Rene replied with feeling. "I'm YOUR best friend, and I'm beginning to feel like I have no best friend at all."

Rene turned on her heel and walked away. Completely baffled, Annie spoke aloud. "Why do people keep stomping off on me?" She again plodded toward home alone. As the tears began to fall, she felt the familiar ache of loneliness.

• • •

The following morning, Annie rose early. Sleep had been elusive. Most of the night had been spent replaying the scene with Kevin. Her biggest concern was that Kevin wanted to end the relationship. A dull feeling of nausea persisted. She could not fathom what she had done to alienate him. Rene presented a secondary worry. While Kevin was a mystery, Rene could be handled.

Dialing her number, Annie was relieved to find Rene nonchalant. They made arrangements to meet for Sunday Mass. Mr. McGowan did not insist on the family attending Mass together, correctly assuming that the battles would undo any possible spiritual benefits. Annie and Rene agreed to meet at their usual halfway point.

Thirty minutes later, Annie waited on the corner. Impatient, as usual, she began to walk in the direction of Rene's house. She finally spotted her friend walking quickly toward her.

"What kept you?" she shouted.

Rene shrugged. Proceeding toward Annie, she countered, "Why are you so early?"

"Rene, I'm going crazy. First of all, what was wrong with you last night?"

"Don't worry about me, Annie. I miss you because you're always with Kevin," Rene spoke with sincerity. "I understand how it must be for you. I only wish you would not stay in because Kevin can't go out. My mother says it's not healthy. You need to be with your friends more."

"Rene, you must know I miss you too. It seems like we don't do much together anymore. It's just that Kevin is going through such a hard time that I hate to make him mad." Annie was definitely upset. She continued, "It might not be a problem any more." She now burst into tears. "I told you exactly what happened, Rene. What did I do that was so horrible? He said some nasty things, too, didn't he?"

Rene nodded. "Annie, you didn't do anything wrong. I think we have to consider that the problem is with him. Maybe he should talk to his mother about this. She must see that he's miserable."

"That's exactly what I suggested, and he nearly bit my head off," Annie explained. Just talking brought relief, and she continued more calmly. "He said she was afraid to say

10

anything to his father, but she's 'the greatest.' I said if she was so great she'd do something. Was that so terrible?"

"Why are you doubting yourself?" Rene asked incredulously. "It's not as if you called her a hooker or something." At this they both giggled, and Rene added, "My mom says men are not sensible about their mothers. Lets talk about the way he treated you in front of everyone. That was really nasty."

"I know," Annie frowned. "It wasn't like him at all. Why do you think he told everyone I said they were boring?" Annie wondered. "He must not have realized it would make everyone mad."

"Annie, he's playing with your head. Don't you see it? Was anything else said between you?"

Annie was quiet for a moment. She instinctively knew not to tell Rene how Kevin told her to go to hell. Rene would not tolerate that type of thing. She pondered for a moment. Would she tolerate it? She dismissed the thought. Rene didn't understand Kevin as Annie did.

"No, I think I've told you everything," she lied. "What should I do?"

"What can you do?" Rene asked logically. "Calling him is out of the question. After the way he acted, he should make the first move." Rene eyed her sternly. "Don't you agree?" A look of pain crossed Annie's face as she nodded miserably. She could not bear the thought of losing Kevin.

"I guess, Rene. I know you're right, but what if he breaks up with me?"

"He won't. I sure of it." Rene spoke forcefully now. "He needs you more than you need him."

Annie was not so sure but said nothing. She felt a little better and was grateful for Rene's empathy. What did people do without best friends? Annie squeezed Rene's arm.

"Hurry up," Annie urged suddenly. "If we miss the gospel, I have to go again." The girls quickened their pace accordingly.

Two days passed with no conciliatory call from Kevin. Annie's misery deepened, with alternate bouts of sadness and anger. How dare he treat her like this? Graduation was only a couple months away. This would ruin it. But then, nothing really mattered. Annie felt as if her life was over at thirteen. She languished on the living room couch until Mr. McGowan suggested she see a doctor. Annie sighed dramatically and shook her head. She wanted only to be left alone.

On the third evening, Rene called her. It was late for a telephone call, and Rene sounded tense.

"Is your father around?"

Mr. McGowan disliked his children on the telephone and thought it the height of rudeness for people to call after eight o'clock in the evening. Normally he turned on the bell silencer, but tonight he was reading in his room and Annie had turned the ringer on low.

"No. He's lying down. Any news?"

"Kind of. I called Terry pretending I had a question about school, you know, to feel him out. I know you're tired of waiting."

Annie felt her stomach lurch. "Rene, what did he say? Don't mess around. Tell me."

"He told me Kevin says you're cranky these days. Kevin is tired of putting up with your moods, but he understands that you miss your mother. He feels bad for you." Rene paused.

Annie remained quiet.

"Are you there?"

"I'm speechless, Rene. He's the moody one. I think Terry got it mixed up."

"It sounds bizarre," Rene agreed. "I did ask him to repeat it, and that's what he said. If it's any comfort, no one is mad at you. They feel bad that you're sad about your mother."

"How nice," Annie said sarcastically. "I'm sad because my friends are all nuts. Rene, am I losing my mind?"

"No, Annie. The whole thing is strange. Even if you were sad about your mom, that's not Kevin's place to tell everyone. Is it?" Rene asked.

"No," Annie replied. "It's nobody's business but mine,

and maybe yours. I'm more confused than before. Did he say anything else?"

"He said Kevin has a lot going on in his life and maybe you two should take a break from each other." Rene spoke in a rush, as though she knew this would hurt her friend.

"I'm glad to hear Terry has everything under control," Annie said angrily. "I hope if Kevin is telling people it's over, he'll have the courtesy to tell me."

"I thought the same thing myself, Annie." Rene sounded relieved. "This is all a bit much. First he gets mad at you for nothing. Then he back-stabs you to your friends. Now he's acting like you have emotional problems. I wouldn't mind, but none of this is true. It's like he's turning the whole thing around on you. Do you think he's just a big liar?"

"No," Annie feebly defended him. "I don't know what to think, Rene. But one thing is for sure. I'm sick of it. Let him say what he wants. Kevin can go to hell."

"Well, I'm glad to hear you say that, Annie," Rene said roundly. "It's not the end of the world. Next year we'll be in high school, going to dances and stuff. We'll meet all kinds of new guys, and they always like you. It's going to be great."

Annie wished Rene did not sound so cheerful. "You're right. We'll have a great time. Rene, I have to hang up before the raging bull finds out that phone security has been compromised." Rene giggled. "I'll meet you for school tomorrow."

Busy weeks followed. Annie nursed her misery in silence. Rene seemed to sense her friend's suffering but did not broach the subject. Annie again became comfortable with the constant ache in the pit of her stomach. She foresaw a life of dignified loneliness. Dramatically, she pictured herself entering a religious order. She turned her focus to school.

• • •

One day, a few weeks later, Annie arrived home close to dinner time. Three hours of volleyball had left her hungry. One sniff assured her dinner would be on the table soon. It smelled like Mr. McGowan's infamous beef noodle casserole. Annie grinned. Most of the McGowan children hated the dish, but it was one of her favorites. Her father had mastered only six dishes. With military regularity they appeared on the table.

"I'm home," Annie shouted.

Mr. McGowan poked his head around the kitchen to identify the owner of the voice. "Annie, my pet. How was your day?"

Annie glanced up suspiciously. Normally the children were greeted by a barrage of orders regarding placement of coats, shoes, and books. Mr. McGowan had long since learned that his children forgot overnight where their things belonged. Like any mother, he reminded them daily.

"Come in and have a chat with me," he requested pleasantly.

"Dad, I swear to God, I didn't take the key to the wine cellar," Annie said vehemently. "I wouldn't drink that poison if it were the last drink on earth. If I were on a desert island, dying..."

"Enough already," her father said in an injured tone. Next to his homemade wine, his cooking was gourmet. "I'm not interested in the wine cellar key. Maureen has it, I think. She's the only one with the cheek to pull it off. Never mind. Sister Aniceta called."

"What?" Annie exploded. Sister Aniceta was her English teacher. "I'm her best student. I'm the only one in her class who actually listens. I swear to God she's lying." Annie spoke with the self-righteous indignation reserved only for the young.

Mr. McGowan lost patience. "Will you, for God's sake, close your mouth and listen! And don't let me hear you swearing to God again, Young Miss. You are not in trouble." He took a deep breath and continued, "She only wanted to say that you are a fine student and doing a wonderful job for her."

Annie eyed him speculatively. Clearly there was more to this.

"She's thinking that maybe you should go to a special high school. Instead of going to St. Clare's with your sisters, maybe we should look into something a little different for you." Mr. McGowan shifted nervously.

"You mean like a school for the mentally retarded?" Annie asked with exaggerated politeness.

"Annie," he began heavily, "mark my words. Your mouth is going to get you in trouble someday." He shook his head and started again. "A better school. There's a boarding school in Peoria, and she thought you might like to see it one weekend."

"Dad, I'm sure you have a point, but what is it? You want to send me to boarding school?" Annie struggled for comprehension. "Am I that much trouble? Is this the absolute worst time of my life or what?" With that she flung her jacket down and ran up the stairs and into her bedroom. The inevitable slam of the door was followed by the sound of her body collapsing onto her bed.

"Doorknobs are a privilege, not a right," Mr. McGowan muttered as he uncharacteristically climbed the stairs. He knocked on the door firmly. "Annie, let me in. Hear me out."

"It's open."

He opened the door slowly, as if afraid. He normally did not mount the stairs, preferring not to see the state of their rooms. "I am not trying to get rid of you," he said wearily. "In spite of your clever mouth, I like having you around. The good sisters think you should consider the school for two reasons. First, it is academically superior, even to St. Clare's. Second, many of the girls who go there have vocations. I told her she didn't know you very well or she wouldn't think so."

"Dad, you can't be serious," she implored. "On my best day I can't imagine having a vocation." Close to tears, she continued. "Are you sure you don't want to get rid of me?"

"I'm dead certain," he said with finality. "Sure, I don't like any of my kids, but I couldn't part with one of them.

Especially not you. I only want to do the right thing here. It's rough without a mother, and perhaps you'd like this. If it worked out, we'd send Eileen as well."

"Sister Aniceta is evil," Annie snapped. "I won't like it, and I don't want to go."

"Don't say that about the good woman." His tone now cajoled. "I'm merely warning you; she's going to bring it up. You make up your own mind. If you want to have a look, fine. If you don't, I'll tell her and that's the end of it. OK?"

"OK. But what about Nellie and Maureen? Why aren't you asking them?"

He chuckled. "Maureen wouldn't last a week. They'd kill her." He considered for a moment. "Nellie's too timid. Besides, they're already in St. Clare's, and Sister said it would be bad to change them." He sounded relaxed and reasonable now. "Are we clear? No one is getting rid of anyone." Annie smiled, and he moved toward the door in relief. "By the way," he paused. "Some guy named Kevin called you last night."

Annie's gasp startled him. "What? Are you sure? Why didn't you tell me?"

"Yes, I'm sure, and I'm not a social secretary," he said irritably. "I told him not to be calling here, bothering me at night." Noting the look of panic on her face, he continued quickly, "He's calling back tonight. I told him to make it before eight, and he said he would. Who is this character? Is he the one who stands out on the corner till you come out?"

"Yes, Dad. That's him," Annie answered, distracted.

"Tell him to summon up his intestinal fortitude and come to the door. I want to get a look at him. Just once, though. I don't want him hanging around the house all the time. We've got enough kids of our own without..."

"Yes," Annie interrupted, "...without some damn neighbor kids destroying our peace."

"That's right, Annie," he said good-naturedly. "I've got your favorite dinner down there. I put an extra can of mushrooms in there for you," he said with a wink. "Don't tell the others."

16

Annie grinned happily. She was the only one who liked mushrooms. As much as she liked them, the others hated the vegetable. "Thanks, Dad."

After he left, Annie let her heart soar. She did manage to wait a full three minutes before darting down the stairs to call Rene. Picking up the only telephone in the house, she jumped at her father's voice.

"Put that phone down whoever you are," he bellowed. "We'll not be disturbed during dinner."

"Dad, it's Annie, and this is an emergency. I have to tell Rene about something for school."

"You just spent ten bloody hours with her," he complained. Peeking around the corner, he observed the intensity on her face and relented. "Make it quick."

Rene's mother answered and called out to Rene, telling her it was Annie. Annie faintly heard Rene's father in the background complaining that the girls had just spent the entire day together. Annie rolled her eyes in exasperation. Honestly! It must be universal. Annie leaned against the wall, waiting for Rene and imagined some Chinese eighth grader rolling her eyes as she waited for her friend to come to the telephone. Maybe not. According to Mr. McGowan the Chinese were all starving due to some "bloody communists." If they were starving, they probably didn't have telephones, she thought idly. Feeling blessed, she made a mental note to get some money from her dad for the pagan babies they adopted at school. Her father always sprang for the missions, despite his contention that no one cared about his starving babies.

"Hi, Annie," Rene's voice popped her reverie.

"Hi," she said frantically. "I can't talk long. The raging bull has dinner ready so I only have a minute. You'll never guess in a million years who called last night."

Rene gasped, "Kevin?"

"Yes. Since my Dad is not a social secretary, he didn't tell me until today. He dropped it casually, right after he told me that Sister Aniceta has decided I have a vocation. They want me to go to some lunatic asylum for high school and become a nun." This was big stuff, but Annie had no time for preliminaries.

"Wait a minute, Annie. What are you talking about?" Rene was in a state. This was too much information too quickly. "My homework is done, Dad," Annie heard her shout. "WHO wants you to be a nun?"

"My dad and the diabolical Sister Aniceta. I'll tell you about it later. Can you believe he called?" she asked. "He told my Dad he would call back tonight. I'm getting off now, Dad," Annie yelled in response to her father's request. "Rene, what should I say?"

Her father's voice boomed from around the corner. "Tell him you're starving because you missed dinner."

"I have to go, Rene, he's listening," Annie whispered. "Come over after dinner."

"No friends in the house tonight," ordered her father.

"Was that your dad?"

"Of course," Annie whispered more quietly. "Come to the basement window, and I'll be waiting."

Annie sauntered into the kitchen and chose a chair. "Dad, did you know it is extremely rude to listen to other people's conversations?"

"Yes, Your Ladyship," he returned flippantly. "And did you know it's extremely rude to tie up someone's business line when they have apartments for rent?" Mr. McGowan was a builder. Since the death of his wife, he maintained the apartment buildings he had, thus enabling him to be home for his children. "I have two units vacant, and callers can't get through here. That leaves me short for the month." So much for the pagan babies, Annie thought regretfully. "And who is telling the callers that the buildings are next to the funeral parlor?"

"But, Dad," Maureen pointed out reasonably, "the buildings *are* next to the funeral home."

"I don't care," he said irritably. "It sounds morbid. And you certainly don't need to tell them we held your mother's wake there when 'she got dead.'" Now he eyed Eileen, his youngest.

18

"She was dead, Dad," Eileen answered cheerfully.

"Yes," he agreed. "I guess she was, Honey. But certain things are none of their business. Do you understand?"

Eileen nodded intelligently. "Are they like the neighbor bastards, Dad?"

The table went up for grabs. He tried in vain to shout over the din. "Be quiet, you jackals," he commanded. "I NEVER said that."

"Yes, you did, Dad. I remember," Eileen said confidently. "You said it when the neighbor lady came over to ask if we were all sorted out for our first day of school. You said she was a nosy bastard, and it was none of her damn business." Eileen did not see the humor but was delighted by the laughter of her siblings.

"Stop the nonsense," he commanded again. "Finish your dinners. Let's talk about the wine cellar key."

A renewed interest in their beef noodle casserole quieted the group. Danny, at eighteen the oldest, politely passed the salt to fifteen year-old Maureen, who offered to get more milk for Nellie, the oldest girl. Annie, whose conscience was clear, enjoyed the scene immensely.

"What happened, Dad?" she asked innocently.

"It was the strangest thing," their father said conversationally. "I had the key on my ring in my pocket when I went up to take a bath. I haven't seen it since. What could have happened to it?"

The resulting stillness was finally broken by Eileen. "Maybe the fairies got it, Dad," she offered gravely. "They got my candy last night."

Annie adopted a thoughtful tone. "She could be right, Dad. Last night I heard a fairy throwing up."

Laughter rung from the ceiling as Mr. McGowan tried in vain to regain control. "Your mouth is going to crucify you, Annie McGowan," he said with feeling, rising to begin clearing the table. Annie saw him turn his head quickly, before anyone saw the smile on his face.

Chapter Three

It was a busy night for the basement window. Maureen and Nellie, currently grounded for a curfew violation, had sneaked out to go for a drive with a newly licensed friend. Annie had been conscripted to provide cover in the event their absence was discovered. Maureen had guts, and Annie admired her. Sixteen-year-old Nellie, on the other hand, was a shy, more studious individual. Nellie hated the escapades Maureen strong-armed her into.

After pulling Rene through the small opening, Annie filled her in on the details. Rene felt that Annie should not worry about the convent threat. Mr. McGowan was not the type to send one of his children away against his or her will. Kevin was the primary agenda item. Rene urged Annie to inform him that rude behavior would not be tolerated. Annie agreed. The last few weeks had given her a better perspective. The tricky part would be getting privacy for the phone call.

Rene wished her well and exited the window.

Annie had just closed the window when she heard her father bellow down the stairs, "Nellie? Are you down there?"

Annie froze. She waited, silently praying he would go away.

"Nellie? Answer me."

Raising her voice tone an octave, Annie answered. "Yes, Dad?"

"Come up here and get these clothes off the stairs before someone kills their self."

"In a minute, Dad. I'm in the middle of something."

"Well, hurry up. It's enough I wash the blasted things. I'm not going to carry them upstairs for you. If they're not gone tonight, I'll throw the lot of them in the garbage." His steps left the doorway. Looking up at the basement ceiling, Annie tracked his footfalls back to the living room.

With a whoosh of relief, she let her breath out. A brisk knock at the window nearly stopped her heart. She went over and pulled it open.

"You're just in time..." she began.

"Shut up, Annie, and help her in," Maureen ordered gently as she pushed Nellie through the open window. Nellie began climbing in feet-first. "Help her down," Maureen instructed. "It's all right now, Nellie. We're home, and no one was hurt."

Annie guessed the situation was dire if Maureen was being so nice. "Come on, Nellie," she coaxed in kind. "Step on to the chair. I've got you. You're almost in." With Nellie safely in and placed on the couch, Annie turned to help Maureen. "What's wrong with Nellie?" she asked. Observing the equally shaken state of Maureen, Annie stated uncertainly, "I'd better go get Dad."

"Yes, Annie," Nellie cried passionately. "Go get Dad. Maureen just dragged me down 65th Street."

"Shut up, Nellie," Maureen ordered. "Annie, don't you dare get Dad. We're not hurt, and it's over. It will only upset him."

"WHAT?" Annie demanded. "Were you attacked?"

"No," Maureen said, collapsing on a chair across from Nellie. "Tom Flynn was taking us for a ride, and a drunk man slammed into us at the intersection. The car is totaled.

Nellie was in the back. I couldn't get her out. I couldn't get the seat up."

Annie's wide eyes rested in a now pale face. "Is she hurt?"

"No," Maureen responded confidently. "Just shaken up."

"Don't talk about me like I'm not here," Nellie sobbed. "We were almost killed! And I am too hurt. My arm is killing me. Look. It's all red." She pushed up her sleeve to reveal a red and slightly swollen wrist.

"It looks like an Indian burn, Nell," Annie said kindly.

"You idiot, Nellie," Maureen snapped. "That's from me trying to pull you over the seat. I thought the car was going to blow up. You're not hurt."

"She wouldn't let us go to the hospital," Nellie cried to Annie. "Even the police said we should go get checked. There could be internal injuries."

"Nellie," Maureen moaned in frustration, "if you were hurt, I would have let you go to the hospital."

"No, you wouldn't have," accused Nellie viciously. "You're a big bully, Maureen. I'm never going out with you again. All you care about is not getting grounded."

"Well, if I'm a bully, you're the biggest baby I've ever met. Shut UP already."

Maureen's patience had exhausted itself, and Annie hastily intervened. "Nellie, you need a nice can of pop and a wet rag for your arm. Maureen would never have brought you home if you were hurt. I'd be upset too, if I was in a car accident. Wait here. We'll be right back."

"Thank you, Annie," Nellie said piteously, as Annie, followed by Maureen, headed for the bottom of the stairs.

Maureen spoke in a low voice. "Jim is still talking to the police. They probably think I had to go to the bathroom, the way I kept trying to leave. They wanted to take us home in the squad car and goofy Nellie was saying, 'Yes, officer. We're much too upset to walk.' I waited until he turned around and literally dragged her home. She cried the whole way, saying we deserved to die for sneaking out."

"It sounds awful," Annie commiserated.

"It was. Remind me never to rob a bank with that girl."

They laughed shortly, then Annie remembered their father. "She'll have to pull herself together, Maureen. Dad wants her to move the clothes off the stairs. He's threatening to throw them in the yard or something. Do you think we can calm her down?"

"Not that quickly. I'll go do it."

Annie hesitated for a moment. "No offense, Maureen, but don't you think he'll wonder why you're doing Nellie's job?" Maureen was not known for her willingness to do her own chores, let alone someone else's.

"I'll tell him I traded her for the dishes," Maureen decided. The girls frowned. The trade value for dishes was much dearer than bringing the clothes up. Another gulping sob from Nellie mobilized them. "Get her some pop and a rag before she faints or something."

"Yes, I will," Annie promised. "But I'm waiting for an important call. I can't stay with her too long."

Maureen nodded shortly. "I heard. Don't be too nice to him, Annie. If someone likes you, they don't try to get you in trouble with your friends."

Annie did not ask how her sister had heard. With the exception of their father, everyone knew everything in their family. The girls separated to complete their respective tasks.

Shortly before eight, Annie headed up the stairs to commence the phone watch. A calmer Nellie agreed that Mr. McGowan should be kept in the dark. While Maureen did have mixed motives, the girls truly wanted to spare their father additional stress. Annie peeked over at the stairs going up to the bedrooms and admired Maureen's moxie. Not only the laundry had been cleared, but shoes, books, and bathrobes had also disappeared. Maureen was taking no chances. Annie found her sitting by the telephone. "Good job on the stairs," she congratulated.

Maureen smiled in return. "He hasn't called yet, Annie. I've been sitting right here. Mrs. Flynn called, though. She said she had a moral duty to talk to Dad about the accident." Annie's eyes widened. "I told her Dad was much too upset to talk and that Nellie was resting. She said if Nellie hit her head she could have a concussion and should be kept awake for at least six hours, then awakened every two hours through the night."

"Dear God," Annie exclaimed. "Did she hit her head?" Maureen shook her head. "Should we ask her if she hit her head?"

"No," Maureen insisted. "Nellie is not quiet about pain. She would have said something. If we bring it up, she'll imagine she did. Just to be on the safe side, we'll have to wake her up every two hours. Mrs. Flynn said to look for strange behavior."

"What would be strange behavior?" Annie asked nervously. Maureen crossed her eyes and repeatedly twitched her head sideways. Annie burst out laughing. "You're beastly, Maureen. I'm serious."

"How should I know?" Maureen said, also laughing. "There must be an obvious reason they call it strange. With Nellie it could be hard to tell. She's always strange. We'll have to wait and see, I guess."

A ring of the telephone made the girls jump.

"Shut it off, Annie. What if it's the police?"

"But what if it's Kevin?" Annie wailed.

Another ring prompted a roar from the living room. "Turn off that damn phone," their father commanded.

The girls jumped as one, but Maureen snatched the receiver first. "Yes? Kevin? Thank God, it's you. Listen, stay on the line as long as..."

Annie grabbed for the receiver angrily. The two hissed at each other for a few moments until Annie succeeded in wrestling it away.

"Hello?" she said sweetly.

"Annie? Is that you?"

Turning her back on Maureen. "Yes, of course."

"What was that all about?"

"Maureen is in a bit of a panic. Nothing new."

"Well, I think we should talk about a few things. Can I

come over?"

Annie grimaced. "Now?"

"Yes. Can you meet me in the alley?"

Maureen would have to do without her for thirty minutes. "Yes, Kevin, but why don't you come to the door?"

"I'd rather meet you in the alley, if you don't mind, Annie."

Annie agreed, resolving to address that issue tonight if everything went well. Taking the phone off the hook, she lay it on the floor. That should take care of Mrs. Flynn, she thought with a smirk.

Ten minutes later, Annie spied Kevin's familiar form out by the alley. Grabbing a sweater, she headed out the back door.

"Hi, Kevin, how have you been?" she asked lightly.

His brown eyes studied her seriously. "It's good to see you again, Annie."

"Well, I didn't exactly move, you know. You could have seen me anytime you liked."

Hands in pockets, Kevin looked down and kicked at the gravel. "After the way you acted, I was pretty sure you wanted nothing to do with me." Kevin now eyed her directly. Sincere, sad eyes rebuked her.

"What are you talking about?" Annie forced her voice to remain neutral. "Explain how you came to that conclusion. The last time I saw you, you completely ignored me, after telling my friends I said they were boring." Kevin began to speak, but Annie continued, "That was shortly after you told me to go to hell." The past few weeks had been torture, and Annie's voice rose in spite of herself.

Kevin looked away. "I knew this was a bad idea. Your temper makes talking impossible." He began to walk away.

Annie panicked and grabbed his arm. "Wait, Kevin. I'm sorry. Don't go." He stopped but stood with his back to her. "Why don't you say what you came over here to say? I'll be quiet."

Turning to face her, he stammered, "I wanted to say...I miss you all of the time. I don't want to fight. I don't want

26

to break up."

Annie's heart soared. "I don't want to break up, either."

"Is there any way we can forget this whole thing ever happened?" Kevin pleaded. "People have fights all the time. It doesn't mean they should break up. Does it?"

Annie felt a rush of pain. The thought of Kevin's suffering as she had was unbearable. "Of course not," she assured him. "We have to know what the other one is feeling, though. Then we won't have misunderstandings."

"I feel miserable," he said emotionally. "I didn't realize how much I needed you, Annie. You're the only one in the world I can talk to."

"I feel the same way about you," she admitted, mentally apologizing to Rene.

"I'm scared, though, Annie." Kevin stretched his knuckles as he spoke. "I know Rene is your best friend. But I don't think she likes me. Next year in high school, she'll want you to go out and meet other guys. I can't bear the thought of losing you."

His meekness melted Annie. "You're not going to lose me. I promise. And Rene does like you. She worries about me, that's all." Annie instinctively knew this was not the time to bring up the idea of going places without him. If he was insecure before, the subject would only make things worse. She also decided not to complain about meeting in the alley. Kevin obviously needed reassurance. He still loved her! That was all that mattered.

They talked. They hugged. They vowed never to let such a silly argument come between them again. How lucky they were to have this wonderful relationship. Kevin felt Rene was jealous. Annie let herself be persuaded that it was possible. Kevin said their friends did not understand how serious their relationship had become. Annie should accept the fact that no one understood. Kevin said he was glad Annie could be trusted not to relay what went on between them. Kevin could never trust someone who did that. Annie smiled and resolved to stop telling Rene everything. Yes, it all made sense now. A small voice whispered that Rene would not be satisfied with Kevin's explanations. Actually, he had made none. Kevin did not want to talk about what had happened.

"What time do you have to be home?" she asked.

"I told my Dad I had to work some cramps out of my legs," Kevin grinned. "He said to take my time walking around the park. I feel so much better now that..."

A light briefly illuminated Kevin's face. Someone was coming toward them through the backyard. Annie recognized Mr. McGowan's camping flashlight.

"I think it's my dad. Dad? Is that you?"

"Annie? What the hell are you doing in the alley at this time of night?" Mr. McGowan answered, proceeding toward them.

She was about to respond when Kevin bolted down the alley. "Where are you going?" she yelled after him. "Come back and meet my dad."

Kevin never paused. He ran until he turned the corner at the end of the block.

"Who might that have been?" her father inquired sardonically.

Annie sighed deeply. "That was Kevin, Dad."

Mr. McGowan clicked off his flashlight and leaned against the fence. "Annie, why does he run away? There's something odd about that lad. I've never seen anything but the back of his head."

Annie leaned over the fence. "I don't know. His father is kind of mean. Maybe he thinks you're the same way."

"Humph," he grunted, unconvinced.

Annie made herself relax. What did it matter if Kevin had not met her father? There was plenty of time now that they were back together. "Should we go in now, Dad?" she asked elfishly. The two stood in the dark alley with Mr. McGowan in pajamas.

Her father chuckled. "Yes, I suppose we should. I was waiting to see if Kevin came flying around a corner. I figured I could wave or something." Annie laughed with him as they made their way through the yard. "By the way," he added, "I don't want you standing out here in the alley at this time of night. If you must talk to Kevin, have him sit on the porch. But not after eight on school nights." He attempted to sound stern, and Annie correctly surmised that Kevin's hasty exit had thrown him.

"I know, Dad," she said placidly. "He had something important to tell me. I won't do it again."

"Fine. Now run upstairs and talk to Maureen. She's playing records and making an awful racket. Poor Nellie is exhausted. She claims Maureen won't let her go to sleep."

Annie felt a wave of pity for her father. He had no idea how much he missed. She impulsively hugged him. "I will, Dad. I'll go right up."

As they entered the back door, Mr. McGowan patted her head. "You're a good girl, Annie," he said affectionately. "We'll not push that boarding school thing. I'll tell the good sister to shove off."

Annie nodded. "Yes, Dad. I really couldn't leave home."

"Of course not, and why should you? Run up there like a good girl and give Maureen a clout."

Annie danced up the stairs. Midway to the top, she paused to check the ache. Sure enough, it was gone. Smiling happily, she proceeded. With Kevin sorted out, she could concentrate on Maureen's dilemma. How on earth would they keep Nellie awake till midnight?

Chapter Four

Peaceful months followed the argument. Annie and Kevin were closer than before. While he still had not met her father, he did stand closer to the house. Soon, they experienced their graduations as a whirl of parties. Kevin was allowed more time for himself these days. He had secured a full scholarship to a prestigious private high school. The coach told Mr. Griffin that Kevin's routine was excessive and to allow the boy more free time. They would be working the players hard in the fall. He did not want Kevin burned out.

And so the summer passed, with long days and lightning-quick weeks. High school was upon them. Annie and Rene gaily made their way to St. Clare's. Annie was secretly glad to go back to school. She had seen little of her best friend and looked forward to spending more time with her. Lately, she found it impossible to keep both Kevin and Rene happy. Kevin preferred they be alone. At least now, Annie and Rene would see each other every day.

Annie wondered what Kevin's new schedule would bring. With practice and homework, she knew he would be busy. Strangely, this did not bother her. It would give her time to do some normal things. There were also a lot of dances scheduled, and Annie was determined to get to one of them. A dance this weekend celebrated the opening of the school year. Rene was planning to go, and Annie had promised that she and Kevin would join her. Now, she had to get Kevin to agree.

As usual, the topic of socializing created tension between them. Kevin often said he was glad Annie was not a flirt like other girls. Rene said that Kevin confused flirting with being social. Kevin said that if Annie had no interest in other guys, she would not want to attend social gatherings. Annie did comment that if he trusted her, he should not mind her going places. Kevin replied that the top priority at most functions was meeting members of the opposite sex. Annie had no response for that.

Kevin was fiercely protective of Annie. One night over the summer, he had knocked a boy to the ground for trying to talk to Annie. The girls at the party had been very impressed, gushing to Annie that Kevin was both gorgeous and romantic. Annie disagreed and challenged him.

"Annie, you are so innocent," he replied. "You don't see things. The guy was coming on to you."

"I think you're wrong, Kevin," she said thoughtfully. "But even if he was, I wasn't letting him flirt with me. Why push him down?"

"Because it's an insult to me."

"How is that an insult to you?" Confusion puckered her brow. "He didn't even know we were dating."

"Give me a break, Annie. He knew we were dating. I don't appreciate someone coming on to my girlfriend."

The whole exchange gave Annie food for thought. She would have to be very careful, indeed, not to talk to other boys. Instinctively, she sensed there was something skewered in Kevin's logic. The tough part was putting her finger on the offensive element.

Toward the end of their first week of school, Kevin called. They spent the first thirty minutes discussing their schedules. His day began at seven in the morning and ended at seven in the evening. His newly supportive father encouraged Kevin to get out and relax over the weekend. Annie thought that boded well for the future. Kevin remained cautious.

Annie purposely kept her voice light and took the leap. "There's a dance at Sacred Heart Academy on Friday. Rene is dying to go. I told her we would go with her. How does that sound?"

After a pause, Kevin replied, "I just told you I couldn't get out."

Irritated, Annie shot back, "You did not. You said your dad told you to go out and relax."

"I hate those dances. You know that, Annie. Let's go up to the park and hang out for a while."

Annie knew she had to play this carefully. "I know you hate dances, Kevin. The thing is, I promised Rene. She doesn't know anyone at school. Besides, why not do something different from the boring old park?" The minute she spoke, she knew she had made a mistake.

"I didn't realize I was boring you, Annie," Kevin said quietly.

"Oh, Kevin, you know that's not what I meant. I meant it might be fun to do something different. Terry and all of them are going. Come on, let's go."

"Well it sounds like you can't possibly miss it, so go ahead."

"Yes, Kevin, I'm going to. I haven't done anything with Rene is an long time. I wish you would come with us. If it's terrible, we can leave. Please come..."

"I've told you three times that I can't. You obviously don't want me to go or you wouldn't sound so happy about it. Have a great time."

Click. He hung up on her. Tears of outrage pricked the inside of her eyelids. She blinked rapidly. The ache crept back into place. Ignoring it, she called Rene and informed her they would be going alone. Rene expressed dismay about Kevin. Annie merely said he did not want to go.

Annie did not tell Rene about the fight.

• • •

On the night of the dance, the girls dressed at the McGowans'. Mr. McGowan had agreed to drive them. Rene chattered happily, and Annie attempted to get into the spirit. It was exciting. This was their first official high school function. Annie wished sadly that Kevin was not mad at her. He might ignore her again or break up with her. The thought of being without him frightened Annie, but she could hardly stop her life.

"Let's go, Rene. Your hair looks fine," she said impatiently.

The girls were dressing in Maureen and Annie's cluttered bedroom, utilizing every toilet article they could lay their hands on.

"Easy for you to say, Annie. I look like I just came through the wax cycle of a car wash."

Annie glanced at Rene's hair. "Good God. What did you do to it?" Rene's naturally curly hair reacted badly to any dampness, but it was now matted.

"I put some of your sister's spray on it. What is that stuff?"

"Probably deodorant," Annie quipped with a chuckle. "I'm sorry, Rene, but you look like a second grade boy making his first communion." Rene shot her a hopeless look, and Annie got serious. "Come into the bathroom, and we'll rinse it out. Let me find Maureen's hair dryer."

Annie took control, and in thirty minutes Rene was satisfied. On the way down the stairs, Annie shouted to Mr. McGowan, "We're ready, Dad."

"I'm coming. I'm coming," he muttered as he came out of his bedroom. "Why I have to chauffeur you girls around is beyond me. You both look lovely, but don't think I'll be driving you every weekend."

Annie made a face behind his back but answered sweetly, "Of course, we don't think that, Dad. You're the nicest man in the world. I bet there is not one other father in Chicago willing to drive his kids somewhere. How did we get so lucky, Rene?"

Rene giggled nervously. Annie's teasing made her tense.

Mr. McGowan muttered his way to Sacred Heart Academy accompanied by Annie's soothing platitudes. Rene giggled in the darkness of the back seat until Mr. McGowan asked, "What's so funny back there? Share the joke, or I might think you are laughing at me."

Rene stammered a denial. Midway through her panic, Annie and her father started to laugh.

"He's just kidding. Stop it, Dad," Annie said sternly. "No wonder everyone thinks you're so mean."

"Just kidding, Rene," Mr. McGowan apologized. "Don't be afraid of me. Just don't call my house after eight at night."

"That's not me calling that late. I would never do that," Rene promised him in a cracking voice.

She kept quiet for the rest of the drive, and Annie followed suit. Any more McGowan humor, and Rene would be a wreck. In no time, they were there. After agreeing to be home by ten-thirty, the girls entered Sacred Heart.

Crowds of freshman had gathered in the darkened gymnasium. A disc jockey blared records in one corner. A refreshment stand graced the other.

"Annie, we don't know anyone," Rene whispered. "Where should we stand?"

Annie assumed an air of bravado. "I'm dying of thirst, Rene. Let's go get a coke or something."

The girls aimed for the refreshments. Annie walked casually. Seeing Rene dart off, she hissed, "Don't run, Rene. Walk slowly. Keep talking. You look like you're going to throw up."

"Oh, my God. How stupid of me," Rene babbled. "You're right. Keep talking. I wish I could think of something to say. Oh well ... how do you like school, Annie? I think it's just fine. Let me think of my subjects. Let's see ... math, science, music, what else?"

Annie turned to Rene and burst out laughing. "Rene, stop talking so fast." Rene too broke into loud laughter, and the girls relaxed.

Looking toward the refreshment stand, Annie wondered if she knew one of the girls. This was going to be fun.

"There's Terry and the rest of them," Rene observed. "I thought you said Kevin wasn't coming."

Annie's stomach plunged like a broken elevator. "He isn't. Where do you see him?" Surely Kevin wasn't going to ignore her in front of everyone again. She grabbed Rene's arm. "Rene, if he starts being rude to me, let's walk away. OK?"

Rene looked bewildered. "Of course, Annie. But why would he be rude to you?" Understanding dawned. "Was he mad you were coming with me?"

"He wasn't happy. Let's not talk about it now. Here they come." She had a sinking feeling the whole night would be ruined.

"There you are," Kevin greeted. "We almost couldn't find you with all this fun going on."

Greetings were exchanged as Annie tried to assess Kevin's mood. After a few minutes he was beside her, whispering in her ear. "I'm sorry I was cranky on the phone. I didn't realize how much it meant to you. Are you mad?"

"No," Annie answered honestly. "I thought you were mad at me. But, Kevin, why didn't you call me if you decided to come? I felt terrible."

"I wanted to surprise you," he said sweetly. "I also wanted to make sure you weren't picking up one of these Sacred Heart guys." He spoke with mock sternness. Turning to Rene, he grabbed her arm. "Rene, you look gorgeous. Will you dance with me? I won't get the chance once these guys get a look at you."

Rene looked pleased, if surprised. She followed him out to the dance floor. Annie recognized the peace offering and hoped Rene would respond in kind. She was not disappointed. Kevin was charming, and Annie saw Rene smile warmly at him. Annie felt her heart lighten and happily made small talk. Kevin could make her so happy when he wanted to.

Later, in the bathroom, Rene chattered as she wet her hair down for the fourth time. "Annie, sometimes I don't know what you see in Kevin. Other times, he's so sweet, I wish I had someone like him. You're very lucky."

Annie smiled. "I know, Rene. He gets caught up in the mess at home sometimes."

"It's such a shame," Rene agreed. "Why doesn't his mother tell his father to lighten up?"

"I guess she is afraid to. Kevin says she's nice, though. Like tonight ... she told his father Kevin had to go help his older brother work on his basement." Annie spoke slowly, measuring her words. It was strange, and she did not pretend to understand it.

Rene's baffled frown met hers in the mirror. "What possible objection would his father have to a school dance?"

Annie shrugged. "I can't imagine. The mysterious part is this. They don't even ask him. Kevin said his mother would not permit him to. She said it would only start a fight." The girls exchanged blank looks. "It's weird, I know," Annie continued. "Look at it this way, Rene. What did my mother have against bowling alleys? Parents are not to be understood."

Rene nodded in agreement. There was no explaining the notions of one's parents. The main thing was, Kevin had come and they were having a great time.

• • •

Kevin's aversion to high school activities was limited to dances. He had no problem with sporting events, and Annie adjusted her tastes accordingly. She attended his football games and quickly learned to like the sport. She now spoke knowledgeably about punts, passes, and scrimmage lines. Gradually she let go of her desire to attend dances and limited her own athletic participation to pickup volleyball teams. Rene, on the other hand, had launched herself in high school. She moved purposely from the French club to student council meetings. Annie often teased her but felt small twinges of jealousy. While Annie would not have traded her life in a million years, she did envy Rene the apparent lack of conflict. She was in high school; therefore, she did high school things. Annie felt sure that when Rene began college she would magically turn collegiate.

Annie, on the other hand, felt older than her peers. For some inexplicable reason, she was beyond them. She spent a period of time searching for answers. Was it because she had lost her mother early and was more independent? She considered this a partial explanation. Her high intelligence separated her from others? This she found a more consoling theory. Somehow she was different. Dramatically, she fancied herself a tragic heroine. Except tragic heroines usually died alone. Somehow she had to integrate Kevin into the master plan. She had always felt strong religious leanings but was attempting to quell them. She could not recall reading about a saint who had a grand passion. It was all a bit difficult. Never once did it occur to Annie that most of her peers were struggling with exactly the same dilemmas.

Occasionally she felt nagged by the idea that her life was borrowed from Kevin's. She would not have traded him but thought she should be achieving more. Because of Kevin's intense schedule, she had to be available when he was available. Their time was augmented by the occasional weeknight meeting at the park while Kevin did "light conditioning." Or Kevin shot baskets by his garage. He would call Annie and let her know he was going to be out there. She was then expected to walk the five blocks to his house and meet him. For some reason, his father could not know she was there, so she had to sit on the far side of the garage, out of sight. Also, Kevin did not walk her home, so she went alone, in the dark. She lied in response to her father's inquiries, saying Kevin walked her as far as their backyard. She would have never have admitted to Rene that Kevin let her walk alone. Being embarrassed by this bothered her more than the solitary walk.

One night she told him she would not be coming anymore. As they stood by the side of his garage, she explained she was uncomfortable walking home. She asked if there was any way he could sneak away for ten minutes to accompany her. He became irate and rebuked her for being inconsiderate. Leaving would be disobedient to his father.

"Give me a small break, Kevin," she retorted. "Every time I walk home alone I'm disobeying my father. Not to mention that you disobey yours every time you drink. Frankly, any time you do anything other than sports you're disobeying him."

"Yes, but your father is more understanding," he answered. Annie privately conceded that Kevin's father was more likely to overreact. At the same time, why was it acceptable for her to lie?

"Kevin, I hate to start a fight about this. But it seems to me that we pretty much work around your schedule for everything. Have you noticed that?"

This was their junior year, and Annie was disgusted with Kevin's inability to compromise. The fact that Rene was dating a delightful senior who treated her like a queen did not help matters. Indeed, Annie felt that Rene's romance had shined a bright light on her own. She did not like what she saw. This conversation had been a long time coming, and Annie was determined to get everything out in the open.

"Kevin, did it ever occur to you that I do not like football?" she began. "As a matter of fact, I don't like basketball either. Did you know that? How would you? You've never asked me what I liked. I hate going to football games. It's not enough to freeze my butt off for hours before and after the game. Then we have to go to a party with the intelligent group that is the football team and relive every horrible minute. Every excruciating second lives again. True, we get to watch them shotgun cans of beer and throw up. You can't get fun like that at a dance." Annie paused. Now she spoke more thoughtfully. "I'm sick of everything being about you and your friends." A short glance told her that Kevin's face had grown red.

"Well," he began in an ugly tone, "I had no idea my friends were not intelligent enough for you. Maybe I should be like Rene's boyfriend and sprinkle rose petals in front of you." Kevin had stopped shooting and held the basketball to one side. "Let me ask you this, Miss Intelligence. Have you ever wondered why you have no friends of your own? Let me be the first to tell you. Because people don't like you, Annie. Are you listening? You think you're so superior. But you're not. You're just a snobby little bitch. My friends don't say anything because they know I'd kill them. They don't like you, though, and neither does anyone. Little Miss Intelligence," he mocked her. "You're just stupid Annie. You're just a stupid, snobby little bitch." To underline his point, Kevin thrust his finger directly at Annie's face.

She resisted the urge to step back and faced him directly. "You're right about one thing, Kevin," she said, attempting to maintain a level tone. "I am stupid. Anyone who stayed with you for three years would have to be."

Annie turned her back and started to walk. Suddenly, she was slammed forward. First her shoulder and then her head crashed into the garage. The force of the impact stunned her. Leaning against the garage, she remained motionless. Seconds passed. Slowly she brought her hands up to her head.

"Annie. . ." she vaguely heard Kevin stammering behind her. Resting her head on her hands, she waited for her thoughts to stop whirling. She remembered falling off the bannister as a child and striking her head on the concrete floor. It had felt like this. Strangely detached, she noticed again that Kevin was talking.

"Are you OK? Oh, God. Annie, tell me you're OK. Sit down."

Annie allowed herself to be lowered to a sitting position. She then slapped Kevin's hand away. "Don't touch me, or I swear to God I'll kill you." Surprised at the violence in her voice, Annie rubbed her shoulders where his hands had been, as if to erase the feel of him.

"I tried to grab you, but you tripped and fell forward," Kevin lied earnestly.

Annie looked up at him and felt a rush of rage. "You son of a bitch! You hit me. Admit it, Kevin. You shoved me into the garage." Kevin shook his head. Annie choked back sobs. She could feel her head swelling and tried to calm herself. So many of their arguments left her perplexed. She never walked away from a fight with a feeling of clarity. She would not be misled this time. She shook her head to clear the dizziness. "Admit it, Kevin." Her breath came in spasmodic gasps. Glancing up at him, she noticed he was pressing his hands against his eyes. Emotionally vacant, she pulled him down next to her. "Admit you pushed me."

She waited for Kevin to control himself He curled up with his knees against his chest. Appalled at the ugliness of her thoughts, she looked away. Glancing back, she saw the genuine anguish on his face. With a sinking heart she thought of his home life and how sweet and kind he usually was. Annie pulled him roughly toward her.

"Dammit, Kevin, you're turning into a nut. I know you pushed me. Why do you deny everything? I'm sick of being blamed every time we have a fight."

Kevin hid his face in her shoulder. Annie thought sarcastically that by the end of this she would be apologizing to him. She heard him muffle a sob and felt vaguely disgusted. Ashamed, she pulled him closer.

"Kevin, why did you shove me?" She made an effort to keep her voice gentle. "You owe me a huge apology. We can't go one step further until you admit you pushed me and apologize."

Kevin looked up at her. He made no effort to conceal his pain and said in a choked voice, "Annie ... I didn't mean ... you tripped."

With an abrupt motion, Annie pushed him away. Standing, she towered over his fetal-like form. "Screw you, Kevin Griffin. I hope I never see you again." She stumbled as she turned to leave. "Annie, why are you doing this to me?" Kevin called miserably after her.

Wheeling around, she screamed, "What, Kevin? What horrible thing have I done to you? I'm a human missile, and you're the one crying. Stay away from me! Do you hear me? You're nuts!" Turning, she began to run.

After covering the first two blocks, she paused to catch her breath. The ache returned with a violent force that doubled her over. Tears came. She put one hand up to her head. It was not bleeding but was definitely swelling above her temple. Her first thought was whether her hair would cover the mark. She fervently hoped so. No one must find out. There was not a soul she could tell. The thought enhanced her grief, and her sobs intensified. Attempting to control herself, she tried to figure out what she had done. Kevin had a temper, but he had never hurt her. He often started fights with other guys but always said anyone who hit a woman was a loser. The whole thing was senseless.

Confusion enveloped her, and she gave up. Taking deep breaths, she calmed herself and made her way home.

• • •

Later that night Annie lay awake in the darkness and replayed the scene yet again. It still made no sense. She had insulted his friends. Too bad. Kevin routinely insulted Annie's friends, and she said nothing. Besides, his friends were worthy of insult, and he knew it. He had called her stupid. He had also said she was a snob. Try as she might Annie could not figure that one out. She had never been accused of being a snob and frankly had never been called stupid. His friends did not like her? That was news to Annie. Far from being offended, she decided it was either a lie or the truth. Either way, it did not matter. Annie would treat their dislike as a compliment and think no more about it. A peaceful stillness came over her. It was inevitable. Still, she dreaded it. It was time to think about what he had done.

Staring into the darkness, Annie let the thoughts come. The actual impact of hitting the garage did not immediately present itself. There was something worse. The thought took shape. It was the look on Kevin's face right before she turned to walk away. Annie shuddered. She struggled to define it and wondered if she had imagined it. The truth flitted about the outskirts of her consciousness. Suddenly, it burst through with appalling clarity. Kevin hated her. Kevin had intended to hurt her. Badly. Contemplating the incident, Annie solemnly realized that it was the force of the shove she could not let go of. If her shoulder hadn't hit first, she could have been badly injured. Kevin hated her. Curling up, she began to weep.

Uninvited, another thought jumped into her head. Kevin had called her a bitch. What had she done to deserve this? Stifling a loud sob, Annie heard the bunk bed shift above her. A moment later Maureen's face appeared above her, comically upside-down.

"Annie, I know you're upset about something. Tell me what it is."

Annie shook her head and hugged her pillow to her face.

"I promise I won't tell anyone." Maureen spoke with rare gentleness. "It helps to talk about it. C'mon, Annie. Did you have another fight with Kevin?"

The unexpected kindness, coupled with the loving sympathy of her sister, made Annie cry harder. Maureen waited patiently, peering at Annie from her unlikely position.

"Maureen, he can be such a jerk," Annie exploded. "He goes crazy. Should I never say anything to him? I must be doing something wrong. He's the nicest guy in the world, but somehow I'm making him crazy." Annie spoke in choppy, disjointed sentences.

Maureen listened patiently while Annie spilled everything except the shove. Annie never considered mentioning the push. For some reason she was embarrassed. She also did not want to deal with Maureen's probable outrage.

"Annie, you are a bit of a smart ass," Maureen began judicially. "That sometimes makes people mad. He is a big football player, and it's nice to have your boyfriend in the paper, but think about it, Annie. He's got you to the point where you don't have a life of your own. Johnny would never stop me from going somewhere because he couldn't go."

Annie rolled her eyes in the darkness. Maureen had finished two years of college and come home. Despite her father's disappointment, she could no longer be away from her boyfriend, Johnny. She thought him quite spectacular, and Annie privately dubbed him Mr. Wonderful. She hoped she would not be subjected to a list of his fine qualities tonight.

"I know you think I brag about Johnny too much," Maureen continued.

Yikes! Thought Annie. She's clairvoyant. She had not realized her thoughts were wafting into the top bunk.

"No, Maureen, I think he's great," Annie replied warmly.

Gratified, Maureen continued. "The point is he doesn't control my life. He respects me."

After a short pause, she continued ruthlessly. "Annie, it's time. You've outgrown Kevin Griffin. You know it, and I know it. Think about it, Annie. In three or four years the guy has spoken to Dad twice. That's not shy, Annie. It's rude. You haven't gone to any dances. Just Kevin's stupid homecomings. He gets mad at you for everything and then ignores you for days at a time. Are you getting mad at me?"

"Not at all," Annie said sadly. "I just hate that you're so right. Maureen, he needs me, though, and I'll be so alone without him."

"Are you crazy, Annie? You can have any guy you want." Maureen was incredulous. "Have you noticed you're gorgeous? I see guys looking at you all the time. You don't notice because Psycho Boy will beat them up if they even look at you."

Annie laughed but was grateful. "Maureen, you are so mean. He is not a psycho boy. He's just a little possessive."

"You mean obsessive. Another thing that bothers me about him is the way he is always touching you. Why is he doing that? He always has to have a paw..."

The girls were interrupted by a muffled "ping" against the window.

"Oh great," Maureen said dryly. "Here's Psycho Boy now."

Annie sprang out of her bed. Peeking down from her second story room, she saw that Kevin was indeed standing in the yard. She struggled with the window. There was a loud thud. Maureen slid down from her bed in one smooth, practiced movement.

"We'd better turn on the light before he throws a hand grenade," Maureen said flatly. "That way he'll know he's made contact."

Annie struggled in vain with the window. Mr. McGowan was a fanatic insulator, and Annie couldn't get the caulk off.

"Stand aside, Little Girl," Maureen said, brandishing a knife she kept handy. "You have to peel it out carefully so you can put it back. Otherwise, the warden will put up bars. Annie, do you want me to tell him you don't want to talk to him?" she asked seriously. "You don't have to, you know."

Annie thought of Kevin pressing his hands against his eyes and shook her head. "I've got to, Maureen. I couldn't do that to him."

Maureen nodded in understanding. "OK. Grab your sweater, and I'll tell him you're on the way down. Just a few minutes, though, Annie. And don't wake up Dad." Annie gave her a quick hug.

The girls were not demonstrative, but Annie was grateful. Maureen smiled and pushed up the window. She gave Kevin the thumbs up sign followed by the wait-a-minute signal and closed the window.

Chapter Five

Annie crept silently down the stairs. If she awakened her father, any chance at conversation would perish. Letting herself quietly out of the back door, she took a deep breath and resolved not to get sidetracked. Kevin still stood under her bedroom window.

"Oh, God, Annie, thanks..." Kevin began.

"Shh!" she whispered sharply. Motioning toward the alley, she let him follow her. He looked awful. Unlaced shoes and old sweat pants added to his general air of panic. Annie found it difficult to look at him. Her feelings were so tumultuous that she did not trust herself to speak.

"Annie, hear me out." Kevin spoke in a rush. "Give me a few minutes, and I can explain everything." Annie remained silent with her eyes downward. "The thought of losing you has been making me insane. Lately I get the feeling you're sick of me. I know I'm not like Rene's boyfriend, and I'm sure she is making comments to you about..."

Kevin would have continued, but Annie exploded. "Kevin Griffin, if you dare blame this on Rene, I'll walk away. Do you hear me? I'll walk away."

Kevin put his hands out to placate her. "I'm sorry, Annie. I'm not trying to blame anyone. I just want to explain how I've been feeling. Remember how you said that if I told you what I was feeling, we wouldn't have these problems?"

"The goal was that you share your feelings before you did something nasty, Kevin. It's a little late now, don't you think?"

Kevin put his head in his hands. His voice was muffled and tight with emotion. "Annie, don't leave me. I'm going nuts living there. You know my father has a temper. What you don't know is that he is crazy. He gets mad and throws things. When we were little, he would hit us for nothing. For no reason he would rant at my mom." Kevin stared intently at Annie. In spite of herself, she looked back. "I used to sleep under my bed so that if he got mad and came into my bedroom he wouldn't find me. He must have known I was there, but he never looked for me. If he didn't see me, he started on my brother."

"How old were you, Kevin?" Annie asked.

"I guess about five. That's the first time I remember. I used to keep an old blanket and pillow under there for when they were having fights. My mother cleaned all the time, but she never moved it."

"Kevin, she must have known what he was doing. Did she ever try to stop him?"

"Annie, it wasn't her fault," Kevin sounded tired all of a sudden. "She always came in afterward. She couldn't stop him. She still can't. He doesn't listen to anyone. He's a bastard, and I hate him. No matter what I do, it's wrong. It's so tense there I get stomachaches. What I want you to know is that I will never, never be like him." Annie said nothing. "You have to believe me. I will never lay a finger on you. There's no way I can be without you. If you want me to be like Rene's boyfriend, I will." Kevin paused for a moment and then added, "What queer things does he do? I can read poetry, you know."

Annie laughed in spite of herself. "Kevin, I don't want

you to read poetry. I want you to understand that I have a say in what we do. I want to go to my dances, and I want to go to my friends' parties. And I want you to go with me instead of getting mad and ignoring me for days afterward." Annie spoke gently but felt anxious. The thought of Kevin's sleeping under his bed broke her heart. She could certainly understand now why he was so tense at times. It was a nightmare. Despite this, she was sick of the restraints imposed by their relationship.

"Kevin," she changed the subject, "what about tonight? You could have killed me."

He lowered his head into his hands again. Annie felt his anguish and wondered why it left her cold.

"What you were saying was true. We do everything for me. I felt so guilty, and then when you said my friends were stupid..."

"Kevin, those guys ARE stupid. You're much smarter than they are. I'm not knocking them, but it's true. What's more, you have always said the same thing." Annie now spoke persuasively. "Why would that make you go off on me?"

"Because you're so much smarter than me," Kevin spoke in a rush again. "Annie, you're the best thing that ever happened to me, and I am terrified that some day you'll realize you're too good for me. When that happens, you'll leave. Tonight I figured you had realized it. I'm more sorry than I can tell you. If my dad discovers I sneaked out...you can imagine. I couldn't wait one more second, though. I had to tell you that I love you. I would die for you, Annie. If you live a hundred years, you'll never find anyone who loves you as much as I do." Kevin spoke with certainty. He still respected the distance between them and kept his arms crossed over his chest.

In a rush of emotions too numerous to identify, Annie closed the gap between them and landed in his arms. She finally began to cry and told Kevin that she thought for a minute he hated her.

"Annie," Kevin held her face gently between his two

large hands, "there is nothing in the world, nothing, that could make me hate you. You are the only reason I have ever been happy. Do you understand me? Every day I thank God I have you. Without you I have nothing. From now on my only goal is to make you happy. Whatever it takes. OK?"

Annie nodded. "But, Kevin, I don't want you to do things you don't want to do."

"Well, you do things you don't want to. Don't you? What about reliving every, what was it, 'excruciating second' of my games?" She saw the glint in his eyes, and they both burst out laughing.

Annie felt happy all of a sudden. Kevin understood what he was doing wrong, and he was willing to change. Things were bound to work out. It was true. She could not imagine anyone loving her as much as he did.

"Annie," he broke her train of thought, "I think we have a better shot than most people. I know what it's like to live with a mean person. We're way ahead of the game in that respect. I'll remember what it felt like, and I will never treat our kids like that."

"You're pretty confident in your charms, Mr. Griffin," she teased. "What makes you think we'll have children together?"

"I have it all worked out," he explained. "I'll get a scholarship, and you can come with me. We'll finish school and get married. How does that sound?"

Annie felt a wave of irritation. "Kevin, it's possible I won't want to go to the same school as you. Not because I wouldn't want to be with you but because it might not work out that way. My father would not consider your scholarship as the prime criterion for choosing my school. Quite the contrary."

"Annie, not to be conceited, but I think I can pretty much write my own ticket. You pick your school, and I'll go where you go. How is that?" He looked so handsome and confident, Annie had to smile. She hadn't thought about college in terms of Kevin but could certainly see the advantages of being away together. No Mr. Griffin to drive him crazy. The more she thought about it, the more Annie's spirits rose. Once Kevin was away from his father, everything would change. She was sure of it.

• • •

Glorious days followed the garage door incident. They attended Annie's Junior Prom and spent time with her friends. Kevin was as good as his word and did anything he could think of to please Annie. The two grew closer. Annie felt confident they could weather the adjustment to college. Indeed, it seemed as though nothing could come between them. Kevin reminded her of his commitment to her well-being and often asked if she was happy. Annie truthfully answered "yes."

Enveloped in a romantic haze, the two spent every spare minute together. The only problem from Annie's standpoint was their rapidly developing intimacy. She and Kevin discussed the subject and agreed that sex would have to wait. Feeling quite responsible, they decided to abstain until after they were in college. Then they would reevaluate. Kevin did not feel it was a sin as long as two people loved each other. Annie remarked that most eighteen-year-old men would probably agree. Kevin had laughed ruefully but contended it was only wrong if someone was using someone else. Annie pointed out the church's clear mandate regarding premarital sex. Kevin said that many things they did could be considered sins. Annie understood his logic but felt that there was sin and there was SIN. Because a person stole a candy bar didn't mean he may as well rob a bank. Yes, the subject of sex sparked many lively discussions.

• • •

It was early June, and the two were enjoying the freedom of summer. Both were employed at part-time jobs. Working for money was fun compared to slaving away at school or practice. Kevin's summer conditioning program designed by his father was easy to circumvent because he mostly worked out at the park. Kevin no longer brooded. He further reduced his stress by working as many hours as possible. His father had a great deal of respect for hard work. Kevin said it was a win-win situation. He made money and kept his father happy at the same time. His job at a local gas station was easy and had enabled him to pay for the insurance on his car. The car was old and unpredictable, but it ran and opened up new vistas for the couple. Instead of hanging around at the park, Kevin and Annie drove down to the lakeshore on weekend evenings. Kevin had a Styrofoam cooler and usually kept a six-pack on ice. The nights were passed sitting on the beach. Sometimes they talked, and sometimes they sat silently. On hot days when neither was working, they drove downtown and went swimming at the beach.

One day the beach was particularly crowded. Kevin and Annie surveyed the scene with dismay.

"I guess we could jump in once and leave, Kevin," Annie said doubtfully. "I really don't want to lie around with people walking over me."

"I agree," said Kevin. "But we came all the way down here, and we've already parked. Let me think for a minute. Annie, I have an idea. C'mon. Let's walk this way."

"Slow down, Kevin," Annie said playfully. "You have that criminal look on your face. What's the idea?"

"Have a little faith. Don't you trust me?" He raised his eyebrows and assumed a diabolical air.

He was walking her down Lake Shore Drive, and Annie could not imagine what he was planning. They had very little money and were obviously dressed for the beach. Kevin whistled cheerfully, and Annie gradually caught his mood. It was a beautiful day. It was easy to be impulsive.

Just as Annie began to relax, Kevin stopped dead. They were standing in front of the Hilton Towers.

"Why are we stopping?"

Looking down at her from his six and a half feet, Kevin adopted a mock seriousness. "Annie, did I promise to make you happy?"

"Yes, you did, Kevin. What does that have to do with

anything?" She loved when he was in this mood. He seemed ... happy. That was it. If Kevin was happy, it was impossible not to be happy with him.

"I made a solemn vow to ensure your happiness. I take my vows seriously. You said you wanted to go swimming. I cannot let you languish on the beach with that rabble down there. You're much too good for that. Therefore, we shall swim in the finest pool in the city." Kevin waved his arm in the direction of the hotel. Annie began to shake her head. "No arguments. We cannot, of course, enter through the main doors. You're not that good. I do, however, think that with a little boldness we can access the pool through the parking tower elevators. Follow me, My Lady."

With that, Kevin shifted his Styrofoam cooler to his other hip and proceeded to the parking entrance.

Annie grabbed his arm. "Kevin, you're out of your mind. Look at the way we're dressed."

They were, indeed, underattired. Kevin wore cut-off jeans with flip flops, and Annie wore cut-offs with a T-shirt over her bathing suit. A pony tail and gym shoes rounded off her outfit, and she felt certain they would be thrown out for the vagrants they were.

"Annie, c'mon. If we act like we know where we're going, no one will have the guts to say anything." He gave her an arch look. "No guts, no glory, My Princess. Let's go swimming."

"Well, I guess the worst thing that could happen is they'll ask us to leave," she said hesitantly. "What the hell! We may as well try it."

"That's the spirit," Kevin applauded. No mention was made of the beer in the cooler.

Within ten minutes they were poolside. Their only bad moment had come after they marched confidently into the laundry room. Annie had burst out laughing. True to form, Kevin had greeted the employees as though he were the owner. With great panache he steered Annie on through. Eventually, they spotted a man in swim trunks.

"He's still dry, Kevin. Follow him," Annie whispered.

53

Her tactic was rewarded when they walked out into the sunshine on the roof of the Hilton. Suppressing their delight, they spied two recliners and planted themselves. A few strange looks came their way from the businessman they had shadowed, but he quickly did his laps and left. Looking at each other , they began to roar with laughter.

"This is great, Annie. Come over and look at the view."

Annie danced over to the cement wall. Kevin put his arm around her as they gazed down at the city.

Deepening his voice, Kevin said heavily, "Someday, this will all be yours, Son."

Annie laughed appreciatively. "Watching too many Bonanza reruns, I see. Oh, look, Kevin, there's the rabble." There, indeed, was the beach. Very little sand was visible under the blanket of bathers.

"Kevin, it's brutally hot today. Why do you suppose this pool is empty? I mean, why isn't anyone swimming?"

"I don't know. Maybe there are parasites in the water." Seeing Annie's look of horror, he began to laugh. "I'm kidding. Rich people don't get hot because they have air-conditioning. Also, if you're staying in this type of hotel, you're here to sightsee or conduct business. They don't want to swim."

Annie considered. "I'm glad we're not rich, Kevin. This is fun, and they're missing it."

Kevin looked down at Annie with tenderness. "C'mon, Annie. Back to your lounge chair. Now lie down and close your eyes. I have a surprise for you."

Annie complied. "You're not planning another crime, I hope."

"No, you chicken-hearted wench. Stay here. I'll be back." With that, Kevin walked back into the hotel. Annie silently hoped he would do nothing to draw additional attention to himself. The walk in the hot sun had wearied her, and she closed eyes.

A cool towel placed over her face caused her to jump. "It's me," Kevin assured her. "Keep your eyes closed for one more minute."

Annie listened to a loud scraping. He was moving furniture around.

"OK. Open them up."

Annie looked around her in delight. Kevin had moved a table next to her and covered it with a lovely linen tablecloth. On the table was a red rose in a vase. Also on the table was a cheese tray with crackers and hors d'oeuvres. Kevin bustled to the cooler and soon passed Annie a champagne glass filled with beer. "Not Dom Paraguay or whatever, but I'll have you know Budweiser is the champagne of beers. Only the best for you, Annie."

Annie laughed in pure wonder. "Kevin, where did you get these things?"

"Well, I spotted the tablecloth in the laundry room. I also brought us a couple of bath towels. They're having a conference on the third floor, and the trays were set up in the hallway. I grabbed us an assortment. Cheese alone is so dreary, don't you think?" Kevin had turned English.

"Trying at the best of times, Darling," Annie responded in kind. "Where did you get the rose?"

"I was almost loaded down, but I grabbed it from the maid's cart. She also had the plastic champagne glasses. Are you happy?"

"Delighted." Indicating a variety of small bottles inside the towel, she asked, "What are these?"

"I'm not sure. They were on the cart. They looked kind of female, so I grabbed you a couple." Kevin's smile could not get any bigger. He was quite pleased with himself, and Annie felt a rush of affection for him.

"Kevin, you spoil me. I might get used to this kind of treatment. Then you'll have nothing but trouble."

"I hadn't thought of that. Give me back the beer, and you can keep the shampoo." They laughed again and tried to stop smiling at each other. The afternoon passed leisurely. When they got hot, they swam races in the pool. Annie applauded Kevin's conditioning efforts and remarked that for once he was doing what he was supposed to. After an hour of exercise, they retreated back to the chairs.

"Annie," Kevin asked lazily. "Should we be rich when we get married?"

"I've never really thought about it. Is this like 'What do we want to be when we grow up'?"

"No, I just wondered what kind of a life you want us to have."

"I don't think I have any preference, Kevin. I'd sure like to have enough so we weren't worried about it. Any more than that is irrelevant, I guess." Annie gave it some thought. "We'll have to get real jobs after college," she commented idly.

"You mean I'll have to quit the gas station?" Kevin said in mock horror.

"Well, as much as I'd like a career at Ted's Pizza, I'm afraid we'll have to cast our sights higher."

"I agree. Should we get going, Cinderella?" Annie smiled and nodded her head. She hated for this perfect day to end. Kevin felt the same way. "We'll be back here, Annie," he promised. "Maybe next weekend."

Chapter Six

A few weeks later Rene called Annie with a proposition. Rene's older sister, Patty, was attending a camping weekend sponsored by her college. It was being held at a campground two hours from Chicago, and Rene thought it would be a great chance for them to get away together. They would not have to socialize with her sister's friends but could put their tent close enough for safety. The girls could swim, read, talk, and eat. It sounded great to Annie. The McGowan family had never taken expensive vacations, but they had gone camping every summer, often at this very campground. After determining that Kevin would not be attending, Mr. McGowan granted permission.

Briefly thinking of Kevin, Annie was grateful he had adjusted his previous behavior. A year ago he would have been furious at the very idea. He did say he would miss her, but it was only for three days and the change would do her good. He made her promise she would not let any college boys flirt with her.

Annie laughed. "Kevin, I hate to break it to you, but I'm

not half as appealing as you like to think. "

"Give me a break, Annie. Those guys are vultures, and you are the most attractive girl I've ever seen."

"Thanks for the vote of confidence," she said lightly. "I'll be the most conceited one there anyway."

On the day of their departure, Rene picked up Annie in high spirits. Patty was driving with her friends, leaving the car to Rene. Their parents assumed the two girls were driving together, and the girls had not enlightened them. It was a great adventure. Rene had been driving for a year but currently only obtained the car for trips to the grocery store.

The girls loaded their gear quickly into the car. Mr. McGowan also assumed Patty was the driver. He, too, must be kept in the dark. If he looked out of the window ... the jig was up. Rene surveyed the McGowan's large tent with misgivings.

Annie noted her apprehension and said confidently, "I've watched my Dad put it up a thousand times. It's easy. It looks ghastly, but it will keep us dry, and if we want to invite the whole campground over for a party, we'll have enough room."

Annie ran in and said goodbye to her father. Seconds later they were pulling away and noticed him looking out the window.

"Oh, shit, Annie," Rene said tersely, "he's waving us back. He knows it's me driving."

Annie thought quickly. "Smile, Rene. Smile and wave. Pretend we think he is waving."

The two girls waved and smiled. As they pulled out of sight, Annie noticed her father was no longer waving but shaking his fist. She gave him a huge smile and continued waving. "C'mon, Rene, Move. Bye-bye, Dad." When they were out of sight, the girls burst out laughing. "Rene, I swear I'm going, straight to hell," Annie said, wiping her eyes. "I'll call him tonight and let him know we got there OK. He might call your parents."

"Don't worry, Annie. We're already gone. This is something they haven't covered. Patty and I will act innocent and basically say, 'Oh, now we get it. This is like, a new rule, right?'"

"Well, Rene, I will say this. It's nice to know you guys are as evil as we are," Annie commented with a sigh.

"Annie, all kids are like that with their parents. It's just your family that feels so guilty about it."

"I know, Rene, but my dad has enough to worry about. We really don't like to add to his problems. That sounds funny, doesn't it?"

"Not at all. When my dad was gone for a month, it was that way with my mom. We felt like we had to take care of her or something. And he was only on a business trip. I can't imagine how it would be if he was dead like your mom." Rene always understood. This was going to be a great weekend. The girls headed for the expressway and merged into traffic.

"Let's open the windows and smoke in the car," Rene said recklessly.

"Rene, you're dangerous today," Annie said laughing. For Rene to smoke in her parents' car was extremely rebellious.

"I'm not that crazy, Annie." Reaching under her seat, she pulled out a can of air freshener. "I have a true criminal mind and have planned everything down to the last detail."

The girls settled in to enjoy the ride. Rene was not confident on the highway and alternated between speeding in the right lane and creeping along in the left. They ignored the honking horns and discussed everything from funerals to boyfriends. After what seemed like a short time, they spied their exit. They cheerfully greeted Patty and agreed to set up their tent just up the hill from the crowd. After two hours their temporary home was "viable" as Annie put it.

"It looks like a circus abandoned it," Rene said with a chuckle.

"A very sad and depressed circus," Annie agreed. "Let's get our stuff inside, make the beds, and go swimming. We should also stop at the campground store and buy some wood. We want to have our own fire tonight, don't we?"

"Definitely," Rene answered with a shudder. "Can you imagine sitting with that group all night?"

Annie glanced down the hill and concurred. Patty's friends had set up volleyball nets and a huge scoreboard. "Too collegiate for me."

Donning swimsuits, they bought their wood and spent the rest of the day at the beach. Later they crashed the college wiener roast and thoroughly enjoyed the free meal. After dinner they enjoyed the free campfire. A young man named Harold approached them and struck up a conversation. Surprisingly, he was quite pleasant. They talked about college and camping. He was interested in their college plans, and Annie noticed she had not said a word about Kevin. For some reason she did not want to. This thought made her feel guilty.

"Rene, it's getting late," she said abruptly. "We should go and start our our own campfire."

Startled, Rene jumped up. "Yes, we should, I suppose." She gave Annie a quizzical look but said nothing more.

Harold protested that the night was young, but the girls were adamant. Annie could not shake the mental picture of Kevin. Maybe Kevin was not paranoid after all. Harold was certainly "smooth." He was so smooth that Annie would have liked to sit by the fire with him all night. She could absolutely envision herself going out with him. How did Kevin know these things? This was exactly what he had said would happen. Annie thought about Harold and realized she would love to get to know him better. She felt twinges of disappointment as they built their fire.

"Annie, do you ever get the urge to go out with someone other than Kevin?" Rene asked casually. "I'm just curious. Do you think you can marry him without dating anyone else?"

"I don't know, Rene." Annie answered thoughtfully. "My dad is getting a bit frantic about it. He keeps insisting I date other guys. He even said there was 'no way in hell' I could go to the same college as Kevin." Annie paused. "I could still see Kevin. Just date a couple other people. Kevin would never agree, though."

"No. He sure wouldn't," Rene agreed. "Harold really seemed to like you. It seems like a shame, doesn't it?"

"Yes. It does," Annie said quietly. "But, Rene, I would hate to think of Kevin dating other girls."

"I wouldn't worry about that somehow," Rene said with a smile. "More likely he'd follow you on your dates. I could not help thinking, if Kevin pulled up and saw us sitting there he would automatically assume you were about to start making out with Harold. Did you think of that?"

Annie looked startled. "Yes I did. That's why I came back up. That's an ugly thought isn't it, Rene? What would Tom think if he pulled up?"

Rene rolled her eyes. "You know Tom. He would grab a hot dog and introduce himself to Harold. Tom is not the jealous type. It makes me wonder sometimes." Rene looked pensive.

"Surely you don't think he has to be jealous to like you a lot? Don't compare him with Kevin. Kevin had a lot on his mind from home. It makes him more possessive. I think Tom is more normal. Don't you?" Annie spoke with feeling. She had often wondered why Tom was not jealous. On the other hand, he and Rene did not have huge fights like Annie and Kevin. Their relationship was more peaceful.

"I know what you mean, Annie, and I agree," Rene said slowly. "It's just that you and Kevin seem so romantic. We're not like that. Sometimes I would like Tom to be passionate about me. You know?"

"Yes," Annie sympathized. "When it's good with us, it's good. But when it's bad, it's bad. Kevin has gotten over a lot of that stuff, thank God. You know, Rene, there is nothing stopping you from dating other people." Annie was about to continue when they heard someone shouting her name.

"Who is that? Did you hear someone call your name?" Rene asked.

"Yes," Annie said smiling. "It must be Harold. We're over here, Harold," she shouted into the darkness.

Two figures approached from down the hill. One of the

figures was quite tall. "I hope that's Harold, Annie," Rene said nervously.

"Of course, it is. Who else could it be?" Annie said confidently. "Harold, is that you?" she called out.

As the figures got closer, Annie gasped. "Rene, tell me that's not Kevin. SHIT. How did he find us?"

Rene was aghast. "At least we're sitting up here by our own little fire. Did he say he was coming, Annie?"

"Of course not. I would have told you, Rene. Do you think he heard me calling out to Harold?"

"Don't say anything, and we'll act like he's mistaken," Rene advised.

"I don't believe my eyes," Annie called when they were close. "Kevin, what are you doing here? Hi Terry," Annie said on recognizing Terry Joyce. "How did you find us?"

Greetings were exchanged all around.

"I hope you don't mind us crashing your camp-out," Kevin began. The girls assured them they were most welcome. "We decided we needed some country air."

"But how did you get away?"

The boys began to laugh. "Kevin is staying at my house, and I'm staying at his," Terry answered. "We did not know where you were so we parked down the hill," Terry continued. "We have to go pull the car up and unload the cooler."

Just then a voice rang out of the darkness. "Annie?" Harold called. Kevin shot Annie a level look. She felt a chill as Harold entered their circle of light.

"Hi," he said pleasantly looking at the two unexpected visitors. "My name is Harold." With this he extended his hand to Kevin.

Ignoring him, Kevin looked at Annie. "Who's the loser?"

Harold looked stunned. Rene gasped. Terry shifted his feet around, and Annie said angrily, "Kevin. How rude. This is Harold. Harold, this is my boyfriend Kevin and his friend Terry. They surprised us." Looking at Kevin, Annie explained, "Harold is a friend of Rene's sister Patty. We met him at dinner." Turning to Harold, she said pleasantly,

"What can we do for you, Harold?" Immediately assessing the situation, Harold said quickly, "I just wanted to see if you needed anything. It's kind of lonely up here, and I wanted to make sure you were OK."

"Well, you can see that everything is hunky dory, Harold," Kevin said briskly. "No need to worry yourself. See you later."

Harold began to stammer, and Rene jumped in. "Thank YOU, Harold. Terry, why don't you and I go get the car? We can walk down with Harold. We'll be right back." Rene spoke cheerfully, and everyone hastened to follow her plan. Harold could not leave quickly enough, and Terry looked like he did not relish the thought of pulling Kevin off Harold. Annie gave Rene a grateful wave as they started down the hill. Turning slowly, she faced Kevin in a rage.

"Kevin, how could you? I don't know what to say. I'm glad to see you?" Her voice dripped sarcasm.

"Are you, Annie? I guess I'm wondering if Harold was glad to see me."

"Don't start this, Kevin. I am not doing to defend myself for something I haven't done. Please, for both of our sakes, don't start accusing me of anything." They gazed at each other with intensity. "I'm getting my sweater." Annie turned sharply and entered the tent. Inside she sat down and put her head in her hands.

"Can I come in?" Kevin asked sweetly from the door.

"It depends," Annie answered grimly. "Are you rational?"

"Of course. Why do you always assume I'm going to overreact?"

"Experience, I guess."

"Well, I'm not. I'm glad to see you. I'm glad to be in a tent in the middle of Wisconsin with you. By ourselves. Alone." Kevin assumed a lecherous tone, and Annie laughed. "I'm sorry I was rude to Harvey, Annie. He seemed like a nice guy, but I do not miss him at the moment." Sitting beside Annie, Kevin pulled her into his arms. "Are you mad?"

"His name is Harold. Yes, I'm mad." Kevin kissed her.

"I'm not too mad, Kevin, as long as you're not going to be suspicious. Actually I am happy to see you. If you get caught, you'll have to face the firing squad, you know."

"It would be worth it. How long do you think Rene and Terry will be gone?" he asked becoming more passionate.

"At least thirty minutes. Actually, Rene will stay away longer. I'm sure she thinks you're having a fit about Harvey. Er... Harold. Kevin, maybe we should go back to the fire." Annie suggested. Kevin was a little too pleased to be alone with her.

"Let's stay in here for a little while," he said, kissing her again. "You never let me near you. I know what you're worried about, Annie, but I won't let anything happen. I promise."

Knowing Kevin's feelings mirrored her own, Annie relented. Almost immediately the situation was out of hand. She could have stopped it. Kevin always scrupulously respected her wishes in that regard. For some reason, she let it continue. Later she wondered what was different about that night. She and Kevin were no strangers to passion, but they had always restrained themselves.

Afterward they dressed and sat silently by the fire.

"You're beautiful, Annie," Kevin said lovingly.

"I don't feel beautiful," she whispered.

"Are you sorry?" he asked.

"I don't know. I can't think straight. Kevin, we shouldn't have. I mean. . ." Annie struggled for words. but her voice cracked. Kevin pulled her into his arms and held her. "Annie, it will never happen again. I promise you. It was my fault. Do you hear me?" He pulled back so he could look into her eyes. "Do you hear me, Annie? I won't let it happen again. OK?"

"Kevin, it was not your fault. There were two of us in there. Whatever else we do, we're not going to blame you. It's just that we decided not to do this. We shouldn't have stayed in the tent. Shit."

"I love you, Annie. Do you believe that?"

"Yes," she answered truthfully.

"Then believe me when I tell you it won't happen again. I would never hurt you. You know that. It's all right now. Maybe we got it out of our system."

"You're right, Kevin. We'll be more careful from now on. No more camp-outs for us."

"Annie, I think we can make a case for blaming Rene," Kevin joked. "She ought to be horsewhipped for leaving us alone. I hate Rene. Don't you?" Annie burst out laughing in spite of herself. "That's better," Kevin said kindly. "Now let's have a beer while I plan my next seduction."

"That's not funny, Kevin," Annie said with a hurt look.

"Oh, God. Sorry. It was supposed to be." Kevin had a wild look on his face. "Help me out here, Annie. I'm not sure what to say."

Annie burst out laughing again. "I'm sorry, Kevin. I'm just feeling a little sensitive. I guess I'm waiting for someone to call me a harlot."

"Let's see if we can make Harvey say it," Kevin suggested brightly. "That will give me an excuse to kill him."

"You're outrageous," Annie chuckled. "His name is Harold, and I'm sure he'll run the next time he sees me coming. Honestly, Kevin. Calling him a loser like that ... what were you thinking?"

Kevin smiled. "He was after you, Annie. Couldn't you tell? Let's not talk about Henry, though. Let's get a beer and walk down to meet Terry. Are you OK now, Annie?"

Annie was able to look at him and answer honestly. "I think so. Let's go anyway." Taking her hand, Kevin led the way, and they went off to meet their friends.

The boys stayed for the weekend. Much to everyone's relief, Harold stayed discreetly away. Kevin and Terry were at their funniest, and it turned out to be the best weekend of the summer. Tender and sweet, Kevin made a constant effort to amuse her. Rene voiced her surprise at the turn of events. She candidly admitted that she had been prepared for a midnight flight if Kevin got too aggressive with Harold. "He's certainly acting like a gentleman, Annie," she observed grudgingly. Annie nodded in agreement. He certainly was.

• • •

Summer wore on, and Kevin and Annie prepared themselves for their senior year. College scouts monitored Kevin's progress. He frequently asked Annie about her college plans. Annie was not concerned about making a decision yet. She still had time and figured she would attend school downstate with Nellie. Mr. McGowan was watching Kevin's choice carefully. If Kevin chose the downstate school, Annie could count on a battle.

One evening Annie made Kevin drop her off early. They had gone to a party at Rene's boyfriend's house. Annie had begun to feel sick. Certain she was coming down with something, she asked Kevin to bring her home. Kevin complied and promised to call her later.

On the way up the stairs to her bedroom, Annie doubled over. She felt a sharp pain in her head. Waiting a few moments, she continued up the stairs to her room. Pausing at the doorway, she noticed Maureen reading on her bed.

"Hi," she said weakly. "What are you reading?"

"Nothing good," Maureen answered shortly. "What are you doing home so early?"

"I'm not feeling well," Annie said. She leaned against the doorway and tried to focus on Maureen's face. Strangely enough, it was gone. Annie could only see the bed. "I'm sick," she muttered as she doubled over again.

Annie was vaguely aware that Maureen was screaming for Nellie. It seemed like hours before she felt strong arms pulling her up from the floor. "Annie, Annie, wake up." Annie tried to focus on Maureen's face but gave up. Everything was swimming. She heard Nellie's voice from a thousand miles away. Nellie and Maureen were trying to lift her onto the bed. Annie thought idly that she could not help them. She was concentrating on a more pressing sensation.

"I'm going to be sick," she heard herself say.

Disembodied hands brought her into the bathroom. Someone held her hair, and someone else stroked her arm. Annie felt extremely loved, in a detached sort of way. The nausea passed, and Annie's head cleared. "Can you put me in front of the fan?" she asked weakly.

"Sure. Grab her under the arm, Maureen," Nellie instructed. "Get that washcloth wet, and we'll put it on her head." Nellie was all business, and Annie could only surmise that Maureen was in a panic. Maureen was great in a crisis unless blood or pain was involved. Annie was grateful that Nellie had been close by. Moments later they propped her up on Nellie's bed with every pillow in the house under her head. The sisters kept vigil, waiting for Annie to respond.

"Sorry," she accommodated them.

"No need to apologize," Nellie said gently. "What happened?"

"I'll tell you what happened," Maureen volunteered. "She came to the bedroom door and was messing up her words. Her face was the most ugly gray I've ever seen. Then she doubled up and fell down. I couldn't get to her in time, and she hit her head on the floor. Does your head hurt, Annie?" Maureen shouted.

"Why are you screaming at me?" Annie moaned, putting her hands up to her head.

"She is not deaf, Maureen. She's sick," Nellie snapped. "Annie, did you hit your head?"

"I'm not sure. I felt sick at the party and came home," she answered. "I had sharp pains in my head when I was coming up the stairs. Then I don't remember anything. I'm feeling better now."

"Annie, Dad is riding his bike," Nellie spoke reassuringly. "He should be back in a few minutes, and he can take you to the hospital. Maureen, hop in the car and find Dad." Nellie spoke calmly, but the suggestion put Maureen into a panic.

"Oh, my God. Do you think it's a brain tumor? Should we call an ambulance?" Maureen poised for flight.

"GO, Maureen. Get Dad. I'm sure it's nothing serious, but Dad will know what to do." Nellie looked at Annie and winked. Annie giggled back. Maureen was just the right side of full-blown panic.

"I'm really sick, Nell," Annie said pathetically.

"I know. Don't worry. We'll take you to the doctor and see what he says. Could you drink a little pop?"

Annie nodded weakly. Shortly after Nellie returned, they heard Mr. McGowan's footsteps on the stairs. Moving fast, he blustered into the room and surveyed the patient. Annie was still a funny color, and Mr. McGowan decided to take her to the emergency room for a "quick look." The girls fluttered about, getting her ready.

Four hours later they returned home to find the two sisters waiting up. Their anxious inquiries were met with reassurance from their father.

"She'll be fine," he said breezily. "The doctor said it is a relapse of the mononucleosis she had last year. She's been burning the candle at both ends and needs a lot of rest." He summarized the situation quickly. "What she needs now is to get to bed."

"Did they check her for a brain tumor, Dad," Maureen asked.

Mr. McGowan rolled his eyes. "Maureen, she doesn't have a brain tumor. Headaches come with mono. That's all it is. Now help your sister up to bed and everyone get some sleep."

Annie awoke the next day feeling wonderful. She lay in bed for a moment and discovered she was ravenously hungry. She began to get out of bed and nearly knocked heads with Maureen coming down.

"How are you feeling today?" Maureen asked in concern.

"Actually, Maureen, I feel great. I'm starving, but I skipped dinner last night so I think I need to eat." Annie stretched.

"Annie, I have to ask you something. Promise me you won't get mad." Maureen looked extremely nervous.

"Go ahead, Maureen. What is it?"

"OK. But remember you promised." Maureen paused and chose her words with care. "Are you sleeping with Kevin?"

Annie stared at her blankly. "WHAT?" she asked, in the time-honored tradition of obtaining time to think.

"I know it's ridiculous," Maureen said in relief. Annie's response had negated her suspicions. "I wanted to make sure you weren't pregnant or anything. Sorry I brought it up. It's just the way you fainted made me wonder..." She slid out of her bunk bed and began to dress. "I feel like pancakes. Do you want some?"

Annie groped for an appropriate response. "Uh, sure. If you're making them..." Maureen departed, leaving Annie wrapped in shock. Surely she was not pregnant. It could not be possible. One little time. Annie reeled at the thought. It seemed like seconds before she heard Maureen shouting that breakfast was ready. Annie collected herself and went down to eat.

Chapter Seven

The next two weeks were the longest in Annie's short life. She waited for good news. Kevin called her at least twice a day. Desperately seeking a reprieve, Annie went to the library. She found a book about the female body and read the chapter on pregnancy. It did not look good. Her symptoms were fairly typical. Flipping further, she spotted a chapter on something called hysterical pregnancy. She vaguely tried to imagine any other kind. Yes, she decided, this must be what I have. A hysterical pregnancy. She giggled hysterically at the thought.

"Well, it sounds good to me," Kevin said doubtfully. "How long do these things last? I mean you can't just stay hysterically pregnant for the rest of your life. Can you?"

Annie sighed. "I don't know, Kevin. At some point we are going to have to see a doctor and get a test done."

Kevin's voice held the suggestion of panic that had become so familiar to Annie these last couple of weeks. "What doctor? Annie, they'll tell your dad. We can't let anyone find out about this." Annie suppressed a rolling wave of irritation. "Kevin, this situation is not going to stay stagnant. From what I've observed about pregnant women, they tend to expand horribly. Do you get it? We can't keep this a secret much longer." She eyed him suspiciously. She was tired of his "me first" attitude. His selfishness made her feel bitter.

"Let's give it another week, OK? I'm sure it's the hysterical thing." Kevin was constantly fidgeting with his keys these days, and Annie resisted the urge to snatch them away and throw them out of the car window. They were parked around the corner from her house. Kevin told her he absolutely could not face her father.

"I have a great idea. Let's drive downtown and forget the whole thing," Kevin suggested. "We'll get a six-pack and go to the lakeshore. C'mon, let's do it." he said persuasively.

"Can't drink," she said shortly. "Bad for the baby." Startled, they exchanged looks of mutual horror. It was the first time that the possibility of a baby had been verbalized. "Oh, shit, Kevin..." Annie began.

Kevin started to laugh. "This is a nightmare. Yes, indeed. You're going to have to trust me on this. We need a little bit of fun. Going crazy is not going to change anything so we may as well go get some beer instead." Kevin was acting strangely, and Annie looked at him through narrowed eyes. "Junior will have to cope while Mom, that's you, Annie, and Dad, that would be me, go and get drunk. Are you ready, Mom?" Noticing Annie's accusing eyes, Kevin continued, "Annie, I know what you're thinking. Why is he so upset? I realize that you're the one who is pregnant, hysterical or otherwise, but I'm not going to abandon you. Therefore, I am also pregnant. I realize you get to do the really fun stuff, like actually deliver the baby, but my life is going to change a hell of a lot, too. Add to that the guilt about what I've done to you and the feeling in my stomach about what Grandpa," at this he paused for a nervous chuckle, "is going to say, and I have to admit I am feeling a little...tense. Unless there is a miracle, things are going to get a lot worse before they get any better. Let's go have some fun. OK?"

Annie felt guilty. Grudgingly conceding that this would affect him, too, she decided to stop punishing him. "Let's do it, Kevin. You're absolutely right. Let's go have some fun." Annie smiled as Kevin sighed in relief.

Two hours later he watched helplessly as Annie vomited into a garbage can. "I guess you're right, Annie," he said as they waited for her shaking to pass. "Can you find a doctor that doesn't know you?"

"I'm going to tell Maureen," Annie said with finality. "She goes to a female doctor somewhere in the suburbs. Maybe I can see her." Pale and sick, Annie felt empty, No longer afraid, she just wanted the waiting to be over. Stealing a glance at Kevin, she correctly speculated that he felt the same way.

"Try to make it for a Saturday, and I'll take you," Kevin said without expression. "What will they have to do?"

"According to the book, they'll test my urine. I guess they'll also do some kind of examination. That's the part I dread," she said, equally devoid of expression.

"Let's get it over with. Sorry you got sick."

Annie patted his arm in a distracted manner. "It wasn't your fault. I'm getting used to throwing up. It's not too bad. It was a good idea to try to have some fun, Kevin, but I think I'd like to go home now."

A week later they were waiting in the car outside of a doctor's office. Kevin refused to come in and would not be budged. "I can't believe you're going to make me go in there alone."

"Annie, I can't go in there. Sorry. I'll be waiting right here for you." Kevin looked ashamed, and Annie could have kicked him.

"I wish I could wait here," she said resentfully as she got out of the car. Kevin looked sick but said nothing.

After what seemed like an eternity, she walked back across the parking lot. Seeing Kevin trying to read her face, she shook her head noncommittally. After seating herself in the car, she put him out of his misery. "We have to wait until after four. They won't have the results of the test until then." Annie looked white. "Take me home, Kevin."

"Was it awful?" he asked as he pulled into traffic.

"Yes," Annie said shortly.

"What did she say?" Kevin persisted.

"She said my uterus is consistent with a six-week pregnancy. She also said there could be reasons for that other than pregnancy. She asked me what my intentions were if the test is positive. Apparently she is required by law to ask."

"What did you tell her?" Kevin asked.

"I said 'I guess I'll have a baby.' What else could I say?"

Annie was on the verge of breaking down, and Kevin stopped asking questions. Reaching over, he grabbed her hand and kissed it. "I'll call you at four-fifteen and see what the verdict is. Then we'll go for a walk or drive or something tonight. OK?" he spoke gently, but Annie noticed that his hands were clammy.

"Fine," she agreed tersely.

At four-ten, Annie dialed the number to the clinic. A woman's voice answered and transferred the call to the doctor. "Miss McGowan?" Annie recognized the doctor's voice.

Trying to ignore the nausea, Annie answered, "Yes, it's me."

"You're test was positive. You're pregnant." Hearing no response, she continued. "You'll need to begin taking prenatal vitamins and come back in one month. Do you want me to call in a prescription for the vitamins?"

"Uhm, no. Not today." Annie could not concentrate and clutched the phone. "Thank you," she said shortly and hung up. Reeling, she wandered up the stairs to her room and crawled into bed. She ignored the ringing telephone. Kevin would have to wait. She couldn't move. She heard a voice yelling up the stairs telling her that she had a phone call. Annie heaved herself out of bed and went down to destroy any lingering hope of Kevin's. Her news was met with repeated "Shit, shit shit" on his end, and Annie ended the conversation agreeing to call him later. Finding her way back to bed, Annie fell into a deep and dreamless sleep.

Hours later Annie awoke to Maureen's concerned face staring at her from the side of the bed. "I'm pregnant," she said.

Maureen's face contorted in grief. " Shit, Annie. Shit."

"I can't wait until someone says 'Congratulations.'"

"Give me a break," Maureen said with passion. "Who gets to tell Dad?"

"I thought I'd leave that to you and Nellie," she said in a dead voice. "I don't want to be in the same state when he hears." Annie noted absently that she felt no real emotion. She would have been happy to lie in her bed until she died. "I'm going back to sleep. If Kevin calls, tell him I'll talk to him tomorrow. OK?"

Maureen looked at her in concern. "Sorry, Annie. I don't mean to be nasty. It's just such a shock. It will all work out somehow. I mean this has happened before you know. I have a few friends. . ." she trailed off after observing Annie's look of disinterest. "I'll come up and check on you in a few hours." With that she left the room and turned off the light. Annie rolled over in relief and went back to sleep. She would handle everything tomorrow.

• • •

The following weeks passed in a blur of horrors. Emotional meetings were held with the sisters. It was decided that Maureen would clear the house, and Nellie would do the honors. Annie expressed little concern, and Maureen worried that Annie was having a nervous breakdown. Nellie said Maureen was overreacting. After speaking to Annie privately, she told Maureen that Annie was in shock.

The day Nellie told her father, Annie stayed at Rene's. She wanted to give him time to react. Nellie blessedly refrained from comment when Annie asked how he had taken it. She said he was a little shocked but would be fine in time. Rene had responded to the news the same way everyone else seemed to. Her garbled reaction included the word "shit" at least six times. It seemed to be the word of the hour, and Annie resolved not to tell anyone else.

Her first meeting with her father was uneventful. He

greeted her casually and reminded her of the need to eat properly. He also told her that she would need to get to confession immediately. Annie groaned inwardly. She did not have the heart to tell him she had already gone. Was it a sin to be pregnant? Mr. McGowan asked her one question and never uttered another word of reproach. "Annie, how did this happen?"

"Dad, I don't know," she had responded, legitimately perplexed.

Maureen burst out laughing. "Well usually. . ."

"Shut up, Maureen," Annie and her father replied in unison.

"All right. Never mind," Mr. McGowan continued. "You'll have to make some decisions. The first priority is, of course, confession. I'll take you up there this afternoon."

"Uh, thanks, Dad," Annie stammered. "I'd prefer to go myself."

"I don't want you going alone, Annie," he worried. "You might get upset. Maureen, you go with her. Pop in there yourself while you're at it."

"Remember the motto, Dad," Maureen responded cheerfully. "Mind your own soul. I'm old enough to know when I need to go to confession. I will happily go with you, though, Annie. If the priest starts yelling at you, I'll rip open his door and scream 'FIRE!'"

"Oh, I'm sure he'll just say 'shit,'" Annie said tiredly.

"ANNIE," Mr. McGowan scolded. "Of course, he won't say that. Please do not swear in this house."

"Right, Annie," Maureen responded. "Only Dad is allowed to swear in the house. We have to go outside to swear."

Mr. McGowan drifted into the kitchen, and Maureen hissed to Annie, "'Don't know?' I don't believe you said that." She began to giggle. "Do really think he is going to buy that? Was this, like, the Immaculate Conception?" She paused for a second and said with great gravity. "Just who is that baby you're carrying?"

Annie burst out laughing. "Shut up, Maureen. What was

I supposed to say? 'We did it in the family tent.' Leave me alone. You wait outside the church. You'll make me laugh if you come in."

Later that day Annie and Maureen walked to St. Malachy's. Maureen made outrageous jokes the whole way, and Annie was beginning to get a stomach cramp from laughing.

"I definitely think you should use the Immaculate Conception defense, Annie," she said brightly. "Really give him something to think about. Tell him you don't know how it happened but you suspect divine intervention."

"Maureen, if you don't shut up, I am going throw up on the sidewalk," Annie threatened. She had to serious up enough to go into the confessional. "I mean it. I feel like throwing up."

Maureen immediately stopped joking as Annie knew she would. Vomiting threats were taken seriously these days. Annie left Maureen outside and entered the church. Her anxiety lessened as she observed the short line. She hoped to be last.

Annie's turn came quickly. She slid onto the kneeler and closed the door. She could vaguely hear the mumbling of the penitent on the other side and began to hum quietly. It was not polite to listen to someone else's confession. Alone with a crucifix in the darkened cubby hole, Annie fought off the urge to cry.

The priest slid back the screen and began. Annie made short work of the preliminaries. Getting right to the meat of the problem, she said, "Father, I'm not sure I needed to come again, but my dad wanted me to. I had sex with my boyfriend. I confessed that a couple months ago, but I just found out that I'm pregnant. Anyway, here I am."

"I see," said the priest quietly.

Annie appreciated his response as the first neutral reaction she had gotten to date. Encouraged she continued, "I am not considering an abortion or anything." Did she hear him sigh in relief? "I am going to have the baby, but I haven't gotten any further than that. " They both remained silent for a moment. Stifling a sob, Annie began again. "Father, what bothers me most is the poor baby. It's so horrible that everyone thinks he or she is a tragedy. I know it sounds absurd, but I want this baby. I feel so sorry for it. I would rather not be pregnant, but it's too late for that. I guess I can't expect anyone to be happy, but do they have to be so depressed? If a baby is conceived out of a marriage, is the baby a mistake?" Annie stopped and waited.

"There is no such thing as a baby that is a mistake. I think you are a wonderful person. Let's start with that." Annie began to cry in earnest. "It probably feels very good to cry, and you should do that a lot," he said kindly. "I want to tell you a few things. OK?"

"OK." Annie tried to stop sniffling.

"At the beginning of time God created us. All of us. He took a lot of time because He decided there would be a lot of people. He loved each one of us as though we were the only one He had created. Soon you are going to be a mother. Then you will understand God's love in a special way. You already do, don't you?"

"Yes, Father," she replied solemnly.

"OK. So each soul was created. He knew each soul intimately. He carefully thought about when each soul should be born. At the beginning of time He created the soul of your little baby. He also decided when would be the perfect time to send that precious, innocent soul down to earth. He carefully looked around at all of the souls and decided you were the only one that could be the mother of this baby. He left nothing to chance. He knew this sin would be committed. He loves you like you are His only child. He thought, 'How can I make something wonderful come from something my little angel should not have done?' This baby is no accident, my dear. Your baby was created by God at the beginning of time and has some very special work to do in this world. Work that only he or she will be able to accomplish. Your baby is no mistake. There is no such thing."

A pause gave the young penitent a chance to collect herself.

Then he continued, "Your baby is a precious gift to our world. For your penance I want you to thank God every day for this child. Thank Him for His mercy and thank Him for His constant love. It may be that you'll decide to give this baby up for adoption. Even if you do, remember that you'll be a mother for eternity. God will let you know what is best. Never be afraid of what people think of you. God knows you better than anyone else. He's filled with joy today because you've accepted the gift of this child. That's all that matters. Is there anything else you want to talk about. You've told your parents?"

"Yes. Everything is OK. I'm not going to get thrown out or anything."

"Good. I want you to call the rectory and ask them for the number to Catholic Charities. They can help you to look at all of your options." He hesitated. "Do you want to tell me your first name?"

"Yes, Father. It's Annie."

"OK, Annie. I am going to ask God every day to protect you and your child. He'll take special care of you. Incidentally, are you clear on the rules regarding premarital sex? It doesn't become OK because you're pregnant."

Annie laughed shortly. "I know, Father. I don't know how to thank you. I feel happy. Thank you, Father."

"Thank YOU, Annie. You're a brave and courageous girl. Go in peace."

Annie stumbled out of the confessional. She kneeled down and said her penance. "Thank you, God, for my little baby," she prayed over and over. Her heart felt lighter than it had in two months. The worst was over. Everyone who mattered had been told except for school. The priest did not think she was horrible. On the contrary, he thought her baby was a good thing. "A precious gift" he had called it. Annie smiled to herself. "Thank you, God, for my little baby," she prayed again. Cleansing tears burned her eyelids. She stayed and prayed for thirty minutes. The priest said that it only mattered what God thought. If Annie only worried about what God thought, her worries were over.

God loved her. Of this she was certain. The rest could be dealt with.

With a light heart she skipped out into the sunshine to meet Maureen. "I was just coming in after you," Maureen said grimly.

Annie laughed easily. It felt good to laugh. "Maureen, he said my baby was a precious gift to the world." She did not feel anxious anymore, and her laughter was free of the underlying hysteria.

"Tell me you're joking." Maureen grabbed her arm. "You didn't use the Immaculate Conception defense, did you?"

The intense look on Maureen's face made Annie laugh harder. "But you told me to, Maureen." Maureen's horror forced Annie to relent. "Of course not, you goof. I told him the truth, and he said I am not bad and that the baby is a gift. This baby is not a mistake."

"Annie, of course, you're not bad. No worse than the rest of us who never got caught." Maureen looked worried. "Annie, the baby will be the most adored little monster in the city of Chicago. Can you imagine? We'll spoil her rotten." Seeing Annie's smile, she continued. "If you decide to keep this baby, we'll all help you. Nellie and I did not want to talk about the baby in case it upset you."

"I can understand that." Annie said emphatically. "I've been acting kind of weird. I feel better now. I think everything is going to be OK." She smiled at her sister.

"Of course, it will be," Maureen answered with gusto. "What else can it be? Life has to work out. It doesn't just stop because things get horrible for a while. How's your stomach?"

Annie stopped. After a moment she pronounced it sound.

"My stomach is good. Let's get lunch."

With light hearts the sisters sought out hamburgers.

• • •

While Annie wrestled with her family's reactions, Kevin faced his own struggles. He agreed to tell his mother on the same day Annie went to confession. She waited in vain for

80

his call. Lacking the courage to call him, she waited until the following day. At two o'clock in the afternoon, he called and asked her to meet him around the corner.

"I'm glad to see you're still alive," she began as she got into the car. "How did it go?"

Kevin looked uncertain. "Well, OK, I guess. She didn't say much. She gave me two pills to make me sleep, and I went to bed."

"She must have said something, Kevin," Annie said slowly. "What did your dad say?"

"Nothing. My mom says we're not going to tell him. She says he'll have a fit. We're not going to tell anyone." Kevin looked slightly defensive.

"Kevin," Annie began patiently, "I can understand her wish to avoid a scene, but don't you think he is bound to find out? What about your brother? Won't it be worse if they don't hear it from you."

"Just because you want to tell the whole world does not mean that we have to."

"Pardon me?" Annie asked in disbelief. "My family would eventually have guessed. Contrary to what you might think, Kevin, I don't want to be the poster girl for teenage pregnancies. How could I have not told my dad?"

Kevin's face turned red, and he began to shout. "People don't have to know, Annie. My mother said she would pay for an abortion. I told her you did not want that, and she said to tell you anyway. She said you should not have told your father."

Annie stared at him, white-faced. "Gee, Kevin, I can certainly see why you think she is so cool. Her solution is to chop your baby into pieces." Annie looked out of the window. She felt like a mist surrounded her head. Somehow, it had turned into a nightmare again. "Kevin, would you agree to an abortion? I'm just curious."

Hesitating a moment, Kevin looked like he was about to cry. "No, Annie. If you don't want that then neither do I. She also said you could go away to a home for unwed mothers. You could stay there until you have the baby, then give it up for adoption. No one would have to know that way either."

"Well all I can say is thanks be to God she's not my mother," Annie said with feeling. "For not saying much she sure had plenty of great ideas. What's with the obsession not to tell anyone? Her son looks like a big stud. I'm the one who looks like a tramp, Kevin. Good thing your mother has no daughters. She'd put a scarlet letter on their chest and make them jump off the nearest cliff." Annie was more upset than she knew. She had not expected his family to be happy but had hoped for compassion.

"Annie, I don't want to talk about this anymore," Kevin said putting his arms across his chest.

"Neither do I. Should we talk about the weather? No. Let's talk about football." Annie was not calming down. The more she thought about it the angrier she became.

"Calm down," Kevin raised his voice. "I've had enough of this shit. Don't blame my mother. I admit she was out of line about the abortion thing, but I made it clear we were not considering it. Shut your mouth and listen for a minute. I have to ask you a question." Kevin paused for a breath. He had been pointing his finger in Annie's face.

"Well," Annie said, taking a deep breath, "as much as I would love to hear what you want to ask me, Kevin, I'm afraid I have to leave. Go talk to your mother like that." Annie pulled open the door and started to get out. She felt her head jerked back into the car and slammed against the headrest.

"Let go of me," she said between clenched teeth.

"Shut up, Annie. I asked you to shut your mouth and listen, and you are going to shut your mouth and listen." Kevin had all of the hair on the left side of her head in his hand. Her head was being pressed into the headrest, and Annie could feel hair being pulled out.

"Kevin, you're hurting me," she said in a level voice. He looked like a madman, and Annie knew she somehow had to get away. Her heart was pounding in her chest. Kevin's face was contorted in rage, and she had the fleeting impression that he wanted to kill her.

Still holding her by the hair, he repeated, "Listen to me. I'm going to ask you a question and you're going to tell me the truth. Do you understand? The truth. Are you listening?"

Annie did not hesitate. "I'll tell you whatever you want, but let go of my hair."

"Just so you know, Annie, if you try to get out of this car I'm going to fucking kill you. Do you understand?"

Annie was about to start shouting in outrage. Looking into his eyes, she thought the better of it. She would have to get him off guard and make her escape. She nodded her head. Resisting the urge to glance around for help, she looked directly into Kevin's eyes. "What's your question?"

"What happened with Harold?" Kevin watched her intently.

Legitimately bewildered, she continued to stare. "What?"

"You heard me, Annie. What happened with Harold? Don't lie to me because it won't work. I know exactly what happened. I just want to see if you have the guts to admit it."

Annie frantically searched for a response. What happened with Harold? She thought back. Nothing happened with Harold. Where the hell had this come from? Mental pictures flitted through her head. What had Kevin heard? There had been nothing to hear. Thus assuring herself, she answered with confidence.

"Kevin, I have no idea what you're talking about. Nothing happened with Harold. You do mean Harold from the campground, don't you?"

Out of nowhere she felt Kevin's hand around her throat. His face was right up against hers, and he began to tighten his hand. "Tell the truth, Annie, or I swear I'll choke you. What the fuck did you do with Harold?"

Annie could not speak. She could not breathe. Frantically she clawed at his hand in an attempt to open her airway. Kevin continued to tighten his hand around her neck. She heard sounds coming from her throat and thought about death. Suddenly she was released, and Kevin moved his face back a few inches. Choking, Annie groped instinctively for the door handle. Kevin chuckled. Pulling her hand back, he said, "I don't think so, Miss Intelligence. Do I have to tell you again that you're not getting out of this car until you tell me the truth? You catch your breath and try again. I want to know exactly what happened with Harold. Every little detail." Annie continued to choke while attempting to take breaths. She resisted the urge to attack him, realizing finally that she was completely at his mercy. "That's it," he said. "Get comfortable and start to tell the truth, if you're capable of it."

Looking at him with hatred, she began. Her voice was hoarse as she told him exactly what had happened with Harold. She included every tiny detail she could think of. Harold walked over to them. He began to talk. He got them a drink. He protested when they got up to leave. He came up to their campfire. Annie left nothing out. Finishing the story she stared levelly at Kevin. "Any questions?"

"Just one, Smarty," Kevin began. "Did you really think I was stupid? I've waited for over two months for you to tell me. When we got to the campground, we met Patty. She told us you had just left. She also told us you had been down there the whole night. I arrive and there you are acting so innocent up by your own little fire. You acted like you had been there all night. Didn't you?"

"Kevin, I acted like nothing. I told you we met Harold down by their fire. I did not lie about anything." Annie began to cry. "Why are you doing this to me?" Her body began to react, and she began to shake. "What is your problem? If you had questions, why didn't you ask me then? Two months later you come at me like Gestapo?" Her breath came in gasps. "Do you realize you could have killed me?"

Kevin finally began to look upset. "Annie, I'm afraid I had no choice. You did not tell me the truth, and I had to know. My mother asked me if I was absolutely certain I am the father of this baby." A look of horror came over Annie's face. "I told her yes. I told her I was pretty sure you had never been with anyone else. You're sneaky, but you're not that bad." Annie stared. "Annie, don't get mad at her. She's looking out for me. I told her you weren't like that. I'm sorry I had to get rough with you, but you have to understand that I must know the truth. If we're going to get married, you'll have to get used to telling me everything. Don't be all mad. I didn't hurt you."

Annie looked around her as if to assure herself she was not dreaming. "Sneaky?" she said out loud. "Married?" she whispered to herself. Noticing Kevin groping on the dashboard, she opened the door and literally fell out in one move. He reached over to grab her foot, and Annie kicked at his hand as hard as she could. Rolling over she landed on her knees and stood up. Kevin was leaning over looking out at her through the open door.

"You look pretty funny rolling around in the dirt. You're acting like a nut, Annie," he said quietly. "Get back in the car."

Annie glared at him. She was safe now. A few yards from her house, she would have at least a ten-foot head start on him. "You are out of your mind," she said slowly. She was beginning to feel an emotion pushing itself up from her stomach. She paused briefly to identify it. Rage. That was it. "Kevin, listen carefully. I want you to tell me the truth. Are you willing to go fuck yourself? Because that's what I want you to do." She mimicked his voice. "It's important that you tell the truth now, Mr. Stupid." With that she turned to leave. She heard him calling her name, but she never paused.

Annie stumbled through her house to her bedroom. The mirror confirmed what she knew. Red welts rose up from her neck and throat. "Oh, God. Oh, God," she said over and over. Her eyes appeared too large for her small white face. Her hands still shook, but the ugliest sensation was in her stomach. Within fifteen minutes she would be vomiting. Sitting shakily down on the bed, she put her head in her hands. "Ouch." Her head hurt. Annie moved her hand gently over the left side of her head and came away with a handful of hair. Rolling onto her side, she lay down on the bed. Great gulping sobs racked her as she rolled over again. The left side of her hip was too sore to lie on. She guessed it had happened when she dropped out of the car.

Images popped into her head uninvited ... Kevin's face when he was choking her ... the view out the front window when he had her head pressed against the headrest ... the way he had looked when she was lying on the ground. Annie could not imagine what had happened to Kevin to make him act this way. She imagined herself killing him. If only she were near his size ... that was the extent of her rage. Annie shuddered and was grateful no one was home. Rolling out of her bed, she made the inevitable trip into the bathroom.

Chapter Eight

After the nausea passed, Annie returned to her room. She still shook uncontrollably but no longer mumbled. She had been hysterical. Calming herself, she tried to think. "He's out of his mind," she said aloud. It would have made some sense if he had caught her with another man. But to bring up something that had happened over two months ago?

Had Kevin somehow read her thoughts? How could he know she had liked Harold? Annie gave herself a mental shake and took a deep breath. That was not possible. Even if Kevin sensed something, he would realize all she had to do was break up with him and go out with Harold. Annie wished bitterly now that she had. Then she remembered the pregnancy. So much for Harold, she thought in dismay. Annie was surprised at the brutality of her thoughts. She envisioned Kevin being beat up. Oh how she longed to be bigger! Annie decided she would have nothing to do with Kevin. She wondered if he would try to contact her. Surely not. She thought about his marriage comment and began to laugh. Maybe Kevin had been proposing. The thought made her laugh even harder. I'm losing my mind, she thought wildly. Clamping down the hysteria for the second time, Annie knelt down on the floor next to her bed. "Thank you God for my beautiful baby," she prayed. Pausing for a moment, she continued. "God, will you get Kevin for me? Have someone beat him up." Feeling embarrassed, she amended the request. "Sorry, God. I'll try to forgive him later. Right now I'm too mad. But I can't marry him."

Certain that God understood, Annie got into bed with the intention of taking a nap. Her breath still came quickly, but most of the shaking had passed. Footsteps on the stairs prompted her to turn to her sore left side and face the wall. Conversation was out of the question. She sensed the person coming closer. She remained still, and whoever it was left the room. Annie guessed it was Nellie. Maureen would have asked if she was sleeping. For the next two hours Annie lay in her bed and thought. Prior to this afternoon, she had assumed Kevin would be in the picture. It was a whole new ball game now.

Rolling onto her not-so-sore side, Annie pondered further. For some reason, Kevin was becoming a monster. He said it was her fault. Maureen said she had a smart mouth. Everyone said she had a smart mouth. Was this why Kevin lost it? Annie thought about the whole Harold thing. She desperately played the first night of that momentous weekend through her head. She hadn't done anything too bad. Maybe she should not have been by their fire at all. Maybe she should have walked away when Harold approached them. It had seemed harmless enough then, but Annie did remember feeling guilty. She would like to run it by Maureen, naturally omitting the choking part. Annie felt humiliated. She thought about herself rolling around in the dirt. How mortifying. Thank God, nobody had seen her.

Annie continued to mull it all over. Maybe his mother was the culprit. Imagine asking Kevin if he was certain he was the father. Her face flushed all over again. That had made Kevin violent. Annie seethed with rage. How nice of

Mrs. Griffin to pay for an abortion. Or find her a nice unwed mothers home. Annie considered the concept. Why not send Kevin? He obviously could not bear the embarrassment. Mrs. Griffin could go, too, Annie thought wickedly. She noticed the ache of loneliness in her stomach and began to cry again. The one thing Annie had counted on was Kevin. He was gone now. She was in this alone, and the thought pulled a thick blanket of depression down over her.

The sound of dinner preparations caused Annie to lift her head. The mirror was not her friend. The welts had developed even more, and Annie noticed fingerprint marks on the left side. Feeling herself slipping into hysteria again, she took some breaths and searched for a high-necked shirt. She was tired of crying. She was also starving. Her desire to eat overcame emotional needs, and Annie went downstairs. Their father was not home tonight, thank God, and Nellie was making pizzas.

"Hi, Annie," Maureen greeted her. "Hungry?"

"Starving. When will they be ready?"

Nellie and Maureen stopped.

"What's the matter with your voice?" Nellie asked.

"I don't know." Annie averted her gaze. She sat down at the kitchen table and looked out the window. "I must be getting a cold or something."

"Annie, it's not even September," Maureen noted. "You look awful."

The telephone rang, and Maureen grabbed it. Turning to Annie, she said, "It's Kevin."

Annie felt her stomach lurch. "Let's see," she said slowly. "What should we tell him? I know. Tell him to fuck off."

"Annie," Nellie said reproachfully. Maureen's jaw dropped.

"I'm serious, Maureen," Annie said with a rising voice. "Tell him not to call here. I don't want to talk to him."

Maureen was holding the phone against her chest so Kevin could not hear their conversation. After a moment she lifted the receiver to her mouth and said sweetly,

"Kevin? Annie is not feeling well right now. Can she call you later?" Looking at Annie, she said, "He says it's really important."

Annie slammed her hand down on the table. Rising, she grabbed the phone from Maureen and shouted into the mouthpiece, "Stay away from me, you fucking lunatic." After slamming the telephone down, she sat gingerly down at the table. She was sore. Glancing up she realized her sisters were stunned. Nellie in particular was frozen.

"You better tell us what happened with the fucking lunatic," Maureen said quietly. "Did he finally tell his family?"

"Well, he told his mother," Annie answered. "She took it well, I think. She told him he could not tell his father or brother, but she is willing to pay for the abortion." The girls were motionless.

"She was willing to concede I might not want to do that so she also suggested I find a nice unwed mothers home. Nobody would have to find out," Annie continued bitterly. "The goal seems to be secrecy."

"That bitch," Maureen blurted out.

"Stop swearing," Nellie implored. "It's not going to help anything. What else did she say, Annie?"

"Nothing. Oh yes, she did ask Kevin if he was sure it was his baby."

"That bitch!" Nellie said violently. "You two have been inseparable for years. What a bitch."

"Nel," Maureen said sweetly. "Foul language is not helping anything." Nellie looked white, and Maureen continued, "Let's call her and tell her we're going to name the baby after her. We'll distribute flyers at all the Masses."

The telephone rang again, startling them all. Maureen grabbed it impatiently. After answering she said, "Kevin, did you hear what she said? Which part of 'stay away from me, you fucking lunatic' was unclear?" Hanging up, Maureen sent Annie an apologetic look and started to laugh. "Are you mad?"

"No," Annie replied. "I don't want to talk to him. I don't

90

care if you're mean this time."

"Wait a minute," Nellie said reasonably. "Kevin can't help what his mother does. Can he, Annie?"

"Well he can certainly control what he tells Annie," Maureen argued. "Why hurt her like that? Honestly, Nellie, the hell with him."

"That's not all," Annie offered. She felt compelled to tell them something despite her need to keep the violence a secret. "He accused me of doing something with a guy named Harold the weekend we went camping. He said I was a sneaky liar. He screamed at me, and he would not let me out of the car." Looking at their appalled faces, she stopped.

"Was this the camping trip he crashed?" Maureen asked quietly.

"Yes," Annie told them the whole story excluding only the scene in the tent. They knew about that anyway. "What kills me is that he has not said a word about it for nearly three months. Today he pretended to have some top secret information. He really scared me."

"Well," Nellie said roundly. "I just hope he has the sense to stay away from this house. If he comes near here, I'll call the police."

Annie and Maureen groaned. "Nellie, don't be irrational," Maureen pleaded. "Annie, he does sound frightening. I agree that you should stay away from him. Do you think you can?"

"Does she think she can?" Nellie sputtered. "She has no choice. Don't even put his name on the birth certificate. He'll come after the baby."

"Put Harold's name on the birth certificate," Maureen suggested with an evil glint in her eyes.

Annie and Maureen burst out laughing. "You're burning the pizzas, Nel, " observed Annie.

The conversation continued through dinner. Eileen was out with Mr. McGowan, and Danny was off working out of state. It was decided that Annie would not answer the phone. Their father would only be told that Annie and

Kevin had fought. Annie felt better afterward. She was still depressed, but at least the girls knew about it. Later that night Rene called.

"Did you and Kevin have a fight?" Rene asked bluntly.

"How did you know?" Annie asked in surprise.

"He called me, Annie," Rene related. "He was very upset and said your family was blaming him. He went on to say he had to see you. I'm supposed to call you and talk you into meeting him. He does sound upset, Annie, and I think he was crying. He also said he was acting a bit upset because he was so disturbed about his mother's reaction."

"Rene, I can't believe he called you," Annie began. "Did he also tell you that he called me a liar and a sneak for what I did with Harold?"

"Harold who?"

"Campground Harold. Do you remember? Out of the blue Kevin attacked me for lying about Harold. He said your sister Patty told him we were down by their fire all night." Annie paused for a breath.

Rene sounded uncertain. "Did anything happen with Harold I didn't know about?"

"Of course not," Annie chided. "When would something have happened? I was with you the whole time, Rene. What's the matter with you?"

"I'm sorry, Annie, but what could he possibly have been mad about? That you were talking to him? It doesn't make any sense. I mean... this was months ago. Are you sure there was not something else?"

"Rene, I don't want to talk about this. Kevin is crazy, and I am not going to talk to him. Tell him that. OK?"

"Sure. Annie, is there anything I can do? Do you want me to come over?" Rene sounded concerned, but Annie knew her friend could not begin to understand the situation.

"Thanks, but no," she answered kindly. "I'm all right, Rene. I'm going to bed. I'll talk to you tomorrow. Do you want to pick me up for school?" Tomorrow was their first day of school, and Annie had to tell her advisor about the pregnancy. She was not looking forward to it.

"Yes. I'll be there by eight. Is there anything else you want me to tell Kevin?"

"No. Nothing. I'll talk to you later." She hung up and, after telling her sisters about the phone call, went to bed. It had been a long day.

Sometime during the night, Annie heard Maureen slide out from her bed. Tiptoeing over to the window, her sister studied the darkness.

"What are you doing?" Annie asked.

"Didn't you hear that?" Maureen queried. "Someone threw something at the window. I have a feeling it's Kevin. What do you want me to do?"

"Oh, my God. Maureen, he's nuts. Tell him I'm sleeping and to go away." Annie sat up and pulled the blankets around her neck. Feeling the bruises, she started to cry.

"Don't cry, Annie. I'll get rid of him." Maureen opened the window.

"Go away, Kevin. She doesn't want to see you." Maureen was using a stage whisper. "I said go away. No. She's not coming out. I mean it. Call tomorrow and see if she wants to talk." Turning to her sister, she said, "He looks upset. I hope he has the sense to go away quietly. Let's wait a few minutes." Seeing Annie's white face she remarked, "He can't break in here, Annie. Don't look so scared." At that moment they heard another "ping" on the window. Hearing quick footsteps from down the hall, they exchanged looks of dismay. "Here she comes," Maureen said as Nellie burst into the room.

"Is it him?" Nellie asked tensely. "I heard you talking to someone. I left my window open in case he pulled this. Don't worry, Annie. I'll handle this." Sticking her head out of the window Nellie yelled down. "You better leave right now, Kevin Griffin, or I'll call the police. It's too bad you're grandmother did not have an abortion. Tell that to your mother." Maureen and Annie were speechless. "No," she responded to his request to talk to Annie for one second. "Annie does not want to talk to you ever again!" With that she grabbed a hairbrush from the dresser and threw it out at him.

"Stop her, Maureen," Annie beseeched.

"Nellie," Maureen said, struggling with mirth. "Come in and close the window. I think he got the message."

Just then they heard Mr. McGowan's roar from downstairs. "What the hell is going on up there?" The girls froze. No one answered. "Nellie? What are you doing shouting out your window? Whose grandmother had an abortion? Answer me, dammit."

"Sorry, Dad," Nellie called feebly. "We were just talking."

"Talking to who? The whole city? Go to bed and close the damn window."

"OK, Dad. Sorry." The three girls looked at each other for a moment and burst out laughing. Five minutes elapsed, and still they struggled for control. Mr. McGowan yelled up again. "SHUT UP UP THERE!"

Quieting, Maureen wiped her eyes. Looking at Nellie, she said incredulously, "Your grandmother should have had an abortion? Nellie you're as loony as he is. I can't believe you threw a brush at him." Annie groaned and put her head in her pillow. Then they all began laughing again.

"It's not funny," Annie winced. "Do you think he'll come back?"

"Are you feeling sorry for him?" Maureen asked. Annie shook her head. "I would understand if you did. He looked so pathetic standing out there in the yard."

"Annie, do not back down this time," Nellie beseeched. "He has been mean before, and you always back down. He thinks he can get away with anything."

"Let's go to sleep," Annie suggested. The last thing she wanted was a conversation. Nellie left the room, and they got back into their beds. Annie heard Maureen giggling in her bed, and she started laughing again. "It's too horrible, Maureen. It's like a bad movie."

"I know it is. Nellie's out of control. I hope she doesn't call his mother or anything." Hearing Annie's gasp of horror, Maureen promised, "I won't let her, Annie."

Sleep was a long time coming to Annie. She wondered what Kevin would have said. He had nearly killed her. Annie's thoughts turned round and round until she finally fell into an exhausted sleep.

The interview with Annie's advisor did not go as well as she had hoped. The sister told her that the best solution would be for Annie to get her diploma by correspondence. The school did not have a distinct policy on the subject of pregnancy, but normally the girls were encouraged to stay at home and take the classes through the mail. Annie maintained that she wanted her diploma from Lourdes. After much discussion, it was decided that Annie would remain in school.

"OK, then," the nun replied cheerfully. "Let me talk to the principal. Stop in and see me tomorrow morning."

"I will, Sister. Thank you." Annie left and took a deep breath. Going off in search of Rene, she was relieved they would not throw her out. It was a bad example for the younger girls, and the thought made her ashamed. Still, she reasoned, it was better they see the result in all it's figure-smashing beauty. Annie sighed when she realized that, once again, she was ravenously hungry.

Annie and Rene ambled slowly toward her car. Deciding to go out for lunch, they discussed restaurants and opted for the cheapest one. They were settled in the car when Annie noticed an envelope stuck to the passenger side window. She reached around and grabbed it. It was clearly marked "Annie."

"Rene, it's from him," she said with a shaking voice. "He was here." Annie dropped the envelope on the seat as if it were hot. "You open it."

"Are you sure you want me to?" Rene craned her neck looking around the parking lot. "How did he find my car in this lot ? He must really be on the edge. Doesn't he have school today?"

"No," Annie moaned. "They start tomorrow. He came over last night and threw rocks at the window. I didn't talk to him."

"I think you'll have to talk to him eventually," Rene stated. "It's good to give yourself some time away, but he's obviously frantic. See what he says," she urged, indicating the envelope.

Annie opened it and quickly read its contents. "He loves me and is sorry for the fight. He did not sleep at all, and he feels like he wants to die. If I give him another chance, he promises he will never be rude to me again." Annie looked at Rene dully. "Basically he wants me to make him feel better."

"You're being a little hard on him, aren't you?" Rene asked hesitantly. "I'm not his greatest fan, but this has been a big shock for him, too." Seeing Annie's crestfallen face, she hastened to add, "It's nothing to what you're going through, but he does love you. Also, Annie, he has never acted like he was going to bail out on you. Quite the contrary. Many guys would. He sounds rational."

Annie sighed. "Rene, I may talk to him tomorrow. Right now I don't want to see him." Annie put her hands to her throat and gently felt the bruises. Starting to cry again, she said, "Can you bring me home? I'm not hungry any more."

Rene looked contrite. "I'm sorry, Annie. I'm not sticking up for him. It's just that I hate to see you break up with him now when you need him. Please don't cry. Let's get lunch, and we'll eat in the car. I'm buying."

The next day Annie was informed she was welcome to stay in school. If at any time Annie chose to stop, she could finish the year by correspondence. Annie was to meet with her advisor once a week to make sure everything was going well. She was also informed that the principal's door was always open if she felt the need to talk. Grateful, Annie noticed the irony. Most girls were complaining that they had to come to school. Annie was now thanking her lucky stars they were allowing her to stay. The thought made her feel older than her years.

Mr. McGowan's delight was pathetic. Annie could not bear to talk to him these days. He always treated her as though she were about to cry. She did cry a lot, but everyone annoyed her. She answered his inquiries about Kevin briefly, and he did not pry. The girls must have warned him to leave her alone.

Nellie was going back to school, and Annie would miss her. Thank heavens, Maureen would be around. Eileen had been told and was delighted at becoming an aunt.

Annie wrote Kevin a brief letter explaining that she was not willing to talk to him for one month. If he loved her as much as he claimed, he would respect her wishes. He stopped calling. Consequently, Annie was given time to think. She did little else these days. The situation dragged on. The vomiting had stopped. Annie now felt nearly normal and sometimes speculated that there had been a mistake. Her new doctor burst that bubble. She was progressing normally. Mostly she felt lonely. She missed Kevin more and more.

Kevin made the papers twice for football. He was having a spectacular year. She did not allow herself to think about his mother. She thought with sadness that Mrs. Griffin could at least have called to see how she was feeling. Annie wondered if they discussed it at all. She managed her emotions by shoving them away. Only then could she keep the tears at bay. Time limped by, and Annie slept whenever she could.

The first of October was a Saturday. Rainy and cold, the weather did little to encourage her to get up. Annie stayed in bed as long as her hunger allowed. Finally, she wrapped herself in a robe and dragged down the stairs in search of food. The doorbell rang, and she groaned. Nobody else was home. Annie waited, hoping the caller would leave. It rang again. With a snort of disgust, she opened the door. Kevin stood nervously on the porch.

Chapter Nine

"What are you doing here?" she asked bluntly. Kevin never came to the door. Annie mentally cursed herself for coming down in her pajamas. She cursed herself again for caring.

Kevin looked nervous but determined. "You said to wait one month. I waited. It has been the longest month in my whole life, Annie." Annie shrugged. "Please hear me out. I wanted to respect your wishes. I wanted you to know that I will do whatever you want." With that, Kevin cleared his throat nervously. "Will you please talk to me, Annie?"

Annie sifted through conflicting emotions. He looked terrific. He also seemed calm. She narrowed her eyes. "I'm not getting into a car with you."

Kevin winced. "After the last time, I don't blame you. Do you want to go for a walk?"

"I have to get dressed and eat. You can wait here and watch television." Seeing the apprehensive look on his face, she wondered whether to inform him that her father was out for the day. She decided to let him suffer. Grabbing an apple, she went up to dress.

In the safety of her room, Annie attempted to organize her thoughts. Kevin looked sorry. That was a good sign. She had missed him terribly. There was no question about that. Annie did not want to be alone. That was for sure. On the other hand, she could not tolerate his behavior. He had been hateful and frightening. Annie reminded herself that she had actually believed he might kill her. She must hold on to that during their conversation. She was afraid of him.

"I'm ready," she said lightly as she walked back into the living room.

Kevin looked relieved. "Let's get going. How about a walk to the park?"

"Fine," she responded briefly.

Outside, Kevin began the conversation. "Annie, I want to start by saying I am sorry about the fight in the car. I was out of line. I will never be pushy with you again."

Halting abruptly, Annie looked up at him. "You were not only out of line, Kevin. You could have killed me. Do you realize that?"

"I don't blame you for being upset. I was obnoxious. But, Annie, I think you might be exaggerating a little bit."

"Kevin, if you think I'm exaggerating, I have nothing else to say." With that, she turned to walk away. He grabbed her arm. "Let go of my arm, or I'll scream," she said through clenched teeth. Appalled, Kevin released her. "Annie, I'm sorry. I didn't realize how upset you were. I never meant to hurt you."

Annie was astounded. "Kevin, you choked me. What was it you meant to do when you put your hands around my throat and squeezed?"

"I was half out of my mind that day," he explained emotionally. "I'm sorry. Can we talk about the future?"

Annie composed herself. "Kevin, I cannot plan a future with you. What if you get mad because I have a male doctor? What if you decide I'm flirting with the bus driver?" It was Kevin's turn to roll his eyes. "Your overreaction to Harold was way out of control. Is there anything else you're 'waiting for me to tell the truth' about? I'll never know, will I?"

Kevin's face had turned ashen. "Annie, you were talking to Harold." Seeing her look of rage, he continued quickly. "I'm not saying there was anything wrong with that. I'm just stating a fact. You have told me before that you could not stand my jealousy. Give me a break here, Annie. Didn't I change? I think the Harold thing was just a reaction to the stress. I thought I was going to crack up before I told my mom. Do you know how hard that was? It was a hundred times worse for you. But hear me out. You didn't tell me you were down by the fire that whole night. I'm just explaining how I felt. I never said anything to you because I did not want you to think that I was getting jealous again. I tried to work on that. Didn't I?"

"Yes," she conceded. "Until this thing you were doing pretty good."

"Doesn't that mean I can do it again? There is so much at stake here. I will do anything not to lose you. Especially now. You need me, Annie. Don't push me away." Kevin tried to take her into his arms.

"I don't know." Annie pulled back and crossed her arms. "I was afraid of you that day. I really thought you were going to kill me. I don't think I could live like that." Annie blinked her eyes hard.

"Let me explain why I get so jealous," Kevin said intently. Reaching out to her, he grabbed her hand. "Let's sit on the grass for a minute. You look white." Annie was indeed white. She had the impression that her whole life was riding on this conversation. She allowed Kevin to pull her down to the damp grass. "You are the best thing that has ever happened to me," he began. He took both of her hands gently into his own. "You know that, Annie. But I want to tell you again. I love you more than I ever thought possible. I thought about you constantly last month. I thought about what I would do if you broke up with me. For a second I thought I might be relieved. I'm just telling you my true feelings so don't get mad," he cautioned. Seeing that she understood, he continued. "I figured I would go away to college. No one would know anything. I could start a new life and forget it." Annie kept her expression neutral. "There was only one problem. I could not be happy without you. Never. Besides, now we are going to have a baby. That blows my mind. I have trouble picturing the baby, but I know it's coming. I get jealous because the thought of you with another guy makes me want to die. I know you're too good for me." At this point, Annie groaned. "I know you hate when I say that, but it's true, Annie. You're smart and pretty, and people love you. You could have any guy you wanted."

"Not any more, Kevin," she said blandly.

"Well, that's a good thing because you have me," he said simply. The look of innocent love in his eyes made Annie smile.

"Kevin, I want to believe everything you're saying. I really do," she paused to choose her words carefully. "I guess the problem is, I have to know you'll never lay a hand on me again. How can I know that?"

"I'm telling you right now," Kevin promised solemnly. "I've lived with my father long enough to know that I will never, ever be like him. I wouldn't put you through that, Annie. I do have a temper. I admit that. But you're not perfect either. The fault is not always mine." He looked at her hesitantly. "Admit it."

"I never said I was perfect, Kevin," she said slowly. "The fact remains that you are not afraid of me. I was afraid of you in the car. Everything else can be worked out but that."

"Well, I just worked it out. I promise you I will never lay a hand on you," he said in a deep voice, raising his hand as if to take an oath. "I promise you I will try to control my jealousy even though I'm going to have the most beautiful girl in the world as my wife. How is that?"

Annie smiled in spite of herself. "I guess it's OK. One thing, though, Kevin. If you ever hurt me like that again, it's over. Do you understand?"

"I understand," Kevin spoke gravely. "I hate that you feel you have to threaten me ... but, whatever it takes. Now can we talk about the future?"

"Sure." Annie's spirits lifted. "What new horrors are in store for us?"

"A little optimism, please, or haven't you been reading the papers?"

Annie laughed aloud. "Yes, I know you are a superstar. Trust you to get in the papers to annoy me."

"I had to do something to make sure you were thinking of me," he grinned. "We'll get married after graduation. Hopefully, I'll get a huge scholarship, and we'll go off to college and live happily ever after. I've talked to a few scouts, Annie. There's no question that I'll do good. I like playing again. Now I've got a reason. Motivation helps. It will all work out."

Annie sighed. "I hope you're right. What did your father say about the baby?"

Kevin looked uncomfortable. "We didn't tell him. My mother says not to. I can't go against her wishes. I live in terror that he's going to hear. What can I do? You want to hear something strange, Annie?" She nodded. "My mother has not brought it up once since the first night. I asked her when we were going to tell my father, and she shook her head. She has never mentioned it again."

The look of genuine uncertainty on his face softened Annie's response. "That's bizarre. How horrible for you, Kevin," she said sympathetically. "It's like she's ignoring the whole thing." He nodded his head in agreement. "I suppose telling him on your own is out of the question?"

"No way. She'd kill me. Not to mention what he would do. I'll guess I'll just wait and see. I'm eighteen years old. I'll be nineteen when we graduate. What can they do? We're going away." He looked cheerful all of a sudden. "Won't it be great?"

"I hope so, Kevin. We'll be pretty broke for the first couple years. I suppose I could get a part-time job after school."

"Let's worry about all of that later," he said persuasively. "It's enough that we're back together. I feel better. Do you?"

"Yes," she answered truthfully. "I'm still worried, though."

"Well, don't be. We have at least five months to worry so let's just feel better now. OK?" He looked so boyish that Annie smiled. "OK."

"Oh, by the way," Kevin added. "I think this belongs to you." He pulled a hairbrush from his jacket and handed it to Annie. It took Annie a moment to place it. When understanding dawned, she burst out laughing. Kevin joined her.

Feeling refreshed, Annie wiped her eyes. "Nellie gets a little carried away. Sorry about that."

" You're telling me," Kevin chuckled. " She hit me in the head with it. Then your dad started yelling, and I figured it was time to go." They laughed again. "Things aren't so bad, Annie. At least we can still laugh. The baby will love the Hilton pool. Think how well we'll fit in with a baby. This could work out well..."

• • •

The pregnancy lasted an eternity. Annie faithfully attended school. She stayed small and concealed her condition until nearly her seventh month. After that, she stopped trying. She learned to ignore the stares. Most of her classmates scrupulously avoided looking at her midsection. She was grateful. Her emotions were in a constant state of flux. Countless books on pregnancy persuaded Annie that moodiness was normal. Despite this, she thought the condition tough enough for women without fending off daily crying jags. During this time Annie decided life was hard for women.

She watched Kevin breeze through his last year. Bitterness threatened to overwhelm her, and Annie repeatedly reminded herself that Kevin was doing his best. His car had broken down in November. Kevin's parents drove him to sporting events, and he took the bus to school. Annie suspected Mrs. Griffin of preventing Kevin from seeing her. Kevin agreed but felt his hands were tied.

Kevin had not seen Mr. McGowan since the pregnancy was announced. Never entirely comfortable, he now quaked in fear whenever Annie talked about her father. The result was that they seldom saw each other. Once in a while he walked over. Annie dutifully met him at the corner. For the most part there was nowhere to go. Kevin practiced and played so often that he rarely had free time. In the past, Annie attended all of his games. By Christmas, she only saw him once every two or three weeks.

Time crept by. Christmas came and went. Annie was not due until the first week in February. The girls prepared for the baby. Annie had copied the list of necessities from one of the baby books and would not rest easily until every item was accounted for. Over the holidays, the sisters had a baby shower for her. More horrors. Friends and relatives were supportive, but their kindness did nothing to ease Annie's self-consciousness. The shower, however, did net them quite a few baby things needed to complete the list. Maureen pointed out with practicality that their goal had been achieved. Annie privately believed it would have been less traumatic to skip the shower and rob a convenience store.

Still, she felt more peaceful after the shower. For the first time she believed that people wished her well. Prior to this, she viewed their silence as contempt. Now she understood they were being tactful. Her deep sighs were spontaneous and constant.

Every day she dutifully thanked God for her little baby. She also reminded God that He had put her on earth and as such was responsible for her. So many problems seemed insurmountable. Namely, Kevin's family. No one had been told. The strain on him was tremendous. Scouts were meeting with his father, and Kevin was routinely invited to visit campuses. Mr. Griffin could not understand his son's refusals.

Kevin reasoned there was no point visiting schools until he could inform them he would be bringing along a wife and baby. Annie agreed that honesty was essential but could see no way around telling his father. Kevin looked haggard. Preoccupied by impending motherhood, Annie suggested

Kevin throw down the gauntlet to his mother. He refused. If his mother did not bring it up, then neither would he. Annie tried in vain to convince him he was only hurting himself. He said it was a matter of pride and suffered in silence. As he lost weight, Annie briefly considered calling his mother. Mrs. Griffin's cold reaction stopped her. In a way, she could see Kevin's point. It was a matter of pride with Annie, too.

One day toward the end of January, Annie and Kevin sat talking on the telephone. Annie heard Mrs. Griffin come into the room and speak to Kevin.

"My mom wants to know when you're going to have that baby?" Kevin said somewhat surprised.

"She remembered," Annie said sarcastically. "Ask her why she cares all of a sudden."

Kevin hesitated a moment. "Soon, Mom. Annie says she hopes it's soon." After his mother had left the room Kevin scolded her. "It won't help to be rude. She's only trying to be nice."

Annie held the phone in disbelief. "Kevin, the woman has ignored me for seven months. She has done everything in her power to prevent you from seeing me. Suddenly it hits her. Annie is not going away. She brings it up for the first time, and you want me to be polite?" Annie tried to control the outrage in her voice. "Kevin, I think you should consider the possibility that I will never talk to that woman again."

An ugly fight followed after which Annie tearfully told Maureen she would never speak to either Kevin or his mother again. That would not be a problem, though. Annie was certain her remaining time on earth was short. The baby refused to come, and Annie knew she would die in childbirth. She hated her doctor and hated the nurses. She was sure they would all be mean. There was probably something wrong with the baby, and they were not telling her. Maureen listened with wide eyes. This kind of hysterical outburst was a job for Nellie, who was not around. After calming Annie down with the inevitable can of pop,

Maureen called Mrs. Nolan. The McGowan girls babysat for the Nolans, and Mrs. Nolan had been supportive throughout the pregnancy.

Mrs. Nolan arrived in minutes, and Maureen gratefully sent her up to Annie's room. They talked for two hours. They would have continued, but for Mr. Nolan, who phoned to say he could no longer control their children. Afterward Annie felt like a new person. Everyone thought there would be something wrong with her baby. Nearly everyone hated her mother-in-law at some point. Mrs. Nolan promised Annie the baby would be fine. She also promised to be at the hospital and personally force the doctor to behave. She said the problem with doctors was that they were mostly men. They treated pregnancy like a mechanical process and ignored the emotional upheavals. Annie vowed to be an obstetrician and understand every pregnant woman in the world.

Along with her words of wisdom, Mrs. Nolan brought a strawberry shortcake. Annie pitied Mr. Nolan who would obviously be getting a late dinner, minus the dessert. She ate half of the cake in bed while perusing her newest infant care book. No longer anxious, she was at one with the world. Maureen brought up a half gallon of milk, which Annie swigged from the carton.

"Are you coming to the hospital with me, Maureen?" Annie asked her sister.

"Of course, I'm coming," Maureen said, a little too emphatically. "I would not miss it for the world. I'm hoping your water breaks, and I can do the emergency home delivery." Annie laughed appreciatively. "Just kidding. I've read it about three hundred times. But I would never recover from the grossness. Nellie says I have to go with you and that she'll kill me if I throw up or faint. She says I have to overcome my selfish squeamishness and act like an adult. So there you are, Annie. I'm your girl."

"Well, that's good to hear Maureen," Annie said with trepidation. "Mrs. Nolan said she was coming, too. That won't hurt your feelings, will it?"

Maureen nearly fell over with relief. "Of course not. Great idea. I can be the one who smokes cigars in the waiting room. I'll bring you in pizza or whatever you want."

Annie smiled in understanding. "You're a trooper, Maureen. I know how much you hate this kind of thing. We'll spare you as much grossness as possible." Glad to have settled that, they talked animatedly about the baby. There was no consensus on the name. They decided to reserve judgment until after they got a look at the baby.

That night Kevin called to clear the air. Annie was amazed. Normally, he ignored her for weeks after a fight. She thought with optimism that maybe he was growing up. He said this was not the time to fight. He could not bear the thought of Annie being upset. He understood she was probably feeling emotional, and they would not talk about his mother until things were calmer. He assured Annie that he loved her and that everything would be all right. Annie wondered if he had read Chapter Ten of her baby book. It was the first time Kevin had taken responsibility for an argument. Annie did not retract one comment about his mother. But, in the interest of peace, she let it be.

• • •

Her due date came and went. The doctor explained that a due date was only an estimate. Women routinely delivered late. Annie thought she was going to explode. It was difficult to walk, and she dared not stray far from a bathroom. Everyone around her was nervous. Maureen in particular watched her every facial expression.

Maureen was working downtown these days. She had taken a semester off from school to decide if a major course of study jumped into her head. To date, nothing appealed. Consequently, Annie's sister was now a receptionist in a law firm and immensely enjoyed the regular income. She worried incessantly that she would be at work when Annie went into labor. Every morning she asked Annie how she felt. Annie knew that if she confessed to the smallest of pains, Maureen would shed her professional garb and stay home. Annie noticed cramps all of the time. She had long since stopped timing them because they never got regular. For the most part she now ignored them.

On this particular day, the cramps seemed to have tapered off. Annie assured Maureen that today was not the day and waved her off to work. She lay in bed, idly listening to the morning sounds of the kitchen. Mr. McGowan was force feeding Eileen. Annie decided to take a bath. With a sigh she began the process of exiting the bed. It took some time these days. She eventually stood up and noticed she was all wet. Aha! she thought. A person without her reading habits would think they had wet the bed. Is it clear, colorless, and odorless? But of course. Annie correctly guessed her water bag had finally burst. She held her stomach in excitement. Surely this was the day. Glancing in the mirror she noticed how swollen and blotchy her face had become. Pregnancy played hell with a person's looks.

Because of her extensive reading, she also knew that labor could be hours or even days away. It did look like quite a bit of water, but that could be deceiving. Annie had a morbid dread of going to the hospital and being sent home. She would take no chances. Thank you, God, for my beautiful baby, she prayed absently. Make this baby come today, God, or I'm going to change my mind, she added. Also, please make it quick and painless, preferably a C-section. Annie had read that the best birth was a natural delivery. She had learned all of the reasons why and still thought a Caesarean birth would be preferable.

She would call the doctor and see what he had to say. Chapter Seven was titled "Are you in labor?" She had it memorized. The doctor would politely listen to her symptoms and make an immediate decision. Annie's doctor was unfortunately not like the doctor in the book. He was impatient and sick to death of pregnant women and their mysterious symptoms. Annie resolved to let everything he said roll off. She did not want to get upset today.

Lumbering down the stairs, she met Mr. McGowan coming up.

"How are you feeling?" he asked with his customary "I'm

not worried about a thing" look.

"Pretty good, Dad," Annie answered hesitantly. "I'm going to call the doctor and see what he says. He'll probably tell me to go back to bed and quit complaining. Are you going out somewhere?"

"I don't have to," he answered quickly. "Are you having pains?" His "I'm not worried about a thing" look had become even more pronounced.

"Not really. I just feel kind of funny."

"Well, you're mother did this quite often, Annie. She said no matter how many children she had, it was impossible to know exactly when labor started. Give him a call and see what he says. I'll stick around."

Annie called the doctor. He agreed that her water had probably broken. He was going to be at the hospital all day so it worked out well for him. I'm so relieved, Annie thought with hostility. He told Annie to come right in. Drumming up her nerve, Annie asked if she could stay home until she began having regular contractions. After all her reading, she knew that given the chance, hospital personnel were going to do disgusting things to her if they had the time. She had never had an enema and did not intend to today. She had to arrive strategically late. The doctor sighed, and Annie thought again how difficult he found her. Mrs. Nolan had reminded Annie that she was paying him to provide a service. The doctor eventually agreed to let her wait a couple hours as long as someone stayed with her. He also told her not to eat anything. Annie was ahead of him. Chapter Eight gave specific instructions for the early stages of labor.

"He said not to worry for a while," Annie told her father. "Go ahead and go out," she urged him. "I'll be fine."

"Well, if the doctor thinks you're OK," her father said uncertainly. "I'll only be gone an hour or so."

Annie waved him off and wandered through the house. Everything was in order. The baby would be sharing Annie's room for the time being. Maureen was going to take Nellie's room. Annie thought irrelevantly that she would miss Maureen. A sudden realization hit her. After today, things would never be the same. She would never share a room with one of her sisters again. Annie began to cry. Life was so unbearably painful these days. How did anyone stand it? She wished she could reach Kevin. Feeling a good solid contraction, Annie decided to call Mrs. Nolan and put her on notice. Annie often wondered what she would have done without her these last few months. This is probably what mothers did if you had them, she thought.

Mrs. Nolan answered on the first ring. She was more excited than Annie. She had a babysitter on standby and would call her. Annie cautioned her that it could be several more hours. Mrs. Nolan did not think so. Picking up her sense of urgency, Annie decided to time the contractions. Yikes. Seven minutes apart. They hurt but not too bad. She went back up to her bedroom. Almost immediately she heard her father come back. Up the stairs he came.

"How are you feeling?" he asked quickly. "I think maybe we should run you over. Your mother always said they would not send you home if you were overdue." Mr. McGowan was beginning to perspire. The phone rang, and he sighed. "Maybe that's the doctor. I'll be right back." Annie listened to him going down the stairs. She had no intention of getting there too soon. She heard him on the telephone and listened while he made his way back up the stairs. "That was Mrs. Nolan. She's in a bit of a state, Annie. She's only been through this a few times so she's not as calm as we are." Annie smiled at him. He did not look calm. "Anyway, she says you should go right now. Your mother always went right in if the water broke." Annie knew she had no choice. If she waited any longer there would be two patients. Shit, she thought. They're ruining my strategy.

"OK, Dad," she said heaving herself out of bed. "I'll be down in a minute." She paused. "I really don't want to go, though."

"I can imagine," he said with mingled sympathy and relief. "Your mother always said it was like falling off a cliff.

Once you were pushed there was no way back. Just think, Annie," his voice lightened. "Sometime today we'll have a new little baby. That's a wonderful thing."

Annie wondered if Mrs. McGowan had ever wanted to push him off a cliff.

"Mrs. Nolan wanted to come and get you, but I told her I would drive you over. She'll meet us there."

"Fine," Annie said shortly. "Let's go. I'll probably be in labor until next week. Shit, Dad. Shouldn't we wait a little longer?"

"No. I can't take any more."

Three hours later Annie's baby girl was born. Annie had indeed timed it well. By the time she got there she was too far gone for any preparation, and the doctor told the nurses to skip the enema. Ha, she thought. Later Annie wondered that women did not die from the pain. She was over-whelmed by it. She asked for a Caesarean at least ten times, but the doctor only laughed. He was discussing hybrid tomatoes with the nurse at the time. Annie wanted to kill him. At the very least, she would find out where he lived and destroy his garden. She would have told him so but was fighting her way through another mountainous contraction. When it was over, she had come to her senses. The doctor held all the cards when it came to pain relief. She would have to cultivate him. Mrs. Nolan fixed him by smoking in the room whenever he walked out. Annie smoked with her in defiance to all of the baby books. She wanted all of those people dead, too. How dare they talk about discomfort when referring to childbirth? She resolved to kill them all and write her own book. In the future, girls would know exactly what was in store for them. There would be no such thing as premarital sex after Annie's book hit the stands. Postmarital either, come to think of it. It all came to the same painful resolution. Labor.

When it finally came to an end, Annie looked up to see a small face looking directly into her eyes. The same books that equated discomfort with labor said that babies looked messy and strange directly after birth. They were wrong again. A miraculously perfect little person stared intelligently at her mother. Annie asked the doctor and nurses if they had ever seen such a perfect little girl. To their credit, they all said no. Annie looked down at her doctor busily stitching and wondered why she had ever disliked him. He was the kindest, sweetest man on earth. The nurses were benevolent. Mrs. Nolan had to be led from the room. Annie assumed she had gone to tell Mr. McGowan the news.

"Annie, you did one hell of a job," the doctor praised her. "I'm sorry I was unable give you more pain medication, but you were too close to the end." He had placed the baby on Annie's stomach immediately after her birth and told the nurses to leave her there a while. Annie thought him a saint.

"It was nothing at all, Doctor," Annie said vaguely. "Are all babies this smart?" She missed the smiles exchanged as a nurse's voice answered, no, they were not. Only Annie's.

Eventually they moved Annie to the recovery room. Almost immediately, she was bored. Annie rang the nurse and demanded that her baby be brought back. The nurse patiently informed her that the baby was being cleaned and weighed. Annie repeated that she wanted her baby immediately. A newborn baby needed her mother. The nurse said kindly that she would walk over and see if they had finished with her. Moments later she came in with an impossibly small bundle. Annie gently lifted the blanket off of the child's face. That was her. Snuggling the tiny girl's body warmly against her own, she fell into a sound sleep.

Shortly afterward, the nurse arrived again. She insisted the baby be taken back to the nursery for tests. Also, Annie was going to her room now and would need to rest. Annie did not protest. She was exhausted and starving. Her most pressing need was for pop. Lots of it. She would need ice as well. She asked the nurse but was told she could get a drink in her room. Annie's IV was hurting. The nurse promised her they would take it out when she got to her room. When they were halfway down a long hallway, a man's voice came over the loud speakers. The nurse apologized briefly to Annie and hastily departed. Annie sighed and resumed her wait. Her whole arm throbbed.

"Annie," she heard a voice. Opening her eyes she looked around for Maureen. "OH, MY GOD," Maureen shouted. "My sister is bleeding to death. Somebody help me!"

"Maureen, shut up," Annie said impatiently. "What are you talking about?"

"It's OK. I'm here now, Annie." Maureen looked frantically around for a nurse. "Get a doctor NOW!" she ordered nobody in particular. Annie looked at her arm. The tube holding the clear fluid was now filled with blood. The blood was also all over the floor. Annie groaned. Maureen would never recover from something like this. A nurse came around the corner at a trot. The nurse began a stream of comfortable comments designed to comfort the shaken Maureen. She worked as she talked, and in no time Annie's IV was out and the bloody bag had disappeared. She promised Maureen that Annie would not die from the blood loss. Maureen demanded to know why her sister had been abandoned in a hallway, bleeding and left to die. The nurse explained that an emergency code had pulled the other nurse away. She would take Annie to her room and make her comfortable. If Maureen wanted to go to the waiting room, the nurse would come for her after Annie was settled. Maureen looked at Annie uncertainly.

"You can go, Maureen," Annie spoke firmly. "Find me a can of pop with a glass of ice." Annie paused for a moment. "Better get two or three. And lots of ice. I'm dying of thirst." Given her mission, Maureen departed swiftly. Annie pitied anyone standing in front of the pop machine.

In no time Annie was settled, and Maureen blustered back into the room. Sure enough, she carried a bucket of ice and six cans of pop. She had a wild look in her eyes, and Annie noticed that her clothes were wet.

"Maureen, why are you all wet?"

"I didn't wait for a cab," Maureen answered shortly. "It was raining. I ran from the train." Her eyes were red, and

Annie wondered if she had been crying. "I'm so sorry I wasn't here, Annie," she began. "Dad called me and said you were in the delivery room..." A funny look came over her face. "Did you have the baby?"

Laughing delightedly, Annie nodded her head. "She's the most beautiful baby in the entire world, Maureen."

"It's a girl?" Maureen asked. Annie nodded, and Maureen began to cry. "Oh, it's just too much," she said, sinking into the nearest chair. "Nellie will kill me, but I think I might faint."

Annie sat up in bed. Reaching over, she opened a can of pop and poured a glass. After chugging the first half, she handed her sister the remainder. "You'll be OK. It is pretty shocking, I know," Annie spoke in a comforting voice. "Drink this and you'll feel better. Do you have any cigarettes?" Drinking the pop, Maureen nodded her head. "Can you smoke now?"

"I don't think I'll ask permission. Light one anyway. If they tell us to put it out, we will." Annie wanted to celebrate.

A wan looking woman paused in the doorway. She was evidently walking the halls and stopped to get her breath. "When are you due?" Maureen asked sweetly.

The woman smiled briefly. "I had my baby yesterday."

Maureen looked appalled. "Oh. I'm sure that's why you look so good. I mean ... for just having had a baby..." The woman moved on, and Annie burst out laughing. "I could die," Maureen sputtered. "How embarrassing. The poor woman. She looked like she was still pregnant." She, too, burst out laughing. "This is a horrible place. When can I see the baby?"

Eventually, yet another nurse presented Annie with her baby. Mr. McGowan had seen the baby in the nursery and gone home. Maureen held the baby for over an hour and started crying again when they took her back. Annie rested contentedly. This was without a doubt the happiest day of her life. She noticed in surprise that she did not care about anything. Maureen had called Mrs. Griffin and coldly relayed the news, Annie knew Kevin would come as soon as he heard.

"Her name is Mary," Annie said, softly drifting off to sleep.

Chapter Ten

The birth of their daughter cemented Annie and Kevin. Later. when Annie tried to reconstruct the chain of events leading to Kevin's arrest, she would start with the hospital. It was as if someone sneaked into the room and pushed a fast-forward button on her life. The only constant in the blur of activity was the baby. Pink and helpless, she consumed Annie's focus. A squirming bundle of humanity that required constant feeding and changing. Somewhere in Annie's baby books there should have been a small paragraph. It should have read, "In six months you will feel somewhat normal. Reserve all major decisions until then."

On the evening of Mary's birthday, Kevin blew into the hospital room. Annie watched him as he held his daughter for the first time. Anything short of absolute devotion would have disappointed. A rush of emotions chased each other from his face. She was satisfied. Kevin had not understood before. Fathers did not carry the infants. Annie speculated that fathers only grasped the enormity after they saw their baby. Lying back, she gave him a peaceful smile.

Kevin began talking in a firm voice. Tomorrow he would take the day off school. His father must be told immediately. Kevin planned to sift through his scholarship offers and make calls. Annie let his words flow over her like a soothing balm. For the first time in her life she was content to let someone else take charge. Thirty minutes after visiting hours were over, the nurse forced Kevin to leave.

For the next few days, Annie was kept busy. The phone rang, and flowers arrived hourly. She felt like a queen. Rene came bearing gifts. After briefly admiring the baby, she prattled on about Senior Prom. Feigning interest, Annie found it hard to believe that somewhere there was a world where girls worried about prom dresses. She felt lonely. Trying to imagine herself in Rene's shoes, she got emotional. She would not trade her baby for all of the proms in the world. Still, prom dresses were not frightening. Motherhood was. Once again, sleep proved elusive.

Maureen arrived bright and early the following morning. They were going home. Annie felt strange entering the house. She had left a young girl and returned as a mother. It was late afternoon before she felt remotely comfortable. Annie finished feeding the baby for what seemed like the hundredth time when Maureen called her to the phone.

It was Kevin. Mr. Griffin had been told. Mr. Griffin was ecstatic. Mr. Griffin was insisting that Annie bring the baby over immediately. Kevin's voice was relieved and happy. Annie could hear the babble in the background. She also heard Mary beginning to scream upstairs. Nursing was relentless. Annie informed Kevin that it would be folly to bring the child out in the cold. Besides, she was too sore and tired. Kevin was disappointed but promised that he understood. I should hope so, Annie thought briskly. Kevin promised to be over in a little while. For a moment, Annie marveled that he was no longer concerned about coming to the house. If she ever had a spare moment again, she would think about that.

Moments later, Mary's nursing was again interrupted. This time it was Mrs. Griffin. Kevin's mother begged Annie to bring the baby over. She could not possibly wait another moment to see her little granddaughter. Annie churlishly pointed out that the hospital kept liberal visiting hours. Mrs. Griffin stammered vaguely that life was so hectic these days. Annie said that the baby was crying and she would have to call back.

Cynically apprising her father of the turn of events, Annie received a shock. Mr. McGowan told her to pack up the baby and go over. It was Kevin's daughter, too. These people would very likely be her in-laws for life. Annie must think about Kevin and be charming. Sighing deeply, Annie traipsed back to the telephone. Motherhood was one long martyrdom.

Poor Kevin appeared at the door in minutes. Seeing his relaxed boyish features, Annie mentally thanked her father. Kevin meant everything to her, and his parents were important to him. She realized that she had a lot to learn.

• • •

One month later, they married. A small reception was held at the McGowans'. The elder Mrs. Griffin wore a black pantsuit and a forced smile. The sisters made searing jokes until Annie begged them to behave. The day passed in a blur. Annie worried about the baby. She cried a lot and seemed to be in constant pain. Annie felt certain that Mary suffered from an elusive disease that escaped diagnosis. Mrs. Nolan said she was gassy.

Their weekend honeymoon plans made Annie nervous. Mrs. Nolan had agreed to take the baby. Annie trusted her experience, but vague feelings of foreboding engulfed her. Mary would die before she returned. She was sure of it. The situation was exacerbated by the fact that Annie knew she was irrational. Try as she might, her emotions would not stabilize. The last month had been grueling. The baby slept only two hours at a time. She constantly wanted to eat. Annie seldom got any rest and had dark rings around her eyes. Despite Mrs. Nolan's constant reassurance, Annie felt sure that the problem lay in her youth. She was doing something wrong. Formula supplements helped the baby, but Annie felt like a failure. The books said that babies should go four hours between feedings. Unfortunately, Mary could not read the books, and Annie staggered through each day like a robot, wondering when she would collapse.

Toward the end of the party, Kevin persuaded her to get her bag. She handed Mary over tearfully. In the car. she emotionally informed her husband that she would not get a minute's peace with worrying about their daughter. Seconds later, he gently shook her awake. They were at the Hilton. Legally. Annie managed a tranquil smile. Her honeymoon was one continuous nap. Whenever she awakened, Kevin called for room service. He waved off her apologies. She needed the sleep, and he loved cable television. They were both happy.

• • •

The blur continued after the wedding. Mrs. Nolan watched Mary while Annie finished school. Kevin eventually moved his clothes over to the McGowans'. Mr. Griffin took over the scholarship quest and spent long hours negotiating details. Shortly before their graduation, he presented them with their options.

Kevin, Annie, and Mr. Griffin sat at the Griffin kitchen table. Three schools met their criteria. They were looking for a full scholarship for Kevin, along with housing for the family and a stipend for food. Also considered was the best athletic possibility for Kevin. The schools were in three different states, and Mr. Griffin had arranged the offers in three piles.

Glancing down at the papers, Kevin's responded immediately. "Texas. We'll go to Texas."

Much discussion followed, but Kevin remained adamant. They would go as far as possible. Annie realized with dismay that she had no say in the matter. Kevin politely informed her that the decision was made.

Bristling, Annie asked her husband to clarify which decisions would be joint. Kevin said that as the man of the family, he would listen to her opinions but ultimately was entitled to make the final call. A long, tense, conversation resulted in guidelines, set by Kevin. She was informed that she could make most decisions about the baby and the household. Fearing a full-scale battle, Annie backed down. Options were not available.

It got her thinking. Kevin was wonderful in many ways. He was faithful, devoted, and responsible. He was also a male chauvinist. Marriage was supposed to be challenging, but Annie was stung at just how sticky it could get. Kevin had a temper. That was no secret. But it was not just the jealousy issue anymore. A myriad of topics could now plunge them into war.

The subject of Annie's academic future also proved tricky. Kevin said little. Mr. McGowan brought it up daily. While Annie's first responsibility was to her new family, she should apply for scholarships in her own right. Annie instinctively knew that if she pushed now she would slam into another brick wall. Promising her father she would investigate it further, she bided her time.

That summer Kevin worked in construction. Long days and hard labor exhausted him, but he never complained. He wanted to take as much money as possible to Texas. Annie's father praised his efforts and encouraged Annie to be attentive to her husband.

The last months at home were bittersweet for Annie. Everything was changing. Maureen was going back to school. She and Nellie were saving for a trip to Europe, and Annie tried not to envy them. Nellie had one more year to go, and Eileen was working away at grammar school. Danny was still gone. Occasionally, he called or sent a postcard. Unable to attend their wedding, he promised to surface in the next few months.

Rene would attend school with Nellie, downstate. She frequently stopped by the McGowans', usually to consult with Nellie. Sometimes Annie wished that she had not gotten married. The thought made her feel guilty. She asked Kevin if he ever felt sad at what they were missing. Kevin said sweetly that he figured they were getting it both ways.

They got to go away and be together. Mary was a bonus. This reassured Annie. She would hate to think that Kevin had regrets.

Much too quickly, it was time to go. Mr. Griffin was driving them to school with a trailer attached to the car. Three days of packing brought Annie to the strange realization that everything they owned fit in a tiny pull-along box.

Annie sat on her front porch on the eve of their departure. Her thoughts were heavy and desolate. Hearing the creak of the screen door, she glanced up to see Kevin.

"The baby's asleep," he said quietly. "I think she'll be fine in the car, don't you?"

Annie shrugged. Twenty-four hours of driving would be unpleasant no matter how good the baby was.

"Are you scared, Annie?" he asked gently. When she remained silent, he continued, "I wouldn't blame you. It's far. But I think we'll love it there." As the twilight deepened, he told what little he knew about their destination. Annie listened to his deep voice and felt comforted. Laying her hand in his, she smiled at him as she listened. There was nothing he could say to console her about leaving her family. He did not try. With an ache in her heart, Annie McGowan realized that growing up was painful. For a fleeting moment she wished she could stop the process and remain a child. She understood, yet again, why she was too young to be married with a child. Stifling a deep sigh, she vowed for the millionth time not to let her age affect Mary negatively. Annie would be as good a wife and mother as possible.

Her reverie was broken by Kevin's departure. He wanted to turn in early. Dreaming again, Annie considered her situation. The mothering part was not the problem. Books, advice, and common sense were readily available. It was the marriage part that gave her cause for concern. Kevin was unpredictable. His anger flared unexpectedly. Mrs. Nolan had explained that men were different. Regardless of how many centuries elapsed, they retained some elements of the caveman. Annie listened intently. It made sense.

Annie asked her about the power imbalance. Kevin obviously felt justified in taking complete control. Mrs. Nolan had looked blank. Pressed for examples, Annie related their conversation about the Texas Decision, as she dubbed it. Mrs. Nolan was thoughtful. Annie stated further that Kevin retained strict control of their money. He knew where every penny was spent. Mrs. Nolan suggested that Annie tell Kevin to lighten up a bit. The older woman suggested that Kevin's youth was the culprit. He was overcompensating. It would certainly wear off once Kevin got comfortable with his new responsibilities.

Annie hoped so. As it stood, she felt she had traded her father in for a younger version. At least her father had blind spots and a sense of humor. She rebuked herself. Kevin was not bad. He was still hysterically funny, and he truly loved her. Her father said it was amazing how quickly Kevin had assumed responsibility for his little family. Adjustments were necessary, Annie reasoned. Some would be rocky.

She stared at the trailer. At least she would have her things. Plenty of books had been packed, and no one could take away Annie's reading. The thought cheered her. She would find a library right away. Surely there were buses in Texas. The Griffins would have no car. Kevin's had long since traveled its last mile. Annie felt her spirits rise. The baby could be taken anywhere. They did have a stroller, and Annie did not fear being alone. Her inherent sense of adventure asserted itself. It could be great. Annie resolved to be optimistic and cheerful. Kevin deserved at least that.

Twelve hours later they were on their way. Annie did not cry. Her pain was too deep for tears. Pulling away from her house, she waved briskly to her dad and sisters. Her father's obvious emotion upset her even more. Racing down the highway, she glanced down at Mary. The child slept peacefully in her car seat. So far so good. Opening her book, Annie shut out any further thoughts as she sped toward her new life.

Chapter Eleven

The road stretched on forever. Conversation did not flow freely in the car, and Annie was grateful when Mary woke up and demanded a bottle. Somewhere north of Memphis, Annie persuaded Kevin's father to give her a turn at the wheel. The tension quickly became unbearable. Mr. Griffin was loudly distressed that Annie was not using her rearview mirror properly. Annie always looked behind to check her blind spot. Her father-in-law maintained that if a driver was looking behind, no one was driving the car. He reminded Annie that she could not be looking at scenery while she was operating a motor vehicle. Annie argued back briefly, then closed her mouth. A period of silence ensued.

Another few miles disappeared behind them. Annie was just letting herself feel the exhilaration of the open highway when she heard her navigator grunt. She suppressed an exasperated sigh.

"Did you grunt?" she asked conversationally.

"Pardon me?" he queried politely.

Annie grinned wickedly to herself. The Griffins never

said anything openly.

"I thought maybe you had some more advice for me."

Mr. Griffin spoke considerately. "Well, now that you mention it ... the front end of the car is wobbling. Can you see it?"

Frowning, Annie made a show of concentration. "No, I can't. If I'm staring at the front end of the car ... who is driving the car? I'm on the highway now. This is a motor vehicle. I really can't be looking around at the scenery."

Mr. Griffin began to laugh. "You may be pretty sharp, Annie. But this is power steering. You're jerking the steering wheel back and forth, and the front of the car is wobbling. This is not a go-cart. You don't need to steer it back and forth." He spoke with humor in his voice, and Annie was not offended. "Just take it nice and steady. See what I mean? Now it's not wobbling."

"It was never wobbling. Kevin, did you feel it wobbling?" Annie cast behind her.

"Kevin, look up here." Mr. Griffin requested impatiently. "It's wobbling again. Women can't drive. All they can do with a car is aim it."

Kevin concentrated on the front of the car. He remained silent. Annie was beginning to lose patience herself and toyed with the idea of aiming at a tree. After a tense minute limped by, she said lightly, "You're wife has been driving for years, Mr. Griffin."

"Not correctly. I would never let her on the highway. It's not safe to let bad drivers on the highway."

"Are you implying that I am a bad driver?" Annie asked shortly.

"Annie, that's enough," Kevin spoke sharply. "Hold the wheel steady, and the car won't wobble. You're probably not used to power steering."

"Kevin, do you think my Dad drives a tractor around the city? We have power steering. I'll tell you what," she said bluntly as she put on her directional, "rather than give us all an ulcer, I'll let you professionals handle the driving." Annie spotted a rest area. "I'll just aim for the toilets."

126

When the car was parked, she grabbed her purse and got out. She took herself to the bathroom to smoke a cigarette.

Moments later, Kevin poked his head in the door. "Are you mad, Annie?"

"What do you think?" Annie asked hotly. "What a bunch of bologna! I was driving fine. He just doesn't want anyone else to drive."

Kevin shifted uncomfortably. "I told you he was a pain in the neck. Stop arguing with him." Kevin spoke sharply. "I don't want a stomachache over this, dammit. Get in the car and keep your mouth shut."

Annie frowned. "Keep my mouth shut? That's a nice thing to say. I'll certainly try. Has it ever occurred to any of you that the reason he gets away with so much is because you 'keep your mouths shut'?" Annie ground her cigarette out on the floor and stalked past him. Turning briefly she retorted, "Don't talk to me like that, Kevin Griffin." She strode back to the car and climbed into the back seat. "I'm safely in the back now, Mr. Griffin."

"OK," the older man said pleasantly as he moved over in the seat. Kevin got in on the passenger side. "Why don't we let you pick the restaurant for dinner, Annie? What do you have a taste for?"

Annie wanted to kick both of their back seats. Seeing Kevin's pleading look, she took the olive branch. "I don't care. I love Italian."

"Italian it will be," Mr. Griffin said magnanimously. "How is the baby, Annie?"

"Fine. She'll sleep for at least another hour, I think."

"You're a wonderful little mother, I must say. That's the nicest little baby I've ever seen. That's because you take such good care of her." Annie softened in spite of herself. She was always grateful when someone said she was doing a good job. Annie hoped she was a good mother. She certainly tried hard. She glanced up and met Kevin's eyes. He winked at her and smiled. She made a fist at him and then smiled, too. A trip like this was bound to be tough. Awkward, too. Annie did not want to think about all of them in one hotel room. Surely they would get two rooms. She cursed herself for not making that clear to Kevin before they left. Any more tension, and she would begin to say horrible things. Some people giggled when they were tense. Annie made smart comments. God help us all if we have to sleep together, she thought.

Annie spent the next day comfortably nestled in the backseat. She had insisted on two motel rooms the night before, claiming she would feel terrible if the baby kept Mr. Griffin up all night. After a look of alarm, he quickly agreed and insisted on paying for both rooms. Annie had to keep from chuckling as she unpacked the baby's things. It was very awkward traveling with a baby on formula. Annie had splurged and bought eight-ounce ready-to-feed bottles with disposable nipples. At fifty cents a bottle, they were not cheap. And Annie felt quite rich every time she screwed on a nipple and threw out its predecessor. Kevin said it was wasteful. He had wanted to bring a cooler and make bottles as they were needed. Annie had stood firm on this, though. She told Kevin that if he was not willing to spend the extra ten dollars, he could sit in the back with the baby. He had uncharacteristically backed down. Ha, she thought. Maybe that's the way. Inconvenience him a little.

She also had a long talk with her husband in the privacy of their room. Annie waited until he was relaxed. She then sweetly broached the subject of arguments. She agreed with Kevin that disagreements were inevitable. She wondered aloud if there was anything they could do to keep fights from getting ugly.

Kevin thought about it for a moment. "If you could stop yourself from making smart comments, it would help a lot."

Annie took her time answering. She had read an article on communication in a woman's magazine that said you should listen first and deal with your partner's statements. She was also supposed to reflect on his feelings. Almost as fun as psychology class.

"Does it make you feel minimized when I say something

128

sarcastic?" she asked with great seriousness.

Kevin looked at her warily. "No. I'm not sure what being minimized feels like. The opposite of maximized, I would think. Hmm. Problem is, I don't know what that means either. I do know it pisses me off when you talk back."

Annie bit back an explosive reaction to the term "talk back."

Turning to face him, she said kindly, "Kevin. Do you love me?"

He answered without hesitation. "Yes, I do, Annie. You know that."

"Well, I love you, too. And I don't want us to be at each other's throats. I know we're young, but we don't have to be miserable. Everyone in the world thinks our marriage is doomed because of our age. Wouldn't it be nice to prove them all wrong?" Annie paused. "I know that's not the most important thing. The most important thing is that we make each other happy. I want you to be happy, Kevin. You deserve it more than anyone I know. Help me out here. I can't stand it when you tell me to 'keep my mouth shut.' It's insulting. I know you don't want to hurt my feelings, but it does."

Kevin looked at her for a moment and then pulled her down into the bed with him.

"Kevin," she protested. "The baby is awake." Mary was indeed awake. Annie had her resting on a blanket on the floor.

"Annie, I just want to hold you for a minute," he said in a thick voice. "You're so good. I'm sorry I said that to you. I don't even think about things like that. Does it really bother you?" Annie nodded her head from against his chest. "Then I won't talk like that anymore. I want you to be happy more than anything. We'll have a wonderful marriage. I promise. OK?"

"OK," she said with relief.

Kevin rose up on one elbow. "Just one thing, Annie," he said gravely. "Don't start maximizing me, OK?"

Annie made an attempt to punch him in his chest.

Kevin laughingly pulled her down on top of him. "What was that all about?"

Laughing back, Annie spoke lightheartedly. "I'm trying to communicate with you, Kevin. If you must know, I was attempting to reflect your feelings back to you so you'd know that I heard you."

"Are you going deaf? Why wouldn't you hear me?" he said playfully. "What the hell are you talking about, Annie?"

He was joking, but Annie noticed he looked a little nervous. "Oh, Kevin, I read an article on communication, and I was trying it out." Annie was embarrassed and added defiantly, " I hate the way we fight, and I thought maybe if we could learn how to talk with each other better, we wouldn't fight so badly. Honestly, Kevin. What's the harm in trying to be as good as we can?"

"Nothing, Annie," he responded contritely. "I think it's wonderful. It's a little strange that every time something goes wrong, my wife runs to the library. But that's a good thing. Just explain things to me, and I'll try to learn, too. OK?"

Annie hugged him hard. She thought confidently that they could work out any problems as long as they could talk them out without fighting. They would have to practice. She realized it was not fair to blame Kevin's temper for everything. She, too, had a temper. Annie would try hard to control herself. She thought that the article did one thing for them. Instead of attacking Kevin for being mean, she had opened the door for a discussion. Maybe there was something to it after all. Feeling quite pleased with herself, she organized the room while Kevin showered. Mary smiled up at her from the floor, and Annie felt quite competent.

After their discussion, it was easy to be kind to Mr. Griffin. As good as his word, he had found an Italian restaurant. Mary was actually cranky. Kevin and Annie had to take turns eating their dinners. Annie felt quite mature asking the waitress politely to please leave her salad plate for a few moments while she changed her daughter.

She loved things that made her feel mature. She also loved things that made her feel like a lady. Annie could barely wait until she turned twenty. For some reason she felt sure that at twenty she would feel confident. It sounded old. Like an adult. "Yes," she would respond, "I'm in my twenties." People asked her if Mary was her little sister. Annie hated that. "My goodness, no," she would respond in her most adult voice. It was embarrassing. She did not even look eighteen. She looked more like fifteen. Yes, it was difficult. She had taken to wearing makeup to look older. It did not really help, though. She looked like a girl with makeup on. Mrs. Nolan had promised her that she would be quite happy about her youthful appearance in a few short years. Annie could not wait.

Toward the end of the second day, the travelers blew through Texarkana. Entering Texas gave Annie a feeling in the pit of her stomach. She had tried to watch the countryside change from her rear position, but it had escaped her again. On their family drives to Florida she had always tried to witness the landscape go from northern to tropical. It sneaked up on her every time.

"Is that a cactus?" she asked aloud.

"It sure is, Annie," Mr. Griffin responded enthusiastically. "This state is like a different country altogether." With that, he launched into an educational monologue on the characteristics of Texas.

Apparently, even driving was different here. Vast distances stretched between cities; speed limits were not enforced. It was acceptable to come right up behind someone. Nothing personal. Sort of like a department store's equivalent to "Excuse Me," Annie thought.

Also, Mr. Griffin had been told that wildlife posed a significant hazard to drivers. During dusk and darkness it was not safe to drive without a "spotter." A spotter was kind of like a navigator whose job was to watch the road intently for deer or other large animals. Hitting a deer could kill someone driving at a high rate of speed.

Guns were legal in Texas but could not be concealed. According to Mr. Griffin, everyone owned guns. He pointed out a number of pickup trucks with stocked gun racks. Annie was impressed. She asked why they felt the need to be armed. Kevin's father reckoned it would be handy to have a gun in the event you struck an animal. Annie made a face. No wonder they needed spotters. She reminded Kevin to keep his eyes open. Hopefully, there were not a lot of accidental shootings.

As if reading her mind Mr. Griffin launched into another discussion about boys being taught to handle guns. A deep respect for weapons was instilled in young boys. That same respect prevented the irresponsible handling of guns. Mr. Griffin speculated that the number of accidental shootings in Texas was lower than in places where boys were not familiarized with their fathers' guns. Annie wondered idly if she was a feminist. Being around this man could certainly start a girl thinking about it. He went on to say Texas was the kind of place that respected a man's right to behave like a man. Laws were tough. Responsibility came with those rights, and violators were not mollycoddled like up north. Annie had heard this from her father. He said that Texas knew how to deal with criminals. She yawned. It all sounded very masculine.

Down into the heart of the state they traveled. It was midnight when they arrived in the small college town that was to be home. Exhausted, they spilled into one room. Annie felt twinges of embarrassment at the close quarters but soon fell into a dreamless sleep. The following morning she awoke to Kevin pulling the covers from her.

"Get up, Annie," he commanded. "My dad is down in the restaurant. We have to pack up and go meet him."

"How's Mary?" Annie answered sleepily, peering over at the makeshift bed near the bathroom.

"Fine. I'll get her up and dressed. Get in the shower, Gorgeous."

Two hours later they pulled up in front of their new home. A series of six eight-flats comprised the married housing accommodations. Flush with the west side of the campus, they did not look like university issue. With old red brick and white trim, the buildings looked downright stately. Annie was delighted. Kevin explained that the other married housing units were like small boxes. There was a long waiting list for these, but because Kevin was an athlete ... Kevin could not hide his smile as they inspected their new home.

"Why didn't you tell me how nice they were?" she chided him.

"I wanted it to be a surprise, Annie. I know how worried you've been about coming so far. I figured it would be something nice at the end of it." He checked to see where his father was. Looking out their third floor window, he spotted his father unstrapping the baby from her car seat. He ushered Annie out into the hallway. Swooping her into his arms, he carried her across the threshold. "Now it's official."

Annie smiled. "You're very sweet, my dear. Now put me down and go unpack my stuff. We have to get started."

Kevin came up with the first box. His father followed him in with the baby on one arm and her diaper bag on the other.

"Look who everyone forgot," he cooed. "She was down there by herself, and she's very put out." Annie looked at Mr. Griffin affectionately. How could she dislike anyone who adored her baby so much? "If you'll take this princess, Annie, I'll go find a store and get some pop and ice. Do you need anything for the baby?"

"No," she answered sweetly. "I'll get diapers and formula later. Tomorrow I'll do a big shop for groceries." Annie mused out loud. "Kevin, can you get the baby's bouncy seat on your next trip up?" Kevin nodded cheerfully.

Annie walked Mary around their new home. It was lovely. Annie thought the third floor was just fine. She liked the height, and the view was impressive. Gazing out at the sky, she wondered why it seemed so vast. Shaking off her reverie, Annie got down to business. This was a one-bedroom unit.

When Mary got bigger they would need two, but for now it was fine. A good-sized dining room merged into a large living room. The kitchen was spacious. Muted green tile gave it an old-fashioned feel, which Annie loved immediately. Two large windows overlooked the back porch and the rest of the apartments. Noticing little houses in the yard, Annie watched as a young woman carried laundry inside. Carting laundry up and down would be no picnic, but Annie shrugged. You could not have everything.

Depositing Mary into her seat, Annie put her in a sunny spot with a bottle. Opening the first crate, she talked to the baby as she worked. A beautiful white cloth-covered container came out of the first box. Annie grinned in delight. This was the crucifix that the nuns had given her as a wedding present. Its early appearance was a good omen, and Annie ceremoniously hung it on the wall.

• • •

That evening Kevin and Annie rested in their first home. It was only eight, but already they were sprawled out on the bed. Mary was asleep in her crib in the dining room. Annie was not certain she would keep her there but for now it seemed convenient. She still slept through anything. According to the books it was best to have babies out of the parents' room as early as possible.

Mr. Griffin insisted on staying in a motel room for his three-night visit. He said a young couple needed their privacy. Annie heartily agreed. He was due over early in the morning to take Kevin around the campus. Annie was going to persuade him to take her grocery shopping first. That way she could try out her new kitchen. She also needed a whole list of things from a department store. Why had it never occurred to her that they would need hangers, scissors, and a silverware organizer for the drawer? In unpacking alone she had come up with a list of twenty-two items. She fervently hoped Kevin would not come shopping with her. He was apt to scrutinize every purchase. Annie did not want to have to defend her right to buy a dish drain for the counter.

She rolled over and propped herself up on one elbow. Kevin was looking through a course catalog, and Annie watched him jealously. College would be liberating after high school. Imagine looking through a book and choosing the classes you wanted? Kevin told her it was not quite that easy. For the first two years you had to retake things like English, History, and Speech. Annie did not care. You actually got to pick the times and days you wanted to attend school. She mentally resolved to see an admissions counselor as quickly as possible.

Glancing up at the large double windows in their bedroom, she frowned. She had a bag of cast-off drapes and curtains from Mrs. Nolan and her mother-in-law. Hopefully, she would find a set to fit. The kitchen window would be no problem. Blinds were already in place. Annie loved the clean look of the white blinds against the green walls. The apartment was so airy when it was empty. Annie determined to preserve some of that look. She did not want clutter. Back at the McGowans', her little family had been crammed into one room, and Annie had felt like a hopeless slob. There was simply too much stuff for one room. Seeing their possessions spread around the large flat had shown her that. Here there was room for everything.

"Do you want a glass of pop?" she asked Kevin.

"Sure. Thanks."

Annie really wanted an excuse to wander into her kitchen. What luxury to have your own refrigerator! Opening the door she admired the clean shelves. The case of pop was snug against the open can of formula. It was as if the two items were nervous in that large space.

"Tomorrow you will have plenty of company," she promised them out loud. Feeling embarrassed, she grabbed two cans and quickly closed the door. Opening her cabinet she ran her hand along the shelf paper. The lower cabinets had not been done, and Annie reached over to her list and added thumbtacks. She remembered how embarrassed she had been when Mrs. Griffin handed her two rolls of shelving paper in a store in Chicago. She felt her face burn all over again. "Is it wallpaper?" she had asked. Annie had hoped so because she did have an opinion on wallpaper. Her father said it was crazy to stick paper on a perfectly good wall. Mrs. Griffin rolled her eyes as if searching for patience. Annie wanted to hit her. Feeling tears burning her eyes, she had walked away.

Mrs. Griffin often asked Annie questions she could not answer. One day she asked her if she was going to get a separate beater for her potatoes. Annie was totally nonplused. Mrs. Griffin smiled at the two neighbor women who were there for coffee. They smiled back sympathetically as if to say "What can you do with such inexperience?" Annie had flushed that time, too. Taking the bait, she asked why she would need a separate beater for potatoes? At the McGowans' they used a manual beater for everything. They did not own an electric mixer. They had at one time, but Eileen had taken the attachments into the yard and they had never been seen again. According to these ladies a woman wanted a separate mixer for cake mixes because the one for the potatoes should only be used for potatoes. Annie had replied that she would mash the potatoes by hand, thus eliminating the need for a specialized appliance. The woman had chuckled. Annie was informed that Kevin liked his potatoes very creamy. Annie had replied that she liked hers baked.

Kevin adored his mother, and Annie truly wanted to be friends. She felt her own mother's absence keenly these days. Mrs. Nolan was the closest thing she had. Annie always thanked God for Mrs. Nolan. Mrs. Nolan also thought Kevin's mother was a witch and supported Annie on everything.

Mrs. Griffin had wanted to come for the drive to Texas. Blessedly, Mr. Griffin forced her to wait. He promised to bring her in October for a game. Annie had been tremendously relieved. The last thing she needed was Mrs. Griffin's superior presence while she attempted to get her home up and running. Annie leaned against her counter in her own kitchen and daydreamed. When Mrs. Griffin came in October, she would be ready. She would go to the library and get out books on entertaining. Things with floral centerpieces and candles. Annie would make an elegant dinner, and they would all dine in leisure. A glance into the dining room burst Annie's pleasant daydream. They had a small round white table with two dilapidated red restaurant chairs. Hmm. Maybe a book on Japanese dining. Annie laughed out loud as she pictured Kevin's parents trying to sit on cushions on the floor. Hearing Kevin call to her from the bedroom, she poured the pop into two of her beautiful new glasses. They were clear with large pink flowers. Annie thought them the height of elegance.

Ambling through the dining room, she glanced at Mary. How peaceful babies looked when they rested. Glancing up at the crucifix, Annie held back a gasp. A large, hairy spider about the size of a silver dollar was perched on the top. She bit back a scream and put the glasses down on the table. She had seen pictures of tarantulas. This spider was without a doubt related to the family. The intruder was directly over the crib, and Annie hesitated to move fast for fear of startling it onto the baby. She overcame her panic long enough to pull the crib away from the wall. Reaching in, she grabbed the sleeping child.

Kevin was already off the bed. "Why did you get her up?" he asked in surprise.

Annie quickly sent him into the dining room. He came back with an equally disturbed look on his face. "Give me a shoe," he said.

Annie was close to tears. "Kevin, you can't throw a shoe at the crucifix."

"Don't be a nut. How else am I going to get the damn thing down?"

"Kevin, I mean it. Do not throw that shoe at the cross. It's like throwing it at Jesus." Annie was pale and shaking by this time. "Should I take the baby and get out?"

"Calm down! It's only a spider. It'll go away on its own."

Annie clutched his arm. "Kevin, I swear to you. If you let it go away, I will never sleep a night in this apartment. I mean it. Mary could have been killed. We can't watch her forever." Mary chose this moment to begin a vocal protest.

Kevin looked uncertain. "OK. Put the baby down and come with me. I'll try to scare it off the cross."

Annie quickly put a blanket down on the floor and deposited the screaming infant on it. Following Kevin into the dining room, she held his arm. "Keep your body between the wall and bedroom in case he goes for the baby."

Shaking her off, he yelled, "Shut up, Annie. You're freaking me out." Kevin threw the shoe at the wall directly below the crucifix. Both of them screamed and ran back into the bedroom as the spider jumped from the crucifix to the wall. Bursting into laughter, Kevin prepared himself for a second assault.

"Go, Kevin," she said weakly. "Go kill it. It's not on the crucifix anymore."

"Did you see it jump?" he asked in disbelief "Annie, I don't want to go out there."

Annie remained adamant. "I won't stay here unless I see that thing's dead body. Go smash it quickly before it has a chance to jump again. I'm sorry. I truly cannot go out there."

"Shit," Kevin swore. "OK. But if it kills me, you're going to feel pretty bad. Should I do it with the shoe?"

"No. Use a book." Annie handed him a telephone book from the closet floor. "Do it quick, Kevin. Is it a tarantula?"

"It sure looks like one. Kiss me for the last time, my darling!" he said dramatically. Reaching into his pocket, he pulled out a jaw breaker. "If they take you alive, eat this."

Annie pushed him away. "Hurry UP, Kevin. It's not funny." After he tiptoed out of the room, Annie stuffed a towel against the floor underneath the door. What if it bit him? Laying Mary on the bed, Annie patted her back. Mary immediately went back to sleep. Listening at the door, Annie refrained from asking for a progress report. She did not want to startle it. Suddenly she heard Kevin give a loud shout. She opened the door just in time to admit his flying body.

"Did you get it?" she asked imperiously. Kevin was rubbing his hands all over his arms and legs.

"Gross! Gross!" he repeated.

"What's gross?" Annie asked again. "Did you kill it?"

"I think so, Annie. Go look at the phone book and see if it's smashed."

"I don't want to, Kevin."

"Too bad, Annie. I had to kill it. You go see if it's dead. That's fair."

"Kevin, you're the man of the house. Isn't this your job?"

"Don't change the subject. C'mon. Go check."

Annie went out and confirmed the kill. She made Kevin carry the whole telephone book out to the garbage. She also insisted on bringing the baby's crib into their bedroom. Kevin thought this irrational. Annie did not even pause. Better that Mary be emotionally damaged by sharing a room with her parents than dead from a poisonous spider bite.

Annie lay in bed with her eyes wide open that night. It was a bad omen, and she knew it.

Chapter Twelve

All too soon, Mr. Griffin departed for the long, lonely ride back to Chicago. Annie held Mary tightly as they watched him pull away. She was startled at the burning prick of tears in her eyes. This was her last connection to her father and sisters. She thought sadly that the Griffins' car, a mere collection of metal and glass, would be parked a few blocks away from her family. Irrationally, she envied it. She chanced a look at Kevin. Annie momentarily imagined it was her father pulling away.

"Come on." She shifted Mary and grabbed his hand. "I'll make you a grilled cheese, and we'll go for a walk. You can show me the campus."

Kevin smiled down at her and nodded. "We'll walk to the store and get a TV guide. Can you believe we get free cable?"

Thus cheered, they began their life together.

Initially, all was good. Kevin attended school every morning until noon. He came home for lunch, then went to practice until five-thirty. Annie had a hot dinner ready for him at six. They spent their evenings companionably watching movies or playing Scrabble. The game was not begun until the baby slept. Annie popped corn and made lemonade. Soda was expensive and reserved for special occasions.

Kevin liked school and loved sports. Much of their conversation revolved around his performance and chances of playing. He was a bright individual, and the classes came easily to him. Annie was glad to see him adjusting.

Obtaining groceries presented a problem. The coach arranged for a player to drive Annie to the grocery store on Saturday mornings. But often she needed provisions during the week. Regardless of how completely she made her list, a critical item was forgotten. Annie cheerfully packed Mary into the stroller and walked the two miles but was limited in how much she could carry home. Also, bad weather prevented these trips. Kevin was not interested, repeatedly reminding his wife that it was her dilemma. Annie usually managed but sometimes had to buy milk and bread at the convenience store. Kevin was strongly opposed to this because milk there was fifty cents higher. It was a problem.

Annie spent her days tidying the house and minding Mary. She loved having her own home. Cleaning and laundry could be dealt with by ten-thirty in the morning. Mary was still a good baby, and Annie had no problem getting her work done. It was only in the afternoons that time dragged. Afternoons were open for exploring, and Annie noticed how spread out everything seemed. She grudgingly conceded that Texans had all the room in the world. But it was tough on people without cars. Public transportation was limited to an erratic bus service that actually varied its route as far as Annie could tell.

Only poor people rode buses. Most were Mexicans, and Annie liked them. They smiled a lot and always had children with them. She thought the mothers very affectionate. Anyway, they were poor like her.

She found the public library and obtained a card. It was downtown, about six miles from campus. Kevin told her to use the college library. Someone told him that a "bad element" rode the buses. Annie laughed out loud, picturing the cheerful Mexican mothers with their smiling children. Besides, she could not take books out of the college library unless Kevin was present, plus everyone stared if Mary so much as yawned. Annie loved the little library in town. Her Friday trip for books immediately became a bright spot in her week.

Another highlight was her daily trip to the student center to check the mailbox. Sometimes she browsed in the adjacent bookstore. Once she splurged and bought a notebook for $1.50. It had a beautiful cover with the school logo on every page. Surprisingly, Kevin did not get mad. The Griffins had little money, and Kevin tended to get angry if Annie wasted any.

Letters from home were the ultimate highlight of any day. Eileen wrote religiously. Her younger sister's letters were filled with breezy eleven-year-old nonsense. They came in tubes disguised as Tootsie Rolls or in little boxes with Mickey Mouse labels. Invariably, something for Annie was tucked inside. Sometimes a piece of gum or stickers that smelled like strawberries. Once there were four leaves from the McGowans' lilac tree. Wrapped in plastic wrap and mounted on construction paper, Eileen called them bookmarks. Annie placed these treasures in an honored place on the refrigerator.

Nellie wrote occasional missives with anecdotes about her own college life. Maureen proved to be the correspondent extraordinaire. Filled with local gossip, her letters were racy and fun. She was still outrageous, and sometimes Annie kept these letters from Kevin. They tended to substantiate everything Kevin hated about females. Working in a bar was great fun for Maureen. Still steady with Mr. Wonderful, she made enough money to support herself as she finished college. Because she dealt with liquor salesmen, she received every piece of promotional material offered. Kevin said they would never have to buy T-shirts with Maureen around. Yes, packages from home delighted Annie.

Letters from Danny came once in a blue moon. His mail had a foreign look and bore stamps from places like India and Africa. He was struggling with monsoon season somewhere. He would soon be in New Orleans and promised to drive up to see them. Annie could hardly wait.

• • •

One day Annie marshaled her courage and visited the admissions office. She chose a time when Mary was sleepy and would nap in the stroller. An enthusiastic counselor promised Annie that financial aid would be available. Additionally, the campus sponsored a day-care center where Mary could be deposited while Annie attended classes. The school made every effort to assist mothers in obtaining an education. Annie felt certain that Kevin would not be pleased. She would have to broach it carefully. Finding a quiet bench, she worked steadily until the forms were completed. The counselor told her to look for a response in six weeks.

Annie thought fast on the way home. Kevin's initial complaint would be financial. The best approach was to leave it be until the letter arrived. If she did not land a scholarship, she would keep quiet. If she did, the financial argument was moot.

It WAS possible that Kevin would be supportive. Sighing deeply she quickened her pace. She would have to get dinner in the oven quickly. Tonight was a special night. Maureen was calling. Annie was allowed to use the phone only once a month. Kevin worked out the rate and determined that it was too expensive to call Chicago except in emergencies.

Kevin's bossiness disturbed his wife. They could not afford extras. That was a given. The Griffins were living on a fixed income that had been fixed quite low. But he treated Annie like a child. A bad child. Annie read several books on marriage. When she was honest, she knew they had problems. Communication was difficult. Most disagreements escalated into fights. But the books said every marriage had rocky episodes, and Annie struggled to find the correct method of dealing with conflict.

Kevin was moody. If he was in a bad mood, Annie kept quiet. She could not ask him what was wrong. It made him mad. She had to be careful, too, about reading. Kevin did not like her reading. He accused her of ignoring him. Annie tried postponing her book time until he went to bed. Then he said it was rude not to come to bed with him. Kevin seemed to want sex every night. Annie could go to bed, then get up and read. Unfortunately, that, too, offended him. Annie controlled her anger and matched her reading time to Kevin's studying. So far this had solved the problem. Annie knew she gave in too much, but every book stressed compromise. The problem was, she could not remember a situation where Kevin did the compromising.

Pushing the troubling thoughts from her mind, Annie parked the stroller and carried the baby up the stairs. Within ten minutes dinner was cooking, and the house was tidy. Kevin came home in a mood. He stayed quiet through dinner. Annie tried gently to feel him out. Something was obviously bothering him. Hopefully he would not ruin her phone call. Annie quickly cleared the table and put the baby to bed. Kevin hunched over his books silently. The tension was so thick, Annie wondered why the walls did not blow out.

Finally, she cracked. "Is something bothering you?"

Rage rushed out at her like water from a burst dam. Kevin accused her of complaining. He said Annie was destroying them by her selfishness. Practice and school were draining. All he got when he came home were complaints about how hard it was to get a few groceries.

Annie listened. She knew from experience that the real issue was yet to be revealed.

Annie embarrassed him by taking the bus with the baby. The college library was not good enough for her. She had to haul the poor baby all the way down town on a dirty bus. A good mother would not expose her child to such danger.

At this, Annie exploded. "I'm a bad mother for taking my child on a bus? Why don't you admit you want me locked in the closet?"

Kevin slammed her into the wall and screamed, "That shows what a selfish bitch you are. Being a wife and mother isn't enough." He berated her for thirty minutes. With a sinking heart Annie heard the phone ring. She made a move to answer it but was blocked.

"Don't even think about it," he sneered.

Once again, Annie knew fear. She remembered this Kevin. She remembered him from the front seat of his car. When he finally quieted down, Annie marched into the bedroom and closed the door. Mercifully, Mary still slept. Throwing herself onto the bed, Annie began to cry. The bedroom door burst open. An enraged Kevin grabbed her by the arm. Dragging her off the bed, he pulled her into the living room and threw her onto the couch.

"Listen up, Annie," he shouted. Kevin emphasized his words by jabbing his finger into Annie's chest. "No more waltzing around campus with the baby. No more buying $1.50 notebooks at the bookstore. You're not in college. Your job is here with the baby. Do you understand?"

Annie's voice shook with emotion. "Waltzing around campus?"

Kevin's laugh was ugly. "Don't talk back to me," he threatened. "DO YOU UNDERSTAND?" His right hand shot out and punched the wall above her face. Annie covered her head and waited. "Stupid bitch!" he swore. "What? You think I'm going to hit you? Knock it off, Annie. Quit playing the martyr. Why don't you tell me what you were doing over by the business building?"

Annie looked up and saw hatred in his eyes. Someone had seen her by the business building. If she tried to explain now, she'd get hurt.

"How dare you talk to me like this!" she retorted furiously. "I walk around campus every day. Sometimes I go one way, sometimes I go another. I was also waltzing around by the fine arts building. Yesterday I tangoed by the gym." Seeing his face, she hastened to add, "If the baby gets cranky, I walk. So what?"

146

"So maybe you should tell me so I don't look like a fool when someone says they saw you." Kevin took a deep breath. He lowered his hands to his side. "It looks like my wife is out sneaking around."

"Sneaking around?" she repeated, legitimately puzzled. "Kevin, I swear, I'm not being smart. What do you mean by sneaking around?"

"Annie," he said patiently, "if a husband doesn't know where his wife is, she's sneaking. You never told me you went walking to these places. That means you were sneaking."

Annie shook her head in disbelief. "Are you serious?"

He was getting mad again, and she decided not to push. Kevin sat down next to her. Taking her face in his hands, he gazed at her without speaking. Annie resisted the urge to slap his hands away.

"What's really going on, Kevin?"

"Annie," he whispered. "You act so innocent. You forget. I know you. I know how you can be."

A knot twisted in Annie's stomach. "How can I be, Kevin?"

"Do you think I've forgotten about Harold?"

Annie's eyes widened in disbelief.

"Do you think I'm stupid?" he whispered.

Annie resisted the urge to replay the Harold incident yet again.

Kevin continued. "I forgave you, Annie, but I did not forget. I love more than anything. But I can't trust you. You lie."

The rest of the argument passed in a blur. Three hours later, Annie still sat like a wooden doll. She longed for bed. She attempted to persuade Kevin she was trustworthy. It was futile. Emotionally drained, she stopped caring. Finally he wound down, and they went to bed. Kevin drifted off immediately. Annie stared into the darkness for hours. She must have gone to sleep at some point because her eyes opened to sunlight.

Lying on her side, Annie let her mind dance through last

night's argument. Was she a sneak? She did not think so. She had applied for the scholarship in a secretive manner. But Kevin would have forbidden her had she asked permission. Did that make her sneaky? At any rate, the deed was done. If he thought she was sneaky yesterday, wait until he found out she had applied for school. There was a million dollar question here, and Annie wrestled with it. Did Kevin think Annie was sneaky because of her methods? Or were her methods the result of Kevin's controlling behavior? It was the chicken or the egg problem.

Her mind flitted to the "waltzing around campus" item. How could walking be wrong? Annie would understand if she was seen with a strange man. It never occurred to her that Kevin needed a re-enactment of her every action. Could it be embarrassing when people saw her somewhere? She supposed. The bottom line was Kevin did not trust her. And all because of Harold. Annie tried to recall what Harold looked like. Poor innocent Harold. With one conversation he had dashed any chance of happiness for Annie. Mary, too. And Kevin, for that matter.

Annie rejected such simplistic reasoning. NOTHING HAPPENED, her mind screamed. She quickly skipped away from that old line of thought. The Harold scenario was like a book that had been read too many times. The ending never changed.

Kevin also said she complained too much. Wasn't that part of marriage? Kevin certainly shared his frustrations. Annie wished she had thought of that last night. Kevin talked at length about practice and school. She realized then that there existed an enormous double standard in their relationship.

For a moment, reality shifted. The arguments were too confusing. She felt like Alice in Wonderland. Kevin should be happy that I'm trying to make a life here, she thought bitterly.

Instead, he calls me sneaky and selfish. Annie remembered something else said last night. He said that she was lucky that he married her at all. Annie acknowledged the truth in this. Many men would have fled. I wish he had, she thought darkly. I wish I had never gotten pregnant, she added. She thought of little Mary and nearly drowned in guilt. Annie began to cry. She was as bad as Kevin said.

Rising quietly she went to the bathroom to wash her face. I'm a good mother, she thought defiantly. Taking rides on the bus did not hurt Mary. Annie looked in the mirror. Dark circles ringed her eyes. She wondered how to act. It was Saturday. Unfortunately, Kevin would be around all day. He sometimes accompanied her to the grocery store. Annie prayed he would stay home.

Wandering into the living room, she froze. There was a hole in the living room wall. Hastily, she covered it with a picture. Thinking of the neighbors, her face burned with shame. They must have heard every word of the fight. Annie would have to avoid them. Too bad, she thought wistfully. The wife seemed pleasant, and Annie had hoped to make a friend. Kevin said there was another married player from Chicago on the team. Maybe his wife would be a friend.

Annie opened the blinds and let the harsh sunshine stream through. Squinting at the light, she tried to shift the lonely ache in the pit of her stomach. It was a constant presence these days. She wanted to go home. What if she called and asked her father to send an airline ticket? He would, she knew. She could be home by Monday. For a glorious moment, it seemed like a miracle. Imagine being in her own bed! Annie dismissed the idea. Her father would be worried. He would be disappointed. He would ask what the problem was. Annie did not know herself what the problem was. A failed marriage within a year equaled total disgrace. No. Annie was not going home. That meant she was trapped. Trapped in a bad marriage, she thought dramatically. No wonder there were so many country western songs.

OK, she mused, I'm stuck. So is Kevin. We can either be miserable or make it work. I can't abandon my husband at the first sign of trouble. I promised to love, honor, and obey. What on earth was I thinking? Anyway, there's no point whining because it's not perfect. We can always see a marriage counselor. Annie's eyes opened wide. Why hadn't she thought of that before? There was hope after all. Couples had fights. That was nothing new.

As for the present, should she be mad today? Conciliatory? Gone waltzing? She giggled at this.

Annie heard the baby begin to stir. The bed creaked. Kevin began cooing to Mary. Every morning he reached over and pulled the baby into bed. Hearing him talk softly, Annie felt her heart melt. He loved his daughter. He loved his wife, too, and Annie knew it. She resolved to try to patch things up. From now on she would tell him every single detail of her days. If she dropped a quarter, she would tell him she bent down on Third Street. Annie would make him trust her. A small niggling voice reminded Annie that she had tried this before. Slapping it away, she told herself she had not tried hard enough.

With a false air of briskness, she entered the bedroom. Kevin continued playing with the baby.

"Annie, I'm sorry I got so mad last night," he offered.

"Well," she answered thoughtfully, "you did get carried away. I think we need to talk things out, Kevin. If something bothers you, tell me right away." She searched for words. "I don't mean to complain."

Kevin was facing the wall. His voice was muffled. "You're not complaining, Annie. You're just talking to me. I'm a jag off. Sorry." Annie sat down on the bed and rolled him over on his back. He looked sheepish. "Don't panic and think we've got a bad marriage," he pleaded. "I'll lighten up. I promise. How would you like to go out with that other couple tonight?"

Annie felt her spirits surge. "I'd love it, Kevin. But what about the baby?"

"They have a baby, too," he said lightly. "They're just like us only with rich parents and a car. They said to bring her. They invited us for dinner."

"Kevin, why didn't you tell me?" Annie chided. "What

should we bring? I'll make a dessert." Her mind leapt ahead. "Thank God, I'm going to the grocery store. Should we bring wine?"

Kevin laughed out loud. "Relax. I just found out yesterday, and we weren't exactly talking last night." He considered. "I'd say bring beer. Nobody our age drinks wine. He also said you could go to the store with his wife during the week."

They talked for a while longer. "I wonder if they go to Mass." A sore spot with Annie was her inability to get to church.

"I didn't ask and don't you." Kevin spoke firmly. "It's none of our business. Do you hate me?"

"No." Annie tried to be honest. "I don't like you when you're mean, though. And you called me a bitch."

"I don't know why you stay with me, Annie," he responded contritely. "You're too good for me. It won't happen again, but please don't do things without telling me. OK?"

"I won't, Kevin. Let's get dressed. We're getting picked up in half an hour, and Mary has to be fed."

Scooping up the baby, Annie felt dampness. "You're a wet little peanut, aren't you?" she said affectionately. Mary smiled and grabbed for Annie's nose. "And starving, too, I'll bet." Mary gurgled in joy. Pausing, Annie glanced down at Kevin and smiled.

"I love you, Annie. More than anything."

"I know, Kevin. Don't look so serious. I'm not going to die or anything. Just don't maximize me, OK?"

He laughed appreciatively at their inside joke and began to get up. The day was starting better than Annie had dared hope.

Throughout the day, Annie's mood fluctuated violently. One minute, hope and optimism soothed her. Then, waves of anxiety assaulted. Concentration was difficult. Grocery shopping took forever. Repeatedly, Annie assured herself that Kevin was not mad. The fight was over. But every few minutes, her mind presented a brutal flash of last night's argument. There was a hole in the wall. That message was clear. Next time it will be my face, she thought, frightened. Maybe it was a dream. A nightmare. She would check the wall later. No, her brain insisted.

Kevin had seized her from the bedroom into the living room and called her a bitch. Right now he was pushing the cart ahead of her. He looked relaxed and happy. Mary was chuckling at her dad's funny faces. Annie stared after them, lost in thought. Surely she was overreacting. Pushing up her sleeve, she studied her arm. An angry welt was darkening. Thank God, she thought. I'm not crazy. The bruise was tangible. Wasn't that better than Kevin's verbal assaults? Yanking down her sleeve, she looked around furtively. Her thoughts raced. She could say she banged her arm on the railing of the stairs. Sadly, she realized that nobody cared. She told herself this was a good thing. Imagine the humiliation of someone finding out! A vision of the neighbors slid into her head, causing her face to heat up. Still, Annie allowed for the possibility that the neighbors had not been home.

Consoled, she allowed herself to feel normal. Things were as they seemed. An attractive young wife and mother was shopping on a Saturday morning. Her handsome husband amused their beautiful baby so Mom could concentrate on the respectable task of organizing their nourishment. All we lack are a couple of singing bluebirds, she thought wildly. Bending over to scrutinize a box of rice, she noticed there was something wrong with her throat. Ah, yes, a scream was trying to escape. She snatched a box of rice and clutched it. If she flew at Kevin from behind, she could choke him. Annie stood helplessly, certain she was losing her mind. A cold hand squeezed her heart. Mental illness. People would feel sorry for Kevin. His wife had gone round the bend. She was too young, they would say. She couldn't cope. It would be the ultimate form of control. "No," she blurted out loud. Frightened, she struggled for control. She could not be found talking to a box of rice in the dry goods aisle. Annie giggled. Ragged nerves turned the giggle into a stream of laughter. A shopping cart awk-wardly nosed around the corner. Kevin and Mary eyed her in concern, causing Annie to laugh louder.

"Annie," Kevin hissed. "What the hell is the matter with you?"

Annie stopped laughing and looked at him brightly. "I guess I'm so fucking happy I can't help it. Oops. Bad word choice." The appalled look on Kevin's face increased her mirth.

"Get a grip, Annie! You're acting like a head case. The coach's wife is by the frozen foods. She wants to meet you." Kevin spoke sharply, but his face was wary.

"Am I scaring you?" Annie queried gleefully. "How does it feel, you big jerk?" She took a breath and stopped laugh-ing. "Just kidding, Kevin. I'm a little punchy." She began to walk past him and paused. "Incidentally, don't ever call me a head case, you bastard."

Reshelving the rice, she stalked away. Screw him, she thought. Maybe I'll carry the rice box with me and tell it everything. Annie laughed a little less hysterically as the insanity drifted off. Kevin charged after her with the cart. She turned to scrutinize his face.

"What's the matter with you, Annie?" he said shakily.

Annie shook her head to clear it. "Sorry, Kevin. I'm OK now. Where is the wife?" Brushing her long hair back from her face. she forced a smile. "Honestly. I'm fine."

Kevin bent down and kissed her on the forehead. "You're upset about last night," he said flatly. "It's my fault. I'm sorry, Annie. We'll talk about it at home. Believe me, it won't happen again." He spoke with quiet confidence. "I am the luckiest guy in the world to be married to you. I'm not going to blow it. I promise."

Annie sighed. "I'm not trying to make you feel guilty, Kevin. But your temper is out of control."

Kevin pulled her close and held her. "I'm sorry, Annie."

"Newlyweds!" sang out a woman's voice. Mrs. Nelson, wife of the dreaded coach, appeared. "Only newlyweds hug in the grocery store." Kevin and Annie smiled in embarrassment. "Hello," she continued. "I'm Andrea Nelson. You must be Annie."

Annie extended her hand. The three made small talk while Mary desperately attempted to climb out of the cart. Babies were effective icebreakers, and Annie took stock of the older woman with darting looks. Dressed tastefully, Mrs. Nelson had a feminine drawl and wore a hairstyle that managed to look chic and simple. After telling the Griffins to expect a dinner invitation, she drifted to the checkout.

Inexplicably, Annie felt cheered by the conversation. Mrs. Nelson had treated her respectfully. She had admired Mary and told Annie that great things were expected from Annie's academic future.

Annie grilled Kevin. "What did she mean about my academic future, Kevin?"

"Probably that she heard you were smart," Kevin bragged. "I told the coach your ACT test score." Looking down at Annie, he grinned. "Actually I compared you to Einstein. Coach said you should apply for a scholarship. I told him you were too busy with the baby. Maybe later. Would you like that?"

Annie frowned. This was the time to tell him. Right here in the cereal aisle. The moment drifted on ... and passed. They would have a serious talk, and she would tell him then. It would have to be soon. Kevin would be on good behavior for awhile after last night. The thought jolted Annie. Was this really so predictable? The apologies, the promises, the loving consideration? Well, Annie thought roundly, he's not going to do it again. I'll be very clear about what I'll tolerate in the future.

"I sure would like to think about it, Kevin," she admitted. He smiled down at her. Life slid back into focus. It was a good day. Annie was a happy wife and mother shopping for her family.

• • •

That evening Annie prepared scrupulously for the dinner. A whipped cream pie graced the middle shelf of the refrigerator. Mary's best pajamas were washed and folded neatly.

154

Annie sensed Kevin's tension. Social situations made him uncomfortable, and he made her promise to leave directly after dinner. Cheerfully, she agreed. The prospect of a short night was not disturbing. Any night at all was welcome.

The evening was a success. Greg and Darlene Kemp were friendly and welcoming. Darlene had short brown hair and looked as though she were having trouble taking off the baby weight. Greg was similar to Kevin. Big and handsome. The couples had quite a bit in common, and the conversation flowed. A perceivable difference, as Kevin pointed out, was their obvious financial comfort. The Kemp apartment was furnished, and Darlene wore expensive clothes. She served a chicken casserole and complained that Texans had never heard of pork roasts. Annie could not imagine trying for any roast on the Griffin budget. The couple came from Evanston, a northern suburb of Chicago. Annie listened with pleasure to the familiar accent. She had not realized until now that she missed it.

Both babies slept, giving the mothers time to talk during clean-up. Darlene also disliked her mother-in-law. The Kemps, too, had arguments. Darlene volunteered this information as though it were completely natural. Annie listened intently. Maybe we're not doing so badly after all, she thought. Darlene commented on Kevin's obvious affection for Annie. The young woman actually sighed. Greg was not demonstrative. Darlene said Annie was lucky.

The pie was served in the living room. Both Darlene and her husband praised the confection. Gratified, Annie caught Kevin's wink. Inevitably, the subject of school came up. Darlene was determined to begin after Christmas, and Annie watched in amazement as the couple bantered. They laughed while exchanging pretend barbs. How wonderful, thought Annie. Here they are disagreeing, and nobody is shouting. She glanced furtively at Kevin. Maybe he would learn something.

Two hours after dessert, Annie and Kevin departed. Walking home in the warm darkness, Annie quizzed her husband.

"Did you like them?" she asked neutrally. She knew better than to act too enthusiastic.

"I sure did, Annie. Did you?"

"Yes," she responded. "Darlene is nice. At home I don't know that we would have been friends. You know? But I liked her."

"Greg is nice," Kevin said slowly. "But I know what you mean. I probably would not have hung out with him at home. Darlene sounds like a feminist. Don't you think?"

Annie groaned inwardly. "I did not get that, Kevin. She wants to go to school. That's all. I actually kind of agree with her. As long as we're all here, we may as well get two diplomas. Right?"

"Annie," Kevin said sternly. "If you want to go to school, that's fine. But first you have to come up with the money. And what about the baby? I'm not going to watch her. I have to study. For now, I don't see how it could work."

"I think it could, Kevin," Annie said pensively. This was the time. Right now. She had to tell him. Annie opened her mouth. She really did.

"... anyway," Kevin continued, "I liked Darlene, but I sure am glad that you don't talk to me like that. Kind of bossy, wasn't she?"

"They were just playing, Kevin," she retorted. "Greg did not mind. He was enjoying it."

"What else could he do?" Kevin asked. "She was embarrassing him. Don't get too close to her, Annie. She's a bit much."

Annie arched her eyebrows. "Surely you are not in charge of who my friends will be."

"I don't care who your friends are. Just don't get like Darlene. The pie was great, Mrs.Griffin. I certainly married a good cook."

"Thank you, Mr.Griffin," she responded sweetly. She hated being called Mrs. Griffin. It reminded her of her mother-in-law. Annie shuddered. Kevin's parents had blessedly postponed their visit until after Christmas.

Kevin reached for the baby as they mounted the stairs.

Like babies everywhere, Mary was portable. The child was not aware she was being moved. Annie went ahead and opened the door. She turned on the television while Kevin put Mary to bed. The Kemps had told them that WGN from Chicago came on their cable after midnight. It was mostly old movies at that time, but the commercials were entertaining. Used car dealers hawked their wares in harsh Chicago accents. Annie remarked to Kevin that people watching from around the country probably thought all Chicagoans spoke that way. Kevin said that people thought of Chicago as gangster town. They had a good laugh.

"Annie," Kevin called from the kitchen. "Where is the phone bill?"

"On the counter," she answered.

"I looked there. Find it now," he ordered. "I'm going to pay bills in the morning, and I want them together."

Annie sighed. Rummaging through the kitchen, she found everything but the phone bill. It was gone. She searched drawers, cabinets, even the top of the refrigerator. "Kevin, are you sure you don't have it? I can't put my hands on it."

"Annie, I just told you I did not have it."

"It's one o'clock in the morning," Annie said. "I'll find it tomorrow."

Turning off the television, they went to bed. Annie was exhausted. As she drifted into sleep, she reviewed her list of worries. They had not discussed the fight. They would have to talk about it tomorrow. There was something else. Oh, yes, the phone bill. Surely it would turn up. The real problem was the scholarship application. Kevin would have to be told.

Chapter Thirteen

They never did find the telephone bill. The issue snowballed, resulting in Annie's loss of mailbox privileges. Kevin said this was not the first piece of mail misplaced. How was he supposed to keep things in order if Annie lost correspondence? Annie spent Sunday searching while Kevin berated her. Finally, Annie went downstairs to the garbage bin. Kevin followed her down and said she was an embarrassment.

Shortly before dinner, Kevin implemented the silent treatment and took his books into the bedroom to study. Annie's relief struggled with her anger. She was pulling the drawers out when the phone rang. Maureen was calling with a neighborhood update. Annie cut her off and apprised her of the missing phone bill. Maureen informed Annie that people occasionally lost mail. One simply called the phone company for a replacement. Or, you paid an estimate and caught it up later. Cheered, Annie hung up and shared the information with Kevin. Mistake.

More horrors.

First, he accused Annie of telling her family their problems. Next he said that maybe the McGowans did business that way, but the Griffins were more responsible. Annie retorted that Maureen hardly encouraged them to head for the border. There was simply no reason to make a world event out of a piece of misplaced mail.

Kevin exploded. "You hit the nail on the head," he screamed. "Everyone should be like your family. No one should worry about anything. Let's make a joke and be done with it." Annie remained quiet. Kevin was waving his arms furiously. It was time to back down. "Your father is no Einstein, you know, Annie."

Annie rose from her chair. "That's true," she replied icily. "Nevertheless, he's more successful than your father will ever be."

At that Kevin threw a stack of books against the wall. Annie walked over and picked up the now screaming baby. "Just so you know, Kevin. Start anything, and it will be the last time. Think about that."

Annie walked into the bedroom and closed the door gently behind her. Inside, she comforted Mary. Cursing herself for not leaving the flat, she tried to stop shaking. Annie promised herself two things. The talk would come today, and this was the last time.

Eventually, Kevin began to move around in the dining room. So far so good. His movements were unhurried and calm. He knocked on the bedroom door.

"Can I come in?"

"Are you rational?" Annie countered.

"Perfectly."

"Then come in." He entered the room with a respectful air. "Sit down, and we'll talk. You can go first."

Kevin sat down next to her on the bed and sighed. "I don't know what to say. Tell me one thing. Are you planning on leaving me?"

Annie resisted the urge to qualify her statement. "I meant what I said. What don't you understand?"

"So you're going to leave?"

"No. But if you touch me again, I won't stay." Annie

noted his look of misery and hardened her heart. "Why is it OK for you to say whatever you like? Then, when I respond, you lose it. I've had it, Kevin. What horrible thing did I do wrong on Friday?"

Kevin avoided her direct stare and tried to shift Mary. The child had climbed up on his leg and was beating her little fists against his thighs for attention.

"Annie, we'll talk later when the princess is in bed. I can't concentrate while she is trying to play with me."

Annie swooped the baby into her arms. "I'll give her a bottle of pop and put her down for a nap," she said crisply. "We can talk in the front room."

Annie went into the kitchen and prepared the bottle. She seldom gave Mary anything but milk and juice. This, however, was important. One bottle would not kill her, and separated parents were the greater risk.

Annie lay Mary in her crib. The child's face immediately registered protest. It was not nap time, and she knew it. Annie swiftly put the bottle in her mouth and watched as the little eyes widened. Mary gave her mom a delighted grin. Laughing, Annie closed the door and went into the living room.

Sitting down on the floor by the window, Annie watched Kevin lower himself into the recliner. He reminded her of a man facing execution.

"So," he began. "What do you want?"

Annie let her breath out and checked her response. "Kevin, what do you think I want?"

"I haven't got the slightest idea," he retorted. "You're mad because I insulted your father?"

"No," she replied patiently. "That was mean, but you got it right back. Why did you slam all the books into the wall? Were you trying to scare me?"

"No," Kevin said angrily. "I was pissed off. I'm trying to run a household here, and you're losing mail. Then you go and tell your sister the whole story. She acts like I'm a big loser. She's got all the answers in the world. What's the big deal? I threw a few books." Kevin was talking defensively, but he looked frightened. Annie instinctively knew she had a shot at making her point. She spoke carefully.

"Kevin, I'm sorry if that's how it seemed. That's not how it was intended. You have a right to keep household things private. Is that what you mean?"

"You're damn right it is," he sputtered self righteously. "Every time I make a mistake, it gets blasted all over the south side of Chicago."

"What are you talking about?" Annie asked, flabbergasted.

"You tell them everything," he accused. "I need to know that what happens in this house is between us. How would you like it if I told my friends you lose everything? Or that you don't always keep the house clean?"

"Now what are you talking about?" she asked in dismay. "When isn't the house clean?" A feeling of defeat suffocated her. She frantically shrugged it off. "Kevin, maybe I better go first so we don't get off track. We're talking about this." Bitterly, she pulled up the sleeve of her sweatshirt. A large bruise colored her upper arm. Annie rose abruptly. She pulled the picture from the wall, displaying a large hole. "And this." Taking a few steps into the dining room, she kicked the books. "And these. Kevin, if you want the house cleaner, then tell me. But for right now stick to the goddamned subject. You promised you would never do this. I can't stand it, Kevin. You tell me I'm crazy. Do you want to know something? Living like this would make anyone crazy." She took a deep breath. "I'm not finished, Kevin. I truly believe that our problems can be worked out. I'm willing to go a long way in compromising. But I am not compromising with your temper."

"Are you finished now?" he asked calmly.

"Yes I am."

"I think my wife is a little upset here," he joked. "Is it that time of the month?"

Annie stared at him in disbelief. "Kevin, if you dare make a joke of this, I swear I'll kill you."

"Threatening to kill me?" Kevin said with a wave of his arm. "Annie, listen to yourself. I know you don't like it when I say you're crazy, but admit it. You get a little scary at times." Kevin was looking kind and compassionate. Annie resisted the urge to slap him.

"Answer the question," she demanded. "What are you going to do about it?"

Rising slowly, he put his arms out to her. She stood firm. Kevin turned to face the window. It was possible he would lose his temper, but Annie was unafraid. She was too mad. Marriage is painful, she thought coldly. So is love.

"Kevin," she said, softening a little. "Just so we're clear. I love you very much. I would never WANT to leave you. But I can't be happy if I'm afraid of you."

Kevin nodded his head. Startled, she realized he was fighting tears. She closed the distance between them and put her arms around him from behind.

"Annie, will you help me?" Kevin said as he turned to her. "I don't want to be like my father. I won't lose my temper anymore. I promise."

Kevin and Annie now spoke with humble simplicity. They loved each other. They had everything that mattered in the world. Annie told him about the scholarship application. He was proud of her. He actually said that. She told him how afraid she had been for him to find out. He shook his head in disgust. He said he was really out of control if his wife was afraid to tell him things. The phone bill situation made him feel like he was failing. He wanted to be a good husband and father, but it was scary sometimes. Annie could not believe her ears. She sputtered that she was often afraid she would not be a good wife and mother. Kevin was astounded. He said she always did everything right. That was part of the reason he felt inadequate. Annie promised to mess things up once in a while.

They laughed. They had sex. They woke the baby up and walked up for hamburgers. They had never done that. Kevin said he needed to lighten up about money. He promised that he would try very hard. Annie felt happier than she had in months. Her friend was back. Surely they would have smooth sailing now.

• • •

The next day she went to check the mailbox and discovered that he had stolen her key.

Annie stood staring at the key chain in her hand. She and Mary were in the student center. She looked down at her daughter, nestled snugly in the stroller. "What should I do, Mary?" she asked the baby. "He must have taken it."

Annie scrutinized the ring. It was a Dewars Scotch key chain, courtesy of Maureen, and quite sturdy. The key could not have fallen off. Annie instinctively knew that Kevin had gone along with her last night because he had no choice. He would get her in other ways. Taking her key. Further restricting her freedom.

Annie smiled absently in response to the baby's chatter. Was she paranoid? Kevin was her husband, for heaven's sake. Surely he was not plotting against her. Annie's forehead creased in concentration. She would obviously have to confront him. The thought made her sag wearily against the wall. Annie realized that she needed to talk to someone. A professional.

Walking briskly, she made it home in minutes. Annie put a record on the stereo. Music was becoming very important to her. It reminded her of who she used to be. As she tidied up the house, she felt tears begin to sting her eyes. To keep from getting emotional, she pulled the baby's walker into the kitchen as she prepared dinner. She sang every song to Mary with exaggerated faces and movements. Before long they were both laughing.

Annie screamed when Kevin poked his head around the kitchen corner. He was always so quiet when he came in. He startled her every time.

"Dammit, Kevin," she swore. "If you keep doing that, I'm going to deadbolt the door and make you knock." Leaning against the pantry door she held her hand over her heart. "How was your day?"

"It's not my fault you're half deaf. Do you want me to blow a horn when I come in?" Kevin spoke shortly. He was not in a good mood. "My day was fine. Why is the stereo up so loud? I thought you had a boyfriend over."

"No. Just me and my dancing partner. Say hi to Daddy," Annie instructed. Mary grinned up at Kevin and put her arms out. He picked her up and swung her in the air. The baby laughed in delight. "Mary is having a very happy day today Kevin. But I'm not." At that instant Annie knew how she would handle the situation. "Hand it over, Mister. Give me the key."

Kevin casually opened up the fridge and grabbed the lemonade. Reaching for a glass, he shrugged his shoulders. "What are you talking about?"

Annie felt her stomach tighten. "Give me back my mailbox key, please."

He reached down and picked up the baby again. Looking at Annie, he said quietly. "Annie, don't make an issue out of this. I'm tired of fighting with you. You keep losing mail. That's the fact. From now on I'll get the mail and bring it home. I'll keep the bills and give you any letters. What's the big deal?"

The afternoon sun glinted off his brown hair. Annie squinted against the light in an effort to marshal her thoughts. She was not crazy. Kevin was sinister. If she fought about her right to have a key, he would say she was a feminist. If she confessed her suspicion that he would keep her mail, he would call her paranoid. If she said that she preferred to read her letters first, he would accuse her of trying to hide something. Possibly love letters from Harold. Lifting her chin, Annie stared him right in the eye.

"Give it back."

"No," he said flatly. "In order to avoid any further fights about bills, I'm getting the mail. That's final, Annie. Get over it. What's for dinner?"

"Someday you'll be sorry we went this way, Kevin." With that she turned back to the stove. "Pork chops."

Weeks passed. Annie asked every day if anything had come for her. Every day he said no. One night he took the garbage out and met Greg Kemp in the yard. Annie watched the two men talking. Still looking, she grabbed Kevin's folders and started searching. In the back of the last folder was a letter from Maureen. There was also one from Danny. Both had been opened. Annie replaced them and restacked the pile. Next, she ran into the bathroom and locked the door. Turning the water on hot, she stripped frantically and poured bubbles. She would have to account for her red face.

By the time Kevin started banging on the bathroom door, she was immersed in a sea of bubbles within a virtual sauna. Her eyes were dry.

"What the hell are you doing with the door locked?"

"Taking a bath." She leaned forward and unlocked the door. Settling back into the bubbles, she leaned her head back and closed her eyes.

"Wake up, Annie," Kevin demanded. "Since when do you lock the door?"

Annie answered slowly as if groggy. "Since my husband disappears with the garbage. Anyone could walk in here." She paused. "Where did you go?"

"I was talking with Greg. They want us to come over for dinner tomorrow."

"No, Kevin," she said sharply. "Tell them to come here. We should have asked them sooner."

Kevin sat down on the toilet and stared at her. "What's the big deal?"

Annie opened her eyes and glared at him. It was crucial that he not know she had found the letters. She needed time to think.

Annie redirected her indignation. "Do they think I'm incapable of cooking a dinner?" she snapped. "They can come here or forget it." She closed her eyes and sank back into the bubbles.

She heard Kevin sigh. "Kind of sensitive, aren't we?" Annie ignored him. "OK. I'll tell them to come tomorrow." When Annie again failed to respond, he left. She opened her eyes and saw that he had left the door open. She lurched forward and slammed it. He did not come back.

Kevin was insecure. Annie knew that. She excused his continual bad behavior because of it. At some point, though, he was responsible. She thought hard. He was doing a burn over the college application. It had to be that. He could not find a reason to condemn the action so he was doing nasty things he perceived as safe. It was very important to Kevin that he not look like a nut. He had to appear reasonable and controlled. Annie shuddered. He wanted to cut her off from her family. That was probably why they were here in Texas instead of a midwestern campus. She knew that now. No phone calls. Now he wanted to get the letters. Annie's relaxed body belied the furious activity of her mind.

She was smarter than him. He could not change that. There was no way he could take her mind away. Annie took a deep breath and submerged. She stayed under as long as she could hold her breath. Blowing up through the surface, she took deep gulps of air. She was thinking like a lunatic. This was her husband. Why would he want to cut her off from her family? Annie wondered if he could get to her head. Drive her crazy. The ultimate control.

All right, she mused intently. If she was crazy, she must be paranoid. Kevin had gotten the letters and forgotten to give them to her. After all, she had stopped asking him. This was an oversight, blown grossly out of proportion. He was not diabolical. He was Kevin. Annie shook her head at her silliness.

"Kevin," she called.

Kevin poked his head playfully in the door. "Yes, my little Sybil. What is it?"

Annie smiled easily. "Sorry. Kevin, did you get any mail for me?"

His expression did not change. "No. Nothing."

Annie watched him with a pleasant expression on her face. She would bide her time. A thought popped into her head. Why not get a replacement key? What the hell? Apparently their marriage was destined to be sneaky. She would check the box during the day before he got there. At least she would know how far he was going.

"Kevin," she continued. "I've been thinking. I'm going

to get a job during the Christmas rush. The department stores are hiring part-time help. It'll be a few extra dollars. What do you think?"

Kevin frowned. "Get it out of your head. No wife of mine is going to work in some department store."

He backed out and closed the door.

"Oh, yes, I am," Annie thought grimly.

Chapter Fourteen

The next day, Darlene called to say that the Kemps would not be coming to dinner. Their little boy had an ear infection. Annie was gracious and extended the invitation to the following Saturday. Darlene informed Annie that a mandatory team dinner was scheduled for Saturday. The wives were also expected to attend.

Annie was nonplused. Kevin had not mentioned it. Darlene suggested that he had forgotten. She begged Annie to come so she would have someone "normal" to talk to. Both girls laughed out loud.

"I really can't think of anyone I could get to babysit," Annie hedged.

Undeterred, Darlene said breezily, "I'm using one of the neighbor girls. They live below us. Their mother is in school full-time, and the two girls are in high school. They're both good. Do you want me to call the sister for you?"

Annie's mind raced. It was a bit chancy, not talking about it with Kevin first. The thought of another confrontation was unbearable. At the same time, surely Kevin had meant to mention it.

"Darlene, that would be great. How much do we have to pay them?"

"Well, if we're gone four hours I would say about ten dollars. That way they'll come back when you ask them." Darlene sounded quite efficient. "I usually buy them pop and snacks, too. I'll call her now and call you back."

Annie sat looking at the phone. Ten dollars. He would have a fit. Moments later the phone rang. Darlene had made the arrangements.

Annie hung up and stared. Kevin was at practice. Mary was sleeping. If she was going to make the call, this was the time.

Much thought had gone in to this phone call. On the last visit to Mary's doctor, Annie had noticed a sign on the wall. It gave a hotline number for people in violent relationships. She had heard the term "battered women." Luckily, she did not have to worry about that. Kevin was not abusive. Still, Annie resolved to start there. She needed to talk to a counselor, and maybe they could tell her where to get one. She had looked up the past phone bills. Local calls did not show up. It was safe to call from home.

Before dialing, she ran to the window, just to make sure. This was paranoia. Kevin was not due home for another two hours. He had never missed a practice yet. Not even part of a practice. Kevin played with the flu and sore muscles. Discipline. That was the name of the game. He was doing very well, and it looked as if he would be playing in the upcoming game. He explained to Annie that for a freshman that was exceptional.

Sitting herself down at the desk, she dialed quickly. "Women's Services Center," drawled a soft female voice.

Annie informed her that she needed information. About counseling. After a brief pause the woman asked patiently, "What kind of counseling?"

"Well," Annie spoke in a rush. "actually it's kind of marriage counseling except that I don't think my husband will go. So I guess just counseling for me."

"Are you having marital problems?"

"Not really," Annie said nervously. "Just some adjustment problems. Maybe communication problems. Things like that."

"I see," said the voice. "Did you know that this is an information center for abused women? We have many services that might help you."

"Oh, no," Annie answered hastily. "We don't have THOSE kinds of problems. My husband is not abusive. He's just a little insecure. I am doing something wrong, and I don't know what it is. I thought maybe a counselor could help me figure it out."

"Certainly," the voice agreed. "It's important to know when you need to talk to someone."

Annie was beginning to like this person.

The voice continued, "Would you like to come in and talk with one of our counselors?"

"God, no," Annie blurted. "I'm sorry. But he'd have a fit if he thought I was going somewhere like that. Is there a place that does regular counseling? Like...a regular place?"

"Sure," the voice was not offended. She gave Annie the number of a community services center that offered counseling on a sliding scale. She promised Annie it would be inexpensive. She made Annie promise to ask for a girl named Caroline. Annie agreed. Business taken care of, Annie was loathe to let go of this warm woman. There was a pause.

"What's your name?" Annie asked.

"Dana. Do you mind if I ask your first name?"

"No. I guess not. Is this place confidential?"

"Yes," Dana answered. "Everything you tell me is confidential. I would not ask you for your last name unless you were coming in. Even then, we wouldn't need it. It's just nice to have something to call you."

"I understand." Annie tried not to sound paranoid. "My name is Annie. As long as we're talking, can I ask you a couple questions? Do you have a minute?"

"I sure do, Annie. My job is to answer the phones, and

they're dead quiet. What kind of questions?"

"Well, what kinds of things do these abusers do? Do they beat up their wives?"

"That's part of it," Dana was speaking slowly, as though carefully phrasing her sentences. "But there's a lot more to it. It's a combination of emotional and physical abuse. Mostly, it revolves around the abuser having control of his partner."

"Oh," Annie said in relief. "My husband is not like that at all."

"Annie, I'd like to send you some written information so you could learn more about it. Can I mail it to you?"

"God, no. He took my mailbox key. I'm not allowed to get the mail anymore."

"I see."

"It was my fault," Annie hastened to assure her. "I lose all the mail. Actually, I only lost one little phone bill. I did not even lose it. It was on the counter. I remember because it had cranberry juice on it. It just disappeared. So now he thinks I lose all of the mail. He has my letters in his folder, and he's telling me they never came. Isn't that the meanest thing you've ever heard?"

"It doesn't sound very nice. Annie, Do you work?"

"No. He won't let me. It would help if there was a little more money."

"I can certainly understand that," Dana answered placidly. "Annie, would it be OK if I had a counselor call you tonight? Just to talk things over and make sure you get to the right person."

"No, Dana. Not while he's home. I'll end up trying to explain, and it will start a fight. He's touchy. If he thought I was talking to a women's organization, he'd kill me."

"What do you mean, kill you?"

Annie laughed a bit too hard. "Sorry. Wrong thing to say to a battered women's counselor. I only meant he'd get mad."

"What kinds of things does he do when he gets mad, Annie?"

172

"Oh, let me think. Nothing much. He yells a lot. Calls me names. If he's really mad, he might punch the wall or push me around or something. Nothing abusive. Just nasty."

"How many times have you had bruises after a fight?"

Off guard, Annie answered casually. "A couple of times. One time he nearly strangled me. But that was a long time ago. Lately, just bruises on my arms. Nothing major. He's gotten a lot better about his temper. But I think it's getting bad again."

"Sounds scary," Dana offered calmly.

"That's what bothers me the most." Annie was speaking quickly now. "I hate being afraid every time we get into a fight. It's not fair. Nothing around here is fair. He says it's my fault. There's a million reasons why it's my fault. Some of them make sense, but some of them are absolutely insane. I'd be embarrassed to tell you."

"Is he jealous a lot?"

Annie was stunned. "Yes, he is. He's terribly jealous. Why do you ask?"

"Just wondering. Can he be loving and sweet one minute and be a monster the next?"

"Yes. That's what drives me crazy."

"Annie, there is a profile for this type of person. They tend to be jealous and possessive. They are also controlling. They act like they want to know where you are every minute. Another issue is trust. Abusers will accuse their partners of lying. To avoid arguments, partners stop telling the abuser things. These instances are then used to prove that the wife is untrustworthy. In other words, you're damned if you do and damned if you don't. Women in these relationships say it feels like walking on eggshells. There's much more to it than I can tell you over the phone. Are you OK, Annie?"

Annie was clutching the phone. "Yes," she answered in a small voice. "I'm a little shook up. You're describing my husband exactly."

"I know, Annie. I'm sorry. I don't want to upset you, but

it's important that you know the facts so you can keep yourself safe. Do you think you're in danger right now?"

"No, of course not. He's not even home. He's not like this all the time, you know." Annie was getting angry for some reason.

"I know he's not mean all the time, Annie," the counselor answered compassionately. "If he was, you'd never have married him. I'm sure he can be very loving and sweet. I do think that it's important to look at the signs or symptoms in your home. When you told me he takes your mail and he would not allow you to work, it sounded a bit familiar. Most marriages are not like this, Annie."

Annie sighed deeply. "I know, Dana. It's not supposed to be this way, is it?"

"No, Annie. It's not."

"OK. I'll call this Caroline and make an appointment. It's a start. Do these abusers get better if they get counseling?"

"When they admit they have a problem, they can get better. Usually though, abusers are so busy blaming everyone else, they don't admit they have a problem. Some do, though. Annie, I want you to remember if you ever feel you're in danger, call. If you're ever in immediate danger, call the police. OK?"

"Geez. It's not that bad. Dana, I can't thank you enough. Can I call you again if I think of any more questions?"

"Annie, you can call anytime you want. One more thing. This type of behavior usually gets more frequent and severe. It gets worse. It's important that you know that. Stay safe."

"Yes. Thank you. Goodbye." Annie glanced at the clock. She had been on for over an hour. Feeling guilty, she jumped up and pulled meat out of the fridge. It was chicken. Should she bake it or fry it? She stood in the kitchen. A decision was not forthcoming. Kevin sounded like one of those abuser guys. Call the police? Thankfully Kevin was not that bad. Annie longed to call Maureen. For a second she considered it. This was certainly an emergency but not the kind she could explain to Kevin. She stood holding the chicken for yet another ten minutes. Hearing the baby wake, she jumped again. Good heavens. Where was the time going? She stared at the chicken in her hands. It was too late for baking. Fried it would be. She set it down and went to get Mary up.

Kevin stamped in the door looking tense. A foreign exchange student from class had invited the Griffins to a birthday party for his son. He had been very persistent, and Kevin had finally been forced to agree. Annie had more important issues to consider and told Kevin casually that she was willing to go.

Kevin was nervous. The husband spoke broken English. The wife spoke none. Annie shrugged. She communicated fine with the Mexican moms through gestures and smiles. She told Kevin that women with children spoke a universal language that did not require words. Annie promised Kevin he would be amazed at how much information could be obtained from gestures and voice inflections. Annie decided to bring a small gift for the child. She read books on etiquette and found great comfort in following guidelines.

Kevin came up behind her in the kitchen and put his arms around her from behind.

"Annie, I don't know what I would do without you," he said affectionately. "You're so calm and smart. What do we do about a present?"

"I was just thinking about that," she answered absently. "There is a box from Maureen in the bedroom closet with some kind of toy for Mary. I think it's a blow up doll. We'll wrap it up."

She thought for a minute. "I have birthday paper and some gift stickers."

"You're the greatest wife in the whole world." Kevin said kissing her briefly. Annie smiled. Normally she would have been gratified at the praise. Today it seemed manipulative. It was pathetic how much she desired his approval. Yes, Dana had gotten to her. Kevin was nice when Annie was doing exactly what he told her to. But really. Imagine telling her to call the police? She would talk to another counselor. In the meantime there was nothing to do but act normal.

After dinner, Annie apprised Kevin of the arrangements for Saturday night. He grunted from his textbook.

"Is that OK with you?"

"Fine. We can't make a habit of babysitters, but once in a while it's necessary."

"Kevin, why didn't you mention this party to me?" she asked in a neutral voice. "It was a little embarrassing to hear it from Darlene."

"Now you know how I feel when I hear my wife is over at the business building. It's no big deal. I forgot."

Just like the letters, she thought brutally.

Shortly before seven they left the house. Mary was dressed in a party frock. Annie felt quite together. The gift looked professionally wrapped, and she and Kevin were dressed in casual but nice clothes.

Kevin steered her into a vestibule. "This is it."

"Kevin," Annie whispered, as he rang the bell, "what nationality are they?"

He looked mystified. "I don't know. Lebanese or something."

"Is it Lebanese?"

"What the hell difference does it make? Do you speak Arabic? Just smile and speak that universal language you were talking about."

With that Kevin made an obscene gesture. Annie burst out laughing just as the door opened. With a frozen smile she greeted her host. There had been a tragic flaw with the etiquette book. It had not taken cultural mores into account. Three couples present. All Arabic and formally dressed. The women's hair was elaborately coiffed. Annie thought of her ponytail and wished there was a ribbon around it.

She dared not look at Kevin. He was bound to be in agony. If Kevin found simple social situations disturbing, this would kill him. Deciding to set an example, Annie approached the women and extended her hand to the hostess. All three women began to giggle. None offered to shake. Annie returned to Kevin. He had been given a glass of pop and was still holding Mary.

Standing ramrod straight, he looked like a sentinel by the door. Annie offered to take the baby.

"Not on your life," he said with a fixed grin on his face. "Go talk the universal language with the Mrs. Cleavers."

"I need a baby for that language, Kevin," Annie said sweetly. "Does my smile look as phony as yours?"

They were standing close to each other. It was a dangerous situation. Hysterical laughter was a whisper away. If dressing incorrectly was a social gaff, inappropriate laughter was social death. Sensing they were perilously close, Annie walked back to the girls' side. There was no furniture in the house that Annie could see. Just a large table set up in the living room. It was covered with a beautifully crafted cloth. The fabric was unlike anything Annie had ever seen. As she fingered it lightly, one of the women approached her with a smile. She shyly gestured for Annie to follow. Opening her linen closet she began to pull out various cloths. Annie was amazed. The closet was loaded with exquisite bolts of fabric. They were obviously from her home country. She displayed them one by one for Annie to admire. She nodded and smiled at Annie's admiration. Finished, she gently steered Annie into the bedroom. A double mattress was on the floor. There were no dressers to speak of, just a small table with a lamp. In a bassinet by the bed was an infant. Annie glanced down at the sleeping child. A pink blanket was lightly tucked around the most beautiful infant Annie had ever seen. The soft brown skin was highlighted by a dusting of black fuzz on her head. Tiny black eyelashes were just visible. This baby had been premature. Annie instinctively traced her finger around the child's cheekbone.

"She's beautiful," she whispered reverently.

The young Arab woman smiled in gratitude. Nodding her head, she beamed at Annie. Annie made a gesture with her two hands close together. The woman agreed. The baby was small. Annie gestured to her chest. The woman nodded and rolled her eyes. Gesturing widely, she indicated that the child nursed all of the time. Annie commiserated by making faces. The woman also shared that she had been very sick and had had a Caesarean section. Working furiously, they ascertained that the baby was two months old. Annie told the woman that she looked great. She smiled in gratitude and indicated her rounded waistline. Annie waved it off as if to say, "What can you do?" Bosom friends, they returned to the living room. Ha, Annie, thought. All we needed was a baby.

Kevin was not faring as well. Still clutching Mary and his glass of pop, he looked sick. He stared at Annie, willing her to come back. This was tricky because the hostess was sharing their conversation with the other female guests. They were anxious to talk to Annie now. One had two children, either grown or very large. Annie could not be sure. The other was expecting, but only just. Annie suspected that the husband had not been told. The woman made repeated hush gestures. Then, all three women looked at him and giggled. Annie smiled and smiled. They were regular folks once you got past the language barrier. When she joined Kevin, she was grinning.

"How are you holding up?"

"Annie, we have to leave."

"We've only been here twenty minutes. We have to stay at least ten more. Mary is being good, isn't she?" Mary had not uttered a peep since their arrival. She sat perched on her Daddy's arm like a painting. "What is she staring at?"

"The little boy."

"What little boy?" Annie had seen no evidence of the birthday child.

"He's asleep under the table. See?" Kevin locked his focus so Annie could follow. Sure enough. Under the cloth was a pillow and blanket. Another angelic child was fast asleep there. "It's freaking me out, Annie. I think the kid is dead."

Annie gasped. "Kevin, don't say that. I'm sure he's just

asleep." In spite of this, she could not prevent her gaze from returning to him. He was certainly still. She looked up, as the host approached Kevin. He had not acknowledged Annie's presence yet. Annie had read about some of the Middle Eastern cultures. Not a good place to be a female. Nevertheless, the man seemed jovial enough as he refilled Kevin's glass. Kevin nodded feverishly with the same frozen smile. He was overdoing it.

"Are you OK?" she asked her husband in concern.

Kevin continued his stare. His frozen smile was occasionally reinforced by bouts of frantic nodding. From the side of his mouth he whispered, "This is my fifth glass of Pepsi. I'm on a wicked caffeine high. I think I'm going to wet my pants."

Annie looked up at him in disbelief. "Just say 'No, thank you,' you goof. Kevin, look at me. Give me that baby and go to the bathroom."

"No way. I'm not giving you the baby. What am I going to do if you have the baby?" He was serious, and Annie began to giggle. "Easy for you. You know the universal language. All I know is English, and they don't speak it." Returning a wave to the host, he again nodded and smiled. "See. This is what I have to do. In about thirty seconds he'll come over and give me a refill. I have to chug so I don't offend him. Don't confuse me. Look. I think the kid moved his arm."

Annie glanced down. The boy was indeed waking up. A shout went up amongst the other adults. Kevin jumped as though he had been shot. The three women converged on the boy as one and swooped him into the only chair in the room.

"He must be the little Sultan, Annie." Kevin spoke with no humor in his voice. "See how he's dressed. We've got to get out of here before he orders me beheaded." Kevin gave a sick giggle.

"Kevin, take it easy. He's going to open his presents, that's all. Just keep smiling."

At that moment the host came over with a two liter bottle of Pepsi. "What did I tell you?" Kevin quickly drained his glass and extended it. "Almost caught me, Big Guy. Fill her up." The host did indeed look pleased. For the first time he looked at Annie. Pointing at Kevin, he indicated Kevin's large size and shook his head admiringly. Annie smiled back. The whole thing was exhausting.

The women were making a ceremony out of the presents. To his credit, the boy was polite and amiable if a little sleepy. Annie wondered if he always slept under the table. His mother handed him the Griffins' gift with many warm smiles at Annie and Kevin. Annie smiled back. She felt like her face was going to crack. Just for relief she glowered. Unfortunately the hostess caught her. Stricken, the Arab woman dropped the gift in her son's lap and put her hands over her face. Annie glanced at Kevin in alarm. The host rushed over and took his wife in his arms.

"What the hell is wrong with her?" Kevin asked quietly.

"I don't know," Annie said in consternation. "I stopped smiling for a second, and she caught me."

Kevin looked down at her. "I told you not to do that. You've got to keep smiling. Now you've ruined the whole party." With that, he looked back at the group and resumed his wide grin. Annie burst out laughing. Kevin let out one belt of sick laughter and caught himself. "Please, Annie. In the name of all that's good, don't make me laugh."

Annie laughed harder. The rest of the group was looking at the hostess tensely. Her husband had the situation nearly controlled. Letting go of his wife, he hastily grabbed a glass and filled it with Pepsi. Walking swiftly to Annie, he handed it to her with an apologetic air. Annie politely accepted the drink. Now she understood. The hostess thought she had slighted her guest. Annie took a big gulp and nodded appreciatively. Everyone relaxed. The woman smiled wanly at her. Annie nodded vigorously and took another huge gulp.

"Now you're getting it." Kevin applauded her. "Just keep doing that for an hour, and everything will be fine. If you don't drink enough, you're insulting their hospitality or something. You should probably burp a few times."

Annie glared at him, first checking to see that no one was looking. "I think that's Japanese, Kevin."

"What do you suppose these people do?" he asked with deadly innocence. Annie refused to look at him.

"Stop right there, Kevin. I'm hanging on by my finger-nails."

The boy was opening their gift. Great waves of admiration greeted the wrapped plastic toy. The mother tried to put it aside and hand him the next. He refused. The boy wanted it opened and opened now. The adults made understanding noises and smiled. Their host stepped in to open the package. It was larger than Annie had guessed.

"What is it?" asked Kevin.

"I don't know," she answered tensely. "Some kind of blow up thing."

Their host located the blowing part and began inflating the toy. The boy clapped his hands expectantly. All eyes watched as the form began to take shape. It was getting quite large and looked to be a man. From what they could see, the man had not shaved. He also had a distressingly lecherous expression.

"What the hell is it?" Kevin asked again.

"I'm telling you I don't know," Annie retorted. "I grabbed it from the closet. Maureen sent it."

"Annie, there's writing on it. It's not some kind of obscene thing, is it?"

Annie could not speak. Knowing Maureen, it could well be. Annie's anxiety level escalated. She clutched Kevin's arm. "Let's run out."

He looked down at her and burst out laughing. "Oh, no, you don't. This is too much fun." Any pretense of control evaporated. They laughed hysterically. The other adults in the room began to laugh with them. The whole room was laughing uproariously as the father continued his task. "You thought we could handle it," Kevin continued. "What the hell? Let's have a good time." Kevin was wiping his eyes and trying to regain control. The hands of the form

181

were taking shape. "Ten bucks the clown man is holding himself." With that they burst out laughing again. Again everyone laughed with them. Kevin shot Annie a wild look. "I'm going to throw up," he said urgently. "The clown man is doing the universal thing." Kevin shifted Mary to his other hip. He leaned back against the wall and closed his eyes. Annie wiped her eyes. She was afraid to look at the figure.

"He's holding a glass, Kevin," Annie blurted in relief. "It's all right. He's holding a glass. There is some writing on it, though, and it's definitely not a toy thing." She squinted to make out the writing. "Oh, God, I know what it is. It's a Harvey Wallbanger doll. The writing is the recipe for the drink." She looked at Kevin in dismay. "What should we do?"

"Act like we planned it," Kevin said. "Just smile and act like nothing's wrong. What are the odds they've heard of a Harvey Wallbanger?"

Sure enough, the finished product was a five-foot man holding a tantalizing Harvey Wallbanger. On his stomach was the recipe for mixing the drink. The adults in the room looked puzzled. The host queried Kevin. Kevin shrugged his shoulders. The host began to read the ingredients.

Annie and Kevin remained calm. Their peaceful smiles gave no hint of their inner turmoil. Getting to the bottom of the list, the host paused.

"Hovy Wall-Ban-Ger," he said in slow clipped English. After pondering for a moment, his eyes lit up. "I see. I see." Picking up the doll he bounced it against the wall. "Hovy Wall-Ban-Ger," he said, exultant. "Hovy WallBanGer." The adults roared their approval. The young boy tried in vain to get his toy. The three men took turns banging the figure off the wall. Kevin nodded approvingly. Annie had collapsed in a hysterical heap against the wall.

"Kevin," she gasped. "I'm leaving right now. I can't ... stand it any more." In vain, she tried to control her hysteria. "It's over," she said. "I'm walking out now." With tears streaming from her eyes, she made a movement for the door. Kevin, too, was laughing out loud.

"We're leaving. We really must go," he spoke between giggles. "As you can see, my wife is not well." Annie laughed louder. "Little fits we call them. Little fits." They kept staggering to the door. Annie remembered the last moments of the party as a blur of sweet, concerned, brown faces bidding them goodbye. She literally stumbled into the hallway. Without waiting for Kevin and the baby, she pushed open the door and lurched into the fresh air.

Kevin followed holding the poker-faced Mary and a two liter bottle of Pepsi. "He insisted I bring this," he whispered, indicating the pop. They again burst into laughter.

They walked home like a couple of drunken students. Annie could not remember laughing this hard.

"They were so nice, Kevin. I feel bad," she said regretfully.

"Don't feel bad, Annie," Kevin spoke with confidence. "Right now they're probably imitating me. It's nobody's fault. Different people, that's all. I'm glad we went. I don't think I'm ever going to forget the Sultan's birthday party."

Annie heartily agreed. She felt better than she had in a long time.

"It's good to laugh together. Isn't it nice, Annie?"

"You read my mind, Kevin." She reached over and grabbed for his hand. Shifting the now sleeping Mary, he bent down and gave her a kiss. They strolled companionably home, taking their time. Annie felt tranquil. She resolved not to worry about Dana. If they could still have so much fun together, they could certainly work out their problems.

Chapter Fifteen

Annie did not call the counselor that week. Later, she would marvel at her ability to live in the present. They called it denial. Kevin was sweet and affectionate. He finally gave her Danny's letter, along with two from Eileen. Danny wrote that he would be in Chicago for Christmas.

Annie sighed as she read that. She knew there was no way they could afford to go. It would be different if they had a car. Flying was out of the question.

Annie asked Kevin if there was any sign of her scholarship application. He said no. He did give her another letter from Eileen, leading her to believe he was no longer withholding mail. Annie thus forgot to get a replacement key. She speculated that Kevin had adjusted to the idea of his wife attending school. The worst was over.

On this note she prepared for the party on Saturday night. She and Darlene had decided on skirts and blouses. In a small way, Annie was reminded of her sisters. The McGowan girls always discussed their outfits in advance of an outing.

The babysitter arrived on schedule. After consulting her baby book, Annie had written down all pertinent information on the memo pad by the phone.

Greg and Darlene had offered to pick them up, but Kevin preferred to walk. That suited Annie. She felt strange walking across the darkened campus in heels. Smiling up at Kevin, she reached for his hand.

"It's nice to be going out to dinner, Kevin."

"There's nothing like a free meal," he agreed. "Annie, don't talk too much tonight. OK?"

"What do you mean?" she said in a hurt voice. "Do I talk too much?"

"No," he answered. "It's just that I don't know these people well, and I don't want to be all chummy with them. You know?"

"I wasn't going to invite them all over to see our wedding album," she chided. "Honestly, Kevin. What a thing to say! Do you want me to say anything at all?"

"Don't get all bitchy. I just don't want you to be a social butterfly."

Annie remained quiet. Did she usually talk too much? She was a social person. But people liked it when you made conversation. Still, she would try not to say too much tonight.

Their silent walk ended at the campus center. The dinner was being held in a large room downstairs. Annie quickly spied Darlene and led Kevin over to the table. The Kemps had saved two seats.

"We were right to wear skirts," she whispered to Darlene.

"Thank God," Darlene agreed. "Greg is tense for some reason. Look at him." She inclined her head. Greg did indeed look as nervous as Kevin.

"Don't feel bad," Annie whispered. "Kevin told me not to talk too much."

With that, the girls burst out laughing. They kept their heads together until it was time for the presentations. Darlene made faces, and Annie giggled. It was almost like being with Rene.

There was a lanky boy at their table who looked miserable. Darlene informed Annie that he was from Wisconsin. He had never been away from home and was desperately homesick. Annie leaned over and asked Kevin about him.

"The poor kid can barely get through practice," Kevin confirmed. "He practically cried during the national anthem at the last game. It reminded him of home."

Annie looked horrified. "That's terrible, Kevin. Why don't you invite him over for dinner sometime? It must be horrible to be stuck in the dorm."

"Don't start, Annie," Kevin said shortly. "He'll live."

Annie watched the boy all through dinner. When Kevin and Greg got up to talk to the other players, she leaned over the table. "I'm Annie Griffin. I don't think we've met."

Looking surprised, the boy extended his hand. "I'm Tommy Gill. I've seen you walking with your baby."

"I do a lot of that," Annie replied with warm smile. "This is Darlene Kemp. Our husbands both play."

"Oh, I know who they are," he said enthusiastically. "I'm from southern Wisconsin."

"What part?" Annie asked.

He told her in a wistful tone. She smiled in delight. The McGowans had spent many summers camping ten miles from his home. The boy was delighted. He became animated at once as they discussed his hometown.

"It's very small," Annie noted pleasantly.

"Yes," he agreed. "That's why I like it so much. There's so much to do." He went on to describe the winter activities he desperately longed for. "You can't even tell that time is passing here. The seasons don't change. It's weird."

Annie nodded her head. This had bothered her, too. What on earth would they do at Christmas time? They laughed at the thought. Darlene was listening happily. At that moment, Kevin and Greg walked back to the table.

"Kevin," Annie said excitedly, "Tommy's from near the campground we always went to." After receiving a blank look from her husband, she continued. "You remember.

You met Rene and me there once. That's where he lives." Kevin looked even more blank. An embarrassed silence was settling upon the group. "I'm not making this up," she promised Tom. "Kevin was there once. My family went every summer."

"Let's go, Annie," Kevin said tersely.

Startled, she grabbed her purse. "So soon? OK. I guess I'm ready."

Darlene, Greg, and Tom collectively tried to persuade them to stay. Kevin was adamant. They had a baby to think about, he reminded Annie. Annie's face flushed.

Annie tried to make her goodbyes. It was not easy with Kevin fidgeting by the door. Walking quickly, she caught up with him in the vestibule.

"What's the big hurry?" she asked innocently. She knew what the problem was. Kevin was angry that she had talked to Tommy. Choosing to ignore the obvious, Annie made small talk for the first part of their journey home. Kevin did not respond. Eventually, Annie, too, lapsed into silence. She had a sick feeling in her stomach. Tommy was a nice guy. He was much more like Annie and Kevin than the Kemps. Annie knew she was in for trouble. Hopefully, she thought, Kevin would ignore her for a few days and be done with it.

As they mounted the steps in their building, she remind-ed him that he needed to escort the babysitter home. It was the right thing to do.

Annie greeted the sitter cheerfully. Kevin plopped down on the couch and stared at the television.

"Kevin, are you ready?" Annie asked nervously. "Can you walk Tina home?" Kevin ignored her. Tina was begin-ning to look uncomfortable.

"Mrs. Griffin, it's no problem. It's only across the yard. I can just run."

"Nonsense, Tina," Annie said briskly. "Kevin is appar-ently glued to the news. I'll walk over with you."

Returning, Annie fumed. It was one thing to be mad. She was used to that. But did he have to humiliate her? She decided not to broach the subject tonight. He looked too tense. Tomorrow she would let him have it. Entering the apartment, she went straight to the bathroom and dressed for bed.

Annie was brushing her teeth in the bathroom when she saw his face in the mirror behind her. She was turning to talk to him when she felt her head violently slammed forward.

The toothbrush speared the inside of her upper lip as the side of her face made contact with the medicine cabinet. Still facing the mirror, Annie looked down to see blood streaming onto her pretty green face towels. Instinctively, she whisked them out of harm's way.

Clutching her head, she grasped the sides of the sink. Another glimpse of his face prompted Annie to slither down and away from him. Viciously, he kneed her in the small of her back. A jolt of exquisite pain shot down her legs as she collapsed to the floor. She must have started screaming because Kevin was kicking her, shouting for her to shut up. Annie closed her mouth and curled into a ball. The kicking stopped.

"Slut," Kevin screamed as he backed out of the room. Someone was pounding on the floor. It was coming from the front room. The downstairs neighbors, Annie thought gratefully. Kevin stormed around the living room, pounding back.

"Assholes," he shouted loudly.

Annie became consumed with pain. It was not over. She knew that. Kevin would scream and shout for at least four hours before he would be able to sleep. He's going to kill me, she thought weakly.

Annie scooted over to the tub and pulled herself up. Sitting, she took stock. It was excruciating to sit. She was bleeding heavily from the mouth. Grabbing a washcloth she shoved it in and let it hang out. There was blood all over the sink, floor, and wall. Annie felt a pulsing on the left side of her head. Running her fingers across her face, she was relieved to see no signs of blood. It must all be coming from her mouth. From the sounds of things Kevin was back on the couch. Annie thought of Dana. She wondered what her chances were of reaching the phone. She would have to get to it and dial the operator, then at least shout for help before Kevin reached her. She shuddered. He'd kill her.

Casting around for another plan, Annie decided to make for the back door. Down the stairs and over to ... where? Somewhere with a phone where she could call the police. She tried to think realistically. Kevin was fast. He'd have her in no time. If she could get down just one floor she could bang on the neighbors' door. They thought she was a lunatic anyway. Surely they'd call the police. Annie's heart hammered thunderously in her chest. She thought of poor little Mary sleeping in the bedroom. She had to get the police.

Clenching her teeth, she pulled herself up against the sink. The mirror was a bit of a shock. Her left eye was swelling fast, and her upper lip looked like a harelip. Annie pulled the rag out. It was saturated. She let go of the sink. GO! she told herself. GO!

Annie glided silently out into the dining room. Kevin did not look up. With shaking hands she undid the lock on the back door. "Hey!" She heard him bellow. The lock gave just as she heard his first thunderous footfall. Annie was halfway down the stairs when he caught her by the back of her nightgown.

"Stupid bitch!" he muttered, as he began to drag her back up.

"LET ME GO!" she screamed.

"Fuck you. You're a little slut, and you needed to be taught a lesson. " He grabbed for a better grip on the back of her nightgown. Annie lurched away, half falling, half rolling down the stairs.

"HELP! Help me!" she screamed as loud as she could.

As Kevin struggled for another hold, the neighbors' back porch light went on. Kevin lifted her easily into his arms. With his hand across her mouth he took the steps two at a time. In seconds they were back in the apartment, and Annie was thrown onto the couch. She looked up at him defiantly.

"Get this through your head, Annie." Kevin's chest was heaving, but his voice was surprisingly gentle. His next words dashed any hope that he had calmed down. "I will kill you, yes, kill you dead, if you ever try to leave me again. Do you understand? You can try to hide, but I'll find you. When I do, you'll be sorry you were ever born."

"I'm already sorry," she snapped.

Kevin put his finger against her mouth. "Do you want to live? Don't talk. You are a trashy slut. If we had not left when we did, you would have been making out with Tommy Gill. I should have known better than to leave you alone with Darlene. Five minutes and you're acting just like her. Understand me, Annie. I won't tolerate this. Do I need to say it again?"

"No." Hopefully, he would talk himself down. "I understand."

"Admit that you were attracted to Tommy," Kevin said kindly.

"I was not even remotely attracted to Tommy."

With lightning speed he slapped her across the top of the head.

"That's another problem you have," he sneered. "You're a liar. Next time I ask you a question, tell me the truth. I know that's hard for you. You're a deceitful little slut like your sister Maureen. I've been throwing her letters away. I don't want you reading about her sexual exploits."

"What sexual exploits?" Annie demanded. "Maureen has been steady with her boyfriend for years." She felt a wave of exhaustion. This would go on for hours.

At that moment they heard a knock on the front door. Neither moved. Kevin put his finger to his lips, indicating that she should remain quiet. Annie felt her spirits soar. The knock came again. Louder.

"Police. Open the door," said a deep male voice.

Annie remained expressionless. She looked up at Kevin.

Leaning over, he whispered into her ear. "If you want to die tonight, tell them something." He spoke in a slow and measured voice. "I'll kill you. Now go open up the door."

Kevin went to the farthest corner of the room and sat down. Annie slowly rose and opened the door. Her whole body was shaking. If she told them anything, he'd kill her. Not if he's arrested, she thought. But Annie knew that Kevin would not get life in prison for beating her up. He would eventually get out. And she believed him. He would kill her.

Two uniformed officers stood on the landing. They looked casual and relaxed. One was older, probably late forties. The other appeared to be in his mid-twenties.

"There was a report of a loud disturbance, Ma'am," said the older one, taking charge. "What happened to your face?"

Annie felt her composure slipping. She began taking gulping breaths as she tried to speak. They looked so calm and normal. Still holding the door, she felt Kevin come up behind her.

"Honey, ask them to come in," he said reproachfully. "Please come in, gentlemen. I have to apologize for my wife. We're having an argument, and she's a little upset. She fell coming up the stairs." Annie backed up as they entered the apartment. She felt as though she were in a bad movie. "Sorry about the noise," Kevin continued. "We were at a party and began to argue when we got home."

"What was the argument about?" asked the veteran officer. He was looking at Annie. She shrugged her shoulders. "He got jealous."

The officer looked at Kevin. Kevin smiled sheepishly. "It's not one of my better qualities, I'm afraid. You see, when my wife has a few drinks, she gets a little friendly with other guys. And that's not one of her better qualities. I do tend to get bothered by it, though."

"You're a fucking liar, Kevin," Annie said emotionally.

"Hey lady," the officer intervened. "that's no way to talk to your husband. Watch your mouth." Annie rolled her eyes. "Being a smartass is not going to help matters. Who was screaming for help on the back stairs?"

"That would have been me," Annie answered sarcastically. "It's not one of my better qualities, but when I have a few drinks, I scream for help on the back porch."

"Ma'am, you have a real problem with your mouth," the officer said in warning. "Now we're here to help. Your mouthing off is not going to make it any smoother." He was pointing his finger at her. Annie resisted the urge to slap his hand away from her face. Her husband was trying to placate the man. Kevin was defending her!

"This is insane," Annie cried, sobbing now in earnest.

"Officer, again, I must apologize for my wife," Kevin appealed. "She's homesick and tired. She took a bad fall on the stairs, and it upset her. I'll admit, I lost my temper and started yelling. She ran down the back stairs in her nightgown. I got her back in the house as fast as I could, but it may have upset the neighbors." He had his hand on Annie's back, and he was attempting to comfort her. "It's all right, Annie. You go to bed now and let me talk to these guys."

Annie glanced up at the young officer. He was looking at her intently. With a flash of understanding, Annie got it. He knew.

"Just a minute," the young man interrupted. "Ma'am, can I ask you a few more questions?" Annie froze. "That's a pretty bad split lip you've got there. Where did you fall?"

"On the front stairs there," Kevin answered quickly. "Right down on the first floor."

Annie remained silent. Kevin stood staring at her. She was not looking at him but could feel his gaze.

"Is that what happened?" the officer asked looking directly at Annie. "I guess what I'm wondering is how you split your lip and bashed the side of your head at the same time. Seems a bit awkward. Know what I mean?" She nodded. "Unless someone is fibbing."

"Now hold on a minute," his partner intervened. "Married people have fights. That's not against the law. Young Lady, did someone intentionally assault you and cause those injuries?" Annie was looking down at the floor. Then up at the ceiling. The older officer continued, "Because if they did, you could sign a complaint and that person would be hauled off to jail. He would sit there until a judge set his bail. He would have a permanent arrest record and all because his wife was flirting at a party. See what I mean?"

Annie walked away. She left Kevin talking. They were discussing sports and of course knew who Kevin was. They thought his chances looked pretty good this year. The older policeman told Kevin a joke about Yankees and damn Yankees. The damn Yankees were the ones who never left Texas. He laughingly told Kevin that they had no problem with Yankee athletes, though. Kevin was most welcome in the Lone Star State.

Annie lay on her bed and wondered if this were real. She longingly wished for a hand grenade. At one point it was obvious that the younger guy was putting two and two together. But Annie had presumed the older one was in the dark. Until he told her she could have Kevin arrested. He knew, too. Right from the start. It was all right with him as long as Kevin kept it quiet. Annie figured she was lucky she had not been arrested on a noise ordinance for screaming on the back porch. She fumed. She wanted to kill Kevin. Not painfully. Just dead. Because she was realizing something. Kevin was not going to let her go. Ever. Even if she left him, he would come after her.

Hearing her name, she sat up in bed. Why did they not leave? They weren't going to do anything. She walked back out.

"Yes?" she asked.

"Mrs. Griffin," the nice one spoke. "I've told your husband and I wanted to tell you, you probably need to have your mouth looked at. I'd guess you need a couple of stitches up there."

"Thank you officer. I'll do that in the morning."

He gave her a compassionate smile. "You call us if anything makes you nervous now. Ya hear? We work twenty-four hours, and we're as near as your phone. Understand, Mr. Griffin? We're as near as that telephone on the desk there."

"Sure," Kevin answered innocently. "Thanks for coming. Sorry for the trouble." He closed the door.

Turning toward Annie, he began. "See what you did, Annie. Now they've got my name. You're the biggest embarrassment a man ever had to live with. What the fuck were you thinking? Out in the yard in your pajamas." She leaned back against the wall in shock. "If you ever pull any shit like this again, you're in big trouble. Fucking nut! I don't know how I stand you."

Annie looked up at him. She started doing her usual replay of reality to assess her guilt. She stopped herself. This was not her fault. She had not even called the police. She had only tried to escape. She had done something terribly wrong in her early life, and God was punishing her. God wanted her to be stuck with Kevin for the rest of her life. She prayed, and nothing changed. Kevin was going on about how she would have to try a little harder not to flirt. It would not be hard. This was the last time he would take her out.

Annie tuned him out and continued to think. Did God hate her?

"NO," a voice shouted in her head. Annie was startled. Had the voice been real? She would have giggled, but Kevin might think she was not paying attention.

God wants me to stay with Kevin until he kills me? She tossed it up as an experiment. "No," the voice said more quietly. Annie understood.

"You can't have my soul, Kevin," she interrupted.

"Pardon me?" Kevin asked in a startled voice.

"You heard me," Annie continued flatly. "No matter what you do to me, no matter how often you tell me what a loser I am, no matter how much you twist the truth, you cannot have my soul. So what do you want? Eventually you'll lose me. You know that, don't you?"

Kevin's face paled. "You're talking crazy again, Annie.

Listen to yourself." He made no move to follow her as she walked into their room and climbed into bed.

Annie felt calm. Kevin could not destroy her. He could beat and humiliate her. He could even kill her. But he could never consume her. That was the nameless fear that was driving her crazy. That she would disappear altogether. No, she vowed. God did not want this for anyone. God would help her. So long, Kevin Griffin, she thought. Some how, some way, I'll escape. Annie drifted into a dreamless sleep.

Chapter Sixteen

The following day Annie ignored him. All day. It was Sunday, and there was nothing going on. Her left eye was swollen, and her lip was puffed out. Her back hurt. She was forever shifting to locate a comfortable position. The idea of anyone seeing her like this was unthinkable: she was housebound. Pale and upset, Kevin paced around like a caged bear. He walked into the kitchen while Annie was feeding the baby and looked startled to see her face.

"Why do you make me do it, Annie?" he asked in a strangled voice.

Moving slowly like a robot, Annie pushed past him to get the milk. There was no struggle with depression. Like the tentacles of an octopus, she let it wrap coldly around her. Welcoming the dead heaviness, Annie found it muted the pain. For now, there was nothing worth feeling. Death did not frighten her. She longed for it. If not for Mary, she would be entertaining thoughts of suicide. She entertained them anyway. There were two items, however, firmly barring that option. One, Kevin might get his hands on Mary, permanently distorting Annie's innocent child. With the inherent conceit of every mother, Annie knew that nobody could love Mary as well as she. Two, she doubted God wanted her coming up that way. Suicide was a big sin. Perhaps the biggest. Annie paused momentarily. Was it worse than hurting someone else? Probably they were equal, she mused. She gave herself a mental shake. Wrong was wrong. She was stuck on earth with Kevin. Not for long, she promised herself.

Kevin wrestled with guilt. She sensed it. In a vastly detached way, Annie pitied her husband. The only plight worse than her own would be Kevin's. She shuddered. How tragic to live Kevin's warped and bitter existence. She realized that emotionally she had written him out of her life. Tomorrow she would rethink the marriage thing. It was over. There was no pleasing Kevin, and she might die trying. Her mind lurched backward, reviewing Kevin's accusations.

Even mentally she lacked the strength to defend herself. Well, she thought, there's only one thing for it. I'll accept full responsibility. It can be all my fault, just so it ends. The thought freed her. What had he called her? Spoiled? Annie thought hard. Could she live with that? She was spoiled and sneaky. Yes, she nodded to herself. Spoiled and sneaky was OK. She would be spoiled and sneaky by herself, thus sparing all men from her badness. She would be Jack the Ripper, too, if it enabled her to exit the cruel charade that was her marriage.

Eons later, toward evening, Annie sat sprawled on the bedroom floor with Mary. The contents of the toy box lay strewn about, lending a hurtful cheeriness to the room. Annie heard the couch shift. Kevin had been staring at the television for the last few hours, trying to act normal. Now he opened the door and stood behind her. Annie concentrated on the puzzle in front of her. Children's puzzles were therapeutic. Unlike life, everything fit.

"I'll get my own dinner if you want," he said uncertainly. To her silence he added, "Do you want anything?"

Annie shook her head. Fall over dead in the kitchen, please, she mentally requested. What are the odds? Surely somewhere in the world, a nasty man had fallen dead in his kitchen. Annie thought dejectedly that Kevin was fairly safe working with the butter knife he would certainly use to make a peanut butter sandwich. She shook her head again to scatter the badness. Mary gamely began shaking her head. Annie smiled in spite of herself. Something struck her. She was going to abandon Kevin, no doubt about it. But there was something she could do for him. She could spare Mary. Annie would shield his daughter. Maybe later in life he would understand and thank her.

Mary pushed a book in her face. *Green Eggs and Ham*. Annie sighed deeply and began to read. Sam I Am was kind of like Kevin. Relentless. Galloping through the story, Annie began to use first mad, then pleading voices. Mary laughed in delight. The little pixie face watched Annie's intently for the next change of expression. In spite of herself, Annie came to life. She laughed out loud at the end. On the heels of laughter, tears rushed down. Like sentinels, they had waited steadfastly, knowing their time would come. And so, Annie came to know sorrow.

After distracting Mary with stacking rings, she sat cross-legged on the floor rocking as she wept. The jubilant laughter of a child had liberated her wounded spirit. So free and trusting. The world was a good place to be, and it was wonderful to be alive and loved. Annie grieved the deceit and bitterness of her marriage. She had almost disappeared under it. Someday, she vowed, she would laugh like Mary. Joyfully.

She remembered the voice from last night. Real or not, Annie clutched at it. Whoever it was had said "NO." God did not want this for her. Yes, it was a big mess, but who better than God to clean it up? God did not care if she was rotten. He was looking for faith, Annie knew. Blessedly, she had that. Following that thought, Annie realized that her current risk was that of falling into despair. That would tie His hands. She had to hope, trust, and parachute out of the crashing plane that was her marriage. An unsettling issue popped into her head.

What about the forgiveness thing? Hmm. Surely she could forgive Kevin from a safe distance. Like ... thousands of miles. Annie resolved to pray for Kevin every day. But she had to leave. Lately she had found herself thinking violent, hate-filled thoughts. Enough of that. From now on she would think good, hopeful thoughts. What about the lies? Annie pondered deeply. In order to escape, and she finally understood she would be fleeing for her life, she had to deceive. The question hung in the air as she waited for last night's voice. Nothing. She would take that as a thumbs up. The shortest distance and all that.

Breathing deeply, she gave Mary a genuine smile. She felt cleansed and peaceful. Odds were she would survive this day. Tomorrow she would take action.

• • •

Monday morning, Kevin went off to school as usual. A sickly gray color suffused his face. He looked scared. Annie, on the other hand, was serene. She could hardly wait for him to leave so she could call the counselor. Ignoring his goodbye, she watched through the window as he headed for school. He walked slowly with his head down. Annie beat back feelings of pity.

Popping Mary into the high chair, she steadily spooned fruit into the child. Cheerios came next. That would buy Annie twenty minutes. It was too risky to call Chicago. One expression of sympathy would toss her lightly over the edge. Nervous breakdowns were an unaffordable luxury.

Dialing the number, she asked for Caroline. A woman's voice told her that Caroline was in session and would call her back. Annie thought quickly. Finally, she requested that Caroline call back before noon. She stressed that it would not be safe to call after that. The woman sounded perplexed. Annie said it again, the same way. She thanked the woman for her help and hung up. At this stage Annie did not mind offending Kevin. She did, however, need time to think before any more head-on collisions.

Putting on some music, she cleaned house. Mary began to bellow from the high chair so she picked her up. The baby's clothes were out on the table, and Annie gently laid her down for a change. Her diaper was dirty. Looking at her bottom, Annie decided to pop her into the sink for a quick bath. It was not yet a full-blown rash, but Annie knew it could become one if it was not kept clean. The pediatrician in Chicago had told Annie that the best prevention against diaper rash was a clean bottom. One bad rash had made a believer of Annie, and she silently prayed that the counselor would not call back just yet. Poor little Mary was loudly indignant at a bath that was tantamount to a dunking. Annie wrapped her screaming child in a towel and with one hand made her a bottle of juice.

Annie took a large mixing bowl from the cabinet and filled it with assorted goodies. Placing it on the couch, she helped Mary into a standing position. Mary was just starting to "cruise," as they called it. This meant she was pulling herself up on furniture and walking from piece to piece. Watching her for a moment, Annie decided that cruising was much too smooth a word. Lurching better described the infant's method of travel. Annie sighed. Mary would be walking in no time. Another shower of grief fell down upon her. How sad that Kevin would not watch this beautiful child grow up. Again Annie disciplined her thoughts. Feeling manic, she started to clean with a vengeance. At exactly ten o'clock the phone rang.

It was Caroline. Annie briefly told her that she had spoken with Dana, who had recommended her. Caroline told Annie that she did not have any openings at this time. Annie was silent. This contingency had never occurred to her. Caroline asked her what kind of situation she was in at the moment.

"Uh, I'm not really sure myself," she groped for words.

"Are you having marital problems?" Caroline probed gently.

"The police would think so," Annie began hesitantly. "I don't want to start crying. I'm trying to think of a way to say this."

"Well Annie," Caroline said definitively, "the best way I know is straight out. What's going on?"

"We had a fight the other night." Annie paused. "I lost. I have a bad bruise over my left eye, and I think I should have gotten stitches in my lip but I had no way to get there. He would not have let me go anyway. I also have bruises all over the backs of my thighs and on my back. He was kicking me. I think I need to leave, but he's going to kill me if I do. I'm not sure what I want to do right now ... I feel like it's time I did something." Annie was about to continue when she heard the counselor start to say something.

"Pardon me," Annie said politely.

"Go ahead, what were you going to say?" Caroline waited.

Annie took another deep breath. "As bad as that sounds, I have one bigger problem. I think I'm losing my mind. I mean. I'm really frightened. I might be going nuts."

Caroline burst out laughing. "Annie, I'm sorry. Let me tell you why I'm laughing. You sound like a perfectly sane person to me. It's just that if you told me you felt emotionally great, I might be worried. If you feel like you're going crazy, that's good. It means you're normal. Anyone in your shoes would be losing it right now. Can you get over at twelve?"

"Can you see me?" Annie asked in delight.

"Sure. I can see you during lunch," Caroline said cheerfully. "Will you be able to get here? Where is your husband right now?"

"He's at school and then at practice. He is an athlete and would never miss a practice. I can take the bus, but I'll have to bring my baby. Is that OK?"

"Sure," Caroline responded easily. "We love babies. I might even be able to scare up a babysitter for her. I'll see you at noon, Annie."

Annie hung up the phone and sat with her hand on it. She had done it. No asking Kevin. No fighting about it for six months. She was packing up Mary and going to a counselor. Just making the arrangements made her feel stronger.

She was over eighteen and would do what she wanted. Kevin could not control everything. This would all be great except for two things. One, she still loved Kevin. Two, he would kill her if she tried to leave. Shrugging her shoulders, Annie began to get ready. It was a pretty good day, and you couldn't have everything. She would have to leave soon if she were going to make it on time. Within fifteen minutes, she and Mary were heading to the bus stop.

Annie gave the bus driver the address, and he dropped her off right at the door. She realized with a start that it was probably the black eye and split lip. She kept forgetting that she looked like a prize fighter. She remembered being dragged back into the apartment in her pajamas. Her face flushed every time she thought of it.

After giving the receptionist her name, she sat down. The stroller folded up, and Annie could not decide whether to take Mary out yet. Decisions were impossible these days. Little ones like this. She mulled it over until she heard a woman's voice call her name. Standing up, she turned and saw a woman in her thirties wafting by the receptionist desk.

"Caroline?" she said uncertainly.

"Yes, in the flesh,"the woman answered. "Who is this darling little thing?"

Annie smiled proudly. "This is Mary. Say hello, Mary."

Caroline bent down and took the child's hand. Mary immediately began a long story in baby dialect. Annie chuckled. Mary was usually shy around strangers. Caroline listened seriously and made appropriate responses. "She's wonderful," she exclaimed. "Whatever she's telling me is extremely important." Standing up, she extended her hand. "I'm Caroline Martin. You must be Annie." Annie shook her hand and nodded. She liked this woman immediately. "Come on back to my office. One of the girls is going to hang out with Mary in the playroom if it's OK with you. That will give you a bit of a break so we can talk."

Annie followed her down a hallway to a small room filled with toys. A young girl about Annie's age was hurriedly eating a sandwich.

"Sue," Caroline introduced them, "this is Annie and her daughter Mary. Mary has some important things to say today so I don't think you'll have any problems."

Sue abandoned her sandwich and smiled at Annie. "Great. We'll play in here. Don't hurry. If I need you, I know where to find you.

"Thank you so much," Annie said. "There is a bottle of juice in the diaper bag if she gets cranky. And she's just been changed so she'll be all right until I get back. I'll just back out so she doesn't see me going." Sue nodded. She was already squatted down in front of the stroller with a stuffed porpoise. Mary was chattering away when Annie left. Caroline led her to another small office in the same hallway. Standing back, she motioned Annie in.

Annie settled into a comfortable chair and looked around. The room had a good feel to it. The walls were painted a light mauve, and two country landscapes graced the windowless wall. Their colors blended nicely with the mauve and added to the general serenity of the room. Caroline seated herself across from Annie and smiled.

"Have you ever been to a counselor before?"

"No," Annie answered shyly. "This is the first time."

"Well then," Caroline crossed her legs and became businesslike. "There are a couple things I'd like to fill you in on first." With that she launched into an explanation of confidentiality. Annie listened with one ear. The other ear was enjoying the melodic sound of Caroline's voice. She was not originally from west Texas. That was clear. There seemed to be a bit of eastern seaboard behind the light drawl. The confidentiality was comforting, though. Apparently, Caroline would never tell anyone what Annie said. They would have to torture or subpoena her first. Even then she would not tell unless Annie signed a release of information. Also, there was a sliding scale fee arrangement, which meant that if Annie had no money, she did not have to pay. Annie explained that Kevin dealt with the money and she did not have much extra with her today.

Caroline waved it off. She said they would deal with that down the road.

Caroline went on to talk about scheduling. She was booked at this time. That meant that initially, Annie's appointment time might shift every week. Annie studied her as she spoke. Caroline was very attractive. Taller than Annie, she was thin. Svelte, Maureen would have said. She wore an abundance of light gold jewelry that made constant tinkling noises as she moved her arms and hands. And her head. Feathery gold earrings brushed against her shoulders as her head moved. Annie was enthralled. Shoulder-length light brown hair was pulled back in the front to a delicate arrangement in the middle of her head. Annie would have liked to study it. How on earth did she get it to stay? She passed over a form to read and sign. Annie noticed her hands. Her nails were beautifully manicured and polished in the same mauve shade as the office walls. Her hands, too, were graceful. Annie self-consciously made fists. She had not thought to look at her fingernails in a while. Indeed, it struck her that she barely combed her hair these days. Everything about this woman suggested grace and dignity.

After signing several forms, Annie leaned back in her chair. Caroline shoved them haphazardly into a file folder and also sat back.

"Annie, normally I would get to know you slowly. We would talk about your family life as a child and things like that." Caroline leaned forward and studied Annie intently. "Quite frankly, we don't have time for that. I don't like the look of your face. Let's talk about your husband. Can you tell me what's going on?"

Annie looked down at the floor. She had not even begun to speak, and she was choking up. A warm sympathetic voice was too much. It had been so long since there was someone who seemed to really care about her. Tears began to stream into her lap, and she watched them land on her clenched hands. A box of Kleenex appeared on her lap and she held it like a lifeline.

"I'm sorry."

"Don't apologize. People cry a lot in here," Caroline answered calmly. "Take your time, Annie. I'd guess you've got some pretty good reasons to feel sad."

Annie cried even harder. Caroline waited patiently. After a few minutes Annie felt herself winding down. It felt so good to cry. Kevin became enraged if she cried at home so she seldom did. She had forgotten what a relief it was to express pain.

"I'm losing my mind," she whispered.

"What makes you think that?" Caroline said noncommittally,

"I can't think straight anymore," Annie began. All she needed was a start. After that the words flowed freely. "I could not decide in the waiting room whether or not to take Mary out of the damn stroller. I dwell on little decisions for hours." Annie finally looked up. "Also, I'm having bad thoughts." She waited. So did Caroline. The room was still. "My husband says I'm crazy. Sometimes I want to kill him, and I can actually picture myself doing it. I never would," she hastened to add. "But what kind of person daydreams constantly about her husband's death?"

Caroline looked at her steadily. "The kind of person who is very pissed off and frightened."

"I'm not mad at him," Annie said wonderingly. "I mean, of course, I am sometimes. Most of the time I just don't understand why he gets so mad at me. I wanted my marriage to work."

"Is it over?"

"I don't know." Annie frowned. "I think he might kill me." With that she burst out laughing. "Sorry," she said embarrassed. "See what I mean? I'm behaving like a lunatic."

"Why did you laugh?"

"Did it sound absurd to you?" Annie asked. "I just said I'm not sure if I want to end my marriage. In the next sentence I said my husband might kill me." Annie began to take big gulps of air. "I'm going crazy, Caroline," she sobbed. "How can I not be sure if I want a divorce. He's going to kill me. I thought he would kill me the other night. I can barely sit on this chair, my legs hurt so bad. I think he did something to my back. It's hurting all of the time. I ran out of our apartment in my pajamas screaming for help. What's wrong with me?" Annie's breaths were still coming in gasps, but she was not sobbing. She desperately needed answers. Wrapping her arms around herself, she stopped and waited. "Do you think I'm crazy?"

"Not at all," came the certain response. "I think you're stressed to the breaking point and scared to death. Add to that confusion and loneliness, and I'd say you were pretty much coping the same way any woman would in your circumstances." Caroline paused and stared at Annie until their gazes locked. "Annie, I'm going to tell you a secret. Are you listening?" Annie nodded. "There is nothing wrong with you. Let me repeat that. From what I've seen so far, and what I know about domestic violence, I'd say you were perfectly normal. You're not crazy. Not even a little."

Annie put her head in her hands and cried again. This time she rocked back and forth in her chair. A good few minutes passed before she even attempted to pull herself together. It was like a huge burden had been miraculously raised from her shoulders. She was not crazy. She had never really thought so. Annie's self-esteem suddenly poked up from some buried place. She felt a shred of dignity rising in her chest and actually sat up straighter because of it.

"Thank you, Caroline." Annie spoke gently. Her head was clearing a little. She told Caroline about the fight on Saturday. She left out nothing. Caroline was unshakable. What a relief to tell all of these horrible things and have her look back at you with an intelligent and calm expression. Annie understood that she could tell Caroline everything. Her heart felt connected to the world again. The dirty ugly secrets were in the open, and this diminished their power. When she finished, she looked at Caroline with quiet anticipation.

"OK, Annie. Let me try to explain what is going on in your marriage." Caroline leaned forward, and her jewelry tinkled happily. Even ugly things could not disturb this woman's air of serenity. "First of all, let me say that you are an intelligent and courageous woman." Annie's eyes welled up again. "You probably don't realize how brave you are. You asked me if you were crazy because you ran out in your pajamas. I would have to say No. You made a gutsy attempt to save your life. He could have killed you. You do know that, don't you?" Annie nodded uncertainly. "Annie, let me put it this way. When he slammed you into the mirror, he could have killed you. You've just told me how big he is. He apparently is not exercising self control. He could have crippled you when he kneed you in the back. From now on I want you to practice looking at this clearly. The reality is this. Whether or not he intends to ... and you've told me he has threatened to kill you ... you could end up dead. So if he chokes you just a little and squeezes too hard, the result is a body bag for Mary's Mommy."

Annie shook her head negatively. "I don't mean I don't understand. It's just that I want you to continue. I'll think about how horrible that is later. Please keep explaining."

"OK. This is not easy stuff for you to hear. I want to give you a sheet of information. Men who behave this way, people call them abusers, have a certain set of characteristics. A profile if you will. I want you to look it over and see if any of it sounds familiar."

With that, she handed Annie a sheet of paper. On top was the heading "Profile of a Batterer." Annie winced. Surely Kevin was not someone who could be called a batterer. It sounded awful. She began to read through the sheet. By the time she was on number four, she could feel the color draining from her face.

- Jealous/possessive
- Tries to isolate wife
- Tries to control wife—often financially as well as emotionally
- Jekyll and Hyde personalities
- Explosive temper
- Low self-esteem
- Blamer. Projects own faults onto wife. Tells wife it is all her fault
- Verbal assault/emotional abuse in addition to physical abuse
- Generational. Comes from families where violence was present
- More violent when wife is pregnant
- Denies beatings and their severity *SOMEWHAT*
- May have other problems with the law
- Violence runs in a cycle. Tension building is followed by abusive incident followed by honeymoon phase. Honeymoon phase is characterized by the following behaviors: Apologizes; sends flowers; cries real tears; promises anything including things like stopping alcohol or drug use, attending counseling, family vacations, attending church; and promises never to hit partner again. Often becomes very involved with the children during this phase and attempts to be very supportive of his partner.
- Batterer does whatever it takes to get his partner back, and the cycle repeats itself over and over again

Annie stared at Caroline in disbelief. "This is Kevin. Almost exactly. I don't get it. Is it something they cannot control?"

Caroline was gentle but firm. "Annie, look at it this way. When he hits you, he acts like he's out of control. Right?" Annie nodded. "He pretends that you make him so crazy that he cannot help it. Right?" She nodded again. "Does he ever get really mad at anyone else?"

That was easy. "Yes. He can't stand his coach. He absolutely hates a couple of the guys on the team. They make him crazy. He'll come home and throw things he's so mad."

"Does he ever hit any of them?"

"No. Of course not. He'd get kicked off the team if he did."

Caroline compassionately continued. "That's my point. He hits you because he can get away with it. He makes a choice to be violent. It's not something that's out of control for him. When the police came, he was completely calm and polite. Minutes before he had hit you in the head. If they had not come, he might have killed you. You said yourself he was escalating. Kevin knows exactly what he's doing. It's a power thing. When he feels like he's not controlling you as much as he'd like, he uses violence to bring you around. Get it?"

Annie was pale but deadly calm. "Caroline, that's so manipulative." She searched for words. "It's ... it's diabolical. So if there was a consequence, he would not hit me either?"

"Something like that, Sweetheart. He's very dangerous. You should remember that tonight when he brings you flowers. I promise you this. It's not over. Kevin is not going to help you pack and wish you well. Most women who are killed are killed when they try to leave the abuser. I can't stress that enough, Annie."

Annie was bewildered. "This is too much. That son-of-a-bitch had me thinking it was all my fault. Caroline, I want to kill him again. Why are they most dangerous when you try to leave?"

"Because they can't lose you. That represents the ultimate loss of control. They often say they'd rather kill you than see you with another man."

Annie nodded her pale face. That sounded exactly like something Kevin would say. She sensed emotions swirling around her and squeezed her eyes shut. The room started to spin. Annie felt her head falling into her lap. Suddenly she felt a strong hand on her arm accompanied by the sound of lilting bells.

"Hold on, Annie," Caroline's voice was heavy with emotion. It sounded strong and confident. "You can handle this. You knew all of this anyway. I just put some words on it for you. Nice and slow," she coaxed evenly. Annie began to relax. "It's a lot of information, but we had to move quickly. You're a smart girl. You can cope with this, and I'm going to help you. You're not alone anymore. Don't think I don't understand how you're feeling. Can you sit up?" Annie had her head down in her lap. The dizziness was passing. "I'm going for ice water. Will you be OK for a minute?"

"Yes. I'll be fine." Annie heard her voice and was reassured. It sounded normal. The faintness was passing. "Shit," she swore. No more denial. The truth was right in her face, and it demanded action.

Caroline tried to persuade her to see a doctor. Annie declined. She had neither insurance nor money. A doctor would order X rays. Additionally, Annie did not have transportation. She finally stopped making excuses. The truth was she did not have the energy to deal with the obstacles. She needed every spare ounce of strength to absorb what she had been told.

Caroline also tried to persuade her to go back to Chicago. Another negative response. Annie was going to finish this in Texas. One of the books she had read in the library had talked about jurisdiction. If she ran out of state with the baby, Kevin could file in her absence and get custody. Caroline confirmed that jurisdiction could be a wild card. At any rate, the Griffin budget would not accommodate attorney fees right now. That was a problem in itself.

"Your head is probably swimming, Annie," Caroline said with a worried look.

"No," Annie responded emphatically. "I feel better than I have in ages. Don't worry about me, Caroline. I'm taking it all in. I'll be fine now that I know what I'm dealing with. It's just a matter of sorting everything out in my head and making some decisions."

Caroline insisted they make a safety plan. That was a series of actions Annie would take in the event things looked like they might get out of hand again. She was to put all important papers in one place, along with the bank book and some spare money. Annie had no idea where she would get this spare money, but get it she would. She agreed to come back to see Caroline on Thursday. Three days away. As she walked out the door, she paused.

Turning, she said. "Why did that Dana lady tell me to see you?"

Caroline smiled sweetly. "Someday I'll tell you, Annie. Now stay alive so you get to hear."

Chapter Seventeen

Annie pushed the stroller out into the harsh Texas sunshine and squinted. She felt disoriented. Something huge had just happened. In the ninety minutes spent with Caroline, all dreams were dashed. Like children's bubbles, they had popped and evaporated. Some instinct told her she should feel liberated. Annie just felt weary.

She squinted again. She really must buy a pair of cheap sunglasses. She tried to decide what to do with herself. After a quick inventory of her pocket, she fished out five dollars. Enough for a pack of cigarettes and a counter lunch at Woolworth's. Annie was not hungry, but knew she should be. Turning left, she headed for the dime store. It was a comforting destination. Browsing through countless household items was therapeutic. It also reminded her of her mother. Annie speculated that women the world over went to Woolworth's to gaze absently at the merchandise while mulling over family problems.

Caroline had told Annie that domestic violence was common. Annie's mind rebelled against the facts. How could this type of terror be common? Impulsively, she had vowed to Caroline to help every battered woman she encountered for the rest of her life. Caroline had nodded, setting off a round of tinkling. "That's pretty much the way it works, Honey," she had said affectionately.

Annie bought her cigarettes and rebelliously lit one on the street. Kevin said she could not afford to smoke. Annie heartily agreed. It was a dirty, nasty habit and she was well rid of it. At the same time she wanted to smoke right now. She was also about to blow three dollars for lunch at Woolworth. She no longer feared having to account for the money. Indeed, Annie noticed that she no longer feared Kevin. Physically, of course, he was scary. But Annie knew something. Kevin would not hit her in the next few days. He was on good behavior. She shuddered. It was frighteningly predictable. If she bought the abuser explanation, and she did, Kevin would be violent again. But not for a while. As long as he thought she was staying, she should be safe.

In a matter of minutes, she arrived at Woolworth and stubbed her cigarette out on the pavement. Mary napped soundly in the stroller. Annie selected the last seat at the lunch counter and wedged Mary's stroller between her own seat and the adjacent stool. This would ensure privacy. Ordering a BLT, fries, and a Coke, she settled in to think. Her thoughts were disorderly, and she roped them in. Kevin fit the profile. According to Caroline, the possibility of a spontaneous and miraculous change was remote. Therefore, she had to leave. Period.

She felt tears approaching and pushed them back. Her lunch provided a welcome diversion, and Annie ate as if starved. Everything tasted delicious. Even the pickle and the parsley garnish. Sated, she sat back and lit another cigarette. Caroline said she would have to take it one step at a time. She would need financial help. That meant a phone call to Chicago. What about the mailbox key? The money would have to be wired. She would ask her dad how much he could part with. He would say it depended on how much she needed. A few hundred ought to be enough initially while she decided on a plan. Caroline said they would work on that Thursday, after Annie had some time to think.

Realistically she should go back to Chicago. Why was that thought so terrible? Because Kevin would follow. She knew it. Scholarship be damned, he would chase her back and create havoc there. For some reason, Kevin felt he had certain entitlements to her. Annie would have to explain the whole disaster to her family. How much would they understand about domestic violence? Well, the girls would get it. She thought of Maureen's reaction and cringed. At best it would be more ugliness. At worst, bloodshed. Her father would be mystified. Annie remembered seeing a news program telling about a man who had beaten his wife to death with a bat. Mr. McGowan had shaken his head in bewilderment. "Why would anyone want to hurt his wife?" he had wondered. Clueless. It was beyond his comprehension, and Annie would crack up if she had to persuade everyone that Kevin was the culprit. He was an expert at appearing innocent. By the end of it, he would have her locked up in a psychiatric ward. She would have to work things out here.

Caroline would help her. Annie thanked God for Caroline. Heaving herself out of her stool, she checked the time. Kevin would be home at five. It was nearly four already. Annie decided to go home and make dinner. She did not have to talk to him, but it would help her stay sane if she did something normal. Also, she was worried about him. He looked strained and sick. How bizarre that she could hate him so much and feel so sorry for him. It was a maternal feeling. She was going to hurt him badly when she left. He would condemn her for years. Maybe forever. Nevertheless, leave him she would. Strangely, it was a relief that he had assaulted her on Saturday. Because of that she had taken steps.

The bus ride was soothing. Mary continued to sleep, and the bus driver actually put the bus in Park and lifted the stroller up the stairs for Annie. Leaning back against the seat, Annie sent up a brief prayer. She would need guidance. The open window invited a soft breeze, and Annie let it caress her face sweetly. The answer to her prayer? Someone up there was comforting her. The thought made her smile.

A hand clamped down on her shoulder, and Annie jumped. Soft brown eyes looked down at her. Mexican mom. She had her own infant on her hip and needed the stroller moved. Annie apologized in Spanish and shifted the wheels to grant passage. The woman smiled and then frowned. Reaching down she moved one finger softly along Annie's bruised eye. Making a fist, she uttered what sounded like a Spanish oath. Annie stared at her pleasantly. What the hell was she talking about? The two other Mexican women on the bus behind them burst out laughing. Annie looked at her in bewilderment. Making a motion with her hand, the woman made clutching twisting motions in the air about groin level. Annie got it and burst out laughing. These women knew about domestic violence. Ha, she thought. She was less alone than she thought.

Home at last, Annie parked the stroller and climbed the stairs. Mary was happily groggy. Opening the front door, Annie paused. She heard the scrape of a chair, and Kevin rounded the corner.

"Annie, where have you been?" he blurted out in a tortured voice. His face was gray except for red blotches. Alarmed, Annie set the baby down.

"What's wrong? Did someone die?"

"What?" Kevin sounded perplexed. "What are you talking about? I thought you left me."

With that, he turned sharply and went into the bedroom, closing the door behind him. Annie gave a huge sigh and closed the front door. Carrying Mary into the kitchen, she stopped dead in her tracks.

There were the flowers. Twelve red roses. Kevin had never bought flowers. Not even when the baby was born. What was next on Caroline's list? Annie felt the urge to giggle. She consoled herself with the thought that this was anxiety created by a highly emotional situation. Now, what should she do with the grieving abuser? Batterer? Dr. Jekyll? Mr. Hyde? This was not funny, and Annie had to serious up. He sounded like he was in anguish. Should she remind him about the ban on tears? Annie decided to start dinner and give him privacy. A mean and nagging voice suggested that his tears were manipulative. Ignoring it, she opened the freezer for meat.

She stared into the refrigerator. Absently smoothing her ponytail, she thought longingly of Chicago. At home a person could pick up the phone in times of crisis and order a pizza. The Texans did strange and terrible things to pizza. Darlene heard a rumor, as yet unconfirmed, that they were putting pineapples with Italian sausage. She shuddered. She longed for a gyros, too. Fat chance. Nothing but barbecue and Mexican. Not to be scoffed at but hardly staples.

Mary was standing against the bedroom door, banging it. She wanted her daddy. Annie closed the fridge and picked up the roses. She did own a vase. Mrs. Nolan had sent her flowers in the hospital, and they had come in a beautiful glass vase. Annie could not believe at the time that it was hers to keep.

A paper fell to the floor from under the flowers. Mail. Any mail at all seemed contraband, and Annie picked it up with a guilty glance at the bedroom. Mary was yodeling now. The envelope was addressed to her. It had been opened, and Annie quickly read the letter. Her heart surged. Mrs. Annie Griffin was hereby informed that based on past academic achievements and current financial need, she was awarded a full scholarship. In effect for the spring semester, she would need to apply again next year. There was also a housing stipend for $200 per month, based on the fact that they had a child. It would start in January.

She leaned against the counter. Dear God, she was finally going to school. With a racing heart she headed for the bedroom. With her hand on the knob she stopped. The door opened. Kevin was bent down to grab Mary so she would not fall into the bedroom. He looked up at Annie with a sorrowful face.

"Congratulations. I knew you'd get it."

Annie smiled in spite of herself. "When did it come? Kevin, this means I can go to school."

"Are you going to leave me?" he asked quietly. "I would not hold it against you. I've been worse than terrible." Swallowing heavily he looked down at her sadly. "All I've ever wanted was for you to be happy. If you would be happier away from me, Annie, then go. I'll be here if you want to come back."

He put his hand out and stroked her bruised eye. Annie's heart was once again twisting and turning. This was not Dr. Jekyll or Mr. Hyde. It was not the Abuser. Or even the Batterer. It was Kevin Griffin. Her childhood friend. The only one in the world who knew how terribly she still missed her mother. She let her head fall forward onto his chest.

"Kevin, Kevin," she moaned. "I don't know what to do. I can't handle you anymore. I saw a counselor today."

He stroked her hair gently. "I know, Annie. I'm a little confused myself. How can I hurt you like that when I love you so much? I don't mean to, you know."

Mary began to protest indignantly at being left out of the family hug. Kevin reached down and picked her up. She pulled at his nose and smiled. What was happening? Annie had been so sure in Caroline's office. Now she felt her resolve slipping.

"Annie, you don't owe me a thing," Kevin began. "But in spite of that, will you please talk to me?"

"Kevin, I'm exhausted. I really am. Do we have to do this tonight?" Annie could not talk to him until she had a chance to decide. The scholarship and stipend threw a whole different slant onto the picture. With a job and a little help from the campus nursery, she might have a crack at this.

"That's fine," he said gently. "How about I walk up and get us some hamburgers? Could you eat?"

218

He was so humble. It was hard to see him like this. "That's great. I'll get the house organized."

He was not out the door five minutes before Annie was on the telephone.

"Maureen?" she demanded. "Call me right back."

Seconds later the phone rang. "You're not going to believe this," Annie started. She told her about the scholarship. She knew that her father would be ecstatic, and she wanted him to know right away. Luckily, he was not at home. Annie did not want to talk to him until she made some decisions. Maureen was excited but not surprised. Annie wondered how everyone could have so much faith in her? She told Maureen things were not going well with Kevin. She kept quiet about the fight and the counselor. Instead she said they were considering marriage counseling. Maureen was appalled. Annie ended the conversation with a promise to keep her posted.

Hanging up, Annie went to attend to the roses. She found a small envelope attached to the ribbon. Her mailbox key was taped to a small florist card. "Congratulations! I wish I was worthy of you,"read the card. Annie did not know whether to cry or rip it up. The lack of self-esteem revolted her. Was that number six? The damned abuser list kept popping into her head. Shaking it off, she arranged the flowers in Mrs. Nolan's vase. She placed them on the table and lifted Mary up for a better view. How lovely they looked. Annie felt sorrow coming back. What a happy day this should be in their little household! She glanced up at the crucifix. Maybe there would be a miracle. God could do it. But even He had to contend with Kevin's free will. How wonderful if Kevin was that one in a thousand who decided to change.

Annie forced herself to be realistic. She felt a headache coming on and made a firm decision not to think about it any more today. It was too much.

Kevin came home with dinner, and they ate. Pleasant interactions drew a shutter down over the large issues looming between them. Kevin was polite and attentive. He made the lemonade and poured glasses. He brought Annie a napkin. He cleaned the baby and took her down from her highchair.

Annie's emotions continued to fluctuate. On one hand, she was touched. He was trying so hard. On the other hand, she felt anger. Why did he act like this only when he thought she was going to leave? After the baby was put to bed, he joined her in the living room. Annie was staring blankly at the television.

"Did you get out of practice early today?"

Kevin averted his eyes. "No. I skipped it."

"You skipped it? With the big game next Saturday? Can you do that?"

"I don't care, Annie. I came home for lunch, and you were gone." He met her gaze. "I don't give a shit about playing. It all means nothing if I don't have you. I thought you left me. I sat trying to decide if I should kill myself."

Annie gasped. "Kevin. How can you say that?" Changing her tone, she continued. "Are you serious?"

Kevin looked out the window again. "Annie, if you leave me, I don't want to live. I thought about it and thought about it. We've always known that I need you more than you need me. I have no desire to live if you're not with me." Kevin was matter of fact. He looked at Annie with naked honesty, and she chose her words carefully.

"Kevin, I can't believe I'm hearing this. You're talking about suicide?"

With that, he put his head down into his hands. "I'm sorry. I shouldn't have told you. It'd be better if it just happened."

Annie knelt down in front of him. "That's never the answer. Kevin, do you hear yourself? Even if we don't get along, you're still Mary's father. Can you imagine telling her someday that her daddy killed himself?" Annie forced him to look at her. "It's going to be all right. You're doing well in school. Only a freshman and you're playing on Varsity. What do you want from yourself? We're doing the best we can, Kevin. Go easy. I don't know anyone who has tried harder than you have. Except maybe me." He laughed shortly with her.

"Then why does my wife want to leave me?"

Annie spoke without emotion. "I never said I wanted to leave you." Frowning, she continued. "It's just that I can't live with your temper. You could have killed me the other night."

Kevin looked down again. "I would never have killed you, Annie. You're exaggerating."

"Well, Kevin, let me put it this way. I'm not sure I'm willing to take that chance. You know what I mean?"

She rose and turned away from him. Was she exaggerating? What had she really suffered? A couple of bruises. A bloody lip. Maybe she was overreacting. Maybe Caroline was overreacting. If it were not for that damned Profile, she might be able to convince herself. As it was, Kevin was too typical to pretend this was not happening. Annie sighed deeply once again. What a relief it would be to pretend it had never happened. She got the scholarship. Things would get better.

"Annie," Kevin interrupted her thoughts, "you mentioned marriage counseling once. What about that? I'm game if you are. I mean, what the hell? I will honestly do whatever it takes to keep you." He waited. She remained silent. "C'mon. We've got to try everything before we throw in the towel, don't we? Annie, do you know how much I love you?" She nodded with her back to him. "Then you must know I'll do anything in my power. Counseling might help. You said yourself I had problems with the way I grew up. Give me one last chance. I'm begging you."

"Don't beg me, Kevin," she snapped irritably. "All I want is to be safe in my own home. And to be treated like an adult." She felt her temper beginning to rise. "By the way, thank you for the mailbox key. That's the kind of shit I'm talking about. How dare you take my key away? And I want to get a job, Kevin. We need the money. You never stop talking about how broke we are, yet you forbid me to work. Where is the sense in that?" She paused for a breath.

"While I'm at it, how dare you accuse me of flirting with that poor homesick boy at the dinner! All I did was talk to him. Your jealousy is not my problem, Kevin." Annie heaved herself onto the couch. "Remember, you wanted to talk about this. Not me. I'm not a dog on a leash, and I swear I will never be treated like that again."

Kevin was now sitting directly across from her. He had listened patiently to everything she said. Annie actually felt pretty good. This was how it was supposed to be, she marveled. If you were mad at your husband, you should be able to tell him. Normally she was afraid to.

"Are you finished, Mrs. Griffin?"

"I don't know. If anything else comes to mind, I'll let you know."

"Well. Regarding the mailbox key. You're right. I was wrong. I was simply reacting to my panic at not handling the bills properly. It won't happen again." Annie inclined her head but said nothing. The key was the least of their problems. "Regarding your getting a job. Go ahead. It can probably be worked out if you tell them you can work evenings and weekends. The money would be extremely helpful, and you're right. I'm not the boss." Annie nodded but still said nothing. "About my jealousy. I have no defense except that I'm married to an extremely attractive and outgoing wife. I'm not as confident, and I feel like you'll fall for someone else. That's my problem. I agree. I think the answer is to go out more so I get used to our being around other people, including other men. You were just being nice at the dinner, and I'm sorry. I was a real jerk. It won't happen again." Annie smiled at him but remained quiet. "I think I've covered all of our problems. Have I left anything out?"

"Just one thing. What about the fact that you nearly killed me on Saturday? What are we doing about that?"

"It won't happen again. I promise." Annie rolled her eyes. "Annie, give me a break. I'm promising the moon for a reason. I am going to get used to the idea that you're going to school and working. I can't keep you in the house.

I understand that. I'm giving on everything I possibly can. I'm not going to hurt you again because I know you'll leave. You're going to have to trust me on this. OK?"

Annie rose and again knelt in front of him. "Kevin, how resentful are you going to be if I start school and get a job. You say these things now, but will it last? Last time we had a talk like this you took my mailbox key the very next morning. Why should I believe you?" She thought quickly and made a decision. She summarized the discussion she had with Caroline. Including the Profile. Kevin looked undisturbed.

"Kevin, doesn't it bother you that the Profile fits you to a T?"

"No it does not, Annie." He frowned as he searched for words. "That fits every husband. Every husband gets jealous. Every person in the world has a low self-esteem if you get close enough to know them. Show me a person who is the same personality all of the time. You're certainly not. What does that make you? Dr. Jekyll and Mrs. Hyde? Think about it, Annie. You have a temper, too, and you know it. Who started yelling five minutes ago? It was not me. Did I go psycho and hit you? No. I figured it was your turn to get things off your chest. I've been a jerk, I agree. But I'm not some battering abuser nut. I'm just a guy who got married a little young and is trying to make it work."

Annie was quiet. Inside she was reeling. She had been so sure ... but maybe Kevin was right. Annie certainly was not perfect. She had never pretended to be. At the same time something was terribly wrong.

"Kevin, what about the control thing? Say what you like, but that was true. You try to control me all of the time."

"Annie," he began patiently, "are we in a marriage or not? Look around you. Every spouse tries to control his partner. Yes, I try to control you. But don't you try to control me? You're always telling me how much to drink or not to drink. You're full of orders about how you want the towels laid and where to put my clothes. That's just marriage. Now you're probably thinking those are harmless little things. You're right. I'm willing to agree that I did try to stop you from getting a job. But it didn't work. It's that simple. I tried. You balked. You're getting a job. Honey, I don't think this is as big a deal as you're making it out to be. I adore you, Annie. I'm not going to make you unhappy. I promise."

Annie stared at him with narrowed eyes. He was doing it again. He was waving a magic wand, and everything was going away. It was scary. What about the agony of the last two days? Had she dreamed it?

"Kevin," she persisted, "I'm not trying to be rude, but this has all happened before. Remember? You promised not to hurt me before, and I got hurt again. You're making my head spin, but I'm not going to let go of that."

Kevin rose slowly and came over to where she was sitting. Looking up at him, she thought again how big he was. Right now he was benign. Saturday he had been deadly. That's what she had to hold on to.

Now he knelt down in front of her. "Annie, whatever you think, I'm not letting go of that either. That cannot happen again. I know that, and I agree. Will you hear me out on something?" She nodded her head warily. "I think that a large part of the problem is communication. Apparently, we don't do it well. It's not a huge problem, but it is a problem. If we could talk more about our feelings, I would not explode."

"Let me get this straight, Kevin," she said levelly. "You beat the shit out of me because you can't express your feelings?"

Kevin let out a deep sigh. "That's exactly what I'm talking about, Annie. You get sarcastic whenever I try to make a point. I can't compete with you verbally. So I shout you down." He looked at her sheepishly. "I think we have gotten into some bad habits. If we saw a marriage counselor, maybe he could teach us how to communicate. It's always been a problem for us. Am I right?"

Annie nodded her head reluctantly. It was all true. She would have liked to argue that she was sarcastic because it was her only defense. He shouted her down before she ever got sarcastic. Another puzzling case of the chicken or the egg.

"I don't know," she mused. "You're persuasive. You really think we won't have these huge fights if we learn to communicate?"

He looked at her appealingly. "All I can say is I'm willing to give it my best shot. If I need to change, I'll change. Will you?"

"You know I will, Kevin," she said heatedly. "I just don't want to be the one doing all of the changing." She reached for his hand, and he kissed her fingers. "OK. I'll call this counselor and see if she can see us this week."

"Uhm. Don't get me wrong here, Annie," he hedged. Seeing her eyes narrow, he added quickly, "I would prefer to see a man. That's all. This lady is probably very nice, but she's your counselor. You know? Let's see someone objective. That's all I ask."

"Fine," she agreed. Kevin had made so many concessions, she could not very well object to this little thing.

Annie rose the next morning with a heavy, hangover feeling. Snatches of disturbing dreams flitted through her mind as she groggily commenced her morning routine. Kevin was loving and gentle. Despite this, Annie could not shake the feeling that, once again, she had been had.

After the breakfast was cleared, she called Caroline. She pensively tapped a pencil on the table, waiting for the return call. One thing was certain. If she was going to get a job, she must do it quickly before Kevin changed his mind. She decided to walk up to the closest department store and get an application. They were looking for Christmas help now.

Caroline called and listened carefully as Annie described last evening's conversation. Annie heard her counselor sigh. Caroline cautioned Annie that Kevin was nice because he wanted to be. He could just as easily decide to be abusive. She also said marriage counseling could be downright dangerous in situations like this. With a feeling of helplessness, Annie told Caroline about the suicide threats. Caroline was quiet for a moment.

"Annie, what if I told you that suicide threats by abusers were common?"

Annie sputtered. "You mean it's a form of manipulation?"

"Well, yes. Sort of," Caroline spoke in a measured voice. "That's not to say that they don't mean it, of course. You should never ignore a suicide threat. But abusers will do whatever it takes to gain your sympathy and make you stay. Another thing I want to add. Annie, when Kevin is suicidal, he is very dangerous. He thinks you're staying now so he may be calm. But if he gets the idea you're leaving ... coupled with his suicidal thoughts ... he would be extremely dangerous. Let me say this clearly. It would be so serious, I would encourage you to go into hiding."

"Caroline, you're scaring the hell out of me."

"Good. I'm trying to. Annie, I know that what Kevin is doing is typical. But it's important for you to know, too. Your decision to stay or go is your choice. I'll be here no matter what you do. You're not going to wear me out."

"Thank you," Annie said humbly. "I feel like I have to give it a last shot. He was so sincere, Caroline. I think he meant what he said. He's going to try. How can I walk out without giving him the chance?"

"I understand completely, Annie," Caroline said warmly. "Let me give you a number for the organization that does marriage counseling. They're the same group only a different building. It's the same sliding scale, so don't worry about money. Call me next week and let me know how you're doing. OK?"

"I will. Thank you, Caroline."

Annie called and made an appointment for Thursday with a male counselor named Charles. She also left a message for the babysitter, then loaded up the baby for the walk to the store. Thank God, she had not told Maureen or her father she was leaving. It would be too embarrassing to call back and say she had decided to stay. One could not be too careful about marital problems. Annie could forgive but knew her family might not.

She tried to look on the bright side. Kevin might change. She was going to school and starting a job. She was getting everything she wanted. An instinct told her that she had gained a little ground but remained in the same smoking battlefield. Annie cleared her mind and focused on the present. She was not the same girl who walked into Caroline's office. She was ready to fight if necessary. She thought back on Kevin's explanation of the Profile. Was it possible that all marriages had these struggles? No, she thought grimly. Not like this. Annie never actually knew anyone who had gotten beat up by her husband. But, said the voice, how would you know? How many people know that I'm getting beat up? Outside of Caroline and the police ... nobody. Possibly the neighbors, but Annie refused to think about them. It was too humiliating.

She arrived at the store and requested an application. The girl at the Service Desk was friendly and told Annie to fill it out right away. The manager was scheduling interviews this week. Annie thanked her for the tip and filled out the form. Handing it back, she thanked the woman again. The young girl winked and put Annie's application on the top of a pile. Annie smiled and left.

Walking home she detected a slight mood lift. A job meant freedom. And a paycheck. Annie spent the whole walk home telling Mary how she would spend the money. There was also the stipend. Of course, that would go to Kevin for bills. Regardless, more money would be coming in. Surely the tension would ease.

Chapter Eighteen

Annie landed a job in the camera and jewelry department. She also accepted her scholarship and registered for school. Kevin was being as supportive as possible, and Annie felt her suspicions waning.

Marriage counseling was a disappointment. Kevin ridiculed Charles but otherwise seemed comfortable. Annie was, of course, grateful they were going at all. The problem was, they were not talking about what Annie considered the real issues. Certainly communication skills merited discussion. But Charles and Kevin treated the sessions as though it were the only problem. Annie asked Kevin when they were going to talk about the violence. Kevin got offended and accused her of trying to embarrass him. He remained adamant. Annie was forbidden to bring up violence or suicide. When pressed, Kevin stated that if Annie stayed with him, he would not take his life.

Feeling blackmailed, she bided her time.

Kevin's big game went well, and Kevin received quite a bit of press. Annie dutifully clipped the articles and sent copies to her mother-in-law. The local television station interviewed Kevin at practice so Annie called the station for a copy. For five dollars they made her a tape. They did not own a video tape player, but she figured some day they might.

Kevin cooperated with Annie's work schedule. He got home from practice, and she left for work. She had his dinner ready and the baby fed. The baby went down at seven, and then he studied. He grumbled, but Annie ignored him. College couples had to make sacrifices.

Work became Annie's salvation. It was a fifteen-minute walk to the store if she hurried. She worked from five-thirty until ten. The shift started at five, but the supervisor relented when Annie told him Kevin was an athlete. He, too, followed the progress of the college teams. Annie was competent and quick. She learned the differences in merchandise and took pride in her ability to assist customers. She felt good about herself again. Between earning money and looking forward to the start of her education, life seemed promising. She was careful not to share her exuberance with Kevin. Instinctively she knew if she acted too happy, Kevin would be threatened.

He always asked her if she worked with men. Annie told him to walk up and check. It was all women in her department. He snapped that he hardly felt the need to spy on her. In truth there was a stock boy, or man rather, who had taken a liking to Annie. Bill, the stock boy, as she dubbed him, often stopped by to see if Annie needed anything from the back. He made jokes and flirted, but Annie kept her distance. When she was honest with herself, she admitted he made her feel pretty. That part seemed harmless.

She persuaded Kevin to let her keep the first paycheck for Christmas presents. During breaks she roamed the store in search of bargains. The baby would not require much. Annie had her eye on a beautiful set of Holly Hobby blocks. That would be the big present. Annie would also pick up a couple of inexpensive items to wrap. She needed a big ball and maybe a push toy. Certainly there would be packages coming from Chicago. Babies did not know the difference, she told herself sensibly.

Kevin was a different story. There were all kinds of neat things to buy for him. He complained that he owned no tools. Annie knew full well that Kevin was not mechanically inclined. At the same time he could work a screwdriver, and they did not even own a hammer. She found just the thing. A starter tool kit. At twenty dollars, it was expensive. But Kevin needed to feel like the man of the house. Maybe this would help. She also got him socks and a sweater.

Annie wrapped the presents and hid them in the closet. Kevin was under strict instructions to keep away. Annie loved Christmas. It was magical, and she was determined they enjoy their first Christmas alone together.

The Kemps were flying to Chicago for the holidays, and Annie tried not to be jealous. Their parents had prepaid two tickets, and the baby was free. Darlene searched for presents within their budget. Annie suggested tins of cookies. The tins were on sale at her store, and she picked up ten for her friend. They did not see much of each other these days. Darlene did stop in the store one evening for a visit. Bill, the stock boy, chose that moment to make an appearance with a Coke for Annie. Darlene raised her eyebrows and smiled.

"Who is your friend?" she asked archly.

Annie shrugged her shoulders. "He's a stock boy. He's like that with everyone."

"He seems to like you, Annie," Darlene said conspiratorially.

"I think he might have a small crush on me," Annie acknowledged in spite of herself. "I barely speak to him, but he keeps coming back. The other night he asked if he could give me a ride home. Can you imagine?"

The girls giggled. Then Darlene sighed. "How fun, Annie! I'm sick of being at home. I would love to tell Greg that someone was flirting with me. Maybe it would wake him up a little."

Annie looked at her in amazement. "If I told Kevin that Bill was flirting with me, he'd beat him up. I can't believe you would tell Greg that."

"Greg wouldn't care. He'd say something like 'How fun for you.'" Annie looked astounded. "Seriously, Annie, Greg is not the jealous type. I wish he was. At least you know Kevin cares about you."

Annie shook her head. "I don't know, Darlene. I would rather know that Kevin trusted me."

Darlene looked impatient. "Well, of course, he trusts you. What's not to trust? You never even go to a movie with me. Kevin should lighten up a little."

Annie bristled in spite of herself. "He tries, Darlene. He does. He's just insecure."

Darlene smiled. "The grass is always greener they say. Call me tomorrow. I want you to taste my latest cookie creation. I'm thinking of putting them in my mother-in-law's tin." Both girls shuddered. Darlene's mother-in-law was an extraordinary baker so that tin was important.

"Why don't you buy some exquisite cookies from Marshall Field's bakery when you get to Chicago?" Annie suggested. "Let your mother-in-law think you are a superb baker."

Darlene's eyes lit up for a moment. Then she frowned. "No way! She would ask for the recipes. Besides, she practically owns stock in Marshall Fields. Too risky."

A customer coughed politely, signaling the end of their conversation.

"I'll see you tomorrow, Annie," Darlene said hurriedly. "Look out for Bill."

Annie smiled impishly. As she displayed cameras for her customer, she thought about Darlene. The young Mrs. Kemp was nice enough, but Annie did not trust her. She should not have said anything about Bill. Surely she would not tell Greg who surely would not mention it to Kevin. Annie's stomach squeezed for a moment. Should she request that Darlene keep quiet? No, she decided. That was like entering into a conspiracy. Darlene would say nothing. Annie certainly would not if the situation were reversed. She was being paranoid. And so Annie put it from her mind.

Annie attended to her job duties. Cheerfully waiting on Christmas shoppers, she had no inkling that one brief conversation had jeopardized her very life.

• • •

Rain spattered her face as Annie hurried home from work. It was Thursday. She was fifteen minutes late. A co-worker with romantic troubles had delayed her. Kevin got insecure if Annie was even a few minutes late. The thought of another fight prompted her to quicken her pace even more.

It was four days before Christmas. The temperature was in the sixties, which was helpful. Colored lights festooned houses, and each street lamp sported either a snowman or a bell. How silly, Annie thought. The children here had never seen a snowman. It did not feel like Christmas, and Annie knew it was better that way.

Hurrying up the stairs, she prayed Kevin would be in a good mood. Tension was rising, and a sixth sense told her that Kevin's good behavior was wearing thin. If she questioned him, he would say he could not be perfect all of the time. Annie's brow furrowed. Her marriage was complex at the best of times. Lately, she lived in fear of toppling into a hidden trap.

She paused on the landing. Voices came from her apartment. Annie opened the door and stepped in, and her eyes widened in delight. Her brother Danny was sitting at their kitchen table. Dropping her purse on the floor, she ran to him and was snatched up in a bear hug.

The three laughed and talked at once. He just knocked on the door, Kevin said. Danny said he wanted it to be a surprise. He drove straight through from Chicago and had no idea what time he would arrive. If it had been any later, he would have gotten a hotel room. Annie scoffed at that. She said she could not believe she would be with family at Christmas. Danny's smile vanished.

"I'm leaving in the morning, Annie," he said sadly.

"What?" she demanded. "You are not! You're staying for Christmas if I have to tie you down."

They all laughed merrily. Annie sat down at the table,

and Kevin came around and took her jacket.

Annie smiled up at him. "I got stuck talking to Lorena in the parking lot," she explained. "Her boyfriend went back to Lubbock, and she's devastated."

Kevin rolled his eyes. Seconds later, he placed a mug of beer in front of Annie. "We're drinking, Mrs. Griffin."

"Fine by me," Annie said gaily. "I'll drink all night if Danny tells me he'll stay." Turning to her older brother, she beseeched, "Danny, rearrange whatever nonsense you've got planned." Pausing, her expression changed. "Hey, I thought you were staying in Chicago for Christmas. What are you doing here?"

Kevin and Danny burst out laughing. "Annie," Kevin scolded. "Hush for a minute, and let the man explain. He's trying to tell you."

They all laughed again, and Annie made a zipper motion across her mouth. "Speak."

Danny began to explain. He had intended to stay in Chicago until after the New Year. Unfortunately, a call had come in from his company a few days ago. Some kind of problem had risen involving a boat accident. The bottom line was, Danny would be flying to Japan tomorrow night to bring a boat back. It was an emergency situation, and he did not like to turn them down.

Annie looked perplexed. "Are you flying from here?"

"No," he answered patiently. "I'll be flying from New Orleans. I have to stop by my apartment and take care of some business tomorrow."

Annie remained bewildered. "How did you get here? You drove?" He nodded as he took a long swallow of his beer. "You mean you have to drive to New Orleans by tomorrow afternoon? That's ridiculous, Danny. There's no way you'll make it."

"Annie, Darlin', I'm not driving to New Orleans. I have a reservation in the morning from your little airport. I'll be there in a little over an hour."

"Oh," she said in relief. "That sounds safer than racing across Texas." She frowned again. "What about your car?

How are you going to get it home?"

Danny frowned. "I hadn't thought of that. Shit."

Kevin chuckled. "Annie, he's leaving his car with us. He drove it down here to give it to us."

Annie was delighted. "But we could not let you do that," she protested. "What will you have?"

Danny shrugged. "I'm buying another one, Annie. I hate to sell the Dodge because it's been so faithful. It has a lot of miles on it, but it's in great shape. The insurance has been paid for a year, oil's changed, title is all signed over, and she's yours. I'll be gone for at least two weeks on this trip. When I get back to New Orleans, my new car will be ready. I planned on stopping here for a few days after Christmas, but the plans changed. It worked out great. All you have to do is drive me to the airport in the morning."

"Thank you, Danny," she said quietly. "It will mean a lot to us."

"Forget it," he said pleasantly. "Kevin, I'm thinking we need more beer. I have a feeling it's going to be a long night. Can you run up to the store for us?"

"I'm way ahead of you," Kevin said happily. Stepping out of the kitchen he put his arms out. His coat was already on. "I'll be back in twenty minutes or so." Opening the door, he paused. "Wait a minute. Where are my car keys?"

They chuckled again. Laughter flowed so freely during a reunion. Danny tossed the keys over with a grin. "I'll never drive it again. Kind of sad."

"You're breaking my heart, Danny," Kevin jested. "Tell your sister what kind of car you're buying."

"I'm getting a new Corvette," he said matter-of-factly. "I've always wanted one, and I figure, what the hell, I've got the money."

"Well, I agree," Annie said vehemently. "If you want one you should have one, Mr. Money Bags." Kevin walked out, and they waved to him. "How come you're so rich all of a sudden?"

Danny abruptly changed the subject. "Annie, Kevin will be right back. What happened to your face?"

"What?" The bruise was now so faint she thought it invisible.

"Forget it," Danny took a another long drink and set his beer down. "Here's the deal. Maureen is worried about you. So is Nellie. And now, so am I. Why don't you come with me in the morning? We'll drive, and you can fly home from New Orleans. I've got the money."

Annie sputtered. "Danny, I don't ... I can't just ... What do you mean?"

Danny eyed her intently. "Do you want to tell me about it?"

Annie rose and went into the kitchen for an ashtray. "Do you still smoke?"

"I do, I do," he said regretfully. He pulled a pack of cigarettes from his pocket and set it on the table. Gazing at Annie he continued. "There's another option here. We could take the baby and leave tonight. Or you could come down to New Orleans and stay in my apartment until I get back."

"But why, Danny? What would I be doing there?" Annie said helplessly.

"From the looks of things, you would be hiding," he retorted.

"No." Annie shook her head vigorously. "We're seeing a counselor and trying to work things out. I have to give him this chance, Danny."

"I understand completely. Get me a piece of paper," he ordered as he pulled out his wallet. "Hurry. He'll be back any second."

Annie sprang out of her chair and went to the desk. Grabbing a memo pad, she handed it to Danny with a pen. He pulled a card out of his wallet and scribbled something on the paper. He handed it to Annie and reached back into his wallet again. "Get an envelope." Annie jumped up nervously again and grabbed an envelope out of the desk drawer. Danny pulled out a small stack of bills and placed them in the envelope. Reaching down he added the piece of paper and sealed the envelope. "Go hide this where Kevin won't find it."

"Danny, I can't..." she began.

"Just do it, Annie. If you don't, I swear I'll take you and Mary with me in the morning."

Annie ran to the bedroom and looked around. Where wouldn't he look? She moved quietly so as not to wake the baby. Seeing the diaper holder, she made a decision. The pile never ran all the way down. Annie placed the envelope between two diapers near the bottom. Back in the dining room, she eyed Danny quizzically.

"What's on the paper?"

Danny spoke fast. "A phone number. In New Orleans. His name is Buddy, and he's a good friend of mine. He's a tough guy, but you'd never know it to look at him. If you get nervous, give him a call. He can help you out with anything you need. There's $500 in the envelope. If you get into a spot and need more, call Buddy. I'm serious, Annie. If you think you might get hurt again, get the hell out of here. OK?"

"Yes," Annie said miserably. "Thanks, Danny. I'll feel much better with the car and some money. He's not that bad."

"Annie," Danny warmed. "I like the guy. Don't defend him. No one knows what goes on between two people. But there are some guys who beat up on women. Just because. Kevin is a good guy, and I know he loves you and Mary. You'll work it out. Now, let's get another beer. You won't believe who Dad is dating."

With that he adroitly changed the subject. By the time Kevin returned, they were in stitches at Mr. McGowan's latest romance. Their father was quite in demand and enjoying it immensely.

And so the night passed. It was three o'clock before they went to bed. Annie lay her head on the pillow contentedly. She had her emergency money.

At seven o'clock Annie opened her eyes to Mary's demands for breakfast. Her mind interrupted sleepy thoughts. Something wonderful had happened. In a flash, she remembered Danny, sleeping on the living room couch.

She grabbed Mary from her crib and closed the bedroom door behind her.

"Do you want to see your Uncle Danny?" she asked the baby.

Mary smiled tranquilly. Annie loved her daughter in the mornings. Full of sunshine and happiness. It was too bad everyone could not wake up this way. Still holding the baby, Annie sat down on the coffee table.

"There he is, Mary," she cooed. "He drank too much last night. We might not be able to get him up."

A groan came from under the blankets. "Why do you always get up so early, Annie?" moaned her older brother.

"Ask my daughter," Annie responded cheerfully. "Or don't you want to see the most intelligent child in Texas?"

Danny poked his face out. "She looks like a kid," he said in delight. "Hi, Mary. When did you grow up." Mary let her gaze roam over the newcomer. "She's looking at me like I belong on a garbage dump."

"I know," Annie sighed. "Sometimes she does that with strangers. It takes her a while to warm up."

Danny sat up and put his arms out to her. Mary surveyed him even more skeptically. Raising her eyebrows, she looked away. Danny burst out laughing. "I'll be damned. She's too good for me. The way I feel right now, she's probably right. Do you have any aspirin in the house?"

"Yes. Exactly what time does your flight leave?"

"Ten. It's not going to be pretty."

Annie stood Mary against the coffee table and rose to get the aspirin. "You'll be fine. You need a hot shower and some breakfast. Then I'll run you out to the airport." She kept talking as she rummaged through the kitchen cabinets. Raising her voice an octave, she continued. "I can't believe you're abandoning me so fast. Only you would come for a thirteen-hour visit."

"Don't yell, Annie," he beseeched from the living room. "If I had it my way, I would be here at least a few days." He paused. "I think Mary would spit on me if she knew how."

Annie reentered the living room to see Mary still standing at the coffee table. She was glaring malevolently at her uncle. Annie scolded her gently. "Mary, be nice."

"She's trying, Annie." Danny spoke woefully. "I think she knows things about me. You're a scary little princess. Aren't you, Mary?"

Mary launched into streams of laughter. Danny and Annie exchanged startled looks. "Annie, this it too much on a hangover." Danny chuckled. "Why is she laughing at me?"

"I don't know," Annie said mystified. "I think she's playing with your head. Come on, Mary. Time for breakfast." Annie scooped her up affectionately. "Do you want to jump in the shower, Dan?"

"Yes. Good idea." Danny said briskly. "Do you have any tape? I'll need to fasten my head so it doesn't fall off when the water hits it."

Annie laughed and went to make Mary's breakfast. Within minutes she heard the water running. Seconds later, Kevin staggered out of the bedroom. Annie smiled and handed him the aspirin. "Danny's carrying his head under his arm. How does yours feel?" Kevin grunted and accepted the tablets. Annie hoped her husband was in good mood. His bad moods were like cold showers.

"Did I hear you mention breakfast?"

That sounded friendly enough. "Yes. Give me a minute to get Mary fed, and I'll start ours. I'll make a feast." Studying him more closely, she added. "If you want to go back to bed for an hour, it's fine with me."

"No. Danny's leaving in a couple hours. You can take him to the airport, and I'll stay here and nap with my little beauty queen." Kevin turned to Mary and began to play hide-and-seek with her spoon. "Do we have to see Herr Charles today?"

"He's not German, Kevin," Annie said impatiently. "Yes. We have a one o'clock appointment. We can actually drive."

"That's right," Kevin said without emotion. "We're just like rich folks now. Did you line up Tina to babysit?"

Annie nodded. Since Kevin was playing with the baby, she handed him a bowl of yogurt to feed her. He grimaced but pulled up a chair and began to shovel it in. Mary liked to feed herself, but the yogurt needed an adult.

Thirty minutes later, they sat down to a large breakfast. Afterward, Annie did not bother clearing. They remained at the table and talked. Danny looked like a new person. Clean and fed, you would never guess he had had a late night. At twenty-eight he looked more like twenty. Kevin, on the other hand, looked a little wan.

"Do you want to shower before I leave to take Danny?" Annie asked him.

"I might as well wait until after I nap. I'm going to take Mary out in the yard and get her tired." Kevin rose from the table and went off in search of clothes for the baby. Annie held her seat. Kevin never dressed Mary, but he could certainly do it today. She was reluctant to miss even one minute with her brother.

Kevin congenially dressed the baby and took her outside. Annie cleared the table and started the dishes. Danny lounged on the counter and smoked cigarettes while she worked. Annie could not stop looking at him. It was hard to believe he was sitting here in her kitchen. They talked quickly, jumping from subject to subject. There was so much to say. He was delighted she was starting school and promised to return within the next few months for a proper visit. He said Nelly wanted to come to Texas for spring break.

"Don't tell her I told you," Danny said nervously. They exchanged a glance and began to laugh. How glorious to share a sense of humor! Annie had forgotten what fun could be had in a simple conversation. It was a family joke in the McGowan house. Everything was a secret, but everyone knew everything. The McGowan family members often forgot what they were supposed to know. Many hilarious episodes were the result of botched attempts to surprise each other. They chattered on. In what seemed like minutes, it was time to go. On the way to the airport,

Danny again introduced the subject of his friend.

"I'm thinking, Annie," he said casually. "Maybe Buddy should call and check in with you once in a while."

"Don't let him call me, Danny," Annie said quickly. "I don't want Kevin getting all wild on me."

"Why would he get wild?" her brother demanded. "This guy is a friend of mine."

Annie shifted uncomfortably in the driver's seat. "He gets jealous, Dan. He'll accuse me of having an affair or something. Don't let the guy call me. It will make trouble."

Danny said nothing. Annie was driving and thought she would die of happiness. The airport was eight miles from the town, and she was flying along a two-lane highway.

"Danny, you have no idea how much this car is going to change my life. It's been horrible trying to get around."

"Yeah. You need a car all right," he agreed flatly. "This car is highway ready, Annie. You can drive it back to Chicago any time you want."

"I get it, Danny. Leave me alone." Annie's affectionate smile took the sting from her words.

They hugged at the airport as Annie fought back tears. Being with Danny had reminded her of how terribly she missed her family. "Remember," he called back to her as he left. "Call Buddy for anything you need. Anything at all. One more thing. The girls put some presents and stuff in the trunk." He turned to leave and stopped again. "Merry Christmas, Annie."

Annie smiled. She was too choked up to speak. She cried on the way home. Danny was off to spend Christmas alone in a Japanese hotel. Would it have been better if she had not seen him at all? Not really. It was nice to know that life could bring such wonderful surprises. Also, being with him, even for a short time, reminded Annie of who she was. For some reason she was losing her identity here. She cheered. In less than twenty-four hours she had a car, a mysterious friend named Buddy, and $500 emergency money in case Kevin got nasty again. Hardly a day for complaining.

• • •

Later, Annie and Kevin departed for their counseling session. Kevin was in a foul mood. Annie shot conversation openers at him but was largely ignored. Normally she agonized during Kevin's silent treatments. Today she felt aggravated. One would think Kevin would realize how sad she felt about Danny leaving, she thought resentfully. He should be grateful they had a car. Instead he was stewing about something, and Annie must be punished. She thought bitterly that he ruined every good event in their lives.

The session started off tensely. Charles asked how their communication exercises were going. Kevin was silent. Annie gave an innocuous answer. Charles asked Kevin if there was something bothering him. Kevin looked away, and Annie could have strangled him. She wanted to tell Charles this was all an act. This was Kevin's way of starting a fight out of nothing. She sat back in her chair and watched angrily as Charles tried to coax Kevin to discuss his feelings.

"Charles," she finally interrupted, "this is Kevin's way of saying he is not pleased about something. He'll stay quiet until he explodes. After that, he'll tell us what's bothering him."

Kevin glared at her with hatred. It wouldn't be long, she knew.

Charles also stared at Annie. "Annie," he said sternly, "Kevin has admitted to us that he has difficulty expressing his feelings. It won't help to be unkind."

"I'm not being unkind," she replied. "I'm informing you that there is a pattern. I'm glad this is happening here instead of at home. Kevin," she said kindly, "tell me what's on your mind. If you're mad about something, this is the place to get it off your chest."

"Some things should be discussed privately," he snapped. "I can't believe you would want me to say certain things in front of Charles."

Charles looked intrigued. "Annie," he said professionally, "is there something you do not want Kevin to discuss in front of me?"

Annie kept her face blank. "I can't think what it would be." She turned to Kevin. "Say whatever you like."

Kevin's face reddened. Annie thought with trepidation that Charles had better be careful.

"Why don't you tell him what you were doing after work last night?"

Annie stared at him. Charles stared at her. In spite of herself, her face reddened. Shit, she thought. She probably looked guilty. "Don't start, Kevin. I was talking to Lorena about her boyfriend, and you know it. Why don't we tell Charles what I can't bring up?"

Kevin chuckled meanly. "Why don't we tell Charles about Harold?"

Charles remained quiet.

"Harold is almost a figment of your imagination, Kevin. But yes, I agree, we should tell our counselor about all of these things instead of hiding the dangerous problems." She addressed their counselor, "Charles, as you can see we have a serious trust issue. Kevin does not trust me. There is absolutely no basis for his constant jealously. He freely admits that. Yet he treats me like a tramp waiting to happen. I think this is good. These things have to be worked out, and we both know it."

Kevin gave Charles a beseeching look. "I think she's having an affair." Choking back a sob, he put his face in his hands.

Annie sputtered in rage. "You liar." She searched for words. "Kevin, you are either mentally ill or the most manipulative person I've ever met. Look at me," she demanded. He kept his head in his hands and shook his head.

Charles intervened. "Kevin," he said gently touching Kevin's knee. "Can you do something for me?" Kevin nodded, head in hands. "Can you look at Annie and tell h[er] how you feel?" He nodded again.

Kevin looked up dramatically. "You're tearing m[e] Annie."

Annie checked her temper. "How, Kevin? Tell me specifically how I'm tearing you apart."

"You know how. The constant flirting and fooling around. I can't take it anymore."

Annie rolled her eyes. Kevin jumped from his chair, pushing it back violently into the wall.

"Did you see that?" he demanded, looking at Charles. "Every time I tell her how I feel, she rolls her eyes at me. She constantly minimizes my feelings. I can't take it anymore." Choking back sobs, he fled the room.

Charles flew out after him. Annie heard him pleading with Kevin in the hallway. Kevin refused to come back and eventually stormed out of the building. Charles came slowly back into the room.

Annie gripped the sides of her chair. She was stunned. Charles, too, looked shaken. He also looked angry.

"It's not his fault," Annie instinctively defended her husband. "He had a lot of problems growing up."

"I don't think Kevin is the problem here, Annie," the counselor said coldly.

"Pardon me?"

"How can you be so insensitive?" Charles asked her. "The man was baring his soul to you, and you rolled your eyes. Are you having an affair?"

Annie was speechless. She sputtered for a few moments and then stopped. "Go to hell, Charles. You're as nutty as Kevin."

Annie rose to leave. Turning back, she added, "Kevin plays you like a violin. I've tried to tell you what's going on. The only thing that matters in this room is Kevin and his pretend feelings. Have you ever once asked Kevin to listen _____ ause he fooled you, too. This is sup- _____ counseling. Kevin is a violent man. _____ d ever focused on my feelings, you _____ out."

_____ her in disbelief. "Are you certain _____ se things to justify some of your

Annie shook her head. "Charles, Kevin knows I'm not having an affair. He does live in fear that I'll find someone else. But he knows I'm not unfaithful. He was saying that for your benefit. He probably thought you were coming on to me or something." It was obvious that Charles did not believe her. "You, Charles, are a lightweight. I just hope you didn't get me killed."

Chapter Nineteen

nnie closed the door on Herr Charles. She stood in the lobby uncertainly. Naturally, Kevin has the keys and the car, she thought resentfully. The car would be one more area of control for Kevin. Annie felt a fleeting moment of despair. She should have gone with Danny.

Taking a breath, Annie left the building. Kevin could ignore her until hell froze over. She would ignore him right back. That small voice told Annie that his silence would be the least of her problems. Annie decided to take the bull by the horns this time. If Kevin began to act violent, she would leave. She had the money. She had the car. She might even be home for Christmas. Annie smiled at the thought. Like submerging in a cold bath, the realization struck her that Kevin would never allow her to leave. She would have to escape.

Mulling it over, she began to walk down the street. Half a block later, the car screeched to a halt beside her. Kevin opened the door on her side.

"Get in," he barked.

"No thank you, Kevin," she retorted. "You just acted a beautiful scene back there. Now you want me to GET IN? Go to hell!" Annie resumed walking.

Her back was to the car. She heard the door slam and turned to see Kevin charging her. "Don't touch me, Kevin," she warned quickly. "I swore to you I would leave, and I meant it." Kevin stopped two feet from her. His face was contorted in rage. He wants to kill me, she thought wonderingly. He really does. "Kevin, take some deep breaths. Let it pass," Annie soothed him. "It's me. I'm not your enemy. I love you, and I'm here because I want to be."

Kevin turned abruptly and got back in the car. Annie stood on the sidewalk. If she had any sense, she would run. She knew that. But Mary was at home. So was the money. And Kevin had the car. Annie needed ten minutes in the house by herself. She also needed the car keys. Kevin must be placated for now. She approached the car.

"Are you calm?" she asked. Kevin nodded his head. "Am I safe to get in the car and go home with you, Kevin?" He nodded his head. Annie took a deep breath and held it. She could hardly make him sign a promissory note. Sending up a frantic prayer, she got in.

Kevin took off from the curb like he had been launched. They nearly collided with a truck at the first intersection when he ran a red light. Annie held on to her seat belt and cursed herself for getting in.

"Kevin!," she shouted. "Slow down, dammit!"

He slammed on the breaks. Annie was braced but still hit her head on the dashboard. "Oh, God," she started to cry. "Why are you doing this to me?"

Kevin punched the seat next to her head. Annie put her hand on the door knob and began to shift her weight. Kevin lightly grabbed her hand and placed it in her lap.

"You're not getting out. And I'll tell you why. I'm not going to hurt you. You have me over a barrel, and you love it."

Annie looked him squarely in the eye. "What are we talking about now, Kevin?"

"I can't lay a hand on you, or you'll leave. Fine. I won't touch you. Even when you deserve it."

"What do I deserve, Kevin?" Annie shouted back. "Why would I deserve to get beat up?"

He spoke through gritted teeth. "Because God only knows what you were doing last night after work. Acting all sweet in front of your brother doesn't cut it. If Danny knew how you were, he would be disgusted."

"What, Kevin? What would I have done in fifteen minutes?"

Kevin sighed and seemed to relax.

"Is it over, Kevin? Can we go home?"

Whenever he wanted to hurt her, he told her things about her family. He said they talked to him about her. He once said that Maureen had admitted Annie was a flirt. Annie assumed he was making it up. It hurt, though, and he knew it.

Kevin put the car in gear and began to drive. He was calm now. Annie looked straight ahead. Hopefully the worst was over. After a couple of miles she felt his hand on top of hers. Annie glanced over at him. He looked at her beseechingly.

"Annie, please don't be mad," he said quietly. "I'm sorry."

"You're always sorry, Kevin."

"How come you did not come home right after work?" he asked in a passionate voice. "Just tell me the truth, and I won't get mad."

"I was talking to Lorena about her boyfriend. He left again, and she's upset."

"Fine. That's all I wanted to hear. Sorry." Pulling her hand up to his mouth, he kissed it gently. Annie compelled herself not to cringe. He was repugnant to her. That nearly drowned her in guilt. "Kevin," she said hurriedly, "we want to have a nice Christmas. Right?"

"Absolutely."

"Let's not fight then. Is it really over?"

"Yes, Annie," he said with finality. "I'm fine. I started

249

feeling insecure seeing you have such a good time with Danny. You never laugh like that with me anymore. I think that's what started it."

"Kevin, Danny is my brother. You can't be jealous of him."

"Stupid," he agreed. "But wait a minute. I got mad and did not hurt you." He grinned at her. "See, I told you I would never hurt you again."

Annie smiled wanly back at him. He had nearly put her through the windshield. She peered into the future. Kevin would not hurt her physically anymore. That would be wonderful, of course, and he did deserve credit. He would, however, torment her emotionally. Depression sat down firmly on her lap. She wondered if he controlled himself today because they were in public. It was possible and did not bode well for the evening.

If the tantrum was indeed over, he would be nice for a couple of days. That ought to take them through Christmas. No more seeing Charles, though. Annie wanted to see Caroline. Looking at her watch, she saw it was nearly three. It was Friday. Christmas was on Wednesday. Caroline would probably not be in until Thursday. Annie felt the old ache of loneliness returning. Caroline was the only one who understood.

Kevin was stroking her hand, and Annie fought the urge to slap him. After a fight he had an intense need for reassurance. Conversely, Annie despised her husband after an argument. He fought dirty and then waved his magic wand. According to Kevin, once he apologized, it was over. No matter what he had done, she was expected to immediately forgive him.

"Annie," Kevin said as they pulled into their parking lot. "I forgot to tell you. I'm going out tonight."

"Fine," she said in surprise. "Where are you going?"

"Any players who did not go home are getting together at a bar. Kind of an informal Christmas party. I'm going with Greg. The Kemps are not going home until tomorrow. You don't mind, do you?"

Annie tried not to be too enthusiastic. "Not at all. It will give me a chance to get ready for Christmas. I need to decorate and look through my cookbook. I got a turkey for our Christmas dinner." Kevin smiled at her affectionately. "Kevin," Annie said suddenly. "We can go to Mass on Christmas day."

Kevin laughed. "We can go to Mass every Sunday if you want. We have wheels, Annie." They both laughed, and Annie felt a little better. She would have the evening to herself. She would think about this fight and what she needed to do for the future. She was always glad to see Kevin getting out. She reasoned that the more he went out, the more he might relax about her getting out. So far it had not happened. He pretty much stayed home.

Annie exited the car. "Are you coming in?"

Kevin remained in the driver seat. "I think I'll take the car out for a ride. I need to do some Christmas shopping and cool down. You know?"

"Good idea, Kevin," she said warmly. "And I do realize that you controlled yourself today. That was good."

He smiled sheepishly and waved. Annie climbed the stairs slowly. Mentally exhausted, she decided to call Caroline. The thought speeded her steps, and she quickly dispatched Tina. Mary was still napping so Annie had peace. Without taking off her jacket, she dialed the number. For the first time she was put directly through to Caroline's office.

Annie told her about the fight. She told her about Danny's money and the car. She asked Caroline if it was terrible that she did not want to see Charles anymore.

"Not at all," came the clipped response. Annie pictured Caroline and could almost hear the delicate tinkling of jewelry. "Honey, you get any more marriage counseling, and you'll end up dead."

"That's how I feel," Annie said in relief. "Kevin uses it to manipulate me or something. I'm not sure what's happening, but it's not good."

"I agree. Annie," Caroline said calmly. "I'm in the office

tomorrow. Why don't you come in and see me? Do you think you can get away?"

"I'll try," she said hesitantly. "I don't know if he'll let me. It might start everything up again."

"I understand," the counselor said easily. "I'm not busy, though, and I'll be here all day. Give me a call if you can swing it. Bring the baby. I'm a little worried about you. Are you sure he's over this last thing? Holidays are a dangerous time for women in your situation."

"Don't tell me that, Caroline," Annie said despondently. "I was just thinking in the car that the reason this whole thing happened was because he knows how excited I am about Christmas. He seems to ruin everything that makes me happy." Annie hesitated. "Caroline," she said in a small voice, "I think he wants to kill me. It sounds insane, but I saw it in his eyes."

"It does not sound insane, Annie. You know him better than anyone. I don't think you're safe there, Annie. That's my gut instinct." Caroline was speaking quickly as though she were afraid to let Annie hang up. "Are you sure you won't consider leaving?"

Annie was staring out of the back window. Letting her breath out, she realized she had been holding it.

"I'd have to get the car keys. Somehow I would have to get out of the house, by myself. With Mary." Annie continued to think aloud. "You know what's weird, Caroline?"

"What's that?"

"Less than an hour ago I thought he was going to kill me. Then he kissed my hand and told me he was going to get me a Christmas present. Before that he told our counselor that I was having an affair and stormed out of the room. Then he drove like a maniac and nearly put me through the windshield. Now I'm sitting here, and I don't know if I should leave or not. I must be as nutty as him."

"It's tough, isn't it?" Caroline empathized.

"Yep. It sure is." Annie frowned in concentration. "Part of my problem is that I'm so tired. I can't decide what to make for dinner never mind whether or not I should grab my child and run for my life. Am I blowing this out of proportion? He did not hit me, Caroline."

"That's true, Annie," Caroline said professionally. "He controlled himself because he wanted to. Will he want to tonight when you're trapped in the apartment with him? He nearly got you killed today. You said yourself that you could see that he wanted to kill you. That stuff does not just disappear, Annie. It's all there, waiting for the next trigger."

"I can't leave him alone for Christmas, Caroline. It would be too mean. I think I'll try to get through the holidays and then take stock. I think it's over, Caroline. I really do. I can't stay with him. It's a matter of doing it as painlessly as possible."

"I see." Caroline said nonjudgmentally. "I know that hurts a lot, Annie. It takes a lot of guts to get out of something like this. Will you do me a favor, Honey?"

"Sure. What?"

"Call me tomorrow and let me know how you're doing. OK?"

Annie promised and hung up. She felt much better. Someone understood. Caroline wanted her to call the next day to make sure she was safe. It was a warm and comforting feeling. Annie wished she could sort out her feelings for Kevin as easily. In the last few hours they had run the gamut. Remembering she had missed a good bit of sleep the night before, she lay down on the couch. Even if Mary got up in ten minutes, she would have a rest.

She dozed fitfully. Thirty minutes later, Mary woke up. Annie entered the kitchen as though in a trance. Her mind jumped from idea to idea. Should she leave tonight? Logically, yes. Kevin's moods were all over the board the last few days. If he left the car and rode with Greg tonight, she would have an opportunity. Annie decided she could drive to the nearest town and get a hotel there. She resisted the urge to call home. There was nothing anyone could do right away. The explanations alone would exhaust her.

At five-fifteen Kevin came in. He looked happy. Too happy. He probably took out a life insurance policy on me,

Annie thought irrationally. He made a big production of hiding her present in the linen closet. Normally, Annie would have been excited. She loved presents. Tonight she felt morbid and depressed.

She threw together sloppy joes for dinner. Kevin raved about them. She made a point to talk about Christmas day so he would not suspect she was considering escape. Kevin chattered. He thought it was great that they were spending the holiday alone. Annie smiled. She was going to love her present. Would Annie like to guess what it was? Annie thought she would fall over dead if she had to play this out much longer. Clothes? Jewelry? Kevin laughed too loudly. She wondered if the hangover was making him manic. She asked him if he felt tired. No. Just excited about going out tonight.

Annie cautioned him against drinking too much. She casually suggested that he let Greg drive so he would not have to worry about driving drunk. No way! he exclaimed. Part of the fun was driving his own car. That settled it. Annie felt relieved. She could decorate the house and go to bed. Everything would seem less sinister in the morning.

"Kevin, I'm going grocery shopping in the morning," she said cheerfully. "Why don't Mary and I let you sleep in? I'm going to try to catch Mass as well."

Kevin poked his head around the corner of the kitchen. "I won't be out late, Annie. I'd love to go to Mass in the morning." He smiled. He was talking too fast again. "Unless you're up to something and don't want me to go." This was intended to be a joke, but Annie sensed the underlying threat.

"Not at all," she said breezily. "Your presents are all bought and wrapped." She smiled at him, deliberately mis-understanding. "I'm not spending another penny."

"Good. We can't afford it. I'm jumping in the shower."

Mary hung on her leg. Annie was preoccupied and opened the pots and pans cabinet. Mary eyed it steadily. Without warning she let go of Annie's leg and toddled over to it. Grabbing the top of the cabinet, she turned to Annie with a look of amazement on her face. Annie cheered and clapped. Mary gurgled in delight, rocking back and forth on her heels. She was walking. After much praise and kisses, Annie went back to the dishes. She wanted to weep. Another joyful milestone and she was too strung out to enjoy it. Kevin went in to the shower happy. For all she knew he would come out with a gun. Maybe he had stopped for the gun after he got the insurance policy. Annie giggled. Kevin would not think it through that much. He would just kill her. While wiping the counters, Annie decided to call home tonight. She needed a dose of sanity. She found a lighter on the counter. Had it really only been this morning that Danny sat there and laughed with her? Annie felt her eyes well up again.

At that moment Kevin came into the room. "What's the matter?" he asked sharply.

She began to sob loudly. "I'm homesick," she burst out. "I miss my sisters and Danny and my dad. And then we had the fight today and Mary started walking and it's all too much."

Blessedly, Kevin did not take offense. Annie usually did not bring up homesickness because it made him feel insecure. Tonight he was touched. "That's why you're acting so strangely. I knew something was wrong," he said as he took her in his arms. "I thought you were planning to leave me." He stroked her head soothingly. "It's OK, Annie. It's natural that you're homesick. I'm a little homesick myself But we've got each other. And Mary." Kevin looked around. "Where is she by the way?"

Annie's voice was muffled by Kevin's shirt front. "In the cabinet. She crawls inside to get the pots out."

"She's quiet anyway." Kevin continued to console her, "Annie, I'm sorry about today. I'm acting mean, and I know it. Maybe it's the holidays. I'm fine now. I want you to have a wonderful Christmas."

Annie nodded her head and let herself be comforted. Maybe he was right. A lot of people got strange around the holidays. He promised she could spend Christmas day on the phone if she liked. Come to think of it, Annie should put the baby down tonight and call home. The hell with the bill, he said. He was going out so Annie should also have a treat. Annie smiled genuinely. "Thanks, Kevin. I feel much better," she said honestly as she wiped her eyes. "I love you so much when you're like this."

A look of pain crossed his face. "I'm not like this often enough."

"You try your hardest, and I know that." She spoke with warm affection.

He pulled her to him again. "Would you rather I stayed in tonight?"

Annie thought about it. Kevin was on best behavior so she was safe. And if truth be told she did not want to leave him. Not now. Not ever. She simply wanted him to be nice.

"No. You never get out. I'm OK." Thinking for a minute, she added, "But Kevin, can you get home by eleven or so? I won't be able to sleep till your home, and I don't want to be up late. Is that fair?"

"Absolutely. If I'm going to be later then ten, I'll call. Deal?"

"Deal."

He went to get his coat. Annie was playing peek-a-boo with Mary who was still inside the bottom cabinets.

"Have a pleasant evening, Mrs. Griffin," Kevin said as he kissed her. "I left a little treat for you by the phone."

Annie raised her eyebrows and waved good bye. She immediately walked over to the phone. There on the handset was a pack of cigarettes. She laughed out loud. This was his way of saying she could stop pretending. Annie raced to the back door and stepped out onto the porch. Kevin was getting into the car. "Thank you for my treat," she called down laughing.

He looked up and grinned. Putting one hand across his chest, he bowed deeply. "Whatever it takes, my lady."

Annie inclined her head in a flirty manner. This was the Kevin she loved. She felt lighthearted and happy. Kevin could be lovely when he wanted to. Annie entered the house with renewed vigor. This was just the kind of pleasant evening she needed.

She filled the tub with a mountain of bubbles. Splashing with Mary consumed the better part of an hour, and it was after eight before she tucked her little one into bed. Annie dragged the presents out of the bedroom so she would not awaken the child later. Wrapped in a warm robe, she contemplated. Should she call home first or decorate the house? There was no tree yet. The Griffins were waiting until Christmas Eve in the hope that prices would be more favorable to their budget. She decided to decorate first.

Garland and ornaments were strewn on the floor. Working steadily, she soon transformed the little flat. A small wreath and a Santa Claus hung on the doors. Bright garland held silver ornaments across the wall in the dining room. Chintzy but festive. She took great care in arranging the Nativity. An old lace drapery folded in fourths covered the television set. It looked pretty, and she figured they could flip it back when they wanted to watch something. She smiled in satisfaction. A few strands of colored lights added the magical quality she had yearned for. This would cheer them up.

She was about to call when she remembered the box from home. Like a child she ran into the hallway and opened it. There were several small packages for Mary along with one marked for Kevin and Annie. Annie held the presents in her hands. Closing her eyes, she imagined her sisters wrapping them. A thought popped into her head, and she turned them over. Sure enough. They were fastened with electrical tape. Annie laughed in delight. The McGowan family never had any tape in the house. True to form, the girls had gone down into Mr. McGowan's tools for the silver electrical tape.

Dropping the presents back into the box, she climbed up onto the counter and grabbed an ashtray. She was ready. For the next thirty minutes she chatted happily with her sisters. Eileen had sent a very special present. It was wrapped in Bambi paper but was for the whole family.

Maureen was on a date, but Nellie filled her in on the local gossip. After thirty minutes had elapsed, Annie reluctantly told Nellie that she had to go.

Annie was still sitting at the table when the phone rang. It was Nellie. She figured they could talk for another thirty minutes on the McGowan phone bill. Annie laughed in delight and settled down for another long chat. Nellie said Mr. McGowan would be calling in the morning. And they would certainly call on Christmas eve and Christmas day. Nellie also informed her that Mr. McGowan had met Mrs. Griffin in the drug store. The two parents agreed to split the difference from now on and fly the young family home for Christmas. That was good news. Next year she would be home. If she was still here at all. She dismissed the depressing thought and promised Nellie that she would stay home in the morning until her father called. Once again, they hung up.

Annie glanced at the clock. It was nearly nine-thirty. Kevin would be home soon. Annie was anxious to fill him in on the news. She turned off the big lights and left only the Christmas lights on. The little apartment looked cozy and warm. Annie stretched out on the couch. Everything would work out, she promised herself. If she were looking on the bright side, she would note that Kevin had indeed controlled himself. Had he really wanted to kill her or was that her imagination? It was too late for those thoughts. She focused instead on the Kevin who had grinned up at her before he left.

She awoke with a start. Kevin was still not home, and Annie wandered groggily into the kitchen to check the time. It was midnight! Annie felt a squeeze in her stomach. If Kevin was still drinking, he would be very drunk. That was not good. Kevin got nasty when he got drunk. Also, why had he not called at ten? Especially after how sweetly he had left her.

The phone rang nearly sending Annie through the roof She grabbed it quickly before it could ring again and wake the baby.

"Annie," said a tense female voice. "It's Darlene. Were you sleeping?"

"No. I was just wondering where Kevin was," she answered honestly. "Is Greg home?"

"Actually, that's why I'm calling." Darlene was very upset. "I was up packing, you know, we're leaving tomorrow at five, and Greg came in. He's kind of loaded but not too bad."

Darlene had a tendency to run on, and Annie was impatient. "Where's Kevin?"

Darlene paused. "That's why I'm calling. Annie, you're going to kill me."

"Why, Darlene?"

"I'm so sorry. Greg and I had a fight the other night. He never gets jealous. He doesn't seem to care about me at all." Annie listened patiently. There was no hurrying this woman. "Anyway, I told him what you said about Kevin. I'm really sorry. I swear it never occurred to me for a minute that he would tell Kevin."

Annie's stomach was now in complete lock down. She held it with one hand while she tried to get more information.

"Darlene, what did I say about Kevin?"

Annie heard Darlene take a breath. "That if he knew about Bill, the stock boy, he would beat him up."

Annie looked around the apartment frantically. "Oh, my God. Oh, God, Darlene, how could you? Tell me exactly what Greg told him. Quick! I have to get out of here!"

Darlene was crying. "Annie, what's wrong with Kevin? Greg said he was freaking out. I would not have called, only Greg made me. He said Kevin was going nuts in the parking lot of the bar. He finally took off in the car, driving like a maniac. Greg said I had to call and warn you. Who is Harold?"

"Harold?" Annie said in bewilderment. "What does Harold have to do with anything?"

"Kevin told Greg that you had an affair with some guy named Harold before you were married and that he suspected you had something going on at work." Darlene

259

stopped talking long enough to give a large sniffle. "Do you, Annie?"

"Kevin is out of his mind. Tell me exactly what Greg said to him."

"He only said that there was some stock boy at work that liked you. He said it as a joke. They were talking about wives and stuff, and Greg was pretending to be mad at Kevin for making the rest of them look bad. He said this guy was flirting with you at work. I swear, Annie. That's all he could have told Kevin because that's all I told Greg."

"Darlene," Annie reminded her, "that's all there was to tell. When would I ever see this guy?"

Darlene's voice warmed. "That's what Greg tried to tell Kevin. Did you know that Kevin checks your pay stubs to make sure you're working when you say you are? Anyway, Greg tried to tell Kevin that it was impossible. He says he talked to him for over an hour, trying to calm him down, but Kevin was nuts. Annie, I'm so sorry." Darlene started to cry again. "I knew right after I told him I should not have. But he didn't think it was a big deal. Honestly. Greg thought the whole thing was a big joke until Kevin went crazy."

"I have to go, Darlene," Annie said tensely. "He's going to kill me. Shit! I should get out of here."

"He'll get over it, Annie," Darlene tried to comfort her. "They get mad, but it blows over."

"You don't know Kevin," she said in despair. "I don't know what to do."

"Are you serious?" Darlene sounded scared. "You're not really thinking of leaving. Are you?"

"Darlene, you don't understand. Kevin is going to kill me. I have to get out of here."

"Well, where are you going to go?"

"I don't know. Can I come to your apartment?"

"Oh, Annie," Darlene said sadly. "You know I'd love to help you. But I don't think Greg wants to get involved. Kevin really scared him. Is there somewhere else you can go?"

"Yes," she said coldly. "I'm sure I'll think of something."

Annie hung up the phone. Her hands were shaking violently. There would be no point explaining anything. This was as close as Kevin had ever gotten to hard evidence. Annie knew from experience that she could talk till the cows came home. She ran to the bedroom. Her breath was coming in shallow gulps. If he got home, she knew, she might die tonight. Pushing her hand into the diaper bag she felt around for the money. She would grab the baby and call a cab. No. She could not even wait that long. She would get out of the apartment first. She could walk to the gas station and call the cab from there. Annie frantically began to pull diapers from the bag. In desperation she turned the bag upside down and emptied it. A small piece of paper fell out. Annie held it close to her eyes. It was in Kevin's hand writing.

"Who is Buddy, and where did you get the money?"

A chill ran through her body. Annie dropped the paper like it was a snake. Kevin had her money.

"Oh, God. Help me, God," she muttered frantically. She opened her drawers and pulled out a pair of pants. Stripping off her bathrobe she pulled the pants up. She needed shoes and a blanket for the baby. She would walk to the nearest street and flag down a car. Someone would take her to the police station, and she would call home from there. Her hands shook violently as she tore through the closet looking for shoes. She ended up with boots and jammed her feet into them.

Frantically, she searched for the baby's jacket. She would have to go without it. Annie ran to the crib and grabbed her tiny daughter. Wrapping the blanket snugly around the child, she cuddled her against her chest. She would not even bother with her purse.

She was two steps from the front door when she saw the knob turning.

Chapter Twenty

Annie stopped breathing. Backing up, she headed for the kitchen door. Footsteps pounded behind her, but she never paused. She was halfway down the stairs when Kevin grabbed a handful of her hair.

Stopping dead in her tracks, Annie said softly, "Let me go, Kevin. You're drunk. I don't want to talk to you like this."

"Nice try, Annie," he said turning her around by her hair. "Don't scream. Walk up the stairs."

"Kevin, let me go," Annie repeated calmly. She was holding the baby snugly to her chest. Her head was being pulled almost sideways but she did not complain. Instinctively, she knew two things. If she made any fast moves or reentered the apartment with him, she would die.

Kevin reeked of alcohol. Annie noted in dismay that the smell was not beer. More like whiskey. She would have to be more careful than she had ever been in her life.

"Up the stairs, slut. Quietly. If you scream I'll kill you and the baby. I don't want to live anymore anyway. Then we can all be together forever."

They were still on the stairs. Annie was in a quandary. He was pulling her steadily by her hair. She was afraid to fight with the baby in her arms. They were on the third floor, and a fall could be fatal for Mary. She remembered Caroline saying something about suicide. Suicidal abusers were extremely dangerous. Annie doubted Kevin would kill himself sober. Drunk ... there was no telling. He pushed her to the railing.

"Walk, Annie or you're both going over."

Kevin made the decision for her. She could not go over the railing with the baby. Her breaths came slowly. Each was separate. A lifetime long. Annie began to climb the stairs. Kevin stayed behind her with her hair in his hand. He had it right by the roots so she could barely move her neck.

"Kevin, don't do this. Let me go put the baby down, and we'll talk. I know you don't want to hurt me."

An ugly laugh exploded from him. "You wish I didn't want to hurt you. Frankly, Annie, the jig is up. Get your ass in the house, and we'll figure out what to do with you." Annie still did not move. "I mean it, Annie." Kevin twisted the handful of hair, and Annie sucked in her breath. "Move now, or I'll hurt the baby, too."

Annie entered the apartment. It would have been better if she had been lying on the couch when he arrived. Seeing her trying to escape had confirmed every bad thought in his head. She should have left this afternoon. She should have left with Danny. She should never have married him after the incident in the car when she was pregnant. She should have....

"Put the baby in the crib."

Annie went to the bedroom. Her whole body seemed suspended. This was a nightmare. Annie was experienced with nightmares. Normally she could wake herself up. She commanded herself to wake up. Nothing happened. Annie put Mary in her crib and gently covered her up. Mary opened her eyes briefly and smiled up at her mommy. "Pray for us, Mary," she whispered. The child closed her eyes peacefully.

Annie closed the door and stood in the hallway.

"Get me a glass," he commanded. There was a bottle of Jack Daniel in front of him. Annie went into the kitchen. She toyed with the idea of a desperate lunge out the back door. Reading her thoughts, Kevin slurred, "If you're thinking of running again, let me promise you one thing. I'll kill Mary if you get away. Just so you know where we stand."

Annie figured as much. This time she knew it was not safe to leave her child. She would have to hope he kept drinking and passed out. She would encourage him to drink. Annie got a large glass and put only two ice cubes in it. Placing it in front of him, she started to head for the living room. The fight must be kept away from the baby at all costs. Kevin rose and walked to the phone. He staggered slightly, and Annie was encouraged. Kevin could hold a mass quantity of alcohol, but he was not accustomed to hard stuff. From the looks of the bottle, half empty, he had a sizable head start.

Reaching the desk he picked up the phone. He smiled over at Annie and with an abrupt motion pulled it from the wall.

"Just in case you get in a chatty mood. Tonight you're going to talk to me." He threw the phone into the kitchen and sat back down. "Sit down here with me and talk. Tell me all about your stock boy. How many times did you fuck him?"

Annie walked over to the table and sat down. "You know I would never do that, Kevin."

"Wrong answer," he yelled. Reaching over he knocked her out of the chair. Annie lay still on the floor. He pulled her up by her shirt and placed her back on the chair. "Let's try it again. How many times did you fuck him?" Annie remained silent. "ANSWER ME!"

"I never touched him, and he never touched me."

Slam. Back on the floor. This time Annie's head hit the corner of the wall. She felt no pain. Only confusion. After he lifted her back onto the chair, she realized she was bleeding. Must be a cut on her head.

"Sloppy bitch," he sneered. "You're making a mess all over the table. Go get a towel."

Annie dutifully went into the bathroom and grabbed a towel. It was one of her guest towels. She used it anyway. She purposely did not glance in the mirror. She had no desire to see the look in her eyes.

Sitting back down at the table she held the towel to her head.

"Poor pitiful Annie," he continued to sneer. "Stuck with a jerk like me. What did you ever do to deserve this? Miss Smarty Pants. Too bad I'm a little smarter than you, Annie. Right?" She remained silent. "ANSWER ME, BITCH, OR I'LL RIP YOUR FUCKING HEART OUT!"

"Yes, Kevin," she said quietly. "You're smarter than me."

"You know it, Annie. Which is why you're in such trouble right now. You were going to leave today. Or tonight. That's why I took the car. You'll never get your hands on this car. Where you're going you won't need a car. You're going to burn in hell. Because that's where you belong. In hell. You should not be allowed to touch that child in there. Your hands are evil. What did you do to Bill with those hands? I can't stop wondering. Tell me what he looks like."

"Kevin, there is absolutely nothing between me and this guy. Let me tell you what happened. OK? It's not as bad as you're imagining."

Kevin considered for a minute. "No. First we're going to open our Christmas presents. Go get them. I want to see what kind of presents my whoring little wife bought me."

"Kevin, let me just tell you..."

"LIES? YOU WANT TO TELL ME LIES?" Kevin was screaming. Lowering his voice, he continued. "Don't tell me one thing, Annie. Just for tonight, do exactly what I tell you. If you talk back or argue or piss me off in any way, I'm going to kill you. You know that. If you want to stay alive ... DO WHAT I FUCKING TELL YOU!" He paused for a large swallow of whiskey. "Go get my presents."

Annie went into the living room and got the presents. It was one-thirty in the morning. He had been drinking for four hours. Annie wondered how long he could hold out. She wondered idly if he would kill her. She did not care anymore. If he killed her, it would be over. She could rest. She thought sadly of Mary. If Kevin killed her, at least he could not get custody of Mary. Mary would go to the McGowans. They would take good care of her, Annie knew. She did ask God for one thing. Mary must be spared. And not frightened. Annie felt a peace come over her. God had heard.

She deposited the presents in front of Kevin on the table. He ordered her to sit down. She did. He began a tirade about Christmas. It would have been wonderful if Annie had not ruined it. At two o'clock he opened his first present. The tool kit.

"How nice," he crooned in an ugly way. Taking them out of the plastic organizer, he threw them at her one by one. Annie covered her face as the metal tools bounced off her head. "Just perfect for throwing at sluts. Look on the package, Annie. What does it say?"

Annie glanced at the box. "Great for household chores."

Kevin hit her in the head with the box. "Wrong again. It says 'just perfect for throwing at sluts.' You're so smart, but you can't read. You're going to flunk out of college. Read it again."

"Perfect for throwing at sluts," she intoned.

Kevin laughed uproariously. "That's better. Maybe I'll let you live."

Annie looked down at the table. She was unprepared for the blow to the front of her chest. She flew backward into the wall and then onto the floor. Her head struck the wall and the floor. Annie felt something snap in her wrist. She was stunned but still felt no pain. She lay on the floor, unable to rise. Kevin loomed above her. He kicked at her gently with his foot.

"Get up, Annie. I want to talk to you."

Annie could not move. She heard him from a distance. She knew she should get up before he got madder. For some reason her body would not respond. Suddenly she felt a brutal kick in her stomach. She curled up instinctively and covered her face. The kicking went on for what seemed like an eternity. Kevin was methodical. He worked his way from the back of her neck down to her feet. Annie remained curled up. The back of her body was preferable to her face and stomach.

Eons passed, and the kicking stopped. Annie lay still. She heard Kevin return to the table and fill his glass. He was breathing heavily and muttering to himself Annie sensed his confusion. She was now mentally alert but remained inert. Let him think he killed her. She thought of a possum and felt pity for the rancorous animal.

Kevin began to cry. She could not make out what he was saying. He repeated a sentence over and over. Whatever it was held no consolation for him because he continued to cry and mumble.

Unaware of time, Annie remained on the floor. Hazy thoughts floated past her. She pictured the Christmas tree in the McGowan living room. One by one, Annie identified the ornaments. There was the fat snowman with the light stuck in the belly. There was always an argument over whether or not to use a colored light. The little snowman. No light necessary. A beat up homemade ornament boasted a picture of Nellie in the middle. This was the result of a Girl Scout craft. How it survived so many years was a mystery. Annie continued to mentally scan the tree. Too much tinsel. Always was. The girls could never agree on when to stop. When their mother was alive, she had set limits.

Under the tree was a white sheet strewn artfully by Maureen. The Nativity was displayed there with its own strand of white lights. There was no real theme to this tree, Annie discovered. Pink balls jockeyed for position with red balls. They all hated the pink balls, but for some reason they never disappeared. Only the nice ornaments broke or vanished. Why was that, Annie wondered. It was the same with sunglasses and socks. You could not lose the obnoxious ones. She realized then a great truth about ornaments, socks, and sunglasses. The cheap ones were also lost. It was only that people failed to notice because they did not grieve the loss. The experience had no impact. Now if a person were to lose a really good pair of sunglasses, or break a treasured ornament, he or she felt sad. They grieved. People remembered feelings of sadness. Annie's head was clearing. She reminded herself to remember this great truth she had discovered. The sisters would find it interesting. Annie allowed her mind to reenter the Griffin household. Kevin was quiet. Was he sleeping?

"Bitch," she heard him mutter.

Apparently not. His voice was terrifically slurred. Annie opened her eyes a slit. There was blood. Lots of it. Also, the tiny act of opening her eyes had awakened the rest of her body. Annie was hurting.

Hearing the scrape of his chair, she closed her eyes again. She sensed him standing over her.

"Are you dead, Annie? Did I kill you?" Kevin was jabbing her mouth with his foot. "Are you faking? I'm not calling an ambulance. Get up."

Annie remained motionless.

"GET UP, I SAID!"

With that, he kicked her in the mouth. Annie shouted out loud and covered her head. She could hear Kevin's ugly laugh. A feeling of rage engulfed her. Let him kill me, she thought. Either way. But I'm not going to die like a dog. Annie rolled into a sitting position with her back against the wall. She spit to clear the blood. Grabbing the leg of an overturned chair, she tried to hoist herself into a sitting position. A spear of pain shot up her left arm. Her hand was not working. The agony made her scream.

"DIE, KEVIN," she shouted. "Die slowly! Kill me, too. I don't care. You're not hurting me because I don't care anymore. If I die, I won't have to be with you."

Kevin backed around the table and sat down again. He never took his eyes off her. Annie held her left arm in her right hand and stared at him. She no longer felt any fear. Just hatred.

"You think you're so powerful because you can throw me around." She paused for breath. Breathing was painful for some reason. "You're not, Kevin. Only bullies and cowards beat up people that can't fight back. It means nothing. Kill me if you want. It won't change a thing."

Kevin drained his glass, and Annie walked past him into the living room. It was five o'clock. There was no sign of the sun yet. If she could stay alive for another couple of hours, something would happen. Surely daylight would end this torment.

Annie lay gently down on the couch and closed her eyes. She did not dare enter the bedroom because she knew it was not over. He was still awake. At all costs she had to keep the fight away from Mary. Hearing him get up, she suppressed a cry. Oh, God, strike him dead! she implored helplessly.

Pulling the rocking chair up to the couch, Kevin lowered himself heavily. He was still drinking but had dispatched with the glass. Annie noticed that less than a fourth of the bottle remained. Maybe I should play quarters with him, she thought darkly. Annie had always beat him at the drinking game.

"Annie," he spoke heavily, "in spite of your brave little speech, this is far from over. I need more information before I decide if I'm going to let you live. Who is Buddy, and why is he giving you money? Are you getting paid for fucking?"

Annie considered. There was no real course of action that would protect her. From what she had seen in the past, she was going to get assaulted no matter what she did. Fighting back? That just delighted him. Attempts at self-defense justified his abuse. The trick was to stay alive. Annie realized at that moment that she had absolutely no control over her life.

"Buddy is a friend of Danny's. I have never met him or spoken with him. Danny gave me the money in case we ever had an emergency. He gave me Buddy's number because Buddy works in the same company. He said if there was a family emergency, like if someone died, we should call Buddy, and he would know where to reach Danny. It's as simple as that."

Kevin stared at her through bleary eyes. An ugly smirk twisted his face. "You're such a good liar, Annie," he said admiringly. "I almost believe you. Were you surprised when you discovered I had found your hiding spot?"

"Yes, I was." Annie kept her tone matter of fact in spite of the hysteria that was lurking beneath her conscious thinking. "I was surprised that you did not mention it to me. If I had found that much money, I would have gone right to you for an explanation. It was meant to be a surprise, Kevin. That's all there is to that."

Kevin chuckled harshly. "Well, if I was a stupid man, I would have let you know I found it. But I thought of something better." He leaned forward awkwardly and put his face right up to hers. "I know you've been planning to abandon me. What a surprise if you had no money when the time came! No money. No Buddy. I'm smarter than you'll ever be," he said complacently leaning back. He took another swig and pondered. "I'm trying to decide what to do with you. If I let you live, you'll leave. Maybe not tomorrow. But some day. I can't watch you forever. I would like to have sex with you one more time, though. Let's have sex, Annie. Want to?"

"Kevin, I'm hurt. Leave me alone. Tomorrow I'll do whatever you want. And I'm not going to leave you. If you promise not to drink anymore, I won't leave you. We'll be OK." Annie was fighting for her life, and she knew it. Kevin was a powder keg. Any breath by Annie could be the match that ignited him. He momentarily closed his eyes. Annie kept talking softly, trying to lull him to sleep. She was still reclining and would have preferred to sit up but knew better. Any movement at all could disturb him. She saw his hand relax. The bottle dropped onto his lap. No response. Annie watched him intently for what seemed like an eternity. At last she sat up. She did not try to be quiet. Better to be acting naturally if he opened his eyes. She sighed noisily. Still no response.

She rose and began to walk to the back door. She remembered running up the McGowan's basement stairs as a child. Certain that a monster was chasing them, the children had pushed their backs as far forward as possible during their flight. This was how she felt right now. At any second she would feel the hand on her shoulder.

Annie was once again inches from freedom when she felt him behind her. She flinched as he grabbed her neck but felt no emotions. She had tried. That's all she could ask of herself.

Kevin squeezed her throat and turned her to face him.

"Last chance, Bitch. I was testing you."

Looking up into his face, Annie saw death. The full force of Kevin's rage exploded as he choked her violently. Annie remembered little after that. At one point she thought she was dead, so relaxed did she feel. But that was only a respite. Kevin was preparing to rape her.

• • •

The sun was well up when she knew consciousness. She was lying on the kitchen floor. Something was holding her feet down, and she kicked it. Kevin's head bounced off her legs. Annie wondered if he was dead. Hearing him snore, she realized he had finally passed out. The bottle of whiskey lay empty beside him.

Annie Griffin felt void of emotion. She rose slowly and checked for injuries. Hard to say. There was more blood on the kitchen floor, but that could have been from her head wound. Head wounds tended to bleed a lot. Her legs were sore, but they seemed to be able to support her. That was a good thing. She would need to walk out of here. Annie stood fully and stepped over Kevin. She unlocked the door and hesitated. There was something she was forgetting. Glancing down, she realized she was naked. Shit. She should probably get some clothes. Annie again stepped over her husband and walked to the bedroom. Mary was there. Annie had forgotten about Mary, too.

Good thing I needed clothes, she thought. I might have

left her. Annie casually dressed herself. Later she would look at the green sweat pants paired with a dressy sweater and wonder who had picked her clothes. Right now she moved like a robot. Simple tasks. She could handle them.

Dressed, she grabbed Mary with her right hand. The left one was giving her trouble. Annie lifted the baby and held her firmly against her chest. Mary was beginning to rouse, but Annie ignored her. These were important tasks that needed to be done, and she could not risk being derailed. If her mind did not concentrate, it would shut down completely. She realized that she was in shock. What a good thing this shock was. Annie felt emotionless but did congratulate God on inventing shock. It helped you to get important jobs done when you needed to.

Stepping over her husband again, Annie left the apartment. Pausing on the landing, she turned around. She had forgotten something important. Returning, she adjusted the baby's weight and found Kevin's pants. Reaching in, she took his wallet and opened it. There was her money and Buddy's number. She also grabbed the car keys. Annie knew she could not drive now. Later she might want to.

Stepping out a third time, she started down the stairs. No hand on the back this time. Kevin would sleep at least four hours. Annie crossed the yard and knocked on Darlene's door. She waited patiently while the Kemps woke up. Mary was trying to peek out from under the blanket, but Annie would not let her. If she looked at her daughter, she would fall apart. The door finally opened. Annie ignored Darlene's gasp of horror.

"Take the baby, Darlene. Greg needs to take me to the hospital." Darlene stepped back and held the door for Annie, hand still over her mouth. "I know you're leaving this afternoon," Annie continued in a dull voice. "If you can watch her for a couple hours ... I think my arm is broken. It won't take them long."

Her last memory was of Mary being lifted gently from her arms. Darlene was crying. She remembered that. Greg was white. She remembered that, too.

Chapter Twenty-one

Annie lay parked in a hallway, waiting for an X-ray technician. Not a word had passed her lips since she was helped into the Kemps' car. There was nothing to say. The examining doctor ordered pictures of her left arm and her chest, along with her neck and spine. In reply to his queries, Annie shook her head. If she tried to talk, she would lose her mind. By staying silent and concentrating very hard, she was able to stay sane.

"Annie, you're obviously traumatized," the doctor said compassionately. "You don't have to talk until you're ready. I just want to let you know what I'm doing." With that he explained his findings. He told her she was going for X rays and they would talk again. Annie nodded her head and pulled the sheet up closer around her neck. "I'm not giving you anything for pain yet," he continued. "I have to make sure you've had no concussion. Do you understand what I'm saying?"

Looking him directly in the eye, Annie nodded her head. She tried to say something, but her voice was too hoarse. Everything hurt so bad. "Sorry," she managed to mutter.

She sounded like a man and looked at him in alarm.

He lay his hand on her leg gently. "Were you choked, Annie?" After her affirmative nod, he added, "That's why your voice is hoarse. It will come back, but I do need to get some pictures of your neck. Your friend Greg tells me that your husband probably did this. Is that correct?"

With one movement, Annie lowered her head into the pillow on her lap. He was going to make her crazy. Annie resolved to keep her head in the pillow until he left. The hand patted her leg again. It felt good. Safe and comforting.

"No more talking now," he said placidly. "I just wanted to make sure you were with us mentally. It's common to feel a kind of detachment. It's called shock. Perfectly normal. I just did not want to confuse it for a concussion. I am calling the police, Annie. It's something I have to do with this level of injury. For right now, lie back and let's see what the pictures say. You're going to be fine. I promise."

She lay back on the gurney and stared at the ceiling. The nurses came and wheeled her down the hallway where she was parked.

The technician disturbed her reverie. After what seemed like a hundred shots, he parked her back in the hallway. Eventually she was propelled back to her small examining area. Rolling onto her side, Annie wondered what would become of her. Poor little Mary was stuck at the Kemps who were leaving for Chicago in a couple of hours.

Suddenly there was a timid knock on the door. Annie rolled over painfully but did not respond. Hospital personnel did not knock. Three more timid knocks, and the door opened slowly. Herr Charles poked his head around the door.

"Annie," he said fearfully, "Your friend Greg told the nurse that you were in counseling, and they called me. What happened?"

Herr Charles' glasses were slipping down his nose, and he nervously pushed them back up. He kept the door open and had one foot in the hallway. Annie felt hatred in the pit of her stomach. An internal prompter told her that Charles was not to blame for this. Kevin was the guilty party. Annie ignored the prompter and found her voice.

"Charles, I think he's communicating better now," she said icily. Her voice was hoarse, startling them both. Annie continued anyway, "I told you, didn't I? I just want you to admit that I told you and you ignored me."

Clutching the door, Charles groped for words. "I'm sorry ... I had no idea ... you must know that I would never have..."

"You ignored me, Charles. You were so impressed with Kevin's athletic ability that you ignored me. I have nothing to say to you."

The door closed quietly. So much for Herr Charles, Annie thought wickedly. No more feeling guilty, she admonished herself. Being nice would get her killed. Thinking about Kevin's Christmas had landed her in the hospital. Annie decided then and there that she would get a divorce. Right here in Texas. According to Caroline, Texas had jurisdiction. Fine. She would finish it here and take her scholarship. He had hit her for the last time, she promised herself.

Annie felt a wave of rage at Charles. He was despicable. And unprofessional. Annie felt her anger bouncing off the walls and rollicking back at her. At that moment there was another knock on the door.

"Come in," she commanded hoarsely. She was ready to talk.

A young police officer opened the door gently and stepped inside. Annie recognized him. He had responded to the call by the neighbors last month. "Hello," he said politely. "I'm here to ask you a few questions. The doctor is concerned that someone did this to you." Annie nodded her head. "My name is Officer Grady. Let's see," he began looking down at a piece of paper in his hand, "you're name is Anne Griffin. Is that correct?"

"Yes," Annie said in a clipped voice. This was the most humiliating experience in her life. She wondered how long it would take him.

"Your name sounds familiar," he said with a puzzled look on his face. "Have I met you before?"

Annie sighed. "Yes, Officer. You met me last month when my neighbors called you to our house. My husband and I had had a fight." He looked blank. "We live on campus, and my husband is an athlete. His name is Kevin Griffin."

Recognition dawned in the young man's eyes, quickly followed by disbelief "What happened to you?" he asked in alarm. "I'm sorry I didn't recognize you, but your face ... you don't look the same," he hastily added. "Let me start again." They smiled, and Annie felt a little less embarrassed. He seemed like a regular guy. Kind of like Danny, who was forever saying stupid things and then regretting them.

"May I call you Anne?" he asked politely.

"Annie. Yes, please," she was equally polite.

"I feel pretty sure your husband did this. Is that true?"

Annie kept her face immobile. "What if he had? What would happen?"

"Well," the officer began with an impatient motion of his hand, "a lot of things could happen. He should be locked up first of all. He apparently tried to kill you from what I can see. What's wrong with your neck?" he asked, indicating the brace around Annie's throat.

"Someone choked me until I lost consciousness," she said flatly.

"OK, Annie. That's what I'm talking about. Whoever did this needs to be arrested and charged. All you need to do is tell me what happened and agree to sign a complaint against him. Nothing would make me happier than to lock up your All-Star husband."

"If it were my husband that did it and I signed this complaint, how long would he stay in jail?"

"Well, that's hard to say. He would have a bond hearing, and the judge would set a bond. Then he would have the opportunity to bail himself out. He would have to have the money, of course." Officer Grady looked uncomfortable. "He would probably be out before his trial."

"He'll kill me if I do."

"We'll give you a restraining order that keeps him away from you," he added quickly. "Then when he comes near you, we can arrest him. You can't let him get away with this, Annie."

"I'm not letting him get away with anything," she said indignantly. "He does not ask my permission before he attacks me. Why didn't you arrest him at my house? You guys asked me right in front of him if he had hit me. What was I supposed to say? He told me before I opened the door that night he'd kill me if I told you anything. He will." Annie looked down at her hands as the young man shifted his feet. "You just admitted he'll bond right out. I'm not sure what to do. Somehow I have to file for divorce."

Officer Grady looked up quickly. "That's the spirit!" he exclaimed. "It's hard for us to intervene when couples are living together. I'm going to go over and talk to him right now. See if he admits anything." He noticed the fear in Annie's eyes and made her a promise. "I'll tell him you refused to talk. Don't you have a baby?"

Annie explained that she had left the baby with neighbors who were leaving town. She told him she had to be home before four to get Mary.

"Annie," he said calmly, "I'm no doctor, but I can't see you being released before tomorrow. They have not even set your wrist yet."

"Is it broken?" she asked in surprise.

"According to the doctor, it is. You also are going to need stitches in two spots in your head. Can someone else watch your baby for now?"

"There's no one," she said despondently. "I have no family here."

The officer cleared his throat and made motions to leave. "Let's take it one step at a time. I have to go talk to your husband. What you need to do now is get treated. I'll be back in a couple of hours to talk to you again. Annie, please think about signing a complaint. I think it's the right thing to do." He smiled and left.

Annie lay back again. Her mind was working quickly. Part of her wanted desperately to sign complaints. The other part of her mind argued it would be too dangerous. He might kill me anyway, she thought in despair. Annie closed her eyes in exhaustion. A restraining order was only a piece of paper. She could hardly picture Kevin being deterred last night by a piece of paper. Still ... it might help to have some consequences. Annie was still wrestling with it when she heard yet another knock on the door.

"Come in," she growled in her new voice.

As the door opened, Annie heard the delightful tinkle of Caroline. "Caroline?"

"It's me," came her voice. A beautifully manicured finger was held up inside the door. "One sec, Annie. I'm talking to the policeman."

Annie felt herself beginning to cry. Just the sound of her counselor's sympathetic voice set her off. If there was one person in the state of Texas who cared about her, it was Caroline. Annie lay back and listened as she spoke to the officer.

"...I certainly appreciate that, Officer, but I'm not clear. Why can't you put him in custody immediately?" Annie could not hear the officer's response—just Caroline's. "Do you usually have a victim's testimony at a murder trial? No. Of course, you don't. The victim here is obviously too injured to deal with these issues." Apparently, the officer agreed to talk to her later. "Thank you, Officer. I'll look forward to that."

Caroline stepped into the room. Looking at Annie, she gasped. "Oh Annie ... I'm so sorry. I knew you were in danger."

Annie sat up gingerly and held out her arms. Caroline stepped closer and lightly held her. Annie cried and sput-tered gibberish for at least ten minutes before they separat-ed. On observing Caroline's equally weepy state, she began to cry again. How wonderful that someone cared enough to cry for her.

"They want me to sign complaints, Caroline," Annie

said fearfully. "He'll kill me if I do."

"Sweetheart, it looks to me like he's going to kill you anyway. If you sign complaints, at least you'll have a restraining order, and he'll know he'll be arrested. Also, sometimes they'll put him out of the house. Have you thought about that? Where are you going to go if he is still at home?"

Annie frowned. "I guess I just assumed that after this ... he would leave."

Caroline pulled up the only chair in the spartan cubicle. Crossing her legs, she brushed out a crease in her expensive silk pantsuit. "Honey, let's talk reality here. I know these guys better than you might think. Right now you're thinking that this thing he did is so bad, he'll have to admit he's a scumbag and give you anything you want. Is that right?" Annie nodded her head wonderingly. Caroline's perception never failed to amaze her. "I'm here to tell you that it's not going to happen. Any remorse he might feel is going to be thrown in the trash as soon as that nice police officer knocks on his door. These guys are out for number one. Period. I know they talk a good line about worshiping and adoring you, but, ultimately, someone who gives a damn about you does not attempt to prevent you from breathing, which, from the looks of your throat and the neck brace, Kevin did. Are you with me?" Annie nodded, and Caroline took a deep breath. "If I'm correct, he is right now explaining to Officer Grady that most of your injuries were either self-inflicted, accidental, or the result of his having to restrain you from doing a Highland Fling in the courtyard naked. Get my picture? He's not going to take responsibility for this. True to form, he is going to blame you and your imaginary boyfriends. He may say you're mentally ill. Or a drug addict. Or maybe an alcoholic. Whatever. What he will not say is that he is abusive and has hopes that eventually he will have the opportunity to destroy you. Wake up, Annie. You're lucky to be alive. Where is the baby?"

Annie was reeling. The abrupt change of subject left her confused. "Mary? Uhm, she's at the Kemps, but they're leaving for Chicago. I have to pick her up. What time is it?"

Glancing down at a delicate jeweled wristwatch, Caroline frowned. "It's after twelve. What time are they leaving?"

"Four or five. I'm not sure. Caroline, I have to get the baby. I can't stay here." Annie's voice was beginning to crack. "There's no one to watch her."

"I know." Caroline was pensive. "Let me go talk to the doctor."

Smiling comfortably, she left the room. Moments later she reappeared. "Annie, he says that the soonest you will be released is tomorrow morning. You've got a broken rib, broken wrist, they're about to come in and stitch your head, and he's worried about internal injuries in your neck and throat. You're not going anywhere, Honey." Annie sighed and lay back down. Caroline continued, "Would you trust me with Mary? It's completely unprofessional, but I don't see any options. Rules were made to be broken and all of that." Seeing the hopeful expression on Annie's face, she continued cheerfully, "She'll fit right in with my monsters. I have a portable crib ... you're not nursing or anything...that's the solution, I'll take her to my house until tomorrow or whenever you get out. It'll be our little secret." She smiled warmly.

"Caroline, what will you're husband say?" Annie spoke hesitantly.

The older woman smiled confidently. "Don't worry about him. He'll ask me first if I'm crazy and second if she's hungry. He's not a problem, Annie."

"What a wonderful marriage you must have," Annie said sadly.

"It is wonderful. And you can have one just as wonderful someday. Marriage is the greatest, Annie. Trust me. All men are not like Kevin."

Annie gave her a wan smile. A thought occurred to her, and she sat up again. "Caroline, when is Christmas?"

"Tomorrow is Christmas eve. Why?"

"You can't have Mary on Christmas eve. It will ruin your holiday."

Caroline gave a snort of disgust. "Don't be absurd, Annie. I would not have offered if it was a problem. Let's take it one step at a time." She paused momentarily. "When Charles called me, I was sure you were dead. Thank God, you're OK."

"Charles called you? What did he say?" Annie was curious. "How did he know to call you?"

"We work for the same agency, Annie. Remember, I told you? Just different buildings. He knew that I was seeing you initially and that you switched to marriage counseling. He's extremely upset."

"He ought to be, Caroline. Do you know what he said?" Annie felt her face beginning to flush. In her opinion, horsewhipping was too good for Herr Charles.

"I can only imagine," said Caroline with resignation. "Don't be too hard on him, Annie. He feels terrible, and I agree that he should. But like many counselors, he knows nothing about domestic violence. He'll learn now."

Annie lay back to rest. Caroline patted her hand absently and opened a book. She told Annie she would wait for the officer to return so they could develop a safety plan. Annie was humbly grateful for her presence. Caroline made everything seem normal. Annie contemplated that Caroline, too, was like a mother. God must be substituting people for the mother He had taken. Annie mentally thanked Him yet again for Caroline.

She must have slept because she awoke to find herself alone. "Caroline," she cried out.

The door opened immediately, and the hand entered. "I'm here, Annie. I'm just talking to Officer Grady."

Annie heard the quiet voices. Caroline sounded tense. Officer Grady sounded apologetic. After a few minutes, they entered.

The young man smiled at Annie briefly and began to speak.

"Well, I spoke with your husband, Annie. He denies assaulting you." He sighed and seemed to measure his next words. "He says you were out drinking and came home like that."

Annie sat bolt upright and then winced at the pain in her back. "That's a lie!" she said with clenched teeth. "I was home all night. Ask the Kemps. He's lying."

Caroline intervened. "We all know that, Annie. We all know Kevin did this to you. Officer Grady is just telling you what Kevin is saying."

Officer Grady smiled gratefully at Caroline and continued. "I was very stern with him, and he's definitely scared. I told him that you were not talking yet, but we hoped you would speak to us soon."

Annie interrupted him. "He's going to come here and try to get me. I'm not safe here."

"No, he is not." The policeman walked to the side of Annie's bed and put his hand over hers. "Annie, if I thought he was going to hurt you again today, I would have arrested him. He's shaken up. He knows he's in big trouble."

Annie stammered for words. "Was he ... did he ask how I was doing?"

Silence fell, and Annie lowered her head. "You mean to tell me he did not even ask if I was OK?"

"No," the man spoke slowly. "He said he was fed up with your drinking and infidelity. He has the baby and says that you are not welcome to come back."

Turning feebly to Caroline, Annie gasped. Caroline quickly put her arms around her and spoke reassuringly. "This is what they do, Annie. I told you. This is not at all uncommon. He's taking the offensive. Officer Grady understands all this, and he believes you. The problem we have is the baby."

Annie sat back and dried her eyes roughly. "What about the baby? Go get her. He's a monster."

Officer Grady sighed and spoke patiently. "Annie, I don't have the right to take the baby from him. Technically, he is the father and has every right to her, with you in the hospital and all. I respect your feelings on this, but there's nothing we can do unless you sign complaints. Then we can get a court order."

"Caroline..." she asked weakly, "is this true?"

"Hold on, Annie," said Caroline efficiently. Annie knew the look on her face. Caroline was so ladylike that Annie suspected people underestimated her. "It's true that Mr. Griffin has every right to this child. Annie certainly would be the first to agree with that. He has not been accused of molesting or injuring the child in any way." She paused and turned to Annie. "Do you think that Mary is safe with him for the night?"

Annie nodded her head affirmatively. Kevin would not hurt Mary sober. Also, if he was blaming Annie, he was not dangerous. Based on what he had told the police officer, Annie knew that he would be playing the role of father of the year.

Caroline continued, "It's obvious to both of us, Officer Grady, that Annie is the undisputed victim. Do you agree?" He nodded his head vigorously. "Now Annie has not decided to sign complaints yet. We need a temporary plan to get us all through the holidays safely. Right?" she queried. He again nodded enthusiastically.

Annie nearly chuckled. She was reeling him in.

"Well, then what needs to happen," spoke the logical Caroline, "is that Kevin has to leave the home tomorrow and give Annie the baby."

He still watched her, but now looked blank.

"Yes." he said thoughtfully, "that's the best solution all right. But how can we make him do that? I mean without a court order..."

Caroline smiled brightly. "Well, I was thinking that you could go over and persuade him to leave. You know ... talk him into it. Let him know that after Christmas he can talk to a judge but that usually in these circumstances, this is how it's done. Tell him that it's not fair and you think he should talk to an attorney after the holidays, but for now he needs to surrender the baby tomorrow and find a place to stay. What do you think?"

He stared at her intently for a moment and then started to chuckle. "You want me to go over there and bully him. Don't you?"

285

Caroline smiled serenely. Annie looked hopeful.

"We-e-l-l. I sure do see your point. It seems like the fairest solution. We can't have Annie here in a motel, with injuries and all, worried about her baby for Christmas." He paused and glanced at Annie. "Is that what you want, Annie?"

"Yes," she said fervently. "I am going home tomorrow whether they like it or not. And I don't mind him seeing Mary. But I don't have anywhere else to go, and he does. He has a lot of friends here. I just need to figure out a way to pay for an attorney so I can file for divorce."

"I understand," he said gently. "Let me run back over there and see if I can shake him up a little." Smiling, he picked his hat up from the chair and turned to Caroline. "You missed your calling, Ma'am. You should have been a used car salesman."

Caroline smiled sweetly at him. "You're wonderful," she said admiringly. "And I'm not just saying that."

He grinned again and left. Annie turned to Caroline, and they discussed the situation. Shortly the nurse arrived with an ominous tray of instruments.

"Stitches," she said briefly. "You can stay, if you want," she said politely to Caroline.

"Thank you ... no." Caroline looked squeamish. "I need to go make some calls." Turning to Annie, she said, "I'll be back when you're finished. And then I'll stay until our Sir Galahad comes back. We'll have this sorted out in no time."

Annie waved to her and steeled herself for the needle. She had never had stitches.

Fifteen sutures later, the doctor agreed to give Annie a shot for the pain. Annie sent the nurse for Caroline. She needed to take care of business first. When Caroline entered with the long-suffering Officer Grady, she looked ebullient.

"It's all worked out," she said. "Tomorrow you will probably be released by eleven. Kevin has agreed to stay at a friend's, the ones who left town, and he'll turn the baby over to you when you get home." Caroline's face turned serious for a moment. "Officer Grady told him he would need to find a friend to hand Mary off so you don't have to see him." Annie smiled at the officer gratefully, and he looked solemn.

"There's only one stipulation here, Annie," Grady began. "He is determined that he have the baby for Christmas. I did not want to rock the boat so I agreed. You're not going to be feeling much better anyway. That way you can rest."

Annie nodded wearily. "That's fine. Christmas is nothing to me now." Looking into his compassionate eyes, she asked, "Will he have a friend pick her up and drop her off on Christmas day?"

"Absolutely! I told him he can have no contact with you at all until we finish investigating the case." Grimly, the young man continued. "Kevin is like a long-tailed cat in a room full of rocking chairs right now. You don't have to worry about him for the next few days. You and I will talk again after the holidays. Get some rest." Nodding briefly to Caroline, he turned to leave. "One more thing," he said at the door. "Annie, you're going to need a new connecter cord for your phone. Somehow the last one was broken. Kevin said the baby must have done it. I'd advise you to get that in the morning." With a reassuring wink, he departed. Both women sighed.

"Well," Caroline said briskly. "Not perfect but better than I dared to hope." She moved over to Annie's bedside. "At least Kevin has been temporarily neutralized."

"I hope so," Annie said quietly.

"You need rest. Now. You've dealt with too much in the last twenty-four hours. Anything else you're worried about before I leave?"

Annie frowned in concentration. "I don't think so. I have money to take a cab home in the morning. Where do I get a phone cord?"

Caroline waved her hand. "Oh, I'll pick that up tonight and drop it off to you. Are you sure you don't want to call your family?"

"NO!" Annie said vehemently. "There is nothing they can do. I don't want my father flying out here on Christmas eve. It would just make everything more complex." Annie glanced at Caroline pleadingly. "You do understand, don't you?"

"Yes, Annie, I do," was the reply. "You're desperately trying to retain some control. And you're doing fine." Smiling affectionately, Caroline bent down and kissed her forehead. "I'll send the nurse in with the shot."

Annie lay back and listened to Caroline's jewelry as she walked down the hallway. She waited for the nurse. The pain was everywhere. Apparently the shock was wearing off because her head and wrist were throbbing. It hurt to breath in. The doctor said that a hairline fracture of one of her ribs was to blame. It would heal on its own. The wrist would be set in the morning when some of the swelling had gone down. For now it was immobilized. The stitches had been awful, and Annie shuddered remembering. The nurse came in and administered a shot, which she said was Demoral. Almost immediately, a peaceful warmth spread through Annie's body.

It was not so bad, she mused. Many people got divorced. But Mary would be from a broken home. Annie grimaced at the mental image of a house cracked in two. Oh, big deal, she thought impatiently. It was better than being dead. She felt her body slip into an even deeper level of relaxation. What a wonderful shot! If she was honest with herself, she would admit she was relieved. "I'm relieved," she said to herself out loud. "I wonder why?" Just before sleep overtook her, she understood. She was relieved because it was finally over. At last Annie McGowan would be free.

• • •

The radio was playing Christmas carols the next evening. Annie sat alone at her kitchen table with the telephone in front of her. She desperately wanted to call home. Mary had been asleep for over an hour. Annie rose finally and pulled the plug on the radio. The mere act of turning the switch was not enough. The joyful melodies forced too stark a contrast to her present mood.

Making her decision, she dialed quickly. She would act normal.

"Hello," came Maureen's breezy voice.

Annie swallowed hard. "Maureen?"

"Who is this? Annie?"

"It's me," she said tearfully. "My voice is messed up. How is everyone?"

"Fine, fine." Maureen said impatiently. "Where have you been? Dad was trying to get you yesterday, and Nellie and I have been calling and calling. What's the matter?"

Annie discarded her resolution and gave in to the tears. "Sorry," she stammered. "I'm homesick, I guess."

Maureen's voice hardened. "You tell me exactly what's going on right this minute, Annie. I mean it. We got a letter from Danny that said he thought we should talk to you about coming home. Why did he say that? Is Kevin being a bastard?"

"Oh Maureen, I don't know where to start." The tears would not stop now, and Annie talked through them. "The last few days have been awful."

"It sounds like it," Maureen said with uncharacteristic calmness. "Start by telling me where you were yesterday."

"I'll tell you, Maureen, if you promise not to scream and yell. And you have to promise not to tell anyone. Not Dad or Nellie or anyone. Promise?"

Silence echoed over the thousand miles separating them. "It's bad, isn't it?"

"Yes, it's pretty bad." Annie collected herself. "But I have it mostly worked out. I don't want anyone to know until after Christmas. Do you promise?"

"Shit, Annie," Maureen said in a frustrated voice. "I guess I'll have to or you won't tell me. I promise. But if it's bad I'm going to tell them right after Christmas."

"Well, between the two of us we'll have to figure out how much to tell Dad."

"Stop it, Annie! What's happening out there?"

Annie took a deep breath and began. "Yesterday I was at the hospital. In summary, Maureen, Kevin... he came home drunk and kind of attacked me."

"KIND OF?" Maureen exclaimed. "You had to go to the hospital? What's wrong with you?"

"Are you going to stay calm? Really, Maureen. I can't take it if you get upset. I'm kind of shaky myself right now."

Maureen lowered her voice. "Sorry. What was hurt?"

"Well, I have a broken wrist, broken rib, lots of bruises, and I had fifteen stitches in my head." She ignored the gasp and continued. "My head is in a neck brace because my neck is sprained. Other than that, I'm just bruised."

"Oh, my God!" Maureen was starting to cry. "I'm sorry, Annie." Her voice changed. "Where is the baby? Did he hurt the baby?"

Annie sensed the panic in her sister's voice and rolled her eyes. Just as she suspected. She would now have to comfort Maureen. "Maureen, the baby is fine. And I'm fine, too. Just sore. And I wish it wasn't Christmas, and I wish I was home." With that, she started to cry again.

Maureen shelved her own emotions. "Annie." she said calmly. "Do you want to come home tomorrow?"

"I can't," she sniffled. "I look like hell. Dad would have a fit if he saw me like this. I have to take care of things here, and I don't want to waste the money. "

"Give me a break, Annie," she said impatiently. "We'll prepay the ticket at this end."

"Who is going to pay it?" Annie said equally impatient.

"Dad, of course. He's loaded, Annie. He just acts poor." Both girls laughed. "I want to kill Kevin, Annie. He's such an asshole."

"Oh, God, don't start. Not now. I agree, but if I get started on that I might never stop. I knew he was getting weird, and I was going to leave. Danny left me money ... I just kind of never actually did it. I should have, I know."

"Well, for God's sake, don't blame yourself. It's a wonder you're speaking at all." Maureen sounded perplexed. "Why did he do it?"

"He thought I was having a fling with the stock boy at work."

"Are you?" she asked incredulously.

"Don't be a jackass, Maureen. Of course not."

"Sorry." Her sister was immediately contrite. "It's just that I don't get it. Why does he always think you're going to have an affair? You're not even a flirt. He would have killed me a long time ago."

"He's a lunatic." Annie said wearily. She was too tired to get into it.

"I told you, Annie," Maureen said stoutly. "Remember I told you he was a Psycho Boy years ago? Tell me what to do."

They talked for another hour. Annie explained her game plan, and Maureen argued. She wanted Annie to pack up and come home immediately. Right after she signed the complaints. Annie explained that she would have to clear things up first. Officer Grady agreed with Caroline that if Annie took Mary out of state without a court order, it could blow up in her face. Kevin could file in her absence and get custody. At best it would be a few weeks before she could leave. Maureen was all for telling their father immediately, but Annie was loathe to spoil his holiday. There was nothing he could do, and Annie was not sure she would tell him at all. Annie felt that Nellie, too, was prone to overreaction but in a more dangerous way. Nellie would promise anything to get the information and then immediately call the Griffins and anyone else she considered at fault.

After agreeing to speak to the rest of the family the next morning, Annie hung up. She felt better. It was comforting that someone in her family knew what was happening. She glanced at the clock. It was only nine, but she was exhausted. She wished she could go to bed but felt sure she would lie awake all night. She had slept well in the hospital. Promptly at eleven this morning, Officer Grady had arrived. He said he was driving by and wondered if she needed a ride. Tears welled up in Annie's eyes at this thoughtfulness. She had thanked him and accepted. The officer waited with her until Kevin's teammate ran across the court yard with the baby. His presence was sending a message, he said.

For the tenth time, Annie checked the doors. They were all locked and chained. Remembering an episode of Dick Van Dyke, she had soup cans stacked against both entries. At least if he broke through, she would have some warning.

In spite of the precautions she was not unduly concerned. Kevin was playing a role now. He would not take any chance at being branded a criminal. Image was important to him. For all he knew, he could be charged with a felony at any time. No. He would not dare approach her until he felt safe.

Annie arranged Mary's presents in the living room. There was no tree. Luckily, Mary was too young to notice. The other presents were shoved into the linen closet. Kevin had cleaned up. Checking his drawer, she noticed he had taken clothes.

With a deep sigh, she went into the kitchen and found the bottle of painkillers. She filled a glass with water and tried to open the container. It was child-proof. "Annie-proof," she noted aloud. Try as she might, she could not get the top to release. The arrows were lined up properly, but still it stuck. Annie felt tears of frustration in her eyes and swore out loud. She leaned against the counter and took a break. After several deep breaths she tried again. Still no progress. Muttering severely, she opened the junk drawer and pulled out Kevin's new hammer. "Perfect for throwing at bastards," she said out loud. A flood of memories overcame her, and she viciously smashed the pill vial. It shattered. Pieces of plastic and pills shot off in every direction.

"Shit," she swore viciously.

Crouching down, she began to pick up the debris. She speculated fearfully that one of the pills might kill a baby. Quickly she tried to sweep the mess into a pile. Crouching low she looked under the refrigerator. Sure enough, there was a tablet. Stretching her hand out did not work. She could not get to it. Annie swore again and collapsed onto the floor. Her whole body was sore, and she had reawakened the pain in her rib by straining.

She gave in to the sobs and slowly pulled herself into a sitting position against the stove. Hugging her legs, she lowered her head onto her knees and cried loudly. "I hate him," she repeated over and over again. When the worst had passed, she looked around her angrily. Reaching up, she felt for the hammer on the counter. Wincing with pain, she grasped it and hurled it with all her might. It made a satisfactory bang on impact. It also made a sizable dent in the cabinet. Ha! she thought. Keep the security deposit. Remembering one of her conversations with Caroline, she tried to decide if she was redirecting or misdirecting her anger. The cabinet was really innocent. Yes, she thought, it's also inanimate and therefore an appropriate target for redirection of anger. Now if she had thrown the hammer at the doctor, that would be displaced or misdirected hostility. Whatever. Inappropriate. That's what Kevin was, she decided. Inappropriately hostile. A nice clinical term. She would put that on the divorce petition. Her grounds would be inappropriate hostility on the part of the husband toward the wife.

She sighed again and looked around her. "Merry Christmas, Annie," she said sarcastically. That made her laugh out loud. "I'm having a Christmas Pity Party." She sighed again. Annie decided she was too tired to attend her own pity party. Bored with high drama, she got a knife out of the drawer without getting up. She quickly swiped it under the refrigerator and recovered the tablet. Rising carefully, she grabbed the broom and swept up the mess. She looked around and remembered sadly how much she had loved her little kitchen. Now she thought, this is where he choked me, or, I was raped over there. It was time to exit the kitchen. She swallowed the prescribed tablets, turned off the light, and went to bed. Certain of insomnia, she reached under the mattress for her flashlight so she could read. She lay back to rest for a moment and almost immediately fell into a deep dreamless sleep.

Chapter Twenty-two

Sunlight streamed through the bedroom window on Christmas morning. Annie opened her eyes and looked to Mary's crib. Mary, too had just opened her eyes and gave her mom a sleepy baby smile. Annie smiled back. She wondered if there was ever a thing so precious as the morning smile of a sleepy child. They were alone in the apartment. There was no Kevin giving her a stomachache. Just clear morning light and an innocent baby.

"Merry Christmas, little Mary," Annie said.

Mary pulled her cover over her head playfully. She peek-a-booed Annie and laughed in delight when Annie put her head right next to the bars to startle her.

"Let's go see what Santa brought you," she said reaching into the crib. Carrying her daughter into the living room, she marveled that life could be so pleasant. Caroline had told her about this. She said it was not difficult to raise a child alone after an abusive relationship. Problems seemed minimal when the constant stress and fear was eliminated. Annie felt something like relief wash over her. Right now all she had to worry about was having fun with her little girl.

Mary rapidly tore paper from the gifts. Once the actual gift was uncovered, the child lost interest and reached impatiently for the next. Annie told her she was missing the point. Mary was unconcerned.

"Good thing I did not spend a lot of money on you, Miss Paper Puller," she said with mock severity. "I could have wrapped up the silverware."

Annie left her playing in the debris and made breakfast. In minutes Mary came toddling in to check the progress. Annie hoisted her into the high chair with her good arm. The cast seemed as if it weighed a hundred pounds, but the doctor said in a few days she would not know she was wearing it. So much the better. Kevin was sending his emissary for Mary at ten. If Annie thought about it, she would get depressed. Caroline had informed her that her moods would fluctuate wildly. Annie had been advised to exult in the positive and wait out the negative. Wise advice and Annie resolved to follow it strictly. It was time for exulting.

"Do you want to sing Christmas carols, Mary?" she asked.

Mary gave her a polite wave of her spoon and continued to shovel down her oatmeal and pears.

"We'd better not," Annie mused. "That would be pushing it."

Mary nodded sagely.

Annie continued, "This Christmas is a blow off, Mary. Let's talk about what we want to do with Christmas Future. Usually we'll have a big tree. It'll have lights and ornaments and tinsel." Mary smiled agreeably.

"At night before you go to bed, we'll read our story in the front room with only the Christmas lights on, and everything will seem so cozy. You'll love it." Mary nodded intelligently.

"We might go live in the mountains somewhere. I wonder where there are some mountains," Annie mused. "We simply cannot celebrate Christmas without snow. Right?"

Mary shook her head vigorously. "You're the smartest baby I ever met, Mar. You won't mind growing up without Daddy. You can still see him and, honestly, Honey, he's kind of a nut."

Mary looked very solemn.

"Sorry, I know he's your dad, and I do like him. It's just that he wants to kill me. You know?" Mary burst into unexpected peals of laughter. Annie joined in.

"Wacky, isn't it? Who would want to kill a nice girl like me?"

"Do you want to wear a frilly Christmas dress today? Your sinister Granny sent it. She hates me, too. Good thing you like me." Mary largely ignored her and concentrated on her breakfast. "I'll put your pretty dress on and send a comfortable outfit. Mary, please understand that the only reason I'm sending you with him is to keep peace. I'm pretending it's not Christmas, and I want you to do the same. Next Christmas will be better." Mary hurled her spoon at the wall. "I take it you're finished, my Princess." Annie gingerly removed her and took her right to the sink. She prepared the bath, and she awkwardly stripped the child. Her neck was hurting, and she knew she should be wearing the brace. She promised herself she'd put it on as soon as Mary left.

After rinsing the baby, she set her down to run naked. It was Mary's favorite pastime. Annie collected the elements of Mary's Christmas apparel while listening to the wild ripping of paper."

After handing Mary off with a loaded diaper bag, Annie sat back to take stock. Were movies playing on Christmas? She'd need a long, preferably tragic, film. That would require a trip to the store for the paper. That would require getting dressed. Annie pondered. Maybe all this activity should be preceded by a little rest. Her rib was painful, and her neck felt terrible. Annie put the brace on and took a pain pill. Grabbing her latest book, she propped herself up in bed. She reminded herself that she had often longed for this type of solitude. Luckily, the book was a Gothic mystery. Annie read with relish an account of the heroine's rapidly deteriorating plight. Someone was trying to kill her, too. Annie speculated that she was more fortunate than this poor girl. Annie at least knew who the enemy was.

She must have dozed because she opened her eyes with a start. The light had a late feel, and Annie went in to check the clock. It was nearly three o'clock. Perfect. She had killed three hours or so. She dressed as rapidly as her injuries would allow. Annie noticed more bruises coming out but ignored them. For some reason she did not want to see the marks. She looked in the mirror only briefly to ensure that her hair was properly fixed. A small section had been shaved, and Annie had a hard time covering the bald spot.

An hour later she was comfortably ensconced in a dark theater with two other unfortunates. A haggard-looking theater attendant sold the tickets, took the tickets, and distributed popcorn to his three holiday guests. He was young, in his early twenties, and Annie speculated that he had tied one on the night before. Probably missed Mass, too, she thought. At that she started. It had never occurred to her to go to Mass this morning. Mortal sin? With Kevin on the loose, this was not the time to abandon the state of grace. No, she consoled herself, God would understand that it was too embarrassing to go anywhere like this. He would probably tell her to buy a box of chocolate almonds to complement her popcorn. Annie rose to get them, much to the irritation of the hung over attendant. He looked at her like a tired mother. Hadn't he taken her money, torn her ticket, and gotten her popcorn? She had no business bothering him for candy now. Annie chuckled at the thought and took her seat again. The movie was *Reds*. Long, tragic, and pretty much uneventful. Diane Keaton worried over Warren Beatty for more than three hours. Warren was really getting too excited over the communist thing. Annie thought she was bored but regretted the closing credits. Walking out, she checked the time. Christmas was almost over, thank God.

298

Driving home, she thought about last Christmas. She had been told to concentrate on positive thoughts. It could be worse, she thought. I could be stuck back in last year and have to live this year all over again. She shuddered. That was kind of a positive thought, and she commended herself. She decided that everyone should spend one Christmas alone. It was good for the soul. Never again would Christmas seem as important. It was only another day. Lots of people were alone on Christmas. At least four that she knew of in this town alone. The poor old man in the movie had blown his nose throughout the whole film. Annie thought sadly that he needed to beef up his denial reserve. It was working great for her.

Realizing she was ravenous, she looked for an open restaurant. No luck. Even the convenience stores were now closed. Annie thought mournfully that she would have to find something at home. That would be challenging since she had not been shopping in days. She sighed. Depressed people should never allow themselves to get hungry, she thought. It made everything seem worse. Coping mechanisms melted in the face of hunger. She would go home and call Chicago.

As she walked up the stairs to her apartment, Annie noticed a package outside her door. It's probably a bomb from Kevin, she thought only half jokingly. No. There was a letter taped to the top. Annie opened the letter and read, "Merry Christmas from Ted and Cindy Grady." The policeman? He was the only Grady she knew. Annie opened the door and put the bag down on the table. Tears were starting, and she felt her denial dissipating. Inside the large bag was a plate piled with turkey, potatoes, and everything else. Another wrapped plate held three desserts. Annie opened the wrapping of what appeared to be a present. Inside was an expensive bottle of bubble bath with matching lotion. Annie sat down at the table and cried for their goodness. Someone close by wished her well, and it tore the veil off her terrible loneliness. The policeman, a total stranger to her, had gone home and told his wife.

299

What a truly wonderful woman she must be, Annie thought tearfully. She's never even met me. Something about the present touched her as well. The whole thing was unnecessary, but even if she had felt compelled to make a gesture, Mrs. Grady did not have to send such an expensive item. Annie knew in a flash that Cindy Grady had wrapped one of her own gifts. The thought made her cry harder. How good people were, she thought. God was good, too, Annie knew, and probably a little sad that Annie was ignoring Him on His birthday. She thanked God for the Gradys and begged Him to bless them. Someday, she promised herself tearfully, someday she would return their kindness.

After eating the delicious dinner, Annie took a beautiful bubble bath with her exquisite gift. She used it sparingly and vowed to say a prayer for Cindy Grady every time she looked at the bottles. After a tearful soak, Annie felt peaceful and relaxed. Strong enough to call home and face the charade.

Annie dialed the phone and in seconds heard Mr. McGowan's gruff voice. "Hello," he said imperiously. Annie laughed out loud. He always answered as though the caller was terribly invasive even dialing his number.

"Merry Christmas, Dad," she said brightly.

"Annie, is that you? Merry Christmas!" He sounded cheerful. "How's my little Mary?"

"She's fine, Dad," Annie said truthfully. "How is everyone there?"

"Fine. We're all fine. What are you doing tomorrow, Annie?"

"Nothing. Why?"

"Can you pick me up at the airport at eleven forty-five?" Annie's mouth dropped open. She remained silent. "If not, I can easily get a cab. Do they have taxis there?"

"Uh, yes...taxis? Uh, yes, I suppose they do." Annie caught her breath. "Did you talk to Maureen, Dad?"

"Maureen should be horsewhipped for not telling me you were in trouble before this. Don't be mad at her, she started crying at the dinner table, and Nellie got it out of her. Would you rather I drove down with a trailer to bring your things home?"

Annie clutched the table and searched for the right words. Her father was calm and logical. It was clear in his mind, Annie knew. If one of his children got into trouble, they needed to come home. He could not begin to understand the complexity.

Misreading her silence, he continued. "Don't tell me you're thinking of staying with that ape. I spoke to Father Tom."

Annie cringed. Father Tom was their uncle and a priest.

"He said these things happen. You can get an annulment. Now, the Holy Father doesn't like these annulments, so we'll need to work fast while we can still get one in this country. It can all be worked out."

Finding her voice, Annie suppressed hysterical giggling. She pictured herself being marched first to confession, that was a given, just on the off chance she was in any way responsible, and then straight to the Tribunal where Mr. McGowan would demand immediate satisfaction.

"Dad," she said hesitantly, "it's not that simple."

"What are you talking about? Maureen said he hurt your neck."

"Well," she began patiently, "Texas has jurisdiction over the marriage. I'll need to get divorced here first."

"Nonsense," he replied quickly. "I'll put a call in to Harry. He'll sort it out."

Annie cringed again. Harry was Mr. McGowan's attorney and dear friend.

She realized what she was up against and spoke firmly. "Dad, you cannot come here tomorrow. It's just not a good time. Really. There is nothing you can do, and I'm just fine. You cannot come."

She heard a deep sigh. "Annie, what the hell can I do? Now I made a reservation, and it's all set..."

"Dad," she interrupted him. "Send Maureen. Could you send Maureen?"

He paused. "I could...sure...I can, but don't you want me?"

Annie rolled her eyes. Give me the words, she prayed. "Of course, I do, Dad, but not right now," she implored. "It would great to have Maureen, though. Would that be OK?"

"Yes," he responded firmly. "If you want goofy Maureen, then you shall have her. Tomorrow at eleven forty-five. Is there anything else I can do? Do you want some money?"

"Not yet, Dad," she replied in blissful relief. "I'll see how much an attorney will cost and let you know. OK?"

"OK, Sweetheart. Merry Christmas. Here's Maureen now."

Maureen came on the line sounding tense. "Are you furious?"

Annie laughed out loud. "Maureen, I could kill you. Is he real upset?"

"He was like a raging bull, but he calmed down after he talked to Father Tom. Now he's busy making plans. Father Tom told him to bring you right home and end the whole thing quickly."

"Did he really tell him that?"

Maureen lowered his voice. "Yes, Annie. He also said that once a husband was violent, they were violent again. He told Dad to get you a lawyer and get you 'the hell out of it.'" Maureen had deepened her voice and assumed the Irish brogue of their uncle.

"He's probably right. What's Nellie's take on the whole thing?"

"I'll let her tell you herself. She's pulling the phone away...Annie, I'll see you tomorrow. I'll have to tell work it's a family emergency. I have to go to Texas and find my sister a new husband."

Annie laughed again and listened to the scuffle at the other end.

"Annie?" came Nellie's authoritative voice. "I told you he was a pig. Thank God, you're getting out now. You can be in school here in three weeks, and Mrs. Nolan will mind the baby."

"Nellie," she beseeched, "don't tell anyone yet. I don't

know what I'm going to do, but I'm pretty sure I'll stay here for at least this semester. I have the scholarship."

"Why, that's nonsense," came the prompt rejoinder. "Dad's made of money. He'll pay your tuition here, and you can live at home. I always knew it wasn't safe to send you so far off with that pig."

"Nellie, please don't call him a pig." Annie again searched for words. "He's not all bad. He's a good father, you know."

"Don't defend Kevin Griffin to me," her oldest sister said stoutly. "I only hope those barbarians in Texas have the sense to lock him up."

Annie basked in the family support. Nellie said that if Annie did choose to stay, as unwise as Nellie thought that was, then she, Nellie, would come down right after Maureen. She felt sure Kevin would respond to her threats. Annie chuckled and promised to talk about it later. Mr. McGowan signed off with the command that Annie tell Kevin not to bother her. Annie giggled. "I will, Dad."

The doorbell rang, and Annie said quick goodbyes. Mary was home, sleepy and soggy. Annie changed her with a light heart. She kept chuckling as bits of the conversation floated through her memory. Mary fell asleep promptly, and Annie lay in bed with a book. The soup cans were back in place, and she felt lonely and scared. Suddenly, she remembered. In a little more than twelve hours, Maureen would be here. The thought made her laugh out loud, and she fell asleep happy.

• • •

On Monday morning Annie cleaned the apartment as quickly as her injuries allowed. Despite the recent tragedy, Annie was a woman preparing her home for a visit from her sister. By ten-thirty she looked around in satisfaction. If she moved fast, she could run through the grocery store on the way to the airport.

She was just grabbing her purse when the phone rang. Annie answered it quickly. A male voice with a deep Texas drawl introduced himself. "This is Judge Dan Wilkes, from down at the county courthouse. I'm sitting here with Ted Grady."

Annie's stomach tightened. "Yes?"

"Well, now to get right to the point, Mrs. Griffin, Ted is darn worried about you. He seems to think we need to look real close at what your husband might get up to in the future. Now, Ma'am, I'll be honest with you. I don't like to interfere in families. And I don't like wasting anyone's time. Mostly in these types of cases, the woman says she wants to sign complaints and then drops the charges. Wastes everyone's time. See what I mean?"

Annie was not certain if she was being supported or reprimanded. "Yes, I can see where that would be ... uhm, a problem."

"Good. Now, I looked over the report and I'll tell you frankly, I don't like the sound of these injuries. Seems to me that Kester needs to be smartened up. These athletes think they can do anything they want. You come on down here and sign these complaints. I think Kester needs to be talking with a man instead of picking on a little lady. See what I mean?"

"Yes," Annie thought frantically. "I'm very grateful, Sir, both to you and Officer Grady. The only problem is ... you see ... my husband tends to get angry. If I did sign complaints against him, I'm afraid he would hurt me."

The older man's voice became impatient. "Well, that's the whole damn reason I'm doing this. Grady here thinks he's dangerous. He says you're a nice lady. A smart lady. Ma'am, let me explain this a different way. If you don't sign complaints, and he keeps bothering you, maybe even hurts you, there's not a damned thing I can do about it. If he comes and takes your little one tonight, ...well... let's just say he has that legal right. If you get down here and sign these complaints, I'll personally issue a restraining order. I will also personally explain to him how we treat ladies in west Texas. The order will give you the home for now, if that's what you want, and talk about how we need Kester to behave in the future. Annie, are you listening?"

"Yes, I am, very carefully."

"Good. Ma'am, there is nothing we can do unless you sign this. Then the next time he bothers you, Grady here can scoop him right up. He needs to be taught a lesson. Don't worry about him coming after you. I'll scare the pants right off him. OK?"

"OK," she said shortly. What else could she say? He made sense. Annie thought briefly of Caroline. This would make her day.

"Now," said the judge with satisfaction. "I told Grady you'd understand a little horse sense. You come on down here this morning."

"Well, I can't come right now, Judge. I have to pick my sister up at the airport at noon."

"Her sister is coming in today, Grady," she heard him say. "That's just fine. Grady was real worried with you being alone and all. Come on down with your sister then, say about one?"

"That would be fine, Judge."

She hung up and put her purse back on the table. She had not realized she was still clutching it. Her hands were shaking. Kevin would kill her. It would have to be a mighty big scare to calm him down, she thought, unconsciously lapsing into the judge's dialect. One thing he said had turned her around. The threat of Kevin trying to take Mary was valid. Annie knew that Kevin would try whatever would hurt her most. Mary was the next logical target. She thought of Kevin in jail and winced. He would never forgive her, and he would blame her all the way down the line. So what? Annie thought rebelliously. He had nearly killed her. And it was far from over, she knew. She glanced down at Mary who was trying to remove her little shoes. There were no options. Annie took a deep breath and reached down to grab Mary with her good hand. She would see what Maureen had to say.

• • •

"I don't see where the decision is, Annie," Maureen said easily. The girls drove down the highway from the small airport. "Have you ever asked Kevin not to beat you up?"

305

"Of course," she answered.

"Well, I guess he's not listening then. This judge makes sense. Kevin's not going to lie down for this. Think about it, Annie. There's a pattern here. Kevin always gets real nice after he's been nasty. You might sucker in again. This way, there's not much chance of him talking you out of a divorce. If your luck holds, he won't be talking to you at all." Maureen paused. "Do you want to get divorced?"

Annie did not even pause. "Maureen, I would love so much to be free of this whole thing. It's a nightmare. Yes, I do want to get out."

"There's your answer, Annie. You sign complaints, and I think you'll get the divorce."

"That's true," Annie responded thoughtfully. "If I sign, we won't reconcile. He'd never forgive me. I'm going to do it. Kevin never listened to me in his life. If I thought he'd leave me alone, I would not do this, Maureen."

"I know, Annie. I know," Maureen confirmed. "He took away your choices. Think of it that way. Kevin tied your hands."

That was a good way to look at it, Annie pondered. He had tied her hands by his last assault. Also, his version to Officer Grady had been absurd, slanderous, and very telling. Kevin was not remorseful. He was dead set on avoiding consequences. She set her jaw and drove with purpose now. It was the only thing to do.

"Annie, this child is so smart looking. And beautiful," Maureen reverted to gushing over her niece. "Why is she stuck in that awkward seat?"

Mary was sitting in an infant seat that was secured in the back by the seatbelt. "I don't have a proper car seat. I have to get one."

"Well, we'll stop and buy one today," said the doting aunt in baby talk. "Is that what you want, Mary? A fancy new car seat? We'll go shopping right after Mommy signs your daddy's arrest warrant. Then we'll all feel like celebrating. Won't we, Pretty Girl?"

"Maureen," Annie scolded. "That's not funny."

"She's smiling, Annie," Maureen continued. "Mary thinks it's funny. She's such a smart little girl! Aren't you, Mary?"

Annie glanced in the rearview mirror. Mary was indeed lapping it up. "You're speaking her language, Maureen. She loves to be admired."

It was wonderful to have someone around who adored her little one, and Annie could not help smiling.

They arrived at the courthouse promptly at one. Maureen stayed outside with Mary while Annie went in. The judge was waiting for her and said that Officer Grady had promised to stop back by if he could. It was all very casual and quick. Annie raised her right hand and swore to tell the truth right there in the judge's chambers. He had already prepared the order. Kester (Kevin, she had been forced to correct him much to her mortification) was ordered to stay away from the apartment and Annie. The petitioner, that was Annie, was awarded temporary custody of their daughter, and Kevin could not harass her in any way.

Sitting back in the plush leather chair, Annie glanced up at the judge after reading the order through. He was in his fifties, she guessed. Gray-haired, he looked very stern. Annie smiled tentatively at him, and his whole face suddenly wrinkled. His eyes nearly disappeared, and Annie suddenly thought him the most handsome man she had ever met.

"You're a nice lady, Mrs. Griffin," he said kindly. "There are plenty of good men out there who would be lucky to call you their wife. Remember that. A leopard does not change its spots, and I don't think any man who is capable of treating his wife like Kevin treated you is worth having."

"Thank you, Judge," Annie struggled with her emotions. She was very raw these days. The slightest kindness set off an emotional fire storm. Collecting herself, she asked, "What if he wants visitation?"

The judge leaned back in his chair and considered. "Well, I'm not inclined to grant him visitation just yet. We'll see how he behaves at the bond hearing." He watched

Annie closely and said, "I'm going to issue a warrant, you know. That way we can serve this order on him in person. I'll tell him if he behaves like a gentleman for a couple of months, we'll consider visitation. How does that sound?"

"Yes, OK, I guess that's fine." Kevin was going to be arrested. Annie was at a loss and turned in relief when Officer Grady walked in.

"Hi, Ted," spoke the judge congenially. "Mrs. Griffin is all set and ready to go. We didn't need you at all."

They all smiled, and Annie rose to leave.

"Thank you, Judge," she said humbly.

"Thank Ted here, Ma'am. He bothered me until I called you. Now you leave this business to us and have a nice visit with your sister."

Annie smiled and backed out. Ted Grady gave her one of his winks that were so warm and reassuring. "I'll follow you out, Annie."

Annie walked quickly down the cavernous, cool, hallway of the County Building. She stepped with relief into the bright light. Maureen was chasing an ecstatic Mary around the lawn of the building.

"Maureen," she hissed as she approached them, "Get off the grass. I'm sure you're not supposed to be on the grass."

Maureen looked unabashed. Annie thought wistfully how relaxed and pretty Maureen looked. "Oh, who cares, Annie. She loves it." Mary took off in a determined toddler trot, and Maureen took off after her. Glancing around, Annie saw Officer Grady approaching her.

"Hello," she said politely. "Thank you so much for the dinner yesterday."

He waved his hand in dismissal. "Glad you enjoyed it. You're doing the right thing, Annie. I know it's probably not easy for you. Is that your sister?" Annie followed his gaze to Maureen who was coming back with Mary on her shoulders.

"Yes," Annie said smiling. "She just got here." As Maureen drew closer, Annie made the introductions. Maureen was charming and in seconds had the officer smiling and chuckling. He walked them over to the car and promised to contact Annie when Kevin was arrested and served.

The girls got into the car. Maureen waved again at Officer Grady and turned to Annie. "He's gorgeous," she said in raptures. "I love how he talks. Did you hear him say 'Ya'll'? He's like something out of a Western movie. Annie, do you have an impossible crush on him?"

Annie laughed out loud in spite of herself. "He's very married. In fact, his wife sent me dinner and a Christmas present last night." She paused. "But yes, isn't he handsome?"

"They sent you dinner and a present?" Maureen was wide-eyed. "Oh, Annie, I could cry. That was so nice. Was this the absolute, most horrible Christmas you ever had?" Without waiting for an answer, she continued. "If it's any consolation, we were all miserable, too. I mean the thought of you here by yourself.. and I didn't even tell them all that he did ... Annie, I can't believe how you look. I mean, I didn't say anything at the airport because I don't want to upset you. But honestly! Do you want my honest opinion?"

Annie looked at her sister cheerfully. "I'm sure it's coming."

"I think he's nuts. I mean certifiable. He nearly killed you. I have a week to work on you, but I might as well start now. You should come home. I'm afraid of what he might do."

Annie rolled down her window and let the mildly cool air blow through her hair. "We have all week, Maureen. Let's go to lunch. Are you hungry?"

Maureen smiled and took the message. "Starved. Dad gave me loads of money so let's go get something expensive. He figured we'd need a good few bucks to sort out your Disasterous Marriage." The girls laughed uproariously. It did not take much. With high spirits they set out to spend some of their father's money.

Within the hour they were seated at a trendy restaurant on the outskirts of the city. Mary was perched in a high chair with Maureen's purse in front of her. Sifting through the contents would keep the child happy until the food arrived. Maureen stared in amazement at the quart glass of iced tea that was placed in front of her.

"Do they really expect me to drink all of this?"

"All that and more," Annie said brightly. "They'll be around with the pitcher to refill it within minutes. People here consume quantities of this stuff."

"Why are they all so slow then?" Maureen asked with a glint in her eye. "If I drink half of this, I'll be flying out of my pants from the caffeine. You'd think they'd be moving a little faster."

Annie laughed appreciatively. Maureen had such a fresh outlook on Texas life. "Just think what they'd be like without it."

"True," she grinned. "Do any of them drink pop?"

"They call it soda and yes, but not as much as tea. Tell me what's new at home," Annie said, settling back for a nice chat. "Is Dad dating anyone?"

Maureen, too, settled in but would not be sidestepped. "First we have to talk about you. I was sent here for a reason. My mission: bring you and the baby home. I have seven days to complete this mission, along with about $500. I am to use any tactics and brook no resistance." Annie was all ears. "Dad says never mind the divorce. You can get it in Illinois, but you'll have to wait a while. You can come home now and start school locally. He said to tell you the first two years don't mean much anyway. It's where you graduate from that counts. What do you think? It would be nice if you agreed now and let me relax for the rest of the week."

Annie chuckled with her but shook her head. "Maureen, if I go home, none of this will be resolved. He'll eventually follow me and make my life hell. Can you see Dad dealing with this?" She indicated the neck brace. "He's too old for this kind of stress. I have a shot here. I have a life. Now I've got the car, the scholarship, and the college nursery for Mary. I might need a job or someone to watch her while I work. I don't know. I haven't gotten that far. But I do know

310

this." She lowered her voice. "Kevin is out of control. Can you imagine him coming to Dad's house? He might kill him or something. He's way out there, Maureen, and he doesn't think he's doing anything wrong. He thinks I deserve it. Imagine what I'll deserve for getting him arrested?"

Her brow creased in concentration, Maureen replied thoughtfully. "I disagree with one point. Kevin knows what he's doing is wrong or he would not be denying it. He's not bothering you now. Right? That's because he knows he's in trouble. As long as you have this criminal charge pending, he'll stay away. Also, why would he tell the cop that you're a slut who drinks too much? To make himself look good. He's like a dog covering his misdeed." Annie wrinkled her face distastefully. "That shows that he knows he's guilty. What a psycho Annie! Was he like this everyday?"

Annie told her everything. Maureen was a sympathetic listener, and two hours flew by. Finally, Mary would not be pacified any longer. The girls paid the bill and departed. A ringing telephone greeted them at the apartment. It was Nellie, calling to inform them that Kevin was back in Chicago.

Chapter Twenty-three

Annie clutched the phone. "What do you mean he's in Chicago?"

Nellie was succinct. "Apparently, he can no longer tolerate your roving eye. According to his evil mother, he's beside himself. You are stressing him out, and he needs a separation. He feels just sick about leaving Mary, but you pushed him beyond endurance." Nellie took a breath, then continued. "She called here to say that maybe Dad could talk some sense into you."

"Bastard!" Annie swore vehemently. "He's such a liar, Nellie."

Maureen was taking the baby's jacket off and nearly beside herself. "What? Why is he a liar?"

Annie ignored Maureen and demanded clarification. "First of all, Nellie, what is he doing in Chicago?"

Nellie's voice was dripping with ridicule. "His mother was beside herself when she heard about the separation. They're all pretty much beside themselves over there. She thought it would do Kevin good to get home and take stock."

"Did Dad...?"

Nellie cut her off. "Of course not, Annie. I told her truthfully that Dad was also beside himself and that he had no desire to talk about any of this until your injuries healed."

"You didn't," Annie gasped.

"Yes I did." Nellie was furious. "I didn't sugarcoat anything. I told her that her mind was remarkably uncluttered by facts. Apparently, Kevin left out the parts about the pending criminal charges and the hospital. She knows now. She said that in the circumstances Kevin could be forgiven for getting a little irate."

"Oh, dear God," Annie said weakly. "Do you see what I mean, Nellie? He's vicious. He'll slander me all over the city."

Maureen demanded answers. "He's slandering you all over Chicago? Damn! I'm in the wrong city. What did the mother-in-law tell Dad?"

Annie told Nellie to hold on and briefly brought Maureen up to date. Maureen's opinion was simple. "So what? Tell Nellie to calm down." Annie stared at her without comprehension. "Annie, let them say what they want. This is war. The truth is, Kevin is going to meet a couple of sheriffs when he does get back. Let the mother explain that away. Let it go, Annie. You don't have to convince anyone you're doing the right thing."

Nellie heard Maureen's advice. She, too, calmed down. "She's right, Annie. We're overreacting. Let the Griffins do what they want with Kevin. The real issue is getting you home alive."

"OK, Nell," she said sadly. "I guess you're right. What about Dad?"

Nellie snorted in disgust. "I can handle things at this end. Mrs. Griffin will have to go through me to get to Dad, and that's not going to happen. Annie, what did Maureen mean about sheriffs?"

Annie handed the phone to Maureen. Too exhausted for additional explanations, she took Mary in for her nap. After a quick diaper change, she put Mary in her crib and lay down on the bed. Her mind was reeling. How terrible that she and Kevin were reduced to this. She heard Maureen laughing in the dining room and smiled. She decided not to cry. It would wear her out. She would see Caroline tomorrow and make sense of it all.

• • •

The next day Annie did have a good cry. Sitting in Caroline's office, she held a piece of paper in her hand. On it was written a name in flowery handwriting.

"She's a good lawyer and a dear friend," Caroline explained. "She'll take your case for free. She calls it pro bono. You have to see her tomorrow in her office, and she'll draw up the papers. There's a filing fee, but she thinks she can get it waived. What do you think?"

Annie was weepy. "I don't know. I'm incredibly grateful." She frowned in tearful concentration. "My dad could give me some money, Caroline, and I have some put aside."

Caroline waved a graceful hand. "Keep it. You're going to need every penny. She WANTS to do this, Annie. She does one case for free each year. When I told her about you, she jumped right at it. She also defends battered women."

"Why would they need defending?" Annie asked perplexed.

"Well, Honey," Caroline explained, "it's not uncommon for a battered woman to defend herself and end up killing him. Many times she feels that the only way out is to kill him while he is sleeping. Or else she's protecting her children. It happens. Then she's charged with murder or attempted murder. I could tell you stories... But let's concentrate on you. Are you feeling ambivalent about getting a divorce?"

"Yes," she said, no longer surprised that Caroline could read her mind. "Isn't that bizarre?"

"Not at all. What specifically is bothering you?"

"It's going to sound strange. On the one hand, I often thought about Kevin dying. It seemed like that would be the only escape. In some ways it still does. I would lie in

315

bed and imagine he had a car accident. Or a heart attack. And then I would feel so guilty. How horrible that a woman would actually want her husband to die. I also thought about killing him. Caroline, I didn't tell you everything that happened that night. There was something else that he did."

Caroline's pained expression suggested to Annie that she had an idea. "Do you want to tell me now?"

"He raped me," Annie said flatly. "He's my husband, right? I did have sex with him on a regular basis. So how come it's destroying me?" With that she burst into sobs and could no longer continue. The box of Kleenex appeared. Caroline said nothing. An occasional squeeze of her arms told Annie that she was with her. "I'm going crazy, Caroline. I wanted to kill him that night. I wanted to kill him when he was passed out on the floor with no pants on. If there was a gun in the house I might have." Her sobs continued. "Here's the really sick part. I'm not sure I want to divorce him. I'm going to because it's the right thing to do. But part of me misses him. I miss being a family. I miss the idea that Mary's father is asleep in the next room while I'm cooking dinner. That someone is around who cares as much about Mary as I do. And he does, Caroline. I know he does. It doesn't mean he's a well-adjusted father. I know that, too. But he does love her, and I miss sharing that with him."

Annie gave up and collapsed into tears. Caroline sat, peacefully solemn. After the storm passed, Annie raised her eyes. "I think I'll stop crying now. I'm wasting time."

"You're not wasting time, Annie," Caroline said grimly. "This is what this time is about."

"I get through the days," Annie said bewildered. "But it's like I'm bobbing around in a sea of denial. There's this horror hanging over my head, but if I looked at it all the time I'd go around the bend. You know?"

"Yes, I do," Caroline said levelly. "What is this thing hanging over your head? Specifically? Close your eyes and turn around. See what it is."

Annie closed her eyes. She squinted as tears struggled to come through. "It's Kevin with the mean face."

"What mean face?"

"The face he had when he was beating me up."

"OK. I take it you're afraid of that face."

"Terrified. I hate that face. I want to kill him, Caroline. So why do I miss him?"

"Because he has been a major part of your life for seven years. Of course, you miss him. It's perfectly normal." Caroline began waving HER magic wand. Unlike Kevin's, it made Annie feel sane. "Annie, have you ever had a tooth pulled?" Annie nodded. "After the dentist pulls it, you're relieved. Right?" Annie again concurred. "Well, how many times does your tongue run itself over the spot where the tooth was? Ten? Twenty? More like a hundred times a day. Just because it was hurting you does not mean you don't notice it's gone and miss it. It leaves a gap, Annie. It's going to take a while. As time goes by, you don't miss it as much. But it does take time. Now, should you have kept the tooth? Of course not. It was causing you pain and might have made you very sick, even killed you. Pulling the tooth was the right decision. But it's going to hurt."

"I take it Kevin is the tooth in this analogy?" Annie said with a grin.

They burst into laughter. "Yes," Caroline confirmed. "He's the tooth. The infected molar." Again they laughed. "Nobody can make you ready, Annie. It's up to you. Don't feel guilty because you miss Kevin. He's your husband. Part of you is going to feel loyalty for him after he's arrested. What you have to remember is that Kevin is getting arrested because he committed a crime. You are getting divorced because Kevin is abusive. Yes, I agree he probably loves Mary. But not enough to let Mary's mother live in peace. You're going to have to fight for every ounce of peace, Annie. Backing down will only prolong the agony." Caroline changed gears. "Do you want to talk about the sexual attack?"

"No," Annie nearly shouted. "Not at all. Maybe someday, but not for a while. It was the most horrible thing that's ever happened to me. I have to remember that every time I feel sorry for Kevin. Or I think I miss him. He's a dog, Caroline, and part of me hates him."

They discussed details for the rest of the session. Annie asked Caroline to read into the future and predict Kevin's next move. Caroline said she would be surprised if Kevin bowed out gracefully. She warned Annie not to expect cooperation. That was why the criminal charges were so critical. The restraining order hinged on them.

Annie left feeling tired but clear-sighted.

• • •

Within twenty-four hours, Annie signed another document listing her as the petitioner. Griffin vs Griffin asked the court to grant Anne Griffin a divorce on the grounds of irreconcilable differences. The attorney, Madeline Freeman, a dark-haired woman in a severely tailored suit, informed Annie that the petition would be kept simple. In these cases, she said, the less there was to argue about the better. Her primary concern was Annie's safety, which was currently being monitored by the criminal court's restraining order. She explained that her objective was a speedy divorce.

Annie nervously explained that Kevin could have anything, as long as he left her alone.

The attorney interrupted her, "Sure, sure ... I know. No offense, Annie, but it's best to trust me on this. I'm asking that you maintain the residence. Where are you going to go with a baby? The respondent is also being asked to pay your hospital bills, along with child support at a rate to be determined by the court. You'll, of course, retain full custody with reasonable visitation granted. These are not big requests."

"Kevin is going to be furious," Annie interjected nervously.

Her lawyer did not even look up. "Don't you get it, Annie? A sudden wind change will aggravate Kevin Griffin. He's not exactly going to be pleased about the arrest warrant either. We're throwing in the divorce papers, too, while we've got the restraining order."

Madeline Freeman took Polaroid snaps of Annie's injuries and asked Annie to sign a release of information so she could access the medical records. The photos would be available to the prosecutor's office in the unlikely event that the case went to trial. Annie wondered aloud why her case was not likely to go to trial.

The attorney frowned. "You've got medical reports and pictures. He'll have to plead guilty. He'll lose a trial."

This news consoled Annie immensely. "He's going to say terrible things about me if he can."

Madeline did look up now. "Annie, they all threaten to do that. The only relevant issue at trial will be if the jury or judge believes beyond a reasonable doubt that Kevin Griffin committed the crime he's been accused of. Kevin's allegations that you're sleeping with the chess team ... or whatever he's saying ... are not relevant."

Annie smiled at this. It wasn't far off. Thirty minutes later, she was back in the car heading for home. While stopped at a light, she began to cry. Events were moving too quickly. One week ago she had hurried home from work. Her biggest problem was whether or not Kevin would be angry because she was late. Seven days later, she had a car, she had been raped and assaulted, had been admitted to a hospital, had charged her husband with battery, had celebrated Christmas, and had two visitors from home. Oh yes, she reminded herself, and had filed for divorce.

The light changed. She accelerated, still sniffling. Feelings of loneliness dogged her, and she admitted to herself that she missed Kevin. After a firm mental shake, she forced herself to be realistic. She had been lonely with Kevin, too. Only then she had also been afraid. Caroline's advice was to take it one step at a time. Annie was told to relinquish the things she could not immediately control. Like worries about the future.

Later she and Maureen lay sprawled across the living room floor with Mary. Annie filled her sister in on the details. She was officially getting divorced. How sad it was that Kevin would find out from a stranger.

"What else can you do, Annie?" Maureen asked reasonably. "He's not going to take it well no matter how you wrap it. Let him fracture the sheriff's ribs."

Annie nodded absently. "I know. I know. There's probably not a good way to break this kind of news. Besides, Maureen, what does he expect me to do? He doesn't like me. He wants to kill me. Does he think I'm a moron? I have to leave him."

"Of course, you do," Maureen said sympathetically. "You have to leave him FINALLY, you should say. Annie, he's done this before. I mean, who are we kidding? Kevin's always been kind of abusive. You could never go out unless Kevin was there. That's not right. You know that yourself."

"I know, Maureen," Annie said ruefully. "It was never normal. But who would have guessed he'd get this bad. He was nice in many ways. He loves me so much." Maureen rolled her eyes and Annie exclaimed. "He does, Maureen. I know he does. It's twisted. But part of me thinks he loves me a lot. He doesn't know how to love, that's the problem."

"Any more of his love and you'll end up dead, Little Girl," Maureen predicted darkly. "Dad is going to kill me if you don't come home with me. So I've thought of a solution. Why don't I take Mary as a peace offering? You've got a lot of things to take care of. You're pale, Annie. You need to get better. You also need to start school and make the arrangements for Mary. Let me take her home, and Nellie will bring her back. It'll give you a break."

Surprising herself, Annie agreed. "I know I should argue, but frankly, Maureen, it's a great idea. I would love two weeks to get sorted out. It would simplify things. Do you think she'll be OK without me?"

Maureen was stroking Mary's hair. Mary had crawled into her lap and was lying quietly. The child gazed at her aunt with worshipful eyes. "I kind of think so, Annie."

The girls both laughed. Annie beat back pangs of guilt. Mary adored her aunt. Maureen was full of treats and fun.

320

Annie thought remorsefully that she had not been a very good mother lately. How could I be? she defended herself. Hardening her heart, she nodded. Mary would be best away from her emotional mother right now. Annie would take care of business and prepare a life for them both.

The remainder of the week passed pleasantly. The sisters took Mary for long drives in her fancy new car seat. On New Year's eve, they shared a bottle of wine and watched Channel WGN. Annie wondered with an ache where Kevin was celebrating. Maureen was lighthearted, though, and Annie was much better for spending the time with her. They were just toasting the New Year when the phone rang. Nellie was calling with a full report.

"Kevin's mother called today," she began. "She asked me to inform you that Kevin will be moving in with one of the guys on the team. She also said in view of the circumstances it would be best if you moved back here."

Annie bristled. "Did she really? She has a lot of nerve."

Maureen was immediately frustrated. "Who? Who has a lot of nerve?"

"I think she's amazing, Annie," Nellie agreed. "She said since you already tried counseling, there was no point delaying matters."

Nellie paused, and Annie was alert. "What else, Nellie?"

"Well, she said Kevin does not want a divorce. In spite of the way you've acted, he hopes to work things out. He'll only stay with this guy until you come around."

"I knew it," Annie said quickly. "He's told her horrible things, but he does not want a divorce?" She took a deep breath. "At least he's got somewhere to stay."

Nellie brightened. "I've got good news, too. You're losing Maureen on Monday but guess who's coming to see you on Tuesday?"

"Oh, no," Annie moaned. "Not Dad."

"Annie," Nellie chided. "You're rotten. No. Not your loving father who is worried sick about you. Danny is blowing your way again. I told him it would be extremely rude to come and stay for less than twenty-four hours. He agreed.

Apparently he's staying from Monday until Wednesday. He's driving up from New Orleans in some fancy new car he bought. He has to go right back, of course, and can't come here. But at least you'll have another visitor."

Annie smiled. She felt tears of gratitude in her eyes. How lucky she was to have family. "That's great, Nel. I'll be glad to see him."

"SEE WHO?" demanded Maureen. "You guys are so rude, Annie."

"I hear her, Annie," Nellie said cheerfully referring to Maureen. "I won't keep you. Tell Maureen that Johnny is spending the new year at home. He called today to see if Dad needed any help with the floor in the basement. He's such a brown-nose." Nellie chuckled. "He made a point to tell Dad he was staying in. Dad told him he should go out and have a few drinks while the dragon was away. He laughed hysterically, of course." Annie looked at Maureen and giggled.

"What did she say?" demanded Maureen indignantly. "Is she making fun of Johnny?"

"Annie, don't worry about Mary," concluded Nellie. "We're all delighted she's coming. We'll call you every night if you want."

"Thanks, Nellie. Maureen is clairvoyant," Annie said chuckling. "I'll let you fill her in on the Johnny Sighting."

With that, she handed the phone to the impatient Maureen. Plopping down on the couch, she thought hard. Danny was coming for a reason.

• • •

"You have to learn to shoot, Annie," Danny said impatiently. "I like Kevin as much as I like anyone. But he does not like you." Glancing at her cast, he added, "One might suggest that Kevin hates you. We've been over this before. If you want to stay, you'll need protection."

Annie sighed. They were sitting at her kitchen table. Maureen and Mary had departed yesterday. Danny arrived today, Tuesday, and characteristically, was getting right to the point.

"I'm not disagreeing with you," she said thoughtfully. "I just wonder if I could shoot it."

"Think back a few days," her brother said dryly. "Would you have used it the night he pulled this?" He again looked pointedly at the cast.

Annie concentrated. "Yes," she said firmly after a pause. "I thought he was going to kill me. I would have shot him."

"Of course, you would have," said her brother in satisfaction. "Now I'll take a short nap, and then we'll find a field or something."

"OK, Danny," Annie said affectionately. "Go ahead and take my bed." Danny had departed New Orleans at two o'clock the previous morning and made record time. On Friday he would leave the country again. Deep disappointment had lined his face on hearing that Kevin was out of state. Annie could not help but wonder what his intentions had been.

A stillness settled over the tidy apartment. Annie relished the quiet and sat down on the couch to think. Kevin would be back in town by Thursday night. He had practice on Friday. Once he was arrested, anything could happen. He would be served with the restraining order. That should spell out the rules to him. Annie considered her husband for a moment. She shook her head negatively to the empty room. Kevin would not respect the rules forever. And paper would not stop him. Yes, she would take the gun. If only to scare him.

• • •

The sun slipped predictably toward the horizon, softening the rough beauty of the cactus field. Annie shifted her weight, in an effort to frighten away the rattlesnakes she was certain lurked underfoot.

"Do you have any anti-venom in your death bag, Danny?" she asked her older brother.

He replied lightly. "No. But not to worry. We can amputate any affected area with a little whiskey and a pocketknife. Now pay attention. Guns are no joke." He muttered sternly as he unpacked a black leather bag. Annie sighed and tried to concentrate.

"This is a .22 caliber Ruger. It has a clip and is semiautomatic. It's a small weapon but should bring down a big man if you aim it right." He glanced down at his younger sister.

"OK," she summarized. "The clip holds the bullets, which are rounds. Depending on my mood, I can shoot once or seven times. What if I miss, and he's really mad? Can I shoot over my shoulder while I'm climbing out of the window?"

Danny frowned. "Stop messing around. Do you want to die? I can't stay with you, and he's coming back. You said yourself he might kill you next time. Concentrate, Annie! This may come down to him or you." Danny's manner softened his tone. "You're a sitting duck. If you insist on staying, you have to learn to use the gun."

Annie met his gaze directly. "What if I kill him, Danny?"

"Then our problems are solved, and we'll throw a party," he said gaily. "C'mon. Pay attention." He gingerly turned the gun over in his hand and continued his instructions. "This is the safety. When the safety is on, the gun won't fire. Click it off with your finger, and she's ready. Always click the safety on when you're finished. I cannot stress this enough. Whenever you even look at the gun, check the safety. Guns are not bad, Annie, people are. You have to be serious about guns. They can save your life or get you killed. Take it. Let's try one."

He gently handed the gun to his sister. She felt the weight of the weapon in her hand and began to put her finger on the trigger.

"Safety!" he barked. "Check the safety!"

Startled, she jumped back and nearly dropped the gun.

"Dammit, Danny. You scared me to death. I hope whoever I'm shooting has the courtesy to keep quiet."

"Take it nice and easy until you're comfortable handling it."

She carefully turned the gun and checked the safety. "Safety is on," she said lightly. "Life as we know it, may continue."

"Let me show you how to aim," Danny resumed his lesson. "Another crucial point: Never point a gun at anything you do not intend to shoot. And never, never shoot at anything you don't intend to kill. I don't care if it's a squirt gun. Guns go off, especially in shaky hands like yours. Are you ready? Raise the gun and aim." He pointed to the cactus targeted for destruction. "That's your bad guy. Aim a little low. This gun has a kick."

"What's a kick?"

"When you fire, the gun jumps up a little. If you're aiming for the chest, shoot a little lower." In response to her look of bewilderment, he added, "Have you ever seen a woman fire a shotgun in a western movie? The gun jumps up when she fires. That's why you aim a bit lower. Another important point about aiming: always aim at the biggest part of a person's body. That's the middle. Let's assume you want to hit the bad guy in the chest. Aim a little lower, and you have a snowball's chance in hell of actually hitting him. Understand?"

"Implicitly. Aim for his genitals, and I'll connect somewhere near the light fixture." She smiled widely.

"Shoot the damn thing," he said rolling his eyes. "You'll see what I mean."

Annie aimed the gun with her good hand and braced it with her cast. Closing her left eye, she carefully squeezed the trigger. BOOM. The gun went off with no apparent damage to the prickly target. "Whew!" she said, letting herself breathe. "I see what you mean. The cactuses in west Texas are safe from the likes of me."

"Cacti is the plural form of cactus," Danny observed dryly. "Not bad, Annie. You didn't faint or anything. Let's try it again."

The lesson continued for two hours. With the sunlight nearly exhausted, Danny cleared up the debris. Annie looked around the field and sighed.

"How did I end up in Texas shooting at 'cacti,' Danny?"

"You married the wrong guy, Kiddo," he said simply. "It's nothing to be ashamed of. People marry maniacs every day. That's why they get guns and divorces."

"Guns stink, Danny," Annie said with feeling. "Maybe if I prayed more, this would not have happened."

"Guns and rosaries, Annie. We need them both. I always carry holy water, and I usually have a gun. C'mon, let's get out of here before the snakes come out. We'll go get a beer. I hear there's a blizzard in Chicago."

They dumped their gear in the car and headed back onto the ranch road. Annie gunned the accelerator and glanced back at the dust clouds trailing them. She let her thoughts wander. Was she really capable of killing Kevin?

Chapter Twenty-four

On Friday evening, Annie waded through bills. Under Caroline's direction, she tackled concrete tasks involving her future. While writing checks and addressing envelopes, she began to achieve Caroline's goal. She felt capable. The helplessness that had paralyzed her was lifting. That afternoon she had opened a checking account in her name. A small deposit satisfied the account manager. Annie was reluctant to put all of her money where she lacked immediate access. There was no telling when she might get in her car and abandon Texas. She resolved to have the car filled with gas and cash ready at all times. She likened it to wearing a parachute in a plane. Odds were against having to use it, but if you needed it, you needed it.

She was just beginning to stretch when the phone rang. She jumped and looked at it uneasily. Kevin would definitely be back in town by now.

"Hello," she answered with a confident voice.

"Annie? It's Darlene. How ARE you?"

"Hi, Darlene," she answered cautiously. "How was your trip?"

"Fine, fine," Darlene said impatiently. "I felt so bad leaving you like that. Are you feeling better? Greg said you had some broken bones."

"Not too many," she answered briefly.

Darlene waited. When Annie failed to supply details, she continued. "Well, I guess practice was interesting today. But you probably know all about that."

Annie rolled her eyes in exasperation. Darlene sounded catty. "All about what, Darlene?"

"Didn't you issue an arrest warrant for him?"

Annie winced in dismay. "Was he arrested?"

"Yes, he was," Darlene said with poorly concealed delight. "In front of everyone. And a restraining order was read out loud to him in front of the whole team. He must have been mortified."

"I see," Annie said weakly. "Darlene, I had no power over how he was served. I signed criminal complaints against him and asked for a restraining order. The judge issued the warrant. I had no idea they would serve him at practice."

"Not only serve him," Darlene said emphatically. "But take him away in handcuffs. Pretty embarrassing."

"I was pretty embarrassed myself at the Emergency Room." She stopped herself. Darlene had a big mouth. It was possible Kevin would hear every bit of this conversation. "Still, I'm sorry it happened that way." She forced herself to refrain from asking questions.

"Yes," Darlene continued. "I guess the coach followed them down to bail him out."

"Well then, he did not have to stay too long. That's good," Annie said politely. "My main concern was the restraining order."

"Annie, are you sure you didn't overreact just a little bit?" Darlene said sarcastically. "I mean Kevin moved out of the apartment. Did you really have to get him arrested?"

"I thought so," she answered with a sinking heart. There would be no friendship with Darlene. She was obviously discussing the matter with Greg, Kevin, and the team. "I did ask Kevin not to attack me, Darlene. You were the one who called to warn me. Remember? You didn't want me to come over because Greg was afraid of him. Greg thought I could handle him, though. Well, as you can see, I couldn't. I don't want that to happen again, Darlene. He told me if I ever left him, he would kill me. I think he meant it." Annie closed her mouth firmly. Darlene would not understand. Most people did not. Caroline had warned her about squandering valuable emotional energy.

"I know you guys had a major fight. But it's over now. Let it go, Annie. You've got him out of the apartment. What more do you want?"

Annie finally understood. Greg was sitting with her. Darlene was calling to get Annie to drop the charges. For Kevin. "I want to start school next week and take care of my daughter. In peace. I don't think Kevin will let me do that unless he's forced to."

"It seems cold. Don't you think?" Annie speculated that Darlene was enjoying her role in the drama. She would give Greg plenty of fodder for tomorrow's practice.

"Apparently you do, Darlene. I'm trying to do what's best for all of us." Annie's voice was sharper than she intended.

Darlene jumped in hastily. "Don't misunderstand me, Annie. I think Kevin has a horrible temper. But why torture the guy? All he wants is to get back with you. If you're going to abandon him, you could at least do it kindly."

"I'm trying to, Darlene. See you later." Annie hung up. She was shaking with rage and despair. Annie guessed Darlene was delighted with the opportunity to get Greg's attention. She could castigate Annie's actions and thereby raise her own self-esteem. Well, let her, Annie thought wickedly. She'll always be insecure. Judging me will only give her temporary satisfaction. Few understood Kevin. She would have to live with that.

Annie cleared the table quickly. The bills were taken care of, and her life was, on paper anyway, in order. She had registered for school and was starting on Monday. Mary was enrolled in the nursery. Both Mary and Annie would attend school from nine until noon. That was a full load and satisfied the terms of the scholarship. Financially, Annie would be solvent for three months. During that time she would need to get a job. She resolved to begin looking next week. Once the baby came back, it would be more difficult.

• • •

The next morning, Annie took laundry down to the wash house. The small load was done in no time, and Annie began to pack up her soap. A slamming door announced company. Darlene staggered in with two highly stacked baskets.

"Let me help," Annie offered, wrestling with the top basket.

"Thanks," Darlene panted, putting down her load. "I'm glad I ran into you. Were you mad last night?"

Annie averted her eyes. "Not at all. I do feel like you're completely sympathetic to Kevin. That's your business, though."

"Annie, that's not true. All I'm saying is this. It's over. He knows that. He's heartbroken. Maybe he deserves to be. But criminal charges? Come on! That's a bit much."

"Darlene, do you really think he's going to leave me alone?" Annie struggled for words. "I know him better than you. He won't. If I could have gotten the restraining order without the charges, I would have. Until I'm convinced he's willing to let it go ... I have no choice."

"How's your arm?" Darlene changed the subject. "Does it still hurt?"

Annie shrugged. "Not really."

Darlene took a breath. "Annie, I've got to tell you honestly. Kevin wants me to feel you out on something. He wants to get counseling with you. He thinks you can work it out."

Annie felt her heart twist. "Don't do this to me."

Darlene exclaimed hastily. "He knows he was wrong. He's sorry, Annie. He really is. He's willing to forget the whole incident."

"I'll bet he is," Annie retorted sarcastically. "Darlene, try to understand. I'm not mad at him. But I can't give him an inch. Not even a millimeter. He's too manipulative. Tell him if he loves me, he should leave me alone."

Picking up her belongings, she turned and left. She would have to avoid Darlene now that she was Kevin's ambassador. The stairs leading to her apartment were littered with belongings. Annie gingerly stepped around boxes. She must be getting a new neighbor. As she neared the top, a face popped out of the door next to hers.

"Hello," said a friendly voice.

Annie glanced up. Her first impression was that she was looking at the back of somebody's head. Tightly permed hair was pushed back, and a face appeared. A woman in her mid-twenties stood with the door propped open.

"Hello," Annie responded easily. "My name is Annie Griffin. Are you my new neighbor?"

"Yes. I hope I'm not bothering ya'll with the mess on the stairs."

"Not at all" was Annie's warm reply. "Are you and your husband moving in today?"

"It's just me. And my six-year-old daughter. I'm divorced."

Annie felt her spirits lift. "Are you? I'm sorry to hear that. I'm getting divorced, too."

The girl rolled her eyes and extended her hand. "My name is Marty. And I'm sorry that you're getting divorced, but if you're anything like me, you're probably relieved."

Annie burst out laughing and shook the woman's hand. "Something like that. Can I give you a hand?"

"No, I'm taking a break. Come on in for some iced tea."

Annie spent the next thirty minutes talking to her new friend. Marty was in the nursing program and had waited for this apartment two years. One year remained of her studies. Then she had to serve an internship. Annie was delighted with Marty. A native Texan, she was warm and genuine. A summary of Annie's dilemma prompted Marty to give Annie her phone number. If Annie had any problems, she should call. Annie thanked her sweetly. It would be nice to know that a friend was so close.

Leaving Marty to her unpacking, Annie went in and called Chicago. Mary was fine. Having a wonderful time, according to Eileen. Annie hung up quickly. She wanted to save her long distance calls for when she was lonely or depressed. She readied herself to go shopping. Groceries were necessary, and she had resolved to buy herself a new pair of jeans for school. She drove away feeling content and hopeful.

. . .

The first week of school flew by. New notebooks and texts were neatly stacked on the desk. By Thursday afternoon, Annie felt as though she had been in college forever. She was just sitting down to lunch when the phone rang. The female caller identified herself as a paralegal for Annie's attorney. She informed Annie that there was an emergency hearing at two. Annie's presence was required.

Annie replaced the telephone with shaking hands. Dialing Caroline's number, she instructed the secretary to cancel her afternoon appointment. She gratefully accepted an appointment for the next day and changed into a skirt and blouse.

An hour later she was again walking up the steps of the court house. Uncertain of a final destination, Annie paused in the vestibule.

"Annie?"

She turned with a sinking heart. "Hello, Kevin," she said weakly. "I don't think we should be talking."

For a moment. his look of pain pierced her armor. "What happened to your arm?"

Annie hardened her heart. "You broke it."

He looked at her in misery. "I'm sorry. You can't know how sorry I am." His brown eyes welled up. "Please listen to me. I love you. I can change. I've done it before."

"Annie," rang out a female voice. Annie turned to see Madeline Freeman walking briskly down the hall. "Come this way."

Turning shakily, she followed her lawyer. Kevin followed

them. "Annie, you've got to talk to me. Right now!"

The lawyer turned abruptly on her heels. "No, Mr. Griffin. You're wrong. She does not have to talk to you. Following her like this could be construed as harassment, which you'll find has been prohibited by the restraining order that was served to you."

Annie held her breath. Glancing back at Kevin, she saw the look of rage on his face. Instinctively, Annie began to walk. She arrived at the courtroom door and looked back. Kevin was pointing down into the face of her lawyer. Annie made out the words "dyke" and "feminist bitch." Her face flushed in humiliation.

The lawyer turned and walked quickly toward Annie. Kevin went the other way.

"Are you all right?" Annie asked sympathetically.

"Fine," Madeline answered through tight lips. "I can certainly see why you're divorcing him."

"I told you," Annie said in dismay. "I'm so sorry."

"No," Madeline held up her hand. "You have no reason to apologize for him. You've done nothing wrong, Annie. Now I can go in and tell the judge exactly what we're dealing with." Taking a breath, she laughed shakily. "Hello, Annie. How are you today?"

They both laughed. "Fine thank you. And how are you?"

She smiled. "Great. Thanks for coming on short notice. Kevin has hired an attorney. The bottom line is this. Kevin's attorney is petitioning the court for emergency relief. He feels that the restraining order, which has precluded him from entering the residence, is placing undue hardship on him." Seeing Annie's look of horror, she went on hastily, "I'm sure this judge will refuse to amend the restraining order. It's not his jurisdiction. Another judge is presiding over the criminal charge and the restraining order. Let's see what happens."

They entered the courtroom and sat down. Moments later, Kevin entered with his attorney and sat down on the opposite side. Annie put her hand on her stomach. She was terrified she would become sick. She felt her knees shaking and clamped them together.

"Griffin vs Griffin," bellowed a clerk.

Annie's lawyer rose and indicated that Annie should follow her. Her peripheral vision assured her that Kevin was doing the same. A middle-aged judge read through a file in front of him. The four interested parties stood before him silently. Everyone waited while he leisurely familiarized himself with the motion.

Finally, he looked up. "What have we got here?" he addressed Kevin's attorney.

"Your Honor," answered the man with Kevin, "my client has been thrown out of his home and denied access to his daughter for over two weeks. We're asking for immediate relief."

The judge turned to Annie's lawyer. "Your Honor," Madeline responded in a firm voice, "Mr. Griffin was legally removed from the residence by a restraining order signed on the 26th of December. That order is running in tandem with a criminal charge of battery under Judge Melbourne. The respondent is currently out on bond. We would strenuously object to any change in the status of that order."

The judge sighed heavily. Turning to Kevin's lawyer, he said in an aggravated tone. "What do you really want, Counsel? You must know I'm not going to change another judge's order."

The man assumed a placating air. "Your Honor, my client wants to see his daughter. It's my understanding that the petitioner does not even HAVE the child. She sent her out of state without consulting my client. Now if the petitioner wants to relinquish custody, my client would be glad to raise his little girl."

"This is outrageous, Your Honor," Annie's attorney jumped in. "The child was taken back to Chicago temporarily while my client recovered from injuries sustained when the respondent assaulted her. I'd like to add that the injuries included several broken bones and two lacerations requiring stitches."

"Your Honor, give me a break here," interrupted the

opposing counsel. "We're not trying the battery case."

"I'm not trying anything, Your Honor," Annie's lawyer said calmly. "I'm merely familiarizing the court with the facts. As for the child, she'll be brought back within the next two weeks. Judge Melbourne denied the respondent access to both the mother and child in the interest of their safety."

"Under the circumstances, it seems reasonable to me," said the judge. "What else can I do for you today, Counsel?"

Annie was trying to breathe slowly. Her anxiety was at such a level as to stop her from breathing if she let it. She wondered idly how Kevin was faring. She dared not hazard a look in his direction.

"There is another matter, Your Honor," said the attorney without missing a beat. "My client is interested in preserving the marriage. He would respectfully ask the court to order some kind of counseling before the marriage is terminated."

"That also seems reasonable," said the judge turning to Annie's lawyer. "What say you, Madame Attorney?"

"No, Your Honor. Absolutely not. My client is only interested in protecting herself and her child. Her decision to file this petition for dissolution of marriage was well thought out and remains irrevocable."

"Your Honor," said the opposing counsel, "would it be too much to ask that my colleague not answer for her client? Surely she can say whether or not she wants counseling."

The judge nodded. "Mrs. Griffin?" he said, looking at Annie. "Are you willing to give this boy one more chance? You look like nice folks. It's hard to be married when you're young. Maybe you two are throwing in the towel too soon. How about seeing a counselor and finding out for sure?"

Annie looked helplessly at her lawyer. The woman winked at her. "You can talk, Annie. Tell them what you think about additional marriage counseling."

"Well, Judge," Annie answered in a shaking voice, "it did not work out the last time. I don't want to."

Annie's lawyer spoke quietly, "Are you afraid of Kevin, Annie?"

"Your Honor," shouted Kevin's lawyer. "She's putting words in her mouth. Maybe she should let the lady answer."

Annie spoke up. "Yes. I'm afraid of him. And no. I have no desire to attend counseling with him. I'm seeing a counselor right now for myself. I won't change my mind."

"Nobody is talking you into this, are they?" queried the judge.

Annie's lawyer tapped her pen in annoyance. "Your Honor, contrary to what my colleague thinks, I do familiarize myself with my client's wishes before bringing a case before the bench. The reality is this. My client has petitioned for divorce and, by her own admission, has no desire to attend counseling with the respondent. I would also like to ask the court at this time to admonish the respondent to refrain from threatening me. Either in this building or outside it. He threatened me in the hallway before this hearing."

"Your Honor," exclaimed Kevin's lawyer. "This IS outrageous. Counsel is attempting to slander my client."

"I'm attempting to protect myself and my client, Counsel."

"HOLD IT," the judge roared. "Stop this nonsense." Turning to Annie's lawyer, he said heavily. "He better have, Miss, or you're in trouble."

"I'm married, Your Honor, so you can call me Ma'am." Annie looked down and noticed that her representative was now clutching her pen tightly. "The respondent was harassing my client saying 'You have to talk to me.' I informed him that she did not HAVE to talk to him. At that point he told me to mind my own business or I would get hurt. Specifically I was told to mind my own 'fucking business' because I was a 'dyke lawyer' and a 'feminist bitch.' I have no interest in being hurt by this man, Your Honor, and would ask the court to firmly admonish the respondent. If he harasses my client in the court house, Your Honor, we can only imagine what he'll do outside of it. Additionally, if I am threatened again, I will bring charges against him."

"Your Honor, Your Honor," said Kevin's lawyer putting his hands out in a placating manner.

"Yes, I see," the judge said noncommittally. He gave a deep sigh and addressed Kevin directly. "Young man, I'm sorry for you. You don't want this divorce. I can see that. I wish I could change your wife's mind, but I can't. Most young people today have no sense of commitment. Obviously, your wife has made a decision. She may be abandoning you without giving you a chance. There's nothing I can do about that. Now, I know you're feeling angry about all of this. I don't blame you. But you can't threaten people or call them names. Try to behave." With this he winked at Kevin. "Send some flowers and hope for the best."

Annie's mouth dropped open. Had she heard him correctly? She began to giggle.

"Court's in recess," said the judge with a bang of the gavel. He left the bench.

"I'm serious about the charges," Madeline said to Kevin's lawyer.

Annie was surprised to see Kevin's lawyer nod his head affirmatively. "I'll sure make that clear to him, Madeline. I myself will firmly admonish him."

"Thanks, Bob," said Madeline gratefully. "See you next month."

Kevin was already walking out of the room. Annie was confused. Was Kevin's lawyer being nice now?

"Madeline?" Annie asked. "I don't understand. Is that guy a friend of yours?" Her lawyer smiled understandingly. "We've been friends for years, Annie. Just because we're enemies at the bench doesn't mean we don't like each other. It went well. Nothing has changed. Are you OK?"

Annie shook her head, dazed. "I guess so. I'm shaking. What was all that about flowers?"

The older woman snorted in disgust. "Just be grateful your restraining order is in criminal court. This judge likes to think he's a traditionalist. That means he's a male chauvinist pig. We're going to keep the divorce simple and leave your restraining order where it is. It will be fine."

They talked some more. Annie's queries were vague, and Madeline told her to write down future questions as she thought of them. They walked together to Annie's car, making certain Kevin was not around. As Annie pulled out, she saw Kevin talking with his attorney. It looked as though they were arguing. She put on her directional and left quickly.

• • •

Annie arrived home and plopped down on the couch. Minutes later there was a knock on the door. Her stomach lurched as she remembered she had not put the chain on. In the split second it took to make a decision, Annie was on her feet and heading for the back door.

"Annie?" called a female voice.

Annie let her breath out in relief. It was Marty. She turned and opened the door. "Hi," she said warmly.

"Hi, yourself. You look like you've seen a ghost." Marty was carrying two large glasses of what looked to be Kool-Aid.

"Come in," Annie said, stepping back. "I thought you were my husband coming to kill me."

"Good God. Why would he want to kill you?" Marty stepped in with the glasses, and Annie motioned her into a chair.

"I just got back from court. He was not pleased." She sighed heavily. "I'm afraid of what he'll do."

"Here, drink this," said her neighbor, extending a glass. "It's my own concoction. Raspberry iced tea with gelatin. It's supposed to be good for your nails." Annie smiled and took a deep drink. "Do you really think he's going to come after you? Even with the restraining order?"

Annie rolled her eyes. "I don't know. That's what's so scary. A friend says he's sane and rational. She swears he won't bother me unless I tell him it's OK. Then again, he just called my lawyer a 'dyke' and a 'bitch.' He did not seem very rational to me."

Marty's eyes were round. "He didn't! What a nut!"

The two young women talked for another hour. Annie explained some of what had gone on before, and Marty shared her story of marital woe. Annie felt much better. It was good to talk. Marty reminded Annie to call her if she got frightened.

After a shower and a light dinner, Annie sat down to her homework. A ring of the telephone interrupted her. Annie hesitated. Darlene would upset her. As would Kevin. Resolving to make short work of either of them, she answered.

"Hi," said Annie's lawyer. "This is Madeline Freeman. Are you by any chance looking for a job, Annie?"

"Yes, I am. Why?"

"Well, I've got a friend," Madeline began. "Her elderly mother recently had heart surgery. She's not dying, but they can't leave her alone. They need someone from one till five Monday through Friday. It pays five dollars an hour—cash. It would start next month. What do you think?"

Annie was delighted. "It sounds perfect. I would have to line up someone to watch my daughter."

"I told them about your little girl. That's no problem. You can bring her along. They think it might be good for the patient to have a child around."

"Yes, yes, I definitely want it," Annie said with surging hope. "My daughter is very good, and she sleeps every afternoon. I could change her bedtime so she would sleep longer during the day."

"You can work that out with them, Annie. You'd also take her to the hairdresser once a week. Things like that. I'll give you the number, and you can arrange an interview. These are great people. They'll love you."

Annie copied the number down. She thanked her lawyer emotionally. After collecting herself, Annie dialed the number. A woman with a soft southern drawl answered, and Annie briefly introduced herself. A ten-minute conversation followed during which it was determined that Annie would come next week for an interview. She hung up the phone with high hopes. The woman sounded warm and friendly. Annie marveled that she was meeting so many great people. She called home and informed Maureen that life was falling into place beautifully.

Later Annie turned off the lights in the living room. She was checking the locks on the front door when she spotted an envelope on the floor. It was addressed to her in Kevin's handwriting. Annie picked it up and put her ear to the door. No sound. She went back to the phone and shakily dialed Marty's number. After hearing the situation, Marty agreed to check the hallway. She told Annie that if she spotted Kevin, she would say loudly, "My goodness, you scared me." That would be Annie's signal to call the police.

Tense moments followed while Annie listened at the door. She heard Marty walking down the three flights of stairs. Running to the front window, she watched as her neighbor walked around the building. Annie ran to the back door and saw her coming up the back stairs. She opened her door.

"No sign of him, Annie. Did you read the note?"

Annie held the door open for her friend and then opened the letter. Marty watched while she read the contents.

Dear Annie,

I am writing to beg you for forgiveness. Surely we have some good memories. After all we have been through together, I can't believe you would let it end this way. I'm willing to see a counselor, and I have promised to change. What else can I do? You are not completely innocent in this. You know that. I understand about the criminal charges, but I do wish you would drop them. Annie, this is not necessary. If you do not want to give it a chance, I will understand. But drop the charges. You owe me that much. Call me. My number is at the bottom of the page. Please. Call me. You'll never find anyone who will love you like I do. Call me. I'm still your husband. All of my love forever,

Kevin

Annie handed the letter to Marty. Weakly, she lowered herself into a kitchen chair. He was not going to let it go. Marty read it quickly and patted Annie's hand sympathetically.

"It does not change a thing, Annie. He can write anything he wants. He's really trying to get you to drop the charges by making you feel guilty. 'You owe me that.' Throw it in the garbage and forget it," Marty advised. "Better yet. Call the police and tell them he was here. Isn't that a violation of his restraining order?"

Annie looked at Marty in surprise. "I don't know. He's not supposed to be here, but couldn't he say he had someone else drop it off?"

Marty was thoughtful. "Yes, I suppose he could. But he's kind of threatening you to drop the charges. Surely that's wrong. Annie, you better give me a picture of him. That way I'll know him if I see him around."

Annie remained pensive as she looked through the desk drawers. The recent pictures were kept there. Strangely enough, she could not put her hands on them. "They're gone. I'm sure they were here a couple of days ago. I must have misplaced them." Annie went to the hall closet and pulled out a photo album. After flipping quickly through the pictures, she selected one and gave it to Marty.

"Here is an older shot. He has short hair now and a mustache. I have a roll that's half taken. I'll get it developed tomorrow and give you a current picture."

Marty studied the photo and nodded. "He looks like a big guy. I'm sure I'll know him if I see him. There's a one-hour developing place at the mall."

"I'll run it over there tomorrow afternoon."

The women talked for a while longer. Marty offered Annie her couch for the night, but Annie declined. Kevin would be waiting for her phone call. She felt she would be safe enough.

Rain fell steadily the next day as Annie made her way to the mall. She had finished her first week of college. The course work was not difficult, and she had little concern about retaining her scholarship. Annie was eager to get

Mary back. The days seemed strangely empty without the constant gurgling of her toddler. She told herself it would not be long. Another ten days at the most. If the job came through, she would be completely settled by the time her daughter returned.

After locating the photo shop, she pulled the camera from her purse. She started to unload the film and glanced down at the counter. It read zero. Puzzled, she shrugged and took the roll out. She thought Maureen had said there was half a roll left. Annie checked it in and promised to return in an hour.

Post-Christmas bargains tantalized her as she wandered through the mall. Today she would window shop. If she landed the job next week, she would splurge and buy herself a whole new outfit. The hour quickly passed, and she returned for the film. She was certain there was a shot of Kevin holding Mary. She remembered it was the first picture she had taken on the new roll.

Annie left the shop and opened the package as she walked. Sure enough, there was Kevin holding Mary by the wash house. Annie smiled as she flipped through several silly shots of Maureen and the baby. Next was a terrible photo of Annie cleaning the toilet. Courtesy of Maureen, the comedienne. The next picture mystified her. It was a picture of the inside of the refrigerator. Had Maureen taken it? Annie shrugged and went on. The next photograph sent off an alarm in her head and caused her to quickly flip through the rest. There was a picture of the inside of her underwear drawer. Another shot showed her marriage license propped up against the dresser. The fourth showed her divorce petition on the kitchen table next to her textbooks. As startling as they were, it was the fifth that turned her blood cold. Placed on her pillow was the daily newspaper. It was opened to the obituary page.

Chapter Twenty-five

Shoppers swirled around Annie as she stood holding the photograph. Her frozen face belied the furious activity of her mind. Kevin was sending her a message. He was going to kill her. The death notice resting on her bedroom pillow made that clear. Also, the marriage license and the divorce decree. He felt justified because she was divorcing him. He had often reminded her of her marriage vow. Now he would kill her for breaking it.

Annie shuffled the pictures again. The underwear drawer. What was the message there? Also, the inside of the refrigerator. Her thoughts jumped darkly. Maybe he was going to kill her in her underwear and stuff her in the refrigerator. Annie giggled aloud. Oh no, she thought. Inappropriate laughter. She stuffed the pictures into her purse. Kevin had been in her house. Recently. He had the key. Annie could hardly chain the door from the outside. She felt like she had been raped all over again.

Jogging across the lot to her car, she threw her purse in and started the engine. A terrible thought struck her, and she opened the door and jumped out. Checking the back seat, she was relieved to see it empty. She settled in again and gunned the engine. She had to do something. He fully intended to kill her. Annie knew most people would think she was unbalanced. But she knew how Kevin's mind worked. He had a criminal charge pending. He was outwardly on good behavior. Annie shuddered at the probable depth of his internal rage.

Annie drove home with a deadly serious frown on her face. She scolded herself for becoming complacent. From now on she had to be aggressive. She could not sit and wait for him to kill her. Not only would she not drop the charges, she would add another charge. He had obviously violated the restraining order this time. He had broken into her home.

Pulling up to the apartment, she allowed another thought to crystallize. Kevin had written a predictable note by normal standards. I love you, I miss you, Give me another chance, etc. He was not afraid of the note's being scrutinized. That was why he left the message on the camera. Only Annie would understand it. Kevin was not acting impulsively. He was thinking things through. The thought chilled her.

Annie was putting her key in the door when another horrible thought struck her. What if he was inside? With shaking hands, she knocked on Marty's door. In seconds, Marty answered, looking fresh and uncomplicated.

"Hi," she said brightly. Seeing Annie's pallor, she frowned and stepped back. "What happened to you?"

Annie entered and haltingly filled her in. Marty looked at the pictures. She too paled.

"Annie, this guy is worse than weird. Do you realize that means that he left the letter after he had taken the pictures? I mean," Marty frowned in concentration, "does think he can threaten you into a reconciliation? He's certifiable."

Annie met her frightened eyes. "I know. That's what scares me. It's like he is trying to say, 'Get back with me or die.' Do you get that feeling?"

Marty stood up abruptly. "Call the police. Right now."

344

Annie followed her to the telephone and dialed the number for the police department. The dispatcher sounded bored. She asked Annie if she was in immediate danger. Annie said no. "Unless he is hiding in my apartment across the hall."

"IS he hiding in your apartment?"

"I don't know. I'm afraid to go in."

"Well," said a bored voice, "If you go in and he's there, call us back. That WOULD be a violation of the restraining order."

Annie stared at the wall. "He's not going to hand me the phone, you know. If he is there, his intentions are not lawful."

"Lady," the voice snapped. "We can't come over every time you get paranoid. I don't know who took those pictures. And neither do you. Those are the facts. And you're complaining because he wrote you a letter? He did not threaten you, he just wants to get back together. Sounds like a perfectly normal divorce to me. Call your lawyer." The phone went dead.

Annie looked at Marty with her mouth open. "Can you believe this?" she asked her friend. "He told me Kevin sounds perfectly normal and I should call my lawyer."

Marty was furious. "That bastard. I can't believe this. What's the point of giving you a restraining order if they blow off every violation?"

Annie shook her head. She had no answers. "Can you walk me home?" she asked in a deliberately pitiful voice. Both burst out laughing.

"Well, I guess so. We may as well do it while I'm good and mad," Marty said jokingly. "I'll kill the son-of-a-bitch if he's in there."

They opened the door talking loudly. The idea was to warn Kevin that they were coming so he would have a chance to run out. Marty went around checking closets. Annie checked the bathroom and then went back and pulled the shower curtain back. The apartment was empty. They threw themselves onto the couch in relief.

"Honestly, Annie," Marty began, "I thought my ex was nutty. I don't know if you're safe. Are you sure you don't want to go home?"

"I thought of that," she answered honestly. "But it makes me so mad! I've got a good setup here, Marty. If I leave now, I'll screw up the divorce and lose the scholarship." She frowned in concentration. "It's not fair. Why should I have to drop my life? I mean, he's the one causing all the trouble. Why can't we make him leave?"

Marty's eyes brightened. "I hadn't thought of that. Let's ask him to leave." The sarcasm was lost on Annie.

"Screw him," Annie swore bitterly. "He's a spoiled baby. And, Marty, he'll follow me anywhere. Especially back to Chicago. I swear I'd be afraid he would hurt my father or something. You know? He's disturbed enough to do it."

Marty sighed. "What can I do?" she asked warmly. "I'm going to leave my front door open. That way you can come in if you need to."

Annie smiled gratefully. "That's great, Marty. If I get paranoid again, I'll stop at your place first."

Rising to her feet, her neighbor sighed again. "OK, Annie. I'm going home to study. My daughter is coming back next weekend so I'm trying to get ahead as much as possible. Call me if you need anything."

Thanking her, Annie closed the door and turned the deadbolt. She contemplated calling home but knew that the latest developments would only underscore their opinion that she should load up the car and come home. How she wished it was not too late to reach Caroline. Annie felt lonely. She pulled out her books, fighting back tears. They came anyway and filled her with rage. She would not let Kevin ruin her life. She would fight back. It was all she could do to restrain herself from calling and telling him. Thoughts of Kevin in the courtroom stopped her. She could not give him ammunition. He would say she was harassing him or something.

The weekend passed uneventfully. Annie spent most of it in the library, after deciding Marty's strategy was sound.

She wanted to be ahead in her studies when Mary returned.

Monday morning Annie dressed carefully for school. The interview was scheduled for 12:30 so she would have to leave right after her last class. Annie was also seeing Caroline after the interview. It was a busy day.

Shortly after noon, she crossed campus. Her car was back at the apartment, and she was not certain about the directions. She hustled accordingly. The weather was warm and sunny as usual. Annie lifted her face to the sunshine and smiled. It was exhilarating to be on her own. She was amazed at the changes in herself. In a few weeks time, she had regained much of her lost confidence. She also felt attractive again. Men smiled at her, and she smiled back.

Arriving at her car, she opened the back door and threw her backpack over the front seat. Glancing up at the apartment, she froze. Had she seen the drapery move? Either way, she had to go. Annie started the car and pulled around the circle driveway. She looked up again and saw nothing. Surely it was the glare of the sunlight. I can't deal with this now, she thought sternly. I have to look sane for the interview. I'm paranoid, paranoid, paranoid.

The interview went well, and Annie was slated to begin in mid-February. The elderly lady was quite genteel, and Annie loved her at once. She was proudly informed that her patient belonged to the Daughters of the American Revolution. Annie smiled and nodded her head admiringly. A middle-aged women, the patient's daughter, winked at Annie. Apparently, this was a big deal so Annie looked even more impressed. Gratified, the elderly woman informed Annie that her little girl was most welcome. They offered her a salary and asked if it was sufficient. Annie schooled her face and nodded affirmatively. Quite literally, it was twice what she had expected.

Spirits soaring, Annie drove to her counseling appointment in prayerful gratitude. It could not possibly be working out any better. With the salary and the stipend, Annie would be completely independent. She rolled down her window and let the dry air blow her hair into a mess.

Thoughts of Rene filtered into her head, and she resolved to call her that evening. Annie missed her. Now that she was on her own, she could call whomever she pleased as long as she stayed within her budget.

Annie drifted into Caroline's office on a cloud. Caroline rejoiced with her. She told Annie she was very proud of her, and Annie choked up. She never understood Caroline's unwavering faith in her. She filled Caroline in on the phantom photography session. The older women was concerned.

"I don't like it, Annie," she said shaking her head. This set off a round of tinkling jewelry, and Annie laughed. "What are you laughing about?"

"Your jewelry. It's lovely. Does the noise ever bother you?"

"No," Caroline answered vehemently. "I love the noise. Remember I once told you that I would tell you why I helped battered women? Well, I'll tell you now. You have probably guessed that I was in a violent marriage."

Annie's eyebrows shot up. "You're joking! I would never have guessed."

Caroline nodded her head affirmatively.

"But you look so normal."

Her counselor rolled her eyes. "How is a formerly battered woman supposed to look, Annie? You look pretty normal yourself."

"I don't feel normal," Annie said chagrined. "I feel half cracked most of the time."

"That's temporary," Caroline promised. "You'll feel normal again, and people will never guess that you married a homicidal maniac the first time." They both laughed.

"Back to my jewelry ... my first husband never let me wear any jewelry. He said only tramps wore jewelry. So when I got divorced fifteen years ago, I went out and bought myself all kinds of jewelry. I've worn it ever since."

"What does your current husband say about it?"

"He says I'm eccentric and that he adores me." Caroline shuddered. "To think I might have stayed with my abuser

... I still have nightmares sometimes. Anyway, I have two wonderful children, and my marriage is better than I ever thought a marriage could be. So there you are, Annie. I never forget what I went through, and I will probably help battered women for the rest of my life. It gets in your blood. I have high hopes for you."

Annie smiled dreamily. "That's wonderful, Caroline. I would love to think that I could be as together as you someday."

Caroline reached over and placed her hand on Annie's. "Annie," she said seriously, "I have no doubt that you will far exceed what I've done. You've got the right stuff, Honey. Much more so than I did at your age."

Annie's struggled with tears. "Thank you, Caroline. You saved my life, you know."

"No Annie. You saved your own life. I'm only pointing out the right roads. Now when you get home, call Grady and tell him dispatchers are blowing you off. See what he says. I'll call him, too."

They spoke a few minutes longer. Caroline warned Annie not to underestimate the danger. She made Annie review her safety plan and nodded approvingly at Marty's offer to leave her front door open. Annie left with undiminished optimism. Kevin would back off. What else could he do?

• • •

Annie pulled up to her apartment and fairly danced up the stairs. She could hardly wait to get the phone to tell her family about the job. She would insist they bring Mary back this week. There was nothing standing in the way now. No more job interviews or appointments. Annie thought cheerfully that she had better call and tell the department store that her temporary leave was permanent.

Opening the front door, she threw her bag of books on the couch. She suddenly noticed that she was starved. Grabbing an apple from the counter, she went into her bedroom and kicked off her shoes. She was just peeling her nylons off when she noticed the toe of a very large athletic shoe sticking out from the closet. Everything immediately stilled.

Her mind, unlike her heart and lungs, was still working. Annie assessed the situation. Kevin was hiding in her closet. The slow motion thing kicked in, and she pulled her nylons off with her head lowered. There was a crack between the panels of the door. He could be watching.

"There now," she said casually, as if she was talking to herself She rose from the bed and started for the bedroom door. SLOW! she cautioned herself She was just leaving the room when she heard a frantic shuffling. Annie ran for the front door with a sinking heart. This had never worked yet. She was just unbolting the top lock when she heard him yell.

"Bitch!"

The door opened as if by magic. No thanks to her violently shaking fingers. Annie flew across the vestibule. Thanks be to God, Marty was as good as her word, and the large wooden door across the hall opened easily. Annie slammed it shut and turned to bolt it. With one hand on the lock, she felt the door pushed violently in. Kevin's hand was on the inside, and Annie reached down and bit it. She heard him swear violently as she tasted blood. The arm was withdrawn for a second. That was all she needed. The door closed easily, and she slid the bolt home.

She heard Marty's voice scream from behind her. "The police are on the way. You won't get away with this, you bastard."

Marty put her arm around Annie tightly, and they listened. A moment's silence was followed by hasty footsteps on the stairs. "You call the police," Marty said tensely. "I'll see what he does and lock the back door."

Annie flew to the phone. Her mind was blank so she pushed 0. The operator came on the line and rapidly connected her. Annie told them in a shaking voice what had happened. The dispatcher agreed to send someone over.

Annie and Marty stood by the window and waited. Both young women shook violently, and Marty placed her arm around Annie. "It's OK," Marty repeated. "They'll arrest him now, and it'll be OK."

Nodding her head, Annie tried to calm her stomach. "I feel sick, Marty," she said in a trembling voice.

"You watch the window, Annie. I'll get you something." Seeing Annie's white face, she added, "The back door is bolted. He can't get in. They'll be here in a second. It's going to be fine. I promise."

Annie gazed out over the campus. Kevin could be anywhere.

Marty came back shortly with a glass of ginger ale and some crackers. "Sit down, Annie," she urged. "He's not coming back. He's psychotic, but he's not stupid. My grandmother always swore by ginger ale. She said the ginger quiets an upset stomach."

Allowing herself to be shepherded into a chair, Annie sipped at the ginger ale. Realizing she had not eaten, she forced the crackers down. In moments she was feeling stronger. "Thanks, Marty," she said solemnly. "I would have been dead if you had not left the door open."

Marty was chalk-white. "I know, Annie," she said, equally solemn. "I almost forgot. I had to go back and unlock it this afternoon." The girls looked at each other. Both felt chills. "I would have heard you banging," Marty said to reassure them both. "I would have opened it right away."

"Then there would have been three of us in here," Annie said quietly. "No," she amended. "He would have dragged me back into the apartment and locked you out."

"I would have called the police, Annie." They both glanced up at the clock. Ten minutes had elapsed, and there was no sign of them. Annie looked at Marty meaningfully. Marty shook her head in disgust. "I know," she read Annie's thoughts. "If he intended to kill you, he could have."

Marty looked again out of the window. "They're here. We may as well let them walk up so the neighbors don't hear."

"I'm sorry, Marty. We'll go into my apartment. This is embarrassing for you."

Marty gave a snort of disgust. "Well, considering you're my only friend, I'm not too concerned. Was he in there when you got home?"

"Marty, I was taking my nylons off, and I noticed his shoe sticking out of the closet."

Marty held her stomach. "Oh, my God. Now I feel sick." She opened the door in anticipation of the officer's arrival. "We're up here," she yelled down the stairs. "They're talking to the downstairs neighbor," she said with a giggle. "The one with the crazy eyebrows and the husband with the roving eye. Do you know her?"

Annie shook her head.

"She thinks I'm a harlot because her husband always looks at me. People like that suspect any divorced woman."

Annie smiled. Marty's irreverence reminded her of Maureen.

Two officers plodded slowly up the stairs. Annie's heart sank when she recognized the older officer who had responded with Officer Grady the first time.

"What's all the hullabaloo about?" he asked tiredly.

Marty took offense. "The hullabaloo is that this woman's ex-husband, who has a restraining order against him, was hiding in her closet when she got home." Both officers looked bored. "He would have killed her if she had not run to my apartment."

Annie stepped forward. Officer Grady had warned her about appearing hysterical in front of police officers. "Thank you for coming," she began calmly. "My husband and I are separated. I've filed for divorce, and I have a restraining order against him. He's not allowed near this property. When I got home, he was hiding in the closet, and I ran here. He tried to follow me in, and I bit his hand and locked the door. He left when Marty," she indicated her friend, "threatened to call the police."

The older officer took the lead. "Where is this restraining order?"

"It's in my apartment. I'll go get it," Annie replied, moving toward the door.

"Let's all go over," the officer said, making a move to follow her. "Thank you for your help Ma'am," he dismissed Marty. "We'll handle it from here."

"I'm sure Annie would prefer me to go with her," Marty said coldly.

Annie smiled gratefully. "Thanks, Marty. I would."

The group stood silently while the police officer scanned the restraining order. He finally spoke.

"It does say that he should not be here. Plain as day."

"Yes," Annie agreed. "Can you go and arrest him?"

The older man exchanged a look of patient frustration with his partner. "Well Ma'am, it's just not that easy. Did anyone actually see him?"

Marty piped up, "I saw him running into the campus. I can tell you exactly what he was wearing."

"You know this man?" asked the second officer.

"I've seen a picture of him," Marty said defensively.

"Officer," Annie began. "I saw his shoe. It was his shoe. I do know this man."

"No offense," said the older officer "but from what I've heard so far, neither one of you can positively identify Kevin Griffin as the man who pulled these shenanigans."

Annie tried hard to control her temper. "Sir, I've known this man for seven years. He called me a bitch. It was his voice. He also stuck his hand in the door. I know my husband's hand."

"But you did not look out of the window. Your friend did. And she doesn't know him."

"Officer," she spoke with thinly veiled contempt. "I recognized his hand, his voice, and his shoe. In addition to that, I can't offhand think of anyone else who would be waiting in my closet to kill me. Can you?"

"Well, Little Lady, I don't know anything about what you get up to in the evenings. For all I know it could have been anyone."

Marty exploded. "How dare you? This woman has a perfectly valid order against this man. Why do you even grant these orders if the offender can do whatever he likes. She bit him. Check his hand. It will have a bite mark on it. Is that positive enough for you?"

Both officers began shifting uncomfortably at Marty's verbal onslaught. Now they turned their backs to her and addressed Annie. She realized they were alienated and spoke quickly. She told them about the pictures and the letter. They were unimpressed.

"Let me remind you," spoke the older officer sharply. "You filed for divorce, Lady. In my experience, divorce is ugly. This is what you get. I understand you already filed a criminal charge against him. Haven't you done enough?"

"Hasn't he?" she asked incredulously. "Does he have to kill me before you'll do anything?"

"You're getting a little excitable." Annie's mouth dropped open. "Calm down, and I'll tell you what to do. Call your lawyer and have her deal with it. It's not a criminal matter as far as I can see."

"How did you know my lawyer was a woman?" Annie asked, watching him intently.

The officer averted his eyes. "This is not a big town, Mrs. Griffin."

The officers turned to leave, and Marty lifted her middle finger at their backs. Annie could not even smile. "Officers," she said calmly. "One more thing. What happens if he breaks in and I shoot him?"

The younger of the two turned and spoke lightly. "If you wound him and he runs out, drag his ass back in. That way you're in the clear." Both men burst out laughing as they ambled down the stairs.

Annie and Marty stared after them, stunned. "I'll be a son-of-a-bitch," said Marty. "He can do whatever he wants, Annie. You may as well use that order for toilet paper." At that moment her phone rang from across the hall. "Come on," she said. "I don't want to be alone yet."

Annie heartily agreed and followed Marty back into her apartment. She threw herself down on the couch only to be interrupted by her friend.

"It's for you, Annie," Marty said suspiciously. "A very

354

polite man. Maybe someone from the police department. Don't you have a friend over there?"

Annie sprang up hopefully. It had to be Officer Grady. "Hello," she said brightly.

"Annie." Kevin's voice was tight. "I see you called the police." He laughed shortly. "Let me guess. There is nothing they can do, right?"

Holding her hand over her stomach, she signaled Marty. "No, Kevin. There's not. How did you know? How did you get this phone number?"

Kevin laughed again. "Think about it, Annie. The cops won't touch me. They think the whole thing is pretty shitty. Those guys love my coach, and they told him not to worry. As far as the number? Do you really think I don't know everything about you? I know what you wore yesterday, and I know what you're wearing today. Did you get my message on film?"

"You're not clever, Kevin. You're twisted. I thought you wanted me back. Is this how you think I'll change my mind?"

"Well, I do want you back." He sounded uncertain. "Are you ready to come back yet?"

"After this, Kevin, I'll never come back. I can't believe you would even ask me."

"Annie," he spoke in a soft voice that was horrifying. "Despite what you think, I still love you. You don't deserve it, you never did. But I do. I don't care how many guys you're sleeping with. I also liked the old lady you're going to work for. I'm up to date."

Annie drew her breath in sharply. She felt hair prickling the back of her neck.

"You're very quiet," he continued. "Do you understand? You can't hide from me. I will always find you. And you're not going to get away with this. Now, if you drop the charges, I might let you live. Call me tomorrow and tell me that they're dropped." Annie remained silent. She was thinking frantically. "Tell me you understand." He waited again. "Do you realize that right now you could be lying on your bedroom floor dead? I'm going to strangle you. That way there's no evidence. I won't get caught, Annie. I'll get custody, and Mary and I will live happily ever after. Trust me."

She tried a different tack. "Kevin, how can you even talk like this? We've been best friends for years. OK, our marriage did not work out. But do you really want to hurt me that badly?"

His voice cracked. "No, Annie. I don't want to hurt you anymore. It would be better if we both died. We'd be together forever. I'm sorry about all of this. But you're forcing me to do it."

"But, Kevin, if you're so intent on killing us, what do you care if the charges are dropped?"

"I don't know for sure if I want to die. But I can't let you get away with this. I have no choice."

"So if I drop the charges, you'll leave me alone?"

"I'll try to, Annie, I really will. If I can, I will."

"Kevin," she pleaded, "get some help. You sound terrible."

He turned ugly. "Fuck you, Annie. You get help. You're the one who needs it."

The line went dead. Annie stood holding the telephone in her hand. Marty stood staring at her tensely. "Marty, he's not making sense. He's going to kill us both so nothing matters. On the other hand, maybe he'll let me live if I drop the charges." Annie's whole body began to shake violently. Marty led her to the sofa. Annie sat down and put her head down into her lap. Cold sweat dripped down her back. Caroline had talked about anxiety attacks. This must be one of them. Soon she felt a cold cloth on the back of her neck. The result was immediate. Annie sat up. "Thanks, Marty," she said quietly. "I'm better."

"Well, I don't wonder you feel sick," Marty said gently. "I feel sick myself, and it's not happening to me."

Annie smiled warmly at her friend. "Marty, you've been a lifesaver. I'm really OK. I'm going to go home and call my lawyer. Maybe she'll have an idea."

Annie rose to leave. Marty's look of concern was genuine. "Are you sure you want to go back in there?"

"Yes, I'm fine."

"I'll check on you in a little while. Annie," she added, "make sure you answer the door, or I'll be scared silly."

Annie promised and crossed the hall. She deadbolted both doors. Next she sat down at the table. Dialing the police department, she asked for Officer Grady. She was informed that Officer Grady was on vacation for the next ten days. Annie politely thanked the woman and hung up.

After a few minutes of deep thought, she dialed her lawyer's number. She was told that Madeline was on another line and would call her back. Annie hung up and remained motionless. When the phone rang, she answered it dully. She did not care if it was Kevin. Instead she heard her attorney's crisp voice.

"Madeline," she asked clearly, "what would happen if I went back to Chicago?"

"You mean before the divorce?"

"I mean tonight," Annie answered flatly.

Madeline grasped the seriousness of the situation and answered professionally. "If you leave the state without notice to the court, he can file in your absence and be granted pretty much anything. For example. I know your first concern is the child. Kevin could go in tomorrow morning and get custody. It happens. Technically, you could be accused of abducting the child. Then he shows up at your father's house with a squad car and takes her. He would have the right to do that. We're working on a law that says a victim can flee from an abusive spouse with her children, but frankly, Annie, we're not there yet." The woman paused. "Tell me what's going on."

"Well, he was hiding in my closet when I got home," Annie heard the sharp intake of breath and told her the details. "The policemen said there was nothing they could do."

"I see," Madeline answered in disgust. "About the best I can do is take it in front of the divorce judge and ask that Kevin be further admonished."

Annie felt as if someone had just clicked off the light at the end of the tunnel.

"That didn't get you very far last time, Madeline." Realizing how that might sound, she added hastily, "I'm not blaming you ... I'm trying to be realistic."

"I know you are, Annie. Don't worry about offending me. The system here is pretty much a 'Good Ole Boys' club. Is there somewhere else you could stay for a while?"

"Yes," Annie said in a hurry now to hang up. "I think so, Madeline. Don't worry."

"You're not going to do anything drastic, I hope."

"Not at all," Annie said. "I'll be in touch."

She hung up and went to the bedroom. Pulling a chair to the closet, she rummaged around until she felt it. Annie pulled down the gun and replaced the chair. Calmly she opened the linen closet and felt around on the top shelf. Locating the box of sanitary napkins, she reached in and grabbed the bullets and clip.

She mentally thanked Danny and proceeded to load the gun. How naive she had been to think Kevin could be controlled by the courts. The system had made a fool of her. Far from feeling shaky about handling the weapon, she only wished she had a few hand grenades. The thought made her chuckle. Hand grenades would be overkill. When the gun was loaded, she checked the safety and set it down on the table.

Annie rose to get her purse. Her movements were unhurried. In a way she was relaxed. Yes, she told herself, it had really come to this. She pulled Buddy's number from her wallet and calmly made her last call of the day.

Chapter Twenty-six

A knock on the door made Annie jump. Shadows darkened the little dining room, and Annie noticed the clock she had been staring at. It was nearly seven. Two hours ago she had hung up with Buddy. Lifting the gun, she faced the door.

"Who is it?" she asked in a confident voice.

'Marty."

"Hold on Marty. I'll be right there."

Annie placed the gun in the top drawer of the desk. She was walking to the door when she thought of Danny. Mechanically, she turned back and opened the drawer again. Turning the gun over, she checked the safety and replaced it. She must know where she stood at all times. Satisfied, she admitted her friend.

"Have you recovered?" she asked Marty lightly.

"Never mind me." Marty said emphatically. "How are you? Have you eaten anything?" The young woman held a plate in her hands. When Annie shook her head negatively, Marty offered the plate. "Great. I figured as much. I brought you some Texas barbecue with beans. It's legendary, and I have a fridge full of it. Granny again. She figured I might neglect myself with the move and all."

Annie smiled and took the plate. "Will you join me?"

"No. I ate. But I'll sit and talk a while."

They sat at the table. Annie lifted the tin foil and realized she was ravenous. She barely noticed when Marty rose to double check the bolts on the door. In less then ten minutes, she sat back with a sigh. Strength coursed through her body.

"Marty, once again. you saved the day. I had no idea how hungry I was. I'm ready for anything."

Marty took her chair again and grinned. "That's how it is in a crisis. You forget to eat and then wonder while you feel so weak. What did your lawyer say?"

Annie outlined the dismal legal situation. Marty's look of concern prompted her to continue.

"Don't worry, Marty. I called a friend of my brother's. He's on his way."

"What's he going to do?" asked Marty hesitantly.

Annie frowned. "I don't know. He sounded normal on the phone." Her frown deepened. "I have a feeling he's going to threaten Kevin or something. I don't care anymore. Kevin's going to kill me if I don't do something. I'm out of options."

Marty became brisk. Standing, she cleared Annie's plate and bustled around the kitchen. "I'm making hot tea. Annie, don't worry about what he does. Leave it to him. Is he from Texas?"

"Originally, I guess. Now he lives in New Orleans. I don't know anything about him. It's kind of weird."

"Not at all," came the smooth response. "Texans have a way of handling these situations, and it does not involve the courts. He'll probably scare the hell out of him. Kevin needs to deal with a man on this. Let him take on someone his own size."

"I couldn't agree with you more," Annie stated firmly. "I don't care who he deals with ... as long as it's not me. I thought of going home, but that muddies up the divorce waters. Kevin will do anything. He's scary."

"Hey," Marty said suddenly. "How did the interview go?"

Annie brightened immediately. She filled Marty in on the details and cheered herself in the process. "So you see," she continued, "if I can just get Killer Kevin to settle down, I should be fixed up pretty nicely."

The girls sat and talked for another hour. Shortly after eight, Marty rose and stretched. "Are you sure you won't take my couch?" she offered. "I'd feel a lot better if you did."

"No," Annie said flatly. "Thanks, but this guy might show up during the night. Buddy, I mean. He said he was leaving right away. How long does it take to drive here from New Orleans?"

Marty pondered. "At least twelve hours, I would guess. Depends on whether or not there are highway patrols out. He won't get here till morning, Annie."

"Still," Annie said firmly. "I'll stay here. I have the doors bolted."

"What you need is a gun, Honey. I've got one, but it's at Mother's. Yanks aren't used to them, but here in Texas we're raised knowing how to shoot. Do you want me to bring it out next weekend?"

Annie internally debated how much to tell Marty. Comning to a decision, she shook her head slowly. "I don't think so. Thanks, though. Let's see what my Buddy can do."

Marty took her leave, promising to leave her doors unlatched. Annie thanked her for the dinner. The emptiness closed in upon the apartment. Annie turned all the lights on. She wanted to watch television but decided against it. The noise might cover sounds she needed to hear. A bath and book would have to suffice.

The hot tap blasted on full. Annie watched it fill and remembered another night in this bathroom. Blood had splattered all over the floor. Her face hardened, and she went into the dining room and pulled the gun out of the drawer. She scolded herself for going even into the bathroom without it. Instinct warned her she would have little time if he struck again. Danny counseled her to shoot first and reminisce later. Tonight it sounded like good advice.

Setting the gun on the toilet, Annie stripped down and climbed into the tub. It was perfect. Scalding hot. She had the bathroom door locked and the gun within reach, but she could not relax. Glancing at the weapon, she realized it was pointing directly at her. She shot out of the tub naked and checked the safety. The room filled with steam. Would moisture interfere with gunpowder? Was gunpowder what made it shoot? Danny had told her how to clean it, but Annie had not listened. At the time she had no intention of using the weapon. Swinging the door open, she wrapped herself in a towel and moved the gun into the living room.

In minutes she was sitting in the recliner. Warm, soft pajamas provided comfort, and Annie reprimanded herself. The bathtub was a dangerous place to be. The only worse location would be the shower. She had seen the movie *Psycho* and had scarcely enjoyed a shower since. She checked the clock. Roughly eight hours to go. She determined she would sit in the chair until Buddy arrived.

Contemplating the mysterious Buddy, Annie wondered if Danny had paid him. A cultured drawl had thrown her when she called him. What had she expected? Honesty prevailed, and she admitted she expected a tough, shady voice. Maybe a mafia type. Voice-wise, Buddy sounded like the first judge Annie had spoken to. Educated and gentle. For a while she considered her brother. Was he tough? Danny was a gentleman in her experience, but how would she know? By his own admission, he carried a gun. Maybe he had been too long in the South. Texans carried guns. Most were law-abiding citizens. Annie seldom heard of shootings here, while in Chicago they were rampant. She gave up the attempt to categorize men.

By nine o'clock she was equally tired of checking the safety and chasing her thoughts. She fought the urge to call Chicago. It was only ten there, but Annie knew she could not keep the situation to herself. Maureen would get everything out of her, and they would worry sick. They would also think she was demented. Annie wrestled with the concept of craziness. Was she nuts? She was sitting in a living room, thirteen hundred miles from home, with a gun on her lap. It did not sound good. On the other hand, what would be a better response? If she left, Kevin would follow her and disappear with Mary. He was unstable. Annie decided she was too weary to scrutinize the situation any longer.

Reaching down she grabbed the first textbook she touched. Psychology. She would study. Opening the pages randomly, she landed on a chapter titled avoidance. Denial was the first subheading, and she threw the book down in disgust. There was such a thing as too much thinking. She needed light reading. Perhaps a Gothic romance. No. Something more modern. A book where the heroine wielded a .22 and took grief from no man. I'm losing it, she thought humorously.

She toyed with the idea of calling Kevin to make sure he was at home. At least she would know he was not lurking around in her vestibule. No. That might inflame him. Buddy had begged her to go stay in a hotel until he arrived. Annie had been adamant. She would stay in her home with the gun ready. Maybe she was behaving irrationally. Too late now, though. Annie was too frightened to open the door and run to the car. Imagine a lifetime of this? she thought in dismay. A person would go stark raving mad. She had done the right thing, she told herself. Danny seemed to think Buddy was the man for the job, and Danny was almost always right.

She thought about saying a rosary but decided her situation was a bit nebulous for prayer. A real Christian martyr would relish the thought of offering up a brutal death. Annie would never make sainthood because she was determined to do some damage to Kevin before he killed her. If she prayed, there was no telling where she would end up. She had a sneaking suspicion God frowned on the whole murder-for-hire thing. Now, in fairness, she had no idea what Buddy had planned. She emphatically told him she did not want Kevin hurt. He had understood completely. Even so, spiritually speaking, she felt the waters getting deeper and murkier. She thanked God for taking care of Mary and then mentally put her fingers in her ears.

"It's not that I'm not interested, God," she said politely out loud. "I'm just too tired to hash it out now."

With a guilty feeling she grabbed her history book and began to study.

At two o'clock she had a glass of juice with a Hostess Cupcake. At three she had hot tea. At four she made soup, and at five she downed two Cokes. Completely wired, she decided to clean out her silverware drawer. Moments later, she decided the job was too loud. Also, she could not see the front door from the kitchen. He could sneak up on her. Annie left the forks, spoons, and knives on the counter and went back to the living room. She had just settled back in her chair when the phone rang. Annie leapt from her chair, spilling her pop, and ran to the phone. Her heart raced as she picked it up.

"Hello?"

"Annie?" asked the soft drawl, "It's Buddy. I'm down the street. I did not want to scare you by coming up. Are you in the apartment with all of the lights on?"

"Yes." Annie said giggling. "I didn't want him to think I was sleeping."

"OK. I recognized Danny's old car. I'll be right over. My car is a blue Thunderbird. All right?"

"Thanks Pal ... I mean Buddy." Annie closed her eyes in dismay. "I'm a little tired."

He chuckled, too. "I'll bet you are. See you in a minute."

Moments later, headlights pulled into the drive. Annie waited for the knock. She could not risk opening the door too soon. Finally a soft knock came, and Annie swung open the door.

"Hello, Ma'am," said a tall athletic-looking man.

Annie looked him over. He was well-dressed in a casual, collegiate way. Light brown khakis were paired with a tan sports shirt. The inevitable belt buckle was small and did not sport a horse. That was a good sign. Annie suspected men who wore large horsy belt buckles. Black hair was shortly cropped above a handsome face. Annie smiled up at him and extended her hand.

"Call me Annie," she said sweetly.

"I will," he replied. "Thank you, Annie. You're brother is a good man, and I owe him. So don't think you need to be thanking me."

"Well, I'm glad you owe him, Buddy." Annie smiled impishly and stepped back. "Enter the hold-out."

He smiled back and preceded her into the apartment. "Is that your gun?" he asked as he walked over to the easy chair.

"Yes," she said ruffling her bangs. "I've been sitting there holding it most of the night. Danny gave it to me."

Buddy picked it up and looked it over. "It's a beauty. I'm sure glad you didn't need it, though."

"Why?" she asked in surprise.

"Because the clip isn't in all of the way. It won't fire like this." He looked at Annie. She gave him a look of comical dismay, and they burst out laughing.

Annie was still wiping her eyes when she spoke. "Well, the joke is on me. That's what I get for thinking I'm so tough. What can I get you?" she asked suddenly. "You must be exhausted."

"Nothing," he said politely. "I've been drinking sodas all night. What are your plans this morning?"

Annie sat down on the couch and waved him into her chair. "Well, I guess I'll go to school in a couple hours. Why?"

Buddy's clear, handsome face crinkled. "I'd rather you didn't, Annie. From what you've said, this guy is on a mission. Danny had no idea he was this far gone, or he would never have let you stay."

Annie considered for a moment what Danny could have done. Thrown her over his shoulder? She dismissed the thought as uncharitable and paid attention.

Buddy continued. "The picture thing is pretty telling. Until I have the chance to talk to him, I'd rather you stayed close to me."

Annie wavered. After making him drive all this way, she could hardly start quibbling about details. "That's fine. Do you think he'd hurt me at school?"

"No," Buddy answered patiently. "He's not brave. Any guy with a little pride would do time before begging you to drop the charges. Of course, any normal guy would keep his hands to himself. He's not a hero, Annie, but he could grab you on campus and haul you off somewhere. I'd feel better if we played it safe."

"Me, too," agreed Annie. "But when will you talk to him?"

"Don't worry," he said with a grin. "From what you told me about yesterday, he's feeling pretty cocky right now. He'll make a move today."

"You think so?" Annie asked with rounded eyes. "He expects me to drop the charges today. Should I?"

Buddy frowned. "No. Only because I don't feel like going down to the courthouse. I've had enough of courtrooms to last me a lifetime. After I talk to him, you can do whatever you like. But let's make him unhappy. OK?"

"Whatever you say," Annie said complacently. It was wonderful to have someone else take the lead. "How about some breakfast?"

"No, thank you. Annie, go ahead and get some sleep. I'll stretch out here on the couch for awhile. You can leave the gun with me."

"I'll never sleep," she said gloomily. "I'm too nervous."

"Give it a try," he encouraged her. "You look tired."

Annie sighed. "Are you sure you don't mind?"

"Not at all," said the young man. "You'll feel better. I'll take you to lunch when you get up."

Annie smiled widely. "That would be great." She was thanking him again when the phone rang. "Who would that be?" she asked Buddy irrationally. He shrugged pleasantly. Annie looked at the clock. It was six o'clock in the morning.

"Hello?"

"Annie," Kevin said calmly. "How are you doing?"

Annie motioned to Buddy. He walked over and stood by

her. He shook his head negatively, and Annie understood she should not tell Kevin she had company.

"I'm fine, Kevin. What do you want?"

"I'm reminding you that you need to be at the courthouse."

"Why?" Annie asked innocently.

"Annie," Kevin said venomously. "Do it today! I'm tired of being nice about this. Drop the fucking charges."

"So if I don't drop the charges today...?" she said for Buddy's benefit. Buddy smiled. Annie suspected this was what he wanted.

"You die, Annie. Any questions?"

"Screw you, Kevin. I hope you rot in jail." She hung up the phone. Her hands were shaking, and she knew that her face was pale.

"Perfect, Annie," Buddy said pleasantly. "Now go get some sleep, and we'll talk about it when you get up."

"I'll lie down," she promised. "But I know I won't sleep."

Annie climbed into her bed and stared at the closed bedroom door. How comforting to know he was out there. She wondered what Danny had done for him. He said he was sick of courtrooms. Was he a criminal? Annie tried to think about Kevin, but her mind refused. She was too tired. Certain she would lie awake for hours, she promptly fell into a deep sleep.

Chapter Twenty-seven

At three-thirty in the afternoon, Annie sat up in bed. Shaking her head groggily, she made a grab at the day's reality. Was there really a strange man sitting in her living room? What was that thing about Kevin? Oh, yes. Today he was going to kill her. It came back to Annie in a sliding way, as it sometimes does when big events precede a deep sleep.

Annie rolled out of bed and groped in her drawer for clothes. Jeans and a T-shirt seemed appropriate. Glancing in the mirror she grimaced. A shower was mandatory. First she would check on her bodyguard.

Annie peeked around the comer. Buddy was looking right at her.

"You're awake," she said in surprise.

"I could say the same about you," he answered easily. "Did you have any trouble sleeping?"

They both laughed. "No, I guess not," she responded ruefully. "I guess we missed lunch. Are you hungry?"

Buddy was sitting on the couch reading one of her textbooks. "We'll get dinner whenever you want," he said politely. "I made myself a sandwich. Annie, do you have an address for Kevin?"

"No," she said apologetically. "I'm sorry, I don't. He'd be at practice right now until five. I have a picture."

Her house guest smiled and nodded. "Great. Can I see it? I'm going to wander near the gym and see if I can get a look at him. I won't be long." He rose and stretched. "By the way, I met your neighbor, Martha."

"Marty?" Annie asked. "She's been a great help to me. He might have killed me the other day if she had not left her door open."

Buddy smiled. "That's what she said." He took the picture Annie offered and put it in his shirt pocket. "Deadbolt the doors after me, Annie. I won't be long."

Annie locked the doors and headed for the shower. The phone rang. She decided to ignore it. She thought of her father saying "I can't think of a soul still on earth I'm interested in talking to."

After showering at high speed with the curtain half open, Annie dressed. She was replacing her silverware when she heard a knock on the front door. She walked to the living room and stood uncertainly.

"Annie?" she heard Marty say.

"Hi, Marty," she responded easily. "Just a minute." Annie unbolted the door and swung it open. "How are you?"

Marty stepped in and looked around. Large curlers rested on her head. "Where did he go?"

Annie laughed. "He's gone out to stalk Kevin. I heard you met him."

Marty rolled her eyes. "That's the understatement of the world. Are you in love? He's gorgeous!"

Annie frowned. "Yes, I guess he is. I hadn't really noticed."

"Let me check your pulse. You must be dead." The girls heard footsteps outside. They froze. A soft knock landed on the door, and they looked at each other in dismay.

"It's Buddy," he said softly.

Annie made a motion to open the door when Marty

grabbed her arm. Her neighbor gestured to her hair and headed for the back door. Annie grimaced and first followed Marty back through the kitchen. After locking her out, Annie returned to the front door and unbolted it.

"Hi," she said smiling. She ruthlessly crushed the urge to giggle but knew her smile was too wide.

Buddy stepped in. He, too, sported a grin but said nothing. Almost immediately the phone began to ring. Buddy went to the couch as Annie reached for the telephone.

"Annie," said her neighbor tensely. "Find out if he's married."

Annie turned her back to Buddy and said flatly. "Not right now, Marty."

"WHENEVER. Find out, or I'll kill you myself." Marty hung up, and Annie felt her face warming up. She replaced the telephone and turned to Buddy innocently.

"Did you see him?"

"Yes," Buddy answered. He was acting normal, but Annie sensed he knew. Her face burned hotter. "He was working out." Buddy continued nonchalantly. "I spotted him right away. I'm going to head back there in fifteen minutes and see if I can find out where he lives. I wanted to let you know what I was doing. If you want to go shopping or anything, Annie, this would be a good time. I'll be right behind Kevin so you'll be safe."

Annie searched for a way to ask her question. "I don't know how to ask you this, Buddy. I don't want to be rude." Buddy's features were inscrutable. Annie dove in. "You're not going to kill him, are you? I know that sounds ridiculous. Of course, you would never do a thing like that..." Annie was babbling, and she knew it. Buddy rescued her.

"Annie." he said kindly. "I know that in spite of everything, you don't have any hatred for this guy. I'm not a killer. I'm only going to talk to him and make sure he understands that you're not alone. He needs to know he's accountable to someone. That's going to be me." At Annie's look of relief, he continued. "I might throw a few punches if he's not listening. Nothing big. He'll survive. I need to make sure he gets the message. OK?"

"Yes," she said, still hesitant.

"What's the problem, Annie?"

"Well, I wouldn't want you to get hurt, either. He's very big, and, Buddy," Annie looked up at him in concern. "I've never seen him lose a fight."

This made Buddy chuckle. "Don't worry, Annie. He's not going to hurt me."

Something about his complete confidence unnerved her.

"What do you do for a living, Buddy?"

"You mean when I'm not killing Yankees?" He spoke innocently, and they both laughed.

"There's nothing mysterious about what I do. How about if I tell you over dinner? I'll be back in an hour, and we'll get something to eat."

"Fine," Annie smiled up at him.

Marty was right. He certainly was likable. After he departed, Annie telephoned next door. A firm scolding was followed by thirty minutes speculation about Annie's visitor. Annie noted the absence of a wedding ring, but Marty said that was meaningless. Something about him made Annie remember that her hair needed to be cut. For the first time in weeks. she wondered where her makeup was. Marty said she was a fool if she did not at least flirt with him. Annie said she felt guilty even thinking about another man. Marty's snort of disgust was audible.

"Get real, Annie. You're getting divorced. If you live through it, you're going to date other guys. Your brother's best Buddy is as good a place to start as any."

Annie found herself laughing hysterically. Marty was great fun.

"Tell him that my anatomy teacher is looking at me funny," Marty said playfully. "I'd like it handled."

Annie ended the conversation in another fit of giggling. She would have to rid her mind of these thoughts, or she would be terribly uncomfortable. She firmly reminded herself that Buddy was here for one reason. He was Danny's friend. He looked young, but Annie guessed he was at least thirty. He carried himself with the confidence of an older man. It was possible he was an "unclaimed treasure," as Marty called him, but it was equally possible he had a beautiful wife and eight children. Annie told herself she was going to begin wearing makeup every day. She may as well start today.

• • •

An hour later, she was still waiting. The phone rang. Buddy kept it short. Kevin had stopped at a bar. Buddy would remain with him until he headed home. At that point Buddy would come back for Annie. He would call again if it got late. Annie said she was going to go get groceries.

Annie ran through the grocery store as though she were being chased. Her mind raced. What if Kevin got hurt? How would she feel? Emotions ebbed and flowed, and the contents of her grocery cart mystified her. Forcing herself to look at a different scenario, Annie stopped in aisle seven. Buddy had been a last resort. Kevin was dangerous. The loving and kind friend she remembered was gone. It was time to be concerned with her future and Mary's. She would have a whole different set of worries if Buddy were not there. No, she thought doggedly. She would not worry. Danny was smart, and he would never have suggested Annie call a man who would kill Kevin. Promising herself it would come out all right, she sifted through the nonsense in her cart and concentrated. She would cook dinner for Buddy at home.

Another hour passed, and Annie sat alone with her tossed salad. Finally, she heard footsteps on the stairs. A soft knock told her Buddy was back. Still, she checked. After positively identifying him, she opened the door.

"Hi," she said brightly. "Are you starving?"

"Yes, are you?" He really had the most delightful set of blue eyes. "I'm sorry I was gone so long. Let's go to dinner."

"I thought we'd eat here," Annie countered. "If you don't mind."

"Even better," he said cheerfully. "I'd rather we stayed by the phone."

"Why?" Annie asked nervously.

"So that you're here if he calls. He's drunk, but somehow I don't think he went to bed. There were a couple of people at the apartment he's staying at. Let's eat."

Annie nodded and waved him into a kitchen chair. The table was set. She pulled the salad from the fridge and put the steaks into the broiler. Conversation flowed more easily than Annie expected. Buddy had attended Texas A&M University. His degree was in law enforcement. Right now he was working on starting his own business, but he did not say what it was. Annie asked him artfully if his wife worked, and he shook his head.

"She stays at home?" Annie probed casually.

"No," Buddy answered. "I'm not married."

"I see," Annie said innocently. "Did you like Texas A&M?" The subject had to be changed quickly. Buddy liked college but had been glad to finish. All that was years ago, he said. Annie refrained from asking how many years ago and changed the subject. How did he know Danny? Buddy said Danny formerly worked for an oil company that had internal troubles. He did not elaborate except to say Danny was a "stand up guy" and not easily intimidated.

"That worked to my benefit," he added mysteriously. Deftly changing the subject, he asked about Annie's classes. After dessert, Buddy thanked her politely. He then folded his napkin with the air of a man who was getting down to business.

"Annie," he said slowly. "Here's what I had in mind. I think Kevin knows you did not drop the charges today. I also think he's wired pretty tightly right now. Let's see if he shows up here tonight. If he doesn't, I'll run over and talk to him in the morning. How does that sound?"

"Fine," Annie said thoughtfully. "But if he's had a few drinks, he'll be even worse. I mean ... he won't be in a good mood when he gets here."

"I'm certain of it," Buddy agreed poker-faced. "From what I saw at the bar, he's feeling a lot of hostility." He returned Annie's smile at his obvious understatement.

"When he comes, you head for the bedroom, and Kevin and I will take a ride. There's nothing to worry about." Seeing Annie's pale face, he continued. "Annie, I know what I'm dealing with. I doubt Kevin is carrying a gun. Even if he is, it's not a problem." He paused and selected his words carefully. "I've done this kind of thing before with tougher guys than your husband. You see, Annie, Kevin is deadly with you. There's no doubt. But when he's up against a guy who's not afraid of him, he's not so scary. Do you mind if I shower?"

"Not at all. Let me get you a towel."

Annie cleared the dinner dishes. A dropped plate nearly sent her through the roof, and she screamed. Buddy immediately opened the bathroom door a crack.

"Are you all right?"

"Fine," she said, wincing. How embarrassing. "I dropped a plate. Sorry."

"I'll be out in a minute, Annie."

"Great," she said fearing she would drop dead from mortification. Walking into the kitchen, she put her hands over her face. Annie decided sternly to be completely calm and rational from this moment on. No more second-guessing him. He was possibly saving her life, and that was that. He was also extremely handsome. That was also that. Annie would forget how smart, funny, cute, and single he was. She would behave sanely if it killed her. Determined, she put the dishes in the sink and blasted the hot water. Hearing him yell, she turned the water off. Wincing again, she walked within five feet of the bathroom.

"Sorry," she shouted.

"That's OK."

Annie's shoulders began to shake with silent laughter. There was something unnerving about having a man in the shower. She went back to the kitchen and tried to stop giggling. Wouldn't Maureen love this story, she thought ruefully. The exact moment she heard the water shut off, she turned on the sink and began to wash dishes industriously. Because of her great speed and diligence, she was finished before he came out. Hesitating only a moment, she dumped the whole drainer back in the soapy water and began again. Buddy came out of the bathroom looking as well-kept as before except with wet hair. He carried an overnight bag and had changed clothes. He smiled at her, and she smiled back.

"Buddy, I have to admit I'm a little nervous."

"I would never have guessed that, Annie." They laughed. What a lovely laugh he had. "I think you're holding up remarkably well. This must be horrible for you."

"It's not so bad anymore," she said in surprise. "I guess I feel relieved that I called you and you're here. I thought about calling you a lot."

Buddy looked genuinely sad. "I'm sorry any of this happened to you." After a moment he continued brightly, "Don't worry, Annie. I know that being a single mother is probably rough, but at least I can guarantee you that from now on he won't bother you. You'll do great in school."

Annie grinned. "I hope you're right. On both counts."

The tension broken, they relaxed. After an hour watching the news, Annie yawned in spite of herself.

"Go to bed if you want, Annie," Buddy said kindly. "I put the gun under your bed. It's loaded, and the safety is on. I'm leaving the deadbolts off the doors, and I'm going to grab a nap on the couch here." Annie made a move to get him bedding. "Annie," he stopped her. "No matter what you hear, stay in your room. Promise?"

She looked directly into his eyes. "If you say so." A thousand questions flitted through her mind. She shrugged and let them go.

Silently, she went to the closet and pulled down bedding. She set it down on the couch next to him.

"Sleep well, Annie," he said whimsically.

"I'll try," promised Annie. "Be careful, Buddy."

Chapter Twenty-eight

Sometime after midnight, Annie heard the screen door
close downstairs. She sat up. Unable to resist, she
opened her bedroom door and peeked out. Buddy's
voice came softly from the darkness.

"I heard it, Annie. You promised."

"I know. I'm sorry."

She closed the bedroom door and sat on the bed. Her
stomach tensed, but she was not shaking. She wondered if
this had been a good plan. On the off chance Kevin got
past Buddy, she was a sitting duck. She remembered the
gun and felt for it under the bed. She felt better holding it.
Listening intently, she heard nothing. There was no sound
whatsoever. She was just lying back down when she heard
Buddy speak.

"You must be Kevin," he said in a normal voice. "I've
been waiting for you."

Annie heard Kevin yell in surprise. "Who the hell are
you?" She noted from his voice that Kevin was far from
sober. Her stomach knotted with abandon. Praying inco-
herently, she clicked the safety off the gun.

"I'm a friend of Danny McGowan," Buddy said conversationally. "He was worried about his sister so I told him I'd stop by and see her. Are you supposed to be here, Kevin? I thought there was a restraining order against you."

Annie listened tensely. Buddy was being extremely polite.

"It's none of your fucking business," Kevin snapped. "Where's my wife?"

"She's sleeping," Buddy said. "And I don't want you to wake her."

Annie noted half hysterically that Kevin lowered his voice. "Get the fuck out of this apartment. I've got business with my wife."

"I don't think so, Pal. You've got business with me. Let's go for a ride."

Annie heard Buddy stand up. Kevin laughed. Next she heard a scuffle, followed by a yelp and a thud.

"Now get up and let's try again, Kevin. I'm serious about this. You do what I say. That's the only rule. Do you have any questions about it? Ask now. If you make noise, the neighbors might call the police. And you're not supposed to be here. I don't want the police to come. That would be bad for you. Let's try it again."

Annie heard the door close behind them.

Two hours passed. Sleep was not an issue as Annie watched out the window. Buddy and Kevin had gotten into Buddy's car. Kevin was driving. Annie could not imagine why Kevin was so cooperative. Then something occurred to her. She hoped fervently that Kevin was afraid. Let him see how it feels, she thought brutally.

Shortly after three o'clock in the morning she heard a car. Racing over to the window, she watched as Buddy jumped deftly from the driver's seat. He was alone. Annie had the door open and met him in the hallway.

"Is everything all right?"

"Fine, Annie. Everything is fine." His handsome face smiled. "Are you still up?"

Annie backed into the apartment. Buddy followed.

"Strangely enough, I had trouble sleeping," she accused.

Buddy closed the door behind him. He turned to Annie.

"I'm going to take off. It's a long drive, and I may as well get started."

Annie's stomach dropped. "So soon?" What had she thought? He would stay and visit for a few days?

He smiled. "Yes. I have to stop by and see my folks. They live in Abilene. Annie, are you calm?"

She looked up at him. "Why? Should I be calm?"

He nodded. "Absolutely. I just want to explain a few things. Kevin will be calling you in the morning. I told him to. And I have his phone number. I'll call you in the afternoon and see how you're doing. After that I'll check in with you every so often. When is your next court date?"

"In two weeks. Why?" Annie felt like she was repeating herself. Wrapped in a bathrobe, she was having trouble taking it all in.

"Write down the date for me. Would you?" He gave her another reassuring smile. Annie turned to comply. "He sees now that he was wrong, Annie. He won't bother you anymore. Obviously, you have my number. If he so much as breathes wrong, call me. OK?"

Annie handed him a piece of paper and nodded her head. "Yes. I will. Buddy, are you sure he won't bother me?"

He gave her a sardonic grin. "I'm nearly certain."

"Where is he now?"

"Probably at the emergency room. He had a fender bender, and I think he hurt his head. " Annie raised her eyebrows. "Annie," he said conversationally, "how many broken ribs did you have?"

"What? Uhm, one I think. Why?"

"Oops. I doubled your injuries. I thought you had two." He frowned in mock regret. "I'm afraid poor Kevin has four." Finishing before Annie could respond, he said, "This stuff is not an exact science." He turned and grabbed his bag, which was by the door. "Annie, my friend, I wish I had met you under different circumstances. But who knows? Life's not over yet."

Annie nodded her head. He was leaving. He walked out into the hallway. Turning one more time, he gave her another grin. "I'll be in touch. Good night, Marty."

The last sentence was spoken loudly. Buddy was barely out of the building when Marty's door swung open.

"How did he know I was there?" asked her neighbor.

Annie shook her head numbly. It had all happened so fast. He was gone. Kevin had four broken ribs. Buddy wished he had met her under different circumstances.

"I'll talk to you in the morning, Marty. OK?"

"Sure," Marty said just above a whisper. "You're OK?"

Annie nodded and shut the door. She went to the window and watched his car disappear. Sitting down weakly on the couch, Annie wondered what to do with herself. Kevin was hurt. Badly enough to go to the hospital. What should she do?

"I'm tired," she said aloud. "I'll go to bed."

And so she did. It was too soon to unload the gun, so she checked the safety and left it on the dresser. A ringing telephone dragged Annie from a sound sleep. She stumbled from her bed and answered it with still-closed eyes.

"Annie," Kevin said weakly. "I'm calling to apologize for everything I've done. You don't have to drop the charges. I'll plead guilty."

"That's fine, Kevin. Are you all right?"

There was silence. Then Kevin spoke bitterly. "Just fine. I had a car accident last night, and I'm in the hospital."

"I'm sorry to hear that," said Annie with her hand over her stomach. "Were you hurt badly?"

"Broken ribs, and stitches in my head. I guess I don't even know you anymore, Annie. I can't believe you would let someone do this to me."

Annie was speechless.

"I didn't mean that the way it sounded." Kevin interjected. "Please don't repeat it. Do you understand? I'm sorry for everything, Annie. I promise I will never bother you again. Ever. If anyone calls and asks, tell them I said that."

"Fine Kevin. And I'm sorry you got hurt."

Annie hung up the phone. Covering her face with her hands, she sank down into the chair. Dear God, she thought. What have I done?

Chapter Twenty-nine

Time passed, as it does. Gradually, Annie McGowan forgot to be afraid. It simply wore off. For awhile, Kevin followed her. But even that stopped.

Buddy remained mysterious. For the first year after her separation, he appeared randomly. On the day of Annie's final divorce hearing, she spotted him sitting in the courtroom. He said he had not forgotten the dinner he owed her. After that, he popped into town every month or so, paid a quick visit to Kevin, and took Annie to dinner. Those were red-letter days.

Life was not easy for Annie. One day, as she brushed her teeth, she felt overwhelmed. There were bills, final exams, and strange spots on Mary's back. Annie felt an unusual wave of self-pity. Looking up into the mirror, she met her reflection. Green eyes gazed back at her. Annie thought for a moment of how she would feel if Kevin were sitting in the living room. She shuddered. Without warning, she began to laugh. What were bills, exams, and probably a case of heat rash? Annie McGowan felt free. No problem was too big. Exulting in her renewed capacity for joy, she again laughed aloud.

A small eager face peered around the corner of the bathroom.

"What's funny, Mommy?" Mary asked, looking expectant.

"You're funny, my little pixie!" Annie swooped her daughter into her arms. "I'm going out for dinner tonight so I'm going to feed you now."

Annie prepared Mary's dinner, only half-listening to her little girl's chatter. Buddy was coming to take Annie out. As usual, she keenly anticipated the evening. But tonight a touch of sadness gripped her. She faced the fact that it might be the last time. Kevin had moved back to Chicago exactly one month ago. If Maureen's intelligence was sound, and it usually was, he was living with his parents on 63rd and Mozart. Annie did feel truly free to finish her education in peace. At the same time, this latest development would surely end Buddy's periodic visits.

When Buddy arrived, Annie was dressed and ready. Buddy looked impossibly handsome and fresh. They dined at a Mexican restaurant, in a darkened room, and Annie tried not to show the bittersweet feelings that threatened to overwhelm her. Conversation flowed, as it always did, and Buddy listened with great interest as Annie described her upcoming finals and hopes for her last year of college. She laughed when he suggested she would become a Pulitzer Prize-winning journalist. Annie was working on the school newspaper and loved the challenge. She knew she must tell him of Kevin's move. But she didn't.

The ride home seemed to take forever yet passed in a blink. Too soon, they were parked in front of Annie's third floor apartment. Buddy turned to her.

"Thanks for a wonderful evening, Annie. I'll probably get back up here next month."

Annie took a breath and plunged in. "I wanted to talk to you about that, Buddy. You see, Kevin moved back to Chicago. I'm really relieved. I guess I'll have peace now." She smiled at him and carefully placed her hair behind her ears. Buddy never broke character from the concerned and caring friend. He never kissed Annie, never hinted that he wanted anything but this brotherly friendship that had seemed to develop. Annie, on the other hand, spent many happy hours thinking of him and wondering what would have happened if, indeed, they had met under different circumstances.

Buddy smiled back at her in the darkness of the car. "I heard that, Annie. 63rd and Mozart, I believe. He's still drinking heavily but seems to be staying out of trouble. It looks like the siege is finally over. Annie, nobody could have handled this situation better than you did."

Annie nodded and acknowledged the praise. He made her feel so competent and smart. She opened the door and began to step out.

She had to say something. Anything. "Buddy, I don't know how to thank you. I wouldn't even know where to start." Words failed her, and she paused.

Buddy leaned toward her. "Annie, don't thank me. Because in a way, I'm glad it happened. Not to you, of course. Not the bad parts..." He shook his head and started again. "I'm glad I met you. Finals are in three weeks, right? How about we celebrate with Italian? I know a great place. It's out in the country a bit, but you'll love it." He frowned, then grinned. "It's up to you, Annie. I'm not sure how to say this."

Annie's heart stopped. Then it raced. Did he mean ... ? "I can't think of anything I'd like more." She smiled. An awkward moment followed, and Annie stepped out of the car. "That's great then, Buddy."

He laughed out loud. "Thanks for a wonderful evening, Annie. I'll call you. And don't worry about finals. I have great faith in you."

Annie shouldered her purse and walked into the building. She knew he was watching her. He always waited until she entered the apartment. She resisted the urge to watch him drive away and ran up the stairs.

Bursting into the apartment she put her hand on her heart. Marty was painstakingly polishing her toenails as their two daughters slept on the couch. "Well," she demanded, "did he kiss you?"

"Marty," Annie exulted, "I think I have a date."

Understanding
Dating and
Domestic Violence

Following are some concrete tools to help you understand dating and domestic violence. Be aware that
while most victims are female, some are male. There
are abusive females, and they wreak the same havoc on the
lives of their partners as male offenders. Additionally, there
are batterers within same-sex relationships. The dynamics are
the same. The only difference is that the victim in a same-sex
relationship is likely to feel even more isolated, more fearful,
will be less likely to seek help, and possibly remain in the
relationship longer because of a fear of exposure.

Please keep this information with you for as long as you
are dating. Reread it periodically so it is fresh in your mind.
Dating and domestic violence can happen to anyone. Don't
let it happen to you.

One more thing. Many people fear that because they do
not come from a perfect family, there is something wrong
with them. This is nonsense. First of all, there are no perfect
families. Secondly, you can be whatever you choose. If you
witnessed or experienced violence in your family, you can be
that much more determined to choose a healthy and nonvio-
lent partner. Don't let a tough childhood define you. Your
future is up to you!

Profile of an Abusive Partner

- *Low self-esteem.* At the same time this person may appear cocky and boastful on occasion.

- *Trouble trusting others, particularly you.* In spite of this, they may say that they know you would never be unfaithful.

- *Jealous and possessive.* Initially, the abuser may say others were coming on to you. Eventually, though, you will be accused of being attracted to other people, flirting, or being unfaithful.

- *Controlling.* Sometimes this can be subtle. You may be changing your behavior without realizing why. For example, you may "decide" not to see your friends too often because you don't want your partner to get mad.

- *Usually comes from a family where there was violence, although they may deny this.*

- *Passionate!* The abusive relationship is intense and passionate. There is usually a Romeo and Juliet quality, which may be noticed by your friends. This intensity does NOT mean you are fated lovers. It means someone is holding on too tightly.

- *Dr. Jekyll and Mr. Hyde personality.* Loving and supportive one minute and cold and hostile, accusing or distant the next.

- *Mood swings or explosive temper.* You think everything is going fine, and suddenly your partner is furious.

- *Macho or super-masculine.* This is sometimes present in male abusers. This boyfriend will have strong opinions about how a man and woman should behave. He will be rigid. You may find yourself saying, "Well, yes, this happened, but there are reasons why." The abusive partner, male or female, will not accept reasons or explanations. Everything is black or white.

- *Isolating.* These partners may want to isolate you from your friends or family. They may always want to be alone with you. Often they will start trouble between you and your best friend. They will be threatened by any relationships you have with members of the opposite sex and may attempt to destroy those friendships by criticizing your friends or pointing out ways in which they have wronged you.

- *Emotionally and verbally abusive.* Sometimes there is no physical abuse until something like a commitment is made, i.e., you have sex, get pregnant, or cut off your friends and family. It could also be as simple as your agreement not to date other people. You don't have to have bruises to be in an abusive relationship.

- *Denial.* This partner will attempt to minimize the violence or behavior saying:

  "I barely touched you."
  "I was just messing around."
  "You can't take a joke."

- *Blamer.* Abusive partners will blame others for their mistakes or problems. Again, it may be subtle. They will blame others for fights if they can.

  "You know how mad I get when you talk back."
  "You make me crazy."
  "I love you so much I can't help being jealous!"
  "If you weren't so beautiful/handsome, I wouldn't be so worried about losing you."
  "Your friends are trying to break us up."
  "That person was coming on to you."

- *When you have a fight, they may try to blame outside stressors.*

  "My parents are making me crazy!"
  "My teachers are making me crazy."
  "I feel like I'm under so much pressure."
  "You don't understand. Nobody does."

  These are pressures with which we all must cope. They are not an excuse to be violent or *abusive.*

- *Alcohol or drug user.* This partner may abuse alcohol or drugs. If so, he or she has a built-in excuse. Remember that many people abuse alcohol and drugs and never become violent or abusive. It's no excuse.

"I was totally wasted."
"I don't even remember this. Did I really do that?"
"I'll never touch that stuff again!"
"I'm such a jerk. Why do you stay with me?"

They may also say things like:

"Hey, you pushed me first."
"What do you expect when you say the things you said."
"You were just as violent as me."

This can get confusing for you. Don't let it. When you are in an abusive or dysfunctional relationship you may begin to act in ways you normally would not.

Something to think about ...

JENNIFER: "After awhile I always felt like I had to reassure him about how much I liked him. I felt sorry for him in some ways, but his jealousy got so bad I wouldn't even talk to other guys. It got like I was always thinking, 'Can I tell him this? Will this make him mad?' I was always trying to prove that I was trustworthy or something. Like if he thought I was sleazy, then I was. If he thought I was a good person, then I was. In a way I didn't have a self-esteem separate from him. Whatever he thought I was, that was the truth. By the end I didn't care if I was the worst person on earth. I just wanted out."

BOBBY: "Her self-esteem didn't seem too low, but she was insecure and needed a lot of reassurance. It was all about her control over me. She didn't trust me. When she got mad she would call me a liar, no matter what I said. Like, for hours. It was OK for her to be around other guys but not for me to be around other girls. She wanted me to quit my job because she thought the waitresses were after me or something. She manipulated me with lies, but I didn't see it that way at the time. My friends knew, though. She always tried to come between us by saying they were talking about me. She even made up things that I said about them to get them mad at me. She was big into mind control."

Behaviors of an Abusive Partner

- They may keep track of your time.

- They may show up somewhere you have said you'll be. They will call this "surprising" you. If you get angry, they will act as though you were doing something you did not want them to see.

- They may stalk or follow you, sometimes calling your home to see if you are there and then hanging up.

- They may buy you a pager or cell phone so they can always reach you. This can start fights if you don't answer or call back right away.

- They may try to intimidate you by punching something close to you, (a wall, car, window) or by driving dangerously, breaking your personal property, shouting in your face, pointing down at you, kicking walls or doors, or threatening to tell secrets to your family or friends.

- They may criticize your clothes, hair, or mannerisms. They may try to take charge of whether or not you drink, use drugs, smoke, or use birth control.

- They may challenge your femininity/masculinity.

- They may act as if they are the boss or in charge. They may want you to talk to them before making decisions about your activities or friends.

- They may invade your privacy by reading notes; going through your room, purse, or wallet; eavesdropping on telephone conversations; or playing back messages on your answering machine.

- They may push your boundaries by tickling you until you are uncomfortable. Another way is wrestling in an aggressive manner that they call playful but you find painful or upsetting.

- They may be pushy about sex. Even though you have agreed on a cut-off point, you may find that they do not respect the agreement. When confronted, they will say you are overreacting.

- They may pressure you to quit your job or outside activities because they do not want you around members of the opposite sex.

- They will be overly jealous. Remember, JEALOUSY DOES NOT EQUAL LOVE!

- If you do not do what they want, they may threaten to break up with you or possibly end the relationship for a while.

- If you try to break up with them, they may threaten to hurt you or your family, to tell your friends or parents that you had sex or did drugs, or even to commit suicide, killing you first.

- Remember that violence progresses in a gradual way. If a new partner slapped you and called you names on your first date, you obviously wouldn't go out with him or her again. It usually starts with emotional abuse and progresses to shoving, grabbing, or restraining. The next step could be slapping, then kicking or biting. Punching and choking may follow after which the abuse usually escalates to beatings with repeated kicks, slaps, and punches.

Once a partner is violent,
he or she is usually violent again!

Something to think about ...

JENNIFER: "He would call me a lot or say I had to call him at nine pm. If I didn't call right on time, he wouldn't answer the phone, and I would have to think about it all night. Like he would be mad at me, and it would bother me all the next day or until I talked to him and explained why I was late. I always had to justify why I did things. But it didn't start like that. In the beginning it was romantic, and I was so happy that he loved me so much. I loved him, too, at the start."

BOBBY: "She was always paging me and would get pissed if I didn't call her right away. She used to check to see if my car was at work when I said I was working. I got paranoid. Like I was afraid of lying accidentally or something. And she would always try to make me jealous. She said it was because she loved me so much that she wanted to make sure I loved her, too. It got so I couldn't concentrate in school. My mind was fried from her."

Types of Abuse

EMOTIONAL ABUSE

- Criticizing
- Calling you insulting names
- Ignoring or ridiculing your feelings
- Making fun of the way you speak or express yourself
- Manipulating you with lies or distortions of the truth
- Leaving you at a party or somewhere dangerous
- Putting you in situations where you get in trouble, for example, keeping you out later than your curfew, making you late for work, etc.
- Ignoring you or embarrassing you in front of others
- Criticizing or teasing you in front of your family or friends
- Telling friends or family things you have said (or allegedly said) about them
- Telling you things that family or friends have said (or allegedly said) about you
- Threatening to break up if you do something they do not like
- Threatening to break up if they feel they need more control
- Mimicking you
- Teasing you
- Minimizing or ridiculing your accomplishments
- Challenging your femininity ("A real woman would not do this") or masculinity ("Only a wimp would act like this")
- Breaking items that are important to you
- Ridiculing your friends or family

- Calling you a liar or repeatedly asking you to "tell the truth"

SEXUAL ABUSE

- Telling jokes that put women or men down
- Treating women as sex objects
- Acting pushy or aggressive about sex or sex acts that make you uncomfortable
- Forcing you to have sex (rape)
- Calling you names like slut, whore, lesbian, or frigid, fag, wimp, or baby
- Publicly showing interest in members of the opposite sex (the flip side of this would be acting intensely loyal to you and showing no interest in other people at all)
- Acting as if you would have sex with other people
- Telling others about your sexual relationship
- Giving you excessive or unwanted "hickeys" or bite marks (they may say they are marking their territory or want everyone to know you are taken)
- Reading or asking you to read or watch pornography

Something to think about ...

JENNIFER: "He would say he wanted to have sex because he loved me so much and that I was the only one he wanted to be with. I kind of wanted to also, but he was pushy. When he got mad at me, he was pushy. He said once that he could tell I wanted to have sex with other people. How could he tell? I don't even think I did, but I started to wonder about myself. He said there were two types of girls. Nice girls and sluts. My friends were sluts and I was nice, but he treated me like I would turn into a slut if he didn't watch me. Like if I got the chance I would go off and have sex with somebody else."

BOBBY: "You may not believe a girl can be sexually abusive. Guys want it all the time, right? Well my girlfriend would scream in my face, calling me a liar, for hours. Then she'd want to have sex. When I didn't want to, she would refuse to get out of my car. She would kind of force me to. Not so much physically, but she would do things like snatch my keys and hide them. One time I just left the car and walked. She constantly gave me big hickeys I didn't want. It only takes about three seconds and you're marked. She was bad news."

PHYSICAL ABUSE

- Pushing
- Shoving
- Slapping
- Kicking
- Biting
- Punching
- Pulling your hair
- Throwing things at you
- Excessive tickling
- Aggressive wrestling that makes you uncomfortable
- Restraining you by holding you by the shoulders or pinning you to the wall or car
- Keeping you in a car or home against your will
- Shoving food or liquid in your face, mouth, or hair
- Hitting you with a weapon or object
- Banging your head against the floor, ground, or car
- Any forceful sex is considered physical abuse as well as sexual abuse

Something to think about ...

JENNIFER: "It started with him holding me by the shoulders and shaking me. Then he would pinch me sometimes. He also held me down, pretending like we were playing, but it hurt. When I tried to make him stop, he would say I was no fun or a baby. By the end he would slap me, pull my hair, choke me, and kick me. He would make fun of me if I cried. I was scared of him, but I still loved him for awhile. And I thought it was wrong, I knew he shouldn't be hitting me, but I figured it was kind of my fault. And after every fight when we made up, I figured, 'That's over. It won't happen again.'"

BOBBY: "I wasn't afraid she would kill me or hurt me or anything like that. But I did have bruises. It's tough because you're not supposed to hit a woman. And as far as she was concerned it was OK for her to hit me, but if I retaliated I was the bad guy. So what are you supposed to do when they're choking you? I pushed her off me. Then she started breaking things in my car."

Teasing

Many people have talked about teasing that is disturbing and humiliating. Others have wondered about an appropriate response. People sometimes fear being labeled a baby, brat, or someone who lacks a sense of humor.

For example, one woman's boyfriend repeatedly called her a wench. When she asked her boyfriend to stop, he said she had no sense of humor and was being a baby. He also suggested she "lighten up." She felt embarrassed and decided she was taking it too seriously. At the same time, her boyfriend continued to address her this way, to the point of never using her name. Eventually, the relationship ended.

How do we know when teasing has crossed a line? Simple. When it stops being funny. If you find yourself going along with the joke but feeling hurt or embarrassed on the inside, a line has been crossed. The teasing is not funny and must stop.

Another person asked, "But how can you make them stop?"

This, too, is a simple answer. You tell them it's not funny, and you don't like it. If they continue, you have a bigger problem than the teasing. They are not respecting your wishes. In this case you say you cannot stay in a relationship with someone who is intentionally hurting you. Overreacting? Not necessarily. If you stay in this type of relationship, you will eventually observe your partner behaving disrespectfully in other areas. The relationship will probably become abusive or end.

Remember also that partners are not mind readers. It is possible your partner is just being playful. If you don't like whatever they are doing, tell them. Be clear and unequivocal. "Don't call me that. I don't like it."

Be aware that you must also be careful about teasing. Anything that might hurt or insult your partner is out of line. You should treat your partner with the same respect you expect and deserve from him or her.

Cycle of Violence

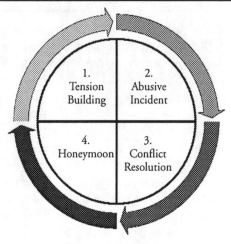

1. Tension Building	**2.** Abusive Incident
4. Honeymoon	**3.** Conflict Resolution

1. TENSION BUILDING PHASE

Characterized by:

- Walking on eggshells
- Criticism

"I'm trying to do everything right, but my partner keeps getting mad at me."

Depending on how far advanced the cycle has become, this phase may include minor incidents such as pushing, tripping, inappropriate tickling, etc. More apparent may be criticism of the victim's behavior. Batterer may get mad quite often and ignore the victim or leave him or her in social situations. (See *Behaviors of an Abusive Partner* for specific behaviors during this phase.)

Victims sometimes think they can diffuse the situation by doing what their partners want and keeping them calm. The victims will try hard during this phase to please the abusers, attempting to see in advance what might anger them.

This phase may be hard to see in the beginning of the cycle but later become more pronounced with the victim often being able to detect when the abuser is getting ready to "go off."

Something to think about ...

JENNIFER: "You're kind of always trying to do the right thing. And everything you're doing you're thinking, 'Will he think this is OK?'"

BOBBY: "You're nervous around them. You're afraid they're going to get pissed off. And you don't know what could start it."

2. ABUSIVE INCIDENT PHASE

Characterized by:

- The big fight
- The explosion
- The break-up
- The violence

"My partner's totally crazy. He/she just exploded!"

Depending on how far advanced the cycle has become, this phase may include violent behaviors such as pushing, shoving, choking, slapping, punching, etc. (See *Types of Abuse* for more specific acts of physical abuse.) The abusive incident is sometimes characterized by the abuser's rejection of the victim, even breaking up with him or her. The abuser may appear out of control during this phase, and the victim may become frightened. The abuser may say someone was "coming on" to the victim or that the victim was flirting with another person. Victim may be called names such as whore, slut, fag, or wimp. Sexual assault may occur during this time.

In the beginning, this phase may seem romantic to the victim, particularly if the abuser is reacting in a jealous way and the violence is limited to shouting, punching walls, restraining, or grabbing. The victim may see it as a sign of the partner's deep love and attachment.

Later, as the cycle progresses, the accusations will become more serious, more frequent, and more violent. This phase is typically short and explosive, but toward the end of the cycle it can become longer, with the abuser even holding the victim "hostage" somewhere for hours or even days while beating and berating him or her.

Something to think about ...

> **JENNIFER:** "Sometimes you could see it coming. But sometimes you'd leave a party, say goodbye to everyone, and then out of the blue he'd come at you for talking too long to one of his friends. It was crazy, and you never knew what was going to set him off. Then you'd think, OK, so now I know that makes him mad so it will be all right from now on."

> **BOBBY:** "It's mostly emotional abuse. But again, if she hits you and you hit her back ... you kind of can't do it. Even if you defend yourself, you're the bad guy. And when they get so jealous you kind of think it's about how much they love you."

3. CONFLICT RESOLUTION PHASE

Characterized by:

- Apology and explanations
- Shared feelings
- Excuses and denial
- Spelling out the rules
- Forcing the victim to admit he or she was partially to blame

"My partner was under a lot of stress, and it didn't help that I was talking to somebody else. He/she is just a little insecure. We worked it all out."

In the beginning of the cycle, the abuser may take full responsibility for his or her behavior, apologizing profusely and offering a list of excuses and reasons for the "fight." "I love you so much that I get crazy with jealousy. I was drunk. You made me furious. I misunderstood something." (See

Behaviors of an Abusive Partner for more on this.) Along with this there may be denial and sharing of feelings, along with explanations. "I barely touched you. You're overreacting. It's just that your friends make me crazy."

As a rule, abusers can be uncommunicative, and the victims may stand on their heads trying to get feelings out of their partners. This phase can lead the victim to think the couple is making progress with intimacy because the partner is so open and responsive. As the cycle advances, though, this phase will be characterized by spelling out the rules. "If you don't do these things, then I won't be violent. It's as much your fault as mine." Initially, the victim may see this conversation as normal struggling to maintain a relationship.

This phase must happen before moving on to the next. Sometimes couples will simply break up. It can be a painful time for the victims while they desperately attempt to figure out why the violence happened and what they should do about it. Reality is shifted in that the victim may know the truth but buy the abuser's explanations. Initially it is a short period, maybe one long conversation, but later, usually after marriage, is characterized by such things as vacations, counseling, and possibly restrictions in the abuser's alcohol or drug use.

Something to think about ...

JENNIFER: "I'd have these long conversations with him discussing why he got mad and what I should or should not do in the future so he wouldn't get mad. I should not 'talk back' when he was mad because I knew that made it worse. One time he told me he would never hit me again if I would never lie again. I said, 'I don't lie.' He rolled his eyes and banged the steering wheel and said, 'You can't even admit you lied! How am I supposed to trust you?' I was totally confused, and it wasn't until I got out of it that I understood how badly he played with my head. Somehow, he always made it seem as if it was my fault and everything would be fine as long as I did or didn't do certain things. I can't believe I didn't break up with him sooner."

BOBBY: "Blaming is a big part of it. They'll take some of the blame but never all of it. She'd convince me it was my fault saying, 'You pissed me off. I shouldn't have hit you, but you shouldn't have said that. I did it out of love, to get you jealous. I don't remember. I was really drunk.' Half the time you end up apologizing to her! It's messed up!"

4. HONEYMOON PHASE

Characterized by:

- Falling in love again
- Getting back together
- Passion

"We were meant for each other. My partner loves me so much."

The abuser is kind, contrite, and, in summary, kissing the victim's backside. If you are a woman, expect things like flowers, candy, compliments, and kindness. If you are a man, you will receive affection, tenderness, and compliments. The relationship is now passionate, and the victim will feel cherished. This is very romantic, and it will not last.

In the beginning of the cycle, this wonderful phase assures the victims that they did the right thing by reconciling. It's so good to be back together, and the abuser couldn't be nicer. Later in the cycle, the victim will enjoy this phase but will know that it will not last. He or she will feel guilt, anxiety, and fear of the next incident.

With most abusive dating relationships, this phase is initially very long. Because of this, the victim thinks that this is the *real partner* and the other behaviors are isolated incidents. As the cycle progresses, this phase becomes shorter and shorter, eventually disappearing altogether, being replaced by blame, blame, and more blame.

Something to think about ...

JENNIFER: "Those were the best times. I would feel lucky to have him then, and we were so close. I mean, you felt like nobody in the world understood or loved you like this person. But toward the end even the nice times weren't so nice. He stopped apologizing or explaining and said, 'See what you made me do. You just don't learn.'"

BOBBY: "It's the same thing over and over again. They're a lot nicer during this phase and they make you feel good about yourself. They compliment you, and you think it's the right thing to do ... going back with them. You kind of think it's a separate incident and that the person is not like this. You blame yourself. It's pretty passionate. You think, 'I'll try harder.' But at the end she knew I didn't want to be with her. I was trapped. She just needed someone because she was so screwed up."

Risk Assessment

Warning Signals

1. Does your parnter call you names?

2. Does your partner say things that will hurt you, then act angry if you get upset?

3. Does your partner tell you things your friends or family have said about you?

4. Would you describe him or her as more jealous or possessive than most people?

5. Does your partner get mad if you have a good time without him or her?

6. Does your partner talk about breaking up when you do something he or she does not like?

7. Does he or she sometimes mimic you or ignore you when you are talking?

8. Does your partner have sudden mood swings?

Something to think about ...

> JENNIFER: "He would get silent. And I would be panicking like 'What's wrong? What did I do?' If it happened to me again, which it won't because now I know the signs, I would say, 'If you're going to ignore me, I'm going home.' I wouldn't go through it again."

> BOBBY: "When you try to walk away, they follow you. If I raised my voice, she'd say I was making a scene. But it was OK for her to raise her voice."

ABUSIVE BEHAVIOR LOW RISK

If you answered yes to any of these questions, your partner may be emotionally abusive.

Most abusive relationships begin with emotional abuse and escalate to physical abuse. If you don't feel you can break up, set some guidelines or boundaries and see how they react. Call them on the emotional abuse. For example, tell them you will not tolerate name calling. Then, the next time they call you a name, walk away. Let them know they owe you an apology. Remember, if they restrain you when you try to walk away, they are being physically abusive. Tell them so. If they threaten to break up with you because you demand respect, let them. It may be difficult to do, but if you do not set limits now, their behavior will get worse.

Danger Signs

1. Does your partner say he or she trusts you but still accuse you of flirting or fooling around?

2. Does your partner check up on you ? Does he or she surprise you by showing up somewhere you have said you will be?

3. Does your partner track your time? For example, do they ask where you were for an hour if it only takes twenty minutes to get home from somewhere?

4. Does your partner isolate you from your friends? Do they hate your best friend or say that your best friend has talked about you?

5. Have they pushed, shoved, slapped, kicked, or punched you? Have they grabbed you by the shoulders to "make you listen"?

6. When you defend yourself, do they say you are "talking back"?

7. Does your partner say he or she would not get so jealous if they did not love you so much? Do they say that you know what makes them mad and you do it anyway, so it is really your fault?

8. Do you apologize to others for your partner's actions? "They didn't mean it; you don't know them. They were just upset."

Something to think about ...

JENNIFER: "He would say my friends were trying to hit on him. Or that they were talking
about me. He wouldn't say it right out at first.
Just things like, 'She's not such a good friend,
you know.' Then I would have to get it out of
him. He talked about my friends, saying
things like, 'You have to admit she's kind of
sleezy.' Or 'I wouldn't trust her. She was flirting with me.'"

BOBBY: "She would say my friends were trying
to hit on her. She hated my friends.
Sometimes she would be nice to them,
though, because it gave her power over me.
Also, she would accuse me of 'liking someone
else.' Not fooling around, just 'liking' them.
How do you fight about that after you've
denied it one hundred times?"

ABUSIVE BEHAVIOR MEDIUM RISK

If you answered yes to any of these questions, you are in an
abusive relationship.

It is not normal for someone to feel the need to check up
on you. A classic sign of an abuser is dislike of the people closest to you. Typically, an abuser will try to separate you from
your best friends by pointing out their faults. It starts with
emotional abuse and moves to physical abuse. After a fight
during which they are abusive, abusers may become apologetic and contrite. They may be extremely loving and promise
all kinds of things. At the same time, they may subtly blame
you for the violence by saying you are making them jealous or
that they love you so much they cannot help themselves.

If your partner is behaving like this, you need to get out. It
will only get worse. Chances are your self-esteem has already
been affected, and you are beginning to feel bad about yourself. Being in an abusive relationship is confusing. You are
never really sure if it is your fault or theirs. You may be think-

ing, "They have a point about some of their arguments." That may be true. You are probably not perfect. Nobody is. But often an abuser will take the truth and twist it so you do not know which way is up. You will find yourself trying harder and harder to please them and being less and less able to. This relationship could destroy you.

Red Alert   Red Alert   Red Alert

1. Has your partner become so jealous that you could describe him or her as paranoid?

2. Do you often find yourself trying to convince them that you did not do anything wrong?

3. Have they ever kept you somewhere against your will (car or house)?

4. Have they ever repeatedly commanded that you "tell the truth" even when you were not lying?

5. Do they say they will die if you leave them or that they cannot live without you?

6. Have they ever talked about killing themselves?

7. Have they ever threatened to kill you?

8. Have they forced you to have sex when you did not want to?

9. Do you have to justify your actions, activities, and time with your friends?

10. Do you want to break up sometimes but feel afraid of what they might do (hurt you, harm your family, or tell others personal things about you)?

Something to think about ...

JENNIFER: "He started following me. Then he told everyone we knew things about me or that I always wanted to have sex. He called and hung up all the time and said that I used to egg him on by saying, 'Hit me, you big fag.' I never did that. Then he would mail me a letter saying how much he loved me. He told me that if I would just learn to tell the truth everything would be fine. I would have said anything to make it stop. It was awful. Then one time, right in front of my dad, he said, 'Should I tell him what you did? Don't you think he should know?' For a long time he followed me and stood outside my job, just looking in at me. Eventually, finally, he started dating someone else. That's when he stopped bothering me. But it hurt more than anything. It took me a long time before I figured him out. I wish I'd known more about it then because I would have broken up with him sooner."

BOBBY: "She was paranoid. She was always telling me to tell the truth. She said she couldn't live without me and that she would kill herself if I broke up with her. She never threatened to kill me, but she threatened to tell my parents things I had done. Things about sex and drugs. She even threatened to make things up. You always feel like you have to justify your actions. Like ... I would change my behavior even when she wasn't around. I would lie about stupid things just so she wouldn't get mad. At the end of it you don't care if they tell personal things. You just want out. So I broke up with her. First, she threatened to kill herself. Then she said she realized what she was doing and that she would stop. When that didn't work, she said she was pregnant. That got to me, but I didn't care. I said I would support the baby, but I still wanted nothing to do with her. So she called my mother and told her."

ABUSIVE BEHAVIOR HIGH RISK

If you answered yes to any of the questions above, you are in danger!

Run for your life! Your partner is extremely abusive and could seriously hurt or even kill you. If your partner is behaving like this, it is no longer safe to date him or her. It is time to get help and end the relationship. You will never convince him or her that you are innocent of their accusations. Until you break up. Then they will say they realize that you are the best thing that has ever happened to them and they are sorry. But that means nothing. As soon as you go back to them, it will all start again.

Many abusers threaten to kill themselves when you try to break up. Will they? Usually not, but it is possible. They need professional help, and you need to tell someone you trust. (See *Safety Plans*.) YOU CANNOT HELP THEM. In cases of dating/domestic violence in which a woman is murdered, the abuser often kills his partner and then himself. This also happens with men, though not as often. That is why it is so risky when your partner is suicidal. The most dangerous time for a female ending an abusive relationship is *when* she tries to leave.

Show your parents this *Risk Assessment* and make a *Safety Plan*. Then call the nearest domestic violence hotline. They can advise you about protective orders and safety strategies. Do not minimize the danger in this situation. It could mean your life!

RED FLAG LIST

Check all that apply:

☐   Your partner has followed you, spied on you, or kept you under surveillance. (This is stalking.)

☐   Your partner seems extremely upset, agitated or paranoid, accusing you of being sexually active or unfaithful with someone else.

☐   Your partner has access to weapons.

☐   Your partner has told you how he or she will kill you, your family members, or someone else.

☐   Your partner is very depressed.

☐   Your partner is obsessed with you.

☐   Your partner has been physically abusive in the past.

☐   Your partner has raped you or forced some kind of sexual activity against your will.

☐   Your partner has injured or killed a pet.

☐   Your partner abuses alcohol or drugs.

☐   You are pregnant. (70% of pregnant teens are abused.)

☐   Your partner has threatened to kill you.

☐   Your partner is suicidal.

☐   You are afraid to disagree with your partner. Your partner may accuse you of talking back.

☐   You are afraid of your partner or of what he or she might do.

☐   You are attempting to break up with an abusive partner.

The more items you checked, the more dangerous your situation.

These are serious danger signals, and you should get professional help. Also reread the *Red Alert* section of the *Risk Assessment* lists.

Something to think about ...

JENNIFER: "When he told me he was going to kill me if I left him, I should have told my parents. They found out anyway after he started stalking me. He said he wanted us to be together forever and the only way to make sure I would never be with another man was to kill me. He said he couldn't stand that thought. He threatened to kill himself if I left him, and he said it would be my fault."

BOBBY: "I don't know about the pet thing. I'd watch out for the pregnancy thing. Guys should always use their own birth control. My girlfriend said she was on the pill. It turned out she was, but she could have gotten pregnant if she wasn't because I never used anything. And the suicide threats. They really tear you up. But you can't help her. If you go back, it's all going to happen again."

"But I was violent, too..."

IDENTIFYING THE PRIMARY AGGRESSOR

When police officers respond to a domestic violence call, they often must determine who is the bad guy or the primary aggressor. In relationship violence, often both parties get violent. This can confuse the victims who may think they are as bad as their partners because they fight back or defend themselves. Following are some points to help keep the issues clear:

- People have the right to defend themselves. Often when someone is attacked, he or she instinctively strikes back.

- When a victim becomes involved with a violent person, his or her behavior may change. When someone is yelling, it's tempting to yell back. When someone is violent, it's tempting to respond violently. These behaviors are learned and can become habits. With a well-adjusted partner, an emotionally healthy person is likely to respond in kind.

- Every relationship has problems and conflicts. Getting angry is not an excuse to assault.

- Nobody is perfect. Many abusers will try to persuade the victim that the abuse is caused by the victim's behavior or faults. This is not true.

- Abusers encourage victims to feel insecure and inadequate. This is manipulation and can cause feelings of jealousy. Unless the other behaviors are present, a victim is not abusive merely because he or she, too, gets jealous.

- Who is usually the abuser or aggressor? The fact that someone hits back during a violent incident does not make him or her abusive. The person who is usually violent is normally the abusive party.

The most telling factor to consider is really very simple. Who is afraid? Are you afraid of your partner? If the answer is yes, then he or she is probably abusive. If your partner is not afraid of you, then you probably are not abusive.

Don't get confused!
If you are afraid, get out now!

Something to think about ...

JENNIFER: "There's nothing anyone can do to make someone beat them up. People get mad. That's life. They have to deal with it. It wasn't my fault. I was just doing the same things everyone else did in relationships. And when I punched his arm during a fight, he said for the longest time, 'You punched me. You're the violent one.'"

BOBBY: "The only time it's OK to hit her is if she has a weapon. Then you're stuck. But I would push her off me. One time I kind of pulled her out of my car and left. You'll know if it's getting out of control and you have to get out!"

Safety Plans

WHAT IS IT?

A safety plan is a series of actions you can take when you feel threatened or afraid. If you are not ready to end the relationship, you can prepare for the next violent episode. If you are breaking up, you can prepare for the violence and stalking that may follow.

WHY BOTHER?

If a plan is prepared in advance, it can maximize safety and prevent panic. Because every relationship is different, safety plans will vary. For this reason it is important that each safety plan be designed by you, the victim, to suit your circumstances.

HOW IS IT DONE?

After identifying your resources and potential danger signals, you can devise your own individual safety plans, including one for breaking up.

A. *Available Resources*
The first step is to identify your resources. What might you possibly need? Who can help and how? Look at the following list and add anything or anyone that might be helpful to you.

1. **Code word or phrase.** A code word or phrase is chosen by the victim to convey a message to family or friends. It can be as simple as, "I'm kind of tired tonight." The meaning is decided on in advance and can mean "Don't leave us alone." There can be varying degrees. For example, "I'm exhausted" can mean either "Come over right away" or "Call the police." You may be with the abuser or in the same room. The code word will help you indicate danger without tipping him or her off.

2. **Cell phone.** A cellular phone is a good idea because you can carry it with you as opposed to finding a pay phone and strug-

gling to locate change. On the other hand, it is a well-known fact that victims go through a lot of phones. The reason for this is that the abuser is not likely to hand you the telephone and wait patiently while you call your parents or the police. (This problem is so prevalent, that the state of Illinois enacted a law that prohibits an abuser from interfering with a victim either calling the police, seeking medical attention, or reporting domestic violence. But quoting statutes won't help you at the moment.) Put important numbers, such as parents, friends, police, on the speed dial. And give yourself a couple of options in case of a busy signal. On the flip side, an abuser can use your cell phone or pager to harass you. Part of your Break Up Plan may be to get a new pager or cell phone.

3. **Answering machines**. Use these to screen calls if your abuser begins to harass you by telephone.

4. **Friends**. Let them know your situation and give them the code word or phrase. They can also ensure that you are not left alone with your partner when the situation seems likely to escalate. Friends can run for help and should be told to call police if an assault is occurring. It is a good idea to let them know just how violent your abuser gets so they will take the situation seriously.

5. **Parents**. I know. You're thinking, "No way am I going to tell my parents." But if your partner is really dangerous, you'll have to. They have the power to do lots of things that you cannot. Like change your phone number, pick you up wherever you call from, contact the abuser's family, help you to get charges filed. (Last on your list, I'm sure. But it may come to that, and it is better they be somewhat prepared. Also, the abuser may threaten other family members, and they *must* be made aware of that.)

6. **Teachers, counselors, and school officials**. This is important because the abuser may come to your school looking for you. If he or she attends the same school, he or she may be

violent there, and you have the absolute right to attend school without being afraid. Also, if school personnel are informed of the problem, they will be more likely to react positively and quickly in a dangerous situation. If you get an order of protection, make sure school personnel have a copy. This will enable them to call the police and get immediate action.

7. **Crisis lines or battered women's shelters**. These organizations provide a wealth of information and give you a place to talk. You can call a crisis line anonymously and bounce your situation off someone who is knowledgeable about the problem. Many people call and say, "These are the things my partner is doing. Do you think that is abusive?" Shelters can provide you with legal information about your area and will even go with you to court if you end up there. Call them for help or just to chat.

8. **Police Department**. This may be a hard step, but if you are being assaulted or see someone **else** being assaulted, you need to call the police. Policemen are experienced in dealing with domestic violence and have seen everything. Your situation will neither shock nor surprise them. And they have the power to intimidate where you may not. Also, a run-in with police will indicate that the situation is serious and convey a message to the offender: violence is against the law, and the abuser is going to suffer consequences.

B. *Warning Signals*

The next step is to identify when you may be in danger. Let's review your abuser's warning signals. What are signs that he or she is in the tension building phase? What does your abuser do when angry? Does he or she:

- raise his or her voice?
- go silent?
- stamp around?
- throw things?

- punch walls?
- drive aggressively or dangerously?
- behave in a sexual manner that is pushy or embarrassing?
- get jealous?
- call you names?
- bang on the steering wheel?
- stare at you?

Something to think about ...

JENNIFER: "He would stare at me, real hatefully. I cannot describe it. That was how I'd know he was mad."

BOBBY: "She would go silent and ignore everything I said. She wouldn't look back at me. Then she would kind of stare at the ground. Every once in a while she would give me a mad or sad look. I'd say, 'What's wrong?' And she'd say, 'Nothing.' If this happens, don't ask what's wrong. Stay with your friends if you're at a party."

At this point anything can trigger a violent episode, and you need to be one step ahead. Put yourself in different situations and decide which courses of actions you can take, what kinds of safety plans you can make. For example, if you are:

At a party

1. You can use your code word or phrase to indicate to your friends that it is not safe to leave you alone.

2. You can go to the bathroom and use your cell phone to call your parents. Ask them to pick you up.

3. You can pretend to have a stomachache and ask to be taken home, making sure that you do not go alone with your abuser.

4. If you cannot get away from them for even a minute, you

can tell them you have to call home for some reason and use your code word to let your parents know you're in danger.

5. You can sneak away and ask a friend, or better yet a few friends, to walk or drive you home.

6. You can approach adults at the party, or the host if you are an adult, and either tell them you're sick and would like to be taken home or tell them the truth—that you're afraid.

The nice thing about parties is that there are other people there. Make the most of that and do not leave with your partner to "talk it out." Chances are they are going to say they want to talk to you privately. Stand your ground and do not get into a car alone with them! Also, try to avoid getting trapped in a room, away from everyone else. Tell them that if they want to talk privately, they can go home and call you on the telephone or even call you the next day. As soon as you see your partner escalating, get away and refuse to talk, even if he or she persuades you he or she is now calm. You know the person. If you saw signals, you're probably right, and they are moving toward a violent phase.

In the car

1. Say you're feeling sick and ask to be taken home. Pretend to throw up if you have to.

2. You can act as though you are going along with your partner and wait until you are at a light. Then jump out. Run to the nearest public place like a restaurant, hospital, or even a busy intersection and call the police, your parents, a friend, or maybe a taxi to take you home. Ideally, all of these numbers are on your cell phone's speed dial.

3. If he or she is dropping off friends, get out at one of their houses and refuse to get back in. Then use their phone and call for an alternate ride home. Or try to insist you be taken home first. Chances are he or she won't do this, saying, "Get back in the car. I want to talk to you." Refuse. Better a scene at a friend's house than in a deserted parking lot where there is nobody to help you.

4. Think back to what has helped you in the past. Is it better to cry, beg, reassure, stay silent? If you fight back, do you have a chance? If not, you may be in the unfortunate position of going along with them or trying to get through it without getting hurt. Try to get out, but odds are they may restrain you or lock you in. Do what you can.

5. Think of an excuse to call your parents or a friend and use the code word or phrase.

6. Scream for help. Wave for help. Act hysterical. Go crazy and see if that works.

The best way to avoid being trapped in a car with an abusive partner is to stay out of the car in the first place. This cannot be stressed enough. Cars are dangerous places to be because you can be taken anywhere and be kept in there. He or she can also get you killed by driving dangerously.

Something to think about ...

> JENNIFER: "I wouldn't get into a car with someone like that again. I used to be stuck in there for hours. Even if he knew I was going to be late and get grounded, he wouldn't let me out."

> BOBBY: "Don't give them what they want. If you're late, explain to your parents. Don't even act mad at your girlfriend. Turn off the music and don't talk. Ignore her. The most important thing is to hang on to your keys. If the girl has the car, then get out and walk. If you have the car, wait until she has to go to the bathroom and leave. Say you're feeling sick or you have to go to the bathroom. Just leave somehow."

In your house

1. Stay out of the kitchen. This is a dangerous room because there are items that can be used as weapons.

2. Move the fight to a safer place like the living room.

3. Call a friend and use the code word or phrase.

4. If anyone else is in the house, call for help, loudly and repeatedly.

5. If the situation is still at a low level, for instance, they are not violent yet but you feel it is escalating, move the fight to a room within easy hearing of anyone else in the home. This should force them to quiet down and give you easy access to help if they get violent.

6. If you are alone there, try to move the fight out on the porch, particularly if there are neighbors around. This will give you the chance to run for help if necessary.

7. Say you have to go to the bathroom and call the police with the cell phone.

8. Try to call 911.

At school

1. Move to hallway or other public place.

2. Call for help.

3. If you leave school and your partner is waiting outside, go back in and inform a teacher or administrator or call your parents to pick you up. You can leave by another exit if you're sure he or she won't spot you.

4. Stay with a friend so your partner cannot get you alone.

5. Refuse to go to a secluded spot. Insist on talking in a public place or tell your partner you'll only speak to him or her if your friend stands close by.

C. *Personal Safety Plan*

There are unlimited situations you may find yourself in. Think of them and write safety plans for each one. Following are a few good ground rules.

1. Don't get in a car alone with an abusive partner.

2. Insist on talking in a public place. If you have things to discuss, do it at a restaurant.

3. Keep a cell phone handy if you can.

4. Do not go anywhere alone if you're afraid.

Breakup Plan

Suggestions:

1. Use the buddy system. Have friends with you everywhere so the abuser cannot get you alone.

2. Carry a cell phone with the numbers of people who can help on your speed dial.

3. Inform school and work personnel that the situation is dangerous.

4. Use your answering machine to screen your calls. Also, since telephone harassment is a crime, save answering machine tapes. Keep a notebook by the phone and record the time, date, and whatever the abuser says. It can also be helpful to record your responses to him or her such as "Don't call me again" or "I've asked you not to call here. You're harassing me." Put the abuser's statements in quotes such as "You've got to talk to me." Or "If you don't see me, I'm going to kill myself." Or "I'll kill you, you _____." It is extremely important to record threats.

5. Lock your doors and make sure your family is aware that your former partner may come over.

6. If you get an order of protection, keep a copy in your purse or wallet and on the refrigerator. Make sure that your family knows to call the police if they see the abuser. Also, drop off a copy to your boss at work and to the principal or security office at school.

7. Ask your parents to consider changing the phone number and getting an unlisted one.

8. If you feel he or she may kill you, go into hiding. Stay at a relative's or friend's house. The abuser cannot have access to you when he or she is dangerous or you may end up dead, along with your family members.

9. Either you or your parents should call your partner's parents and see if they can affect his or her behavior.

10. Make sure your partner knows, via friends or family, that any further violence or harassment will be dealt with legally. Threaten.

11. Stalking in Illinois (check your state's laws) consists of two separate followings or surveillances, along with a threat or battery. It is a Class 4 felony, which is serious. So if your partner threatens or strikes you, then follows you twice, he or she can be charged with stalking. The order of the offenses does not matter, so following you once, threatening or striking you, then following you again violates the law. Make sure the abuser knows this and be certain to tell someone when he or she follows you. Document it. Report it to the police if possible.

12. Try to avoid giving your former partner any reason to think you might reconcile. Because victims sometimes feel guilty or think that they are partially at fault, or because they feel sorry for the abuser, they may agree to see the abuser in an attempt to "make things better." You cannot do this without giving him or her the idea that he or she can still get to you. Be strong and do not see or talk to him or her. Try not to get sucked back in.

Personal Breakup Safety Plan

Now it's your turn. Sit down with a piece of paper and do your own personalized safety plan. Do it with someone else if possible because he or she may have ideas that can help you. Following is a rough guide:

1. List your resources.

2. List the possible situations or places where you may be threatened.

3. List your responses to those situations.

4. Have an alternate place to go if it's not safe to go

home and tell the person in advance that you may be showing up.

5. List the things you have to do to make your safety plan work (get cell phone, set speed dial numbers, get order of protection, inform school and work, talk to parents or family members, etc.)

Remember that anything you have to do to stay safe is OK. Never feel guilty for anything you do to get out of a bad situation, including acting crazy. Many victims end up having sex with the offender to stop an assault. If you find yourself in a situation like that, don't feel guilty. You know best how to take care of yourself. Also, in spite of all of your precautions, you may get hurt. It's not your fault. Hopefully, an aggressive response will protect you.

Something to think about ...

JENNIFER: "Don't believe anything he says about how he'll change. And call the police on him if he follows you. You have to try very hard to stay away from him, or it will all happen again. I would tell everyone, including his family, what he was doing. And I would say to him, 'Go ahead. Tell my friends and family anything you want. They all know you're a liar.' Even if he told them things that were true. If they were personal things that were none of their business, I would say they were lies. After some time went by, I would get so mad, thinking about what he had done. And I wished so much that I had called the police, told him off, or got him in trouble somehow. I would lie in bed and think about what had happened on a certain night and think, 'I should have said this, or I should have said that.' But it was too late then."

BOBBY: "A cell phone can be used against you, along with a pager. So make sure it's a new one and don't give the number out to anyone you don't trust. She called all of my friends looking for my new number. I was actually glad when she called my parents to tell them she was pregnant. I was losing it, and once they knew I could tell them everything and they helped me. They got a phone block and my mother handled the whole pregnancy threat by saying she would raise the baby if they wanted to give it up for adoption. But she was never pregnant. She told a friend who told me that she was going to let me sweat for a couple of months. Nice, huh? I stayed away from anywhere I thought she might be. I also stayed away from places I usually went to because I didn't want to run into her. Tell your boss so he can say you're busy if she calls or shows up. Tell your family so they can hang up on her or slam the door if she comes to your house.

This is the most important part. Don't talk to her or see her. You need a full break in contact because when they get you on the phone they 'grab' you. Just talking to her would confuse me. She would start talking about the future or something, and it would get to me. No matter what happens, don't go see her. It will only screw up your head."

Victim Blaming

MYTHS ABOUT DATING VIOLENCE

☐ Violence in dating relationships rarely happens. Not true. *Statistics show that one in every three dating relationships is violent. (Levy, B., Ed.,* Dating Violence: Young Women in Danger. *Seattle: Seal Press, 1991)*

☐ Dating violence occurs only with drug users or poor people who come from "bad" families. Not true. *Dating violence can occur whether or not a partner uses alcohol or drugs. And it can happen if a partner is poor, rich, respectable, an athlete, or a good student.*

☐ Dating violence means a couple having a "fight." Not true. *Dating violence is not about a couple having a fight. It is about one partner threatening, abusing, controlling, and assaulting another.*

☐ Young women are just as violent as men. Not true. *While young women can be violent, statistics show that young men are more violent.*

☐ Dating violence is usually an isolated incident Not true. *Dating violence is a "pattern" of abuse and control and once it starts, it almost never stops.*

☐ Stress causes dating violence. Not true. *Many people are very stressed and never assault their partners.*

☐ Drinking causes dating violence. Not true. *Abusers will use alcohol as an excuse for their violent behavior but will eventually also be violent when not drinking. Additionally, the manipulation and controlling behavior are normally present even when an abuser is sober. Also, think about it. Many people get drunk, but most do not assault their partners.*

☐ People who batter cannot help it. They lose control. Not true. *Usually people who batter do not assault anyone else. They get mad at others but control themselves.*

They assault their partners because they can get away with it.

☐ If victims wanted to leave, they could just break up. Not true. *Often abusers will threaten to kill the partners if they break up and will later stalk them. Also, victims feel sorry for their partners and sometimes even feel guilty, thinking the abuse is their fault.*

☐ If you love someone enough, you can make him or her change. Not true. *It's not that easy. The decision to change must be made by the abuser, and usually this does not happen.*

☐ If the victim did not make the partner angry, he or she would not hit the victim. Not true. *Victims are assaulted regardless of their behavior. If it's not for one reason, it's for another.*

In summary, anyone can be a victim of dating/domestic violence.

Why She Stays

Why does a woman stay in a violent relationship? Below are some possible reasons.

1. He has threatened to kill her if she leaves.

2. She is afraid of him.

3. She thinks he'll get better.

4. He has promised to change, and she believes him.

5. She thinks it is partially her fault because she did want to make him jealous.

6. She loves him.

7. She is afraid she won't get another boyfriend.

8. She thinks he loves her.

9. When he is nice to her, he is wonderful.

10. She doesn't want to be alone.

11. She believes she can help him to change.

12. She has seen this type of violence at home and accepts it as inevitable.

13. She feels that his extreme jealousy is a sign that he really loves her.

14. He has never really "hurt her." Just small bruises and she doesn't really think that low a level violence is abuse.

15. She feels sorry for him.

16. She has a low self-esteem as a result of the abusive relationship.

Why He Stays

Why does a man stay in a violent relationship? Below are some possible reasons.

1. She has threatened to kill him or tell secrets about him if he leaves.

2. He is afraid of her.

3. He thinks she'll get better.

4. She has promised to change, and he believes she will.

5. He thinks it is partially his fault because she tells him so.

6. He loves her.

7. He doesn't want to be alone.

8. When she is nice to him, she is wonderful.

9. He believes he can help her to change.

10. He has seen violence at home and accepts it as normal.

11. He feels the abuser's extreme jealousy means that she really loves him.

12. She has never really hurt him. She just screams, yells, says mean things, and sometimes pushes or slaps him. He does not realize these behaviors are abusive.

13. He feels sorry for her.

14. His self-esteem is low as the result of the abusive relationship.

Something to think about ...

> **JENNIFER:** "I loved him for awhile. And he was going through a bad time and saying it was my fault. He said my leaving him was the cruelest thing anyone had ever done to him. I felt sorry for him, and I was also afraid he would kill himself or kill me. And I believed him when he said he wouldn't do it again. I believed him every time except the last time."

BOBBY: "I thought I loved her, and she was nice sometimes. In the beginning she was great, and when things started to mess up I thought it was my fault. I figured she'd get better, and I thought I could help her to change. I felt sorry for her, and I didn't want to be alone. I figured her jealousy was a sign that she loved me, and I thought she loved me more than anyone else would. My friends and family didn't like her, but I thought that was because they didn't understand her or know her like I did. Plus, we were together a long time, and I kind of thought we had a future."

Helping Friends

What can you do when your friend tells you they are experiencing dating violence?

- Listen, listen, and listen.

- Do not judge. Use helpful statements and avoid unhelpful statements.

- Do not give them a list of solutions right away. Move slowly.

- Do a safety plan with them, even if it is an informal one (for example, what they will do if the abuser follows them to school).

- Stress that they have the right to break up if they are ready.

- Convey that the violence is not their fault, regardless of what they said, wore, or did.

- Give them information about the *Cycle of Violence*, *Risk Assessments*, and the *Profile*.

- Give them the phone number of a local shelter or a hotline. They can remain anonymous or say they are working on a paper for school, if they choose.

- Continue to be their friend if they go back.

- Call the police if you witness an assault. Then honk a horn or scream for help until police arrive.

Because these situations can be dangerous, you should be acutely aware of your own safety. Do not put yourself at risk!

HELPFUL STATEMENTS

1. You don't deserve to be treated this way.

2. It sounds as if your partner is acting worse and worse.

3. I know how much you like him or her. It must be hard for you.

4. It sounds scary.

5. Your partner is acting abusively.

6. Have you thought about breaking up with him or her?

7. Jealousy is one thing. He/she is out of line!

8. Nobody should be pushing or shoving you.

9. Can I help? Is there anything I can do?

10. This sounds familiar. Let me give you some information about this.

11. You're right to be upset. I would be, too.

12. You cannot argue with them if they act like that. It's not fair.

13. You should be able to get mad without getting hurt.

14. I'm worried about you. I think they could be dangerous.

15. You are way too good to be treated like this.

16. There are plenty of people out there who don't act like this.

17. I'm afraid he/she is only going to get worse.

18. I don't think you can help him or her.

19. This must be awful for you.

20. If you don't feel as if you can break up now, make sure to say that if he or she hurts you again it's over.

21. Let's call someone who knows about this kind of thing.

UNHELPFUL STATEMENTS

1. What a big jerk! What a bitch!

2. At least they care enough to get jealous.

3. You're lucky to have somebody, even if they are not perfect.

4. So ... wear what they want. At least they notice.

5. You should just break up. I told you this before.

6. Don't talk back to them.

7. All people are like this when you get to know them.

8. He's really cute, though. She's a fox.

9. If you don't do something, you're as bad as them.

10. It's not like they punched you or anything.

11. I think it's kind of romantic. Give them another chance. They said they were sorry.

12. They love you so much. I wish somebody loved me like that.

13. They are not usually like that. Focus on their good qualities.

14. Stop making them mad. Don't talk to other people if they are around.

15. They wouldn't get so jealous if they didn't care so much.

Something to think about ...

JENNIFER: "I would give the victim all of this information. And I would tell her repeatedly that it wasn't her fault. I wouldn't blame her because I know how confusing it is. I would point out the things he was doing that were wrong, and I would keep showing her how she was getting mixed up. I would also remind her that there are nice guys who are not messed up. An important thing is that when they made up I wouldn't say anything to make her feel stupid. I would just wait for the next time and do the same stuff over again."

BOBBY: "If I saw another guy in my situation, I would tell him to break up and get away. I would explain what I saw and that it might be hard for him to see it clearly. It would have helped me to see this information because it blew me away when I first read it. It all fit her. I would stress that he doesn't owe her anything because that was hard for me. I would tell him he doesn't HAVE to stay with her, and I would get involved if I saw her ripping into him. I would back up the victim for sure. And I would

NOT make him feel like a fool if he went back with her because that can happen, too. One more thing I would do is warn him that she might get crazy when he breaks up. I would tell him to do a breakup plan and think it through. And if she threatened to kill herself, I would tell her to talk to a counselor. They usually don't, and you can't help them. It just gives them control if you try."

Healthy Relationships

The following are characteristics of a healthy relationship:

- Respect
- Dignity
- Trust
- Consideration
- Communication
- Good conflict resolution skills
- Emotional safety
- Consistency
- Honesty
- No physical violence

In a good relationship you will be able to:

- say no to physical closeness or sex without feeling guilty.
- change your mind.
- go out without your partner.
- have your own goals and interests.
- express your opinions.
- have control over your life.
- be equal.
- be safe.
- be respected.
- break up without feeling afraid.

A good relationship does not mean a conflict-free relationship. Conflict is healthy and inevitable. Disagreements should be resolved without violence, though, and each partner should feel safe enough to voice his or her complaints.

Often, people who have been involved with abusive partners think that a healthy relationship sounds boring. *You should not be bored!* There should be chemistry. But a good relationship is constant. It should not have the wild roller coaster ups and downs usually seen in an abusive relationship.

Something to think about ...

JENNIFER: "I have a healthy relationship now. It's not as dramatic, but now I see that it's not supposed to be. This guy is my best friend, and I can tell him anything. When we first had fights, it was a little confusing. I would start yelling, and he would just kind of look at me. Then I figured out that I didn't have to yell. He wasn't yelling at me. I can't describe how much better that is. I just can't. You'd have to go through it to know. He's funny and romantic, and he makes me feel like I'm great. And he doesn't freak out if I talk other guys. And things that I would have been afraid to tell the abusive guy, I can tell this guy without even worrying about it."

BOBBY: "There has to be trust. You should be able to be with your friends and not have to spend every minute with her. She shouldn't want to be with you every second of the day. There should be communication. They need to respect your decisions, especially when you say no to something. And they shouldn't try to get you in trouble with either your friends or your parents. It's got to be fair. So if something is OK for her, it's OK for you."

Unhealthy Relationships

The following are characteristics of unhealthy relationships:

- Suspicion
- Mistrust
- Lack of consideration
- Emotionally unsafe
- Inconsistent
- Poor conflict resolution skills
- Poor communication
- Lack of respect
- Dishonesty
- Verbal, sexual, or physical abuse

Think in terms of fair. If you find yourself thinking your relationship is not fair, you've probably got trouble.

In a poor relationship, you'll often begin to feel unsure. Your partner will keep you guessing a lot and may encourage you to feel insecure. A good rule of thumb is that your partner should make you feel good about yourself. You should not always feel as though you have to try to please your partner. You should not always have to wonder about whether or not your partner will be in a good mood. You should never be afraid during an argument, and your partner should not do things to humiliate or embarrass you. Physical intimacy should never be forced, uncomfortable, or beyond whatever limits you have set.

Questions to Ask About
the New Person in Your Life

Following are some guidelines for determining which people are potential abusers. While you probably won't quiz your dates, be aware of the following problem indicators:

1. Do your new partner's parents argue a lot? Are they divorced? If so, what happened?

2. Does your new partner have a violent father or mother? An overly critical father or mother? While they may not come right out and tell you this, you can usually get a sense of whether or not anyone in the family is afraid of a parent. You should try to spend some time with your partner's family, certainly before a serious commitment is made. Domestic violence runs in families!

3. How was your new partner disciplined? Anything more than mild spanking when very young is suspicious.

4. Does your new partner get in physical fights with siblings?

5. Does your new partner get into fights with others?

6. Was your partner violent in other relationships, even if he or she contends it was not his or her fault?

7. How did your new partner's former relationships end and why?

8. Is your new partner disrespectful or demeaning toward all women or all men?

9. Are they overly interested in pornography?

10. Are they sometimes pushy about sex?

11. Do they abuse alcohol or drugs?

12. Do they ever try to intimidate you to get their way? Emotionally, physically, or sexually?

13. Is your new partner sometimes rigid about how women and men should behave? For example, the way they dress or whether or not mothers should work?

14. Do they have mood swings?

15. Is your new partner extremely possessive or jealous?

16. Do you find yourself surprised by the seemingly innocent things that make them angry or upset?

17. Does your new partner have strong negative feelings about either their mother or father?

Questions for You to Answer at the Beginning of a New Relationship

Often young people spend a great deal of time wondering what other people are thinking. Do they like me? How much? Will they want to see me often? Do they still want to date other people? Take some control! When starting a new relationship, spend some time thinking about the following questions. Decide what *you* want before you get into it.

- How often do I want to see this person?
- How much time do I need for myself?
- Am I willing to date this person exclusively?
- What is a comfortable way to resolve conflict?
- What actions will cause me to end the relationship? (Disrespectful behavior, violence, forced intimacy, or simply falling out of love are a few.)
- How far am I willing to go sexually? (Important tip here. Make a decision about this and stick to it. If you're feeling ready to extend your limit, decide well in advance. Trying to decide while you're in someone's arms is like deciding whether or not to swim after you've jumped off the diving board!)

Questions for Your Partner

If you fear your partner may be struggling with these issues, copy this questionnaire for him or her.

1. Do you have trouble controlling your temper?

2. Do you get into fights?

3. Are you violent when you use alcohol or drugs?

4. Do you believe you are only violent when you are provoked?

5. Are you afraid that if you don't control your partners, they will control you?

6. Do you sometimes throw or break things to get their attention?

7. Are you afraid your partner will be unfaithful?

8. Do you spend a lot of time worrying about where your partner is and whom he or she is with?

9. Have you ever grabbed them by the shoulders or arms to make them listen?

10. Do you feel that you would not get so angry if they would do what you tell them?

11. Have you ever followed or spied on your partner?

12. Have you ever pushed, shoved, slapped, hit, kicked, or choked your partner?

13. Have you ever thought you might kill yourself if your partner broke up with you?

14. Do you sometimes call them names or say things you know will hurt them?

15. Do you ever pretend that you're going to break up with them if they make you angry?

16. Are you more jealous than most people?

17. Do you get angry when your partner does things without telling you?

18. Have you ever forced your partner to do more sexually than they wanted to?

19. Do you believe you are supposed to be in control?

20. Do you believe women or men are manipulative?

If you found yourself having to think about these questions, you may have a problem with relationship violence. Get some help. It doesn't have to be this tough. Talk to someone who is experienced in this field. Violence is a learned behavior that can be unlearned. One person struggling with this problem said the best thing that ever happened was learning they did not have to be in control. You can learn that, too.

Date Rape

DATE RAPE FACTS

- 25% of college women were found to have been victims of rape or attempted rape.

- 90% of these victims knew their assailants.

- 47% of rapes were committed by first dates, casual dates, or romantic acquaintances.

- 90% of the victims did not report the rape.

(1985 study by Dr. Mary Koss of Kent State University. Students were polled at 35 college campuses.)

It can happen to anyone! Remember that you have the right to say no at any time. Practice the following safe behaviors:

1. Group dating is best, at least until you are comfortable with a new boyfriend.

2. Limit your use of alcohol and drugs so you can remain in control.

3. State your limits CLEARLY, even if you feel a little silly.

4. Say NO at any time you are uncomfortable or feel a situation is moving too quickly. Do not try to be nice. Say NO loudly and unequivocally so your partner is not confused.

5. Beware of date rape drugs (see *Date Rape Drugs*).

6. Trust your instincts!!! If you're feeling uncomfortable, there is a reason. Get out of the situation.

Beware of the man who:

- takes everything sexually, even if it is not intended that way.
- is overly aggressive or violent.
- is disrespectful of women.
- tries to get you drunk.
- won't take no for an answer.
- consistently tries to talk you into sex.
- feels women ask for rape by being provocative.

IF IT HAPPENS TO YOU...

If you said no and sex was forced upon you, you were raped You may want to report the assault to the police. If you are not sure about reporting but want to keep the option open for later, the following will help you to preserve evidence:

- Do not eat or drink
- Do not wash your clothes
- Try not to go to the bathroom
- Do not douche
- Do not take a shower or bath

You should get medical attention as soon as possible to check for injuries and to test for pregnancy and sexually transmitted diseases (STD). Being seen by a doctor or at an emergency room does not mean you have to make a police report, but if you tell medical personnel that you were raped, they are required to contact the police. Even then, you do not have to make a report or file charges. You can refuse to talk to the police or simply tell the doctor you had unprotected sex and want to be checked for STD and pregnancy. If you decide to file criminal charges, you have the right to drop them at any time. The decision to proceed legally is yours and yours alone.

Do call a rape crisis line. It can only help you. Women experienced in sexual assaults will answer your questions and assist you in identifying your options. They will even accompany you to court if you choose to go that route.

Victims of sexual assault feel many different emotions afterward. This is normal and should not alarm you. Following are common reactions: fear, anger, guilt, shock, denial, depression, anxiety, embarrassment, shame, helplessness, confusion, and betrayal.

Additionally, many victims also experience trouble sleeping, nausea, nightmares, the need to shower or bathe repeatedly, difficulty in concentrating, bedwetting, loss of appetite or overeating, and difficulty with touching or being touched.

Please do not blame yourself. It is not your fault!

IF YOUR FRIEND TELLS YOU SHE HAS BEEN RAPED...

- Advise her to get medical attention.
- Let her talk about the experience as much as she needs to, but do not press for specific details if she does not share them.
- Tell her that her emotions are a normal reaction to the experience.
- Advise her to get professional help and give her the number of a rape crisis line.
- Do not judge her actions before, during, or after the incident. (Don't tell her she was foolish to go home with him or that she should have fought harder, etc.)
- Advise her about the importance of preserving evidence if she wants to proceed legally.

- Be patient while she recovers. It will take some time.

DATE RAPE DRUGS

Be aware that young women are being raped with the assistance of various "date rape drugs." Sometimes called "chemically assisted rapes," these assaults leave their victims with little or no recollection of the attack.

Rophynol and gamma-hydroxy-butyramine (GHB) are two of the most common drugs to be misused in this way. Similar to Valium, Rophynol is ten times stronger. It is known to cause temporary amnesia, muscle relaxation, sleep, and impaired motor skills. Additionally, alcohol will intensify the effect. These drugs are extremely popular in the Rave scene. People under the influence of these drugs can become agitated, excited, uninhibited, dizzy, confused, have slurred speech, and lose their judgment. Also possible are breathing problems, unconsciousness, and even comas. Fast-acting, Rophynol can take effect in as little as ten minutes. If Rophynol and GHB are combined and alcohol is also present, death can occur. Following are some tips to avoid being attacked in this way:

- Do not take an open drink, especially one offered from a stranger.
- Drink only from tamper-proof bottles or cans. Insist on opening them yourself.
- Never ask someone to watch your drink. Take it with you everywhere, even to the bathroom.
- If a friend asks you to watch his or her drink, hold it or watch it closely.
- Try to avoid mixed drinks or any drinks from wide-mouthed glasses.
- Use the buddy system. NEVER leave a friend who seems wasted. The bigger your group of friends, the safer you are. Stay with at least one other friend at parties or bars and agree that you leave together. Period. Do not let the plans change later in the evening.

A prevention manual for use when presenting
The Breakable Vow as part of an instructional
program is available from

The Breakable Vow
Adams Press
500 North Michigan Avenue, Suite 1920
Chicago, Illinois 60611-3794

info@adamspresschicago.com

A LETTER FROM ANNIE

Dear Fellow Victim,

Welcome to the twisted, confusing, and pain-filled world of domestic violence. Unfortunately, there are a lot of us. Are you tired? I bet you are. Trying to figure out what is going wrong with your family or relationship is exhausting. Are you confused? You have every reason to be. When you're on the inside, still with an abuser, it's tough to sort through the guilt and accusations. Do you have any self-esteem left? Of course you do. You're a wonderful person with lots of potential. Life will get good again. I promise. The fact that you are reading this tells me that you are looking seriously at what is going on in your relationship. You may have been at a courthouse, or a shelter, or even a hospital. Right now it may feel like your life is falling apart. But it's not. This could be the first step toward a better life. Chances are, you'll return to your abuser. We all do. On average, we leave our abusers seven times before we leave for good. Don't worry about it. Do whatever you have to do, and remember, nobody knows what is right for you but you.

One thing to shoot for in your next honeymoon phase is counseling. Since domestic violence only gets worse (more frequent and severe), you should try to get him to go into a counseling program for abusers. Counseling with just anyone won't work. And don't do marriage counseling. It almost got me killed. Marriage counseling does NOT work in violent situations. Tell him you'll go to marriage counseling after he completes an abuser treatment program. If he loves you as much as he says he does, he'll agree to go. He won't go easily, but he may go and it may help.

I'm going to tell you about your partner. If any of what you read sounds familiar, you may be in the same sinking boat that I was in. While every abuser is different, most have similar beliefs and behaviors. Following are some common characteristics.

Your partner may have been abused as a child or saw his mother abused by his father, even though he may deny it. He may not feel good about himself. You probably find yourself trying to make him feel better about himself or increase his self-esteem. It's probable that he is jealous and possessive. He will accuse you of flirting, having affairs, or wanting to have affairs. He may treat you as if you would like to flirt or have affairs, even though he says he knows you would never do that. Maybe he says someone was coming on to you. It might be irrational stuff, like "No other man would put up with your behavior." If you were having half the fun he accuses you of having, you wouldn't be so depressed.

He is probably demanding of your time. Abusers need a lot of attention and will get angry if you spend time with friends or family members. Sometimes an abuser will even get mad if you are paying too much attention to your children. Often an abuser will want you to stop seeing your friends or stop going out without him. If you go anyway, he'll get angry and accuse you of fooling around. Or he'll pretend to be mad about something else. These people tend to be suspicious. Abusers often accuse you of doing things you did not and may say, "It doesn't take you an hour to drive from here to there. Tell me the truth. Where were you?"

An abuser will blame others for his problems. They will blame you for everything toward the end. Often they will say they were violent because you were being a smartass, talking back, lying, etc. No matter what you say to defend yourself, he will shout you down. He may make statements like, "If you didn't make me so mad, I wouldn't hit you. You know what makes me mad, and you keep doing it." Abusers are rigid. It's their way or no way.

Male abusers often have a low opinion of women, saying women are sneaky or manipulative. While the abuser may think it's cute, he feels he must watch the victim closely. Abusers will often act as if nobody understands them. They are alone on the planet. Somebody needs to tell them that we all feel that way.

He may treat you like a child or a possession. He can sometimes be critical and difficult to please. He may say you are great...except for certain flaws that he is willing to help you correct. You sometimes know what will set him off. Sometimes you may not tell him things that will make him mad. When he finds out, he accuses you of lying. It feels like you are damned if you do and damned if you don't. Abusers can get mad every quickly and easily. What seems like it should be a little thing may set off an explosion. You and your children often feel like you are walking on eggshells. Children say they don't like when Dad comes home.

Abusers can be boastful and arrogant and may make comments like "Somebody has to be in charge." This person may be pushy or forceful about sex at times. He may not trust people, thinking that everyone has an angle or is trying to put one past him. If your partner is like this, he will be more violent and emotionally abusive while you are pregnant and right afterward. About 25 percent of us will lose at least one child to miscarriage. Isn't that terrible? They're murdering our babies!

He may deny the violence saying, "I barely touched you. You're the one with the problem, not me. I'm the victim here." It's very confusing and makes you feel like you are going nuts. They have their own reality. While his side of the story is usually not true, he will stick to it in spite of every argument. They are often threatened by your success. For example, if you consider returning to school, or something that will increase your earning capacity or independence, he will ridicule your achievements or try to mess it up for you, maybe by keeping you up all night before a test. All the while he may be saying, "Go for it. You'll do fine." Be clear. The actual paycheck does not offend them. It's the thought of you breaking away, even a little bit.

Your partner may make fun of you or ridicule you. He tends to be demeaning and say cruel things. He may call you names or embarrass you in front of people. Sometimes it's hard to put your finger on it, and he will say that you have no sense of humor or that he was only joking. But the idea is to make you feel stupid or bad about yourself. Most of us agree that this can be worse than the physical abuse, and when we have to watch him do this to our children it's agony. He may ignore you for days at a time because you put the wrong size bulb in a lamp or ground your 12-year-old for a month because the child was five minutes late for dinner. If you argue, he'll say the kids misbehave because you are a lousy mother. Remember, according to him, it's all your fault. You are not perfect. Nobody is. And your abuser will NEVER let you forget it.

Does any of this sound familiar? Stay with me another minute.

An abuser is impossible to fight with. He will not argue about the violence. If a fight is about money, for example, he will focus on your spending habits. You might try to defend yourself and explain where the money went. The abuser will not listen, saying things like, "All I know is that you are out there blowing money. You think money grows on trees..." And on and on and on. Maybe this goes on for hours, or days, or weeks. He will pick one point and keep coming back to it. Later, after a violent episode, the abuser will say things like, "I admit, I lost my temper a little, but you know how I feel about money, and you just keep on spending it." Blah, blah, blah. Never mind that the kids needed milk money. He will always bring the focus back to your behavior and avoid talking about the violence. It makes me tired just to think about those conversations.

If I were to give one major red flag I would say to beware the partner who accuses you of "talking back" when you are having an argument or discussion. Who usually says we are talking back? Parents, teachers, and other authority figures. If your partner says you are talking back, or says he lost his temper because you were talking back, you have trouble! In an equitable relationship both people are allowed to say what they want to say.

In this type of relationship the power is so unbalanced, in the abuser's favor, that you might be afraid to defend yourself, or to say what needs to be said. You might be thinking "That's not fair." You're right. It's not.

Now, for the really confusing part, we'll talk about how the abuser acts after a fight or when he's not mad at you or the kids.

The abuser is so loving and supportive that you are certain nobody will love you as passionately as he does. He applauds your every breath. He's grateful and blessed to be your husband/boyfriend, (or in some cases girlfriend). In short, he's kissing your...This happens for a while. Some call it the honeymoon phase. But trust me. It will change. After a while he won't be so apologetic and humble. He'll blame you for everything and stop apologizing. If you are like me, you'll eventually feel like you don't care if it's your fault. You will just want to get away. But he's not going to let you go with any dignity. You'll never prove to him that you are fair, nice, and trustworthy. Stop trying. Let him say whatever he wants. Just get away. You will be amazed how much better you are going to feel when you let go of trying to please him. Even if you're broke. Remember to be careful if you are leaving. Most of us who get killed are killed right after we have left. Is that a reason to stay? No way. You may be killed then, too. See what I mean? You'll always be damned if you do and damned if you don't with this guy. Most of us do leave and most of us stay alive. You will, too.

Get all the help you can. Call a shelter. Call a hotline. Call the police. Ask them about the law in your state and how to handle the situation after you leave. Stalking is a crime now, thank God. So if he follows you, calls you a thousand times, or bothers you at work, he can be arrested. One more thing I forgot to tell you. The only thing the abuser understands is consequences. He has to know that something bad will happen to him if he bothers you. Like...he'll be arrested. If you feel so sorry for him you cannot stand it, pray for him. He needs prayers. Because there is a God. And He's watching. He entrusted your children to you, and you have an absolute moral duty to protect them. Good Luck! You can do it! I know you can because I did it and I was a mess. Once you're on your feet, help another battered woman to escape. That's how it works.

May God bless you and protect you,

Annie